KIDNAPPED FOR THE ACOSTA HEIR

SUSAN STEPHENS

RIVALS AT THE ROYAL ALTAR

JULIEANNE HOWELLS

MILLS & BOON

First published in Great Britain 2023
by Mills & Boon, an imprint of HarperCollins*Publishers* Ltd,
1 London Bridge Street, London, SE1 9GF

www.harpercollins.co.uk

HarperCollins*Publishers*, Macken House, 39/40 Mayor Street Upper,
Dublin 1, D01 C9W8, Ireland

Kidnapped for the Acosta Heir © 2023 Susan Stephens

Rivals at the Royal Altar © 2023 Julieanne Howells

ISBN: 978-0-263-30679-8

05/23

This book is produced from independently certified FSC™ paper
to ensure responsible forest management.
For more information visit: www.harpercollins.co.uk/green.

Printed and Bound in the UK using 100% Renewable Electricity
at CPI Group (UK) Ltd, Croydon, CR0 4YY

KIDNAPPED FOR THE ACOSTA HEIR

SUSAN STEPHENS

MILLS & BOON

Huge thanks to you, my loyal readers,
for loving my Acosta guys. I thought there
would be five Acosta stories, but with your
encouragement those sizzling-hot bad boys
just kept leaping onto the page!

Thanks to my family for their good humour and
patience, and my friends for the same. Not forgetting
my scrupulous and effective editor Nic, and every
member of the team it takes to make a book.

And, of course, my husband
for his unstinting love and support.

Happy reading, everyone!

CHAPTER ONE

HE BURNED LIKE a fire in the centre of the room. Outwardly cool and contained, and good-looking beyond the bounds of reason, Alejandro Acosta was rugged and tanned like a man who spent less time behind a desk than he did riding horses on the vast landholding he ruled over in Spain.

And his eyes. *Dark eyes that seemed to plumb her soul.*

What did she know about him? Apart from the fact that he had been her late brother Tom's best friend and was a member of the immensely powerful Acosta family, Sienna knew precisely nothing.

His glance washed over her with indifference. 'Won't you sit down?'

Acosta's voice was deeply masculine, and almost insultingly brusque. She'd heard it said that Alejandro had continued to work for the army long after he left the forces. Tom had let slip that having made a fortune in tech, prior to his service in the regiment, Alejandro had recently been tasked with trialling a special type of drone on the battlefield. Tom had explained that Alejandro was one of many subcontractors, drafted in to fulfil a specific task for the military. It must have been this that had brought them together on that fateful night. With his first-hand knowledge of the army's requirements, and one of Alejandro's companies being a world leader in the field of drone surveillance, he was the perfect man for the job.

But not the perfect man to be standing to attention along-side, Sienna seethed as he continued to try and stare her down. 'I'm happy standing, thank you.'

The disapproving lift of one sweeping ebony brow was his answer to that.

He didn't trouble to hide the fact that he found the pres-ence of a stranger in his London home distasteful. Hos-tile vibes pinged off him in waves. Sienna wasn't exactly thrilled to be revisiting her grief at the loss of her brother in front of such a cold man. It was only a matter of weeks since Tom had been killed, and his funeral was still a raw memory. She'd rather be anywhere than here in Alejan-dro Acosta's plush study, being confronted by an ice king, and a cold-faced solicitor, for the reading of her brother's will. She'd rushed here half dressed for the club where she sang each night, because this was the only time that suited Señor Acosta, his PA had informed Sienna. The fact that the timing couldn't have been worse for Sienna didn't seem to register. Acosta issued orders, and everyone snapped to attention, she presumed.

The most enigmatic of the Spanish Acosta brothers, Ale-jandro Acosta was so powerful, so rich, he was untouch-able, and had made himself unreachable to all except the privileged few. For the short time she was here, Sienna was briefly one of that small number.

'Sit.'

She jerked to attention at the sound of his voice, and im-mediately wished she hadn't. What a rude man. Fortunately, their paths were unlikely to cross again, as they inhabited two very different worlds. Sienna's was hand to mouth, but full of drive and optimism, or it had been until Tom's death, while, according to the press, Alejandro's financial worth was incalculable, but his wealth didn't seem to have made him happy.

A glance at her watch told her what she already knew. She was going to be late at the Blue Angel, where she was the headline act. The club was on the other side of London, and the manager was strict about timekeeping. Sienna was too. She cared deeply about her audience, and couldn't bear to think about them being disappointed, simply because Alejandro Acosta cared for nothing and no one but himself. And there were practical concerns. If she lost her job at the club, how would she pay her final college fees? The bursar had been understanding up to now, in allowing Sienna to spread the cost of her.course, but without that precious certificate to prove she was a qualified music therapist, years of study would be wasted.

As the seconds ticked away Sienna's panic mounted. Respectable singing jobs were hard to find. The last place she'd attended for an audition had told her that entertainers were only hired to keep their punters happy. It hadn't seemed important if she could sing or not, and although the Blue Angel wasn't the type of sophisticated venue she imagined Acosta frequenting, neither was it a seedy cover for anything else. People came to the club to eat good food, and listen to great music, not to hit on the staff.

The glance at her wristwatch had drawn Acosta's attention. Lifting her chin, she stared back. She had never encountered a man so aloof and cold, who could, she admitted now, be so dangerously sensual too. The very model of a billionaire, he had dressed for the occasion in an impeccably tailored dark suit. Black diamonds flashed at the cuffs of his pristine white shirt, in a reminder, had she needed one, that the man's tailoring alone had probably cost more than she earned in a month. Another anxious glance at the door drew his scathing look.

'Are we keeping you, Ms Slater?'

His voice was a low, husky baritone, betraying barely the hint of an accent. 'Sienna, please,' she said politely. They could at least make the pretence of being civil to each other in front of the solicitor. 'I explained to your PA that this is the worst possible time for me.'

'I'm sure you'll *make* time to hear the detail of your brother's substantial bequest in your favour. Oh, and please,' he added with a sarcastic edge, 'call me Alejandro.'

She could think of something else to call him. The expression on his face was distinctly mocking. No wonder, she conceded, when she had dashed here, half dressed for the club, looking like a party girl, fun interrupted on a Friday night, calling in to hear what her brother, barely cold in his grave, had left her.

The cool grey gaze of the lawyer, seated in Alejandro's place behind his desk, added to her discomfort as he levelled a silent reprimand on her face. 'Please carry on,' she said in an attempt to ignore Alejandro's lowering presence.

This request was directed to the solicitor, but as his droning delivery started up again she was uncomfortably aware of Alejandro's primal heat and clean man scent as it filled her senses. Turning her thoughts determinedly to Tom, the brother she'd adored, Sienna could only marvel at how different Tom had been from Alejandro, his so-called best friend. Her brother's appetite for life had been insatiable. Full of kindness and laughter, Tom had had a wicked sense of humour that could always make her smile—

'Something amusing you, Ms Slater?'

Alejandro's question put her on edge. Her only crime was smiling as she thought about Tom. 'I was thinking about my brother, and how much I loved him. And how Tom could always make me laugh.' She might have been diminished by grief, but she hadn't been destroyed by it, and neither Alejandro nor the solicitor could find a clever answer to that.

Hearing the contents of Tom's will left Sienna stunned. She'd had no idea that her brother had accumulated so much money, or that he would leave it all to Sienna. Since the day their parents were tragically killed in a car crash, when she was fourteen, and Tom just four years older, Tom had promised to look after her, but this was on another level. All she wanted was some small memento from Tom, and an expression of love. Her troubled gaze landed on an army photograph, standing square on Alejandro's desk. Alejandro spearheaded the squad of good-looking men, but Tom stood out with his easy smile, and boy-next-door good looks. Once again she asked herself: how could Tom buddy up with this cold man?

Looking back, she'd been muddled by grief and shock when the officers from Tom's regiment had told her the terrible news. They'd said something about Alejandro being involved... Her questioning glance clashed with his. She held his stare steadily. Why, oh, why hadn't Tom saved himself first?

Trouble. That was the first thing that came to mind when he assessed Tom's sister, Sienna. A pale scrap of a woman with long, fiery red hair, she had dressed as if she intended to party hard on the news that Tom had left her a great deal of money, together with Tom's substantial landholding on an island off the coast of Spain—an island Alejandro owned half of. He had successfully avoided feeling anything for years, but Tom's death had opened old wounds that threatened his control in front of this woman.

Returning his attention to the solicitor, who had just asked them both to please sit for the reading of a letter from Tom, he informed the man, 'I'll remain standing.'

He had to hide his shock as the solicitor read on. The contents of Tom's will had been bad enough, and, in fairness, Tom's sister appeared equally perplexed as she listened to the contents of the letter.

Alejandro, I'd trust you with my life, but don't mess with my sister.

Was he to take that as a challenge from the grave? It was followed by some mush for Sienna, along the lines of: I'll always love you, and all I ask is that you follow your dreams.

There were tears in Sienna's eyes. She needn't worry. Tom could have spared himself the trouble of writing those words. Snagged black stockings, a too tight skirt, teamed with a garish, sequined top, brought only one thought to Alejandro's mind: 'Not a chance.' In fact, he found it incredible that, thanks to the terms of Tom's will, he now owned the island he loved jointly with this woman. And there was more to it than that. Tom had got lucky on the stock market, and had wanted to do something useful with the money. They'd come up with the idea of building a rehabilitation centre for veterans on the island. Alejandro had been delighted that Tom had seized upon this idea, as he'd hoped they'd found something at last to save Tom.

That project would still happen, he silently pledged. Nothing and no one would stand in his way. A living testament to Tom would still be built.

And Sienna? What would she have to say about it?

Life was full of challenges. She was just one more.

As if reading his thoughts, she glanced up. Challenge flared in her eyes. He was instantly suspicious. What was she up to? His body didn't care, and responded with enthusiasm to the defiance in her steady gaze. Naturally, his mind overruled his body. She simply wasn't his type. Tom had described his sister as zany and fun, though she could be stubborn, Tom had excused. From what Alejandro had seen, Sienna Slater was unpredictable and bold, which could be a problem. When he'd asked Tom where she worked, Tom had been evasive. 'She works in a club,' Tom had said. 'Tells me she has a really big secret to share with me very soon.' Tom had laughed rather awkwardly as he'd said this, adding, 'I hope she hasn't got herself pregnant.' There hadn't been much Alejandro could say to that.

Returning his thoughts to the island he and Tom's sister now shared, he realised the solution was simple. He'd buy her out. Tom would applaud his decision. It would ensure that Sienna had everything she could possibly need going forward into whatever murky style of life she chose. Tom's last words on the battlefield, his last thoughts, had been for Sienna.

'Tell Sienna I love her, and always will, wherever this new adventure takes me.'

Alejandro had heard it said that people could find no fault in those they loved in their last moments. That had certainly been true in Tom's case. In respect for his friend, Alejandro would do everything in his power to make sure that Sienna was safe, and wanted for nothing—

His chin jerked up. 'You're leaving?' he asked with surprise as she made for the door.

The solicitor was also packing up, he noticed now.

'These documents are for both of you—a copy each,' the lawyer said on his way out of the door. 'Mull them over at your leisure.'

'Thank you...'

Sienna's soft tone captured Alejandro's attention, and he

was forced to admit that he'd never seen anyone look quite so sad before. In that moment, he was glad she hadn't seen her brother's broken body, or been forced to endure the terrible silence when he'd gone. He wouldn't tell her. It would break anyone's heart.

It wasn't his job to mend hearts, but it was his responsibility to keep a watching brief on Sienna.

"'Until my sister feels comfortable with her new situation, I'm entrusting my friend Alejandro with the management of Sienna's inheritance...'"

The solicitor had sighed with disapproval as he'd read this out, but it did mean that Alejandro had the final say when it came to any plans Sienna might have for the island, as well as how she used her newly inherited wealth. The lawyer had gone on to explain that he'd dealt with many similar wills where the deceased had unintentionally, if with the best of intentions, made things difficult for those left behind.

The wall clock behind him began to chime, which was Sienna's cue to exclaim with concern, 'I'm late.'

He bridled. What could possibly be more important to this woman, than the reading of her brother's will?

'I'm singing tonight,' she explained to the room at large.

With an angry gesture, he exclaimed, 'For goodness' sake, go!' Bad enough he should be forced to expose his feelings for Tom, without Tom's sister insinuating that he was keeping her here under duress. Tom wasn't supposed to die. Tom's sister wasn't supposed to inherit half the island. The fact that he, Alejandro, the most meticulous of men, had overlooked the possibility that such a disaster could occur only made his growing tension blaze higher.

But then he saw her face.

Riven with shock, she looked broken. What was wrong with him? They had both lost a piece of their life. Sienna had lost a brother. He only had to think back to how broken his siblings had been when their parents were killed to know how long grief took to heal.

'Before I go...' There was no challenge in her voice now.

'Yes?'

'I know how close you were to Tom.' She said this staring straight into his eyes. 'I want to thank you for everything you did for him.'

'Thank me?' He drew back. 'Thank me for what?'

'For taking my place with Tom at the end,' she explained.

What did she know about *the end*? What could anyone know? Sienna would have been informed in the broadest terms about Tom's injuries, but did she know that the real battle had been in her brother's mind? It wasn't up to him to tell her. How would it benefit Sienna to know?

He made a dismissive gesture in an attempt to close the subject. 'You don't have to thank me for anything.' The island he'd shared with Tom had been intended to restore her brother to the man Sienna thought she knew. It was a blessing she'd never seen how the weight of battle had crushed Tom, who was not just a brave soldier before his mind crashed, but a man who always went above and beyond for his comrades. Alejandro would remember Tom as a hero, a man who battled demons both real and imagined, and who was like a true brother to him. He would always be in Tom's debt.

'I'll say goodbye, then...'

He turned to see Sienna standing at the door. What did she want from him? 'You do realise Tom's money won't come through immediately?'

'I know that.'

She flinched as if he'd hit her, and her voice sounded raw,

but he pushed on. 'I'm happy to extend a loan, for however long you might need one…'

She frowned and looked perplexed. 'A loan for what?'

He gave a casual shrug. 'For whatever you might need.'

'I don't need anything, thank you.'

He was still suspicious. What did he know about her? Would Sienna be able to resist the lure of his wealth? 'Think about my offer, and come back to me if you need help.'

'I don't need to think about your offer,' she assured him. 'I can't think straight about anything right now, let alone money, but one thing I am sure about is that I don't need your help.'

'Don't be too hasty,' he advised. 'You'll soon have responsibilities—'

'Which I'll handle when I have to,' she interrupted. 'Believe me, I won't be rushing into any hasty decisions.'

A strength had come into her face he hadn't seen before. 'I'm trying to make things easy for you,' he explained.

The cynical lift of one finely drawn brow was accompanied by a cryptic question: 'Are you judging me on appearance, and thinking me needy?'

'No.' Yes, he was. 'Do you intend to hitch a lift to Spain— to visit your land?'

Her answer was a huff of incredulity. 'You have no idea of my means, and although I'm *very grateful* for your offer, please don't trouble yourself to make another, as I can't envisage any situation where I'd seek help from you.'

'We all need something, *señorita*,' he observed, resting back against the wall. 'And you may change your mind. Call me if that happens.' Reaching into the breast pocket of his jacket, he pulled out a card.

Taking the card without looking at it, she moved past him to the door. He opened it for her, and as they brushed against each other her cheeks pinked up. His reaction was more primitive. 'One last word of advice,' he offered through gritted teeth. 'Don't discuss your windfall widely.'

'My *windfall*?' she challenged, swinging around. 'Are you suggesting I regard my brother's bequest as nothing more than a tax-free win?'

'I *suggest* that you are wilfully misunderstanding me.'

'Am I?' she added with bite.

If looks could kill, but, *Dios*, she was beautiful. Younger than he'd imagined. *Had Tom said twenty-four?* If so, she was a very young twenty-four. Innocence blazed as fiercely as the anger in her eyes. 'I understand that you're upset—' She huffed at this, but, keeping his voice level, he continued, 'I intend no offence, and my offer remains open without time limit—' Was she even listening now? 'Don't forget to take your copy of Tom's letter with you—'

He fully expected her to snatch it from him, and stuff it in the envelope containing her brother's will, but instead she gripped it tightly, as if the paper it was written on contained some remnant of Tom. Her hands were shaking, he noticed, and she seemed emotionally deflated. Even he found it hard not to feel something when tears began to fall unchecked down her face. Examining Sienna's stricken eyes, he knew with certainty that he would never tell her the entire truth about Tom's death.

Reaching past her, he opened the door, but, perhaps remembering the last time when they'd touched, she lifted her hands up as if to ward him off, and her tone was very different as she said, 'I'll be sure to dress appropriately the next time we meet—'

What did he expect her to wear, sackcloth and ashes? But, bizarrely, the notion of a *next* time appealed to him.

'Tell me one thing, Alejandro,' she said, surprising him by stopping dead on her way out of the door.

The passion in her eyes transfixed him. 'Yes?'

'How could a man like you be my brother's best friend?'

He didn't take offence, because he'd asked himself that same question many times. Tom had released something in him, he supposed, until darkness had finally descended on Tom, and there was no lightness left in him.

'Tom was wonderfully warm and funny,' Sienna continued, unaware of the terrible irony in her words. 'My brother was the kindest person I ever knew. He lived in the light—lived *for* the light. He didn't dwell in darkness like you!'

'Upsetting yourself won't bring Tom back,' he cautioned. His concern was growing that Sienna might actually blunder into the road in this state and do herself some damage.

'Don't tell me to calm down,' she snapped. 'I'm grieving, heartbroken—stressed out with all the information you and the lawyer expect me to digest in an instant—'

'You're obviously distressed—'

'No!' she flared, brushing his hand from her shoulder. 'Don't you dare touch me! How do you think I feel in your gloomy house, with these heavy curtains and blinds shutting out the world? And—' She seemed at a loss for a moment, before blurting, 'And your butler wears white gloves.'

Hysteria born out of grief, he supposed, deciding to treat it with gentle humour. 'You take exception to white gloves?'

'I take exception to this hideous house,' she retorted.

His London residence had been decked out by an award-winning interior designer, who, she had told him, had taken great pains to reflect his personality. Unfortunately, he could see now that Sienna had a point, saying it was gloomy.

'And this!' she continued, jolting him back into the moment. Sweeping aside the curtains, she allowed the acid light of street lamps to flood into the room. 'I take exception to you! If you allowed some light into your life, perhaps you'd see things more clearly.' And with that, she stormed into the hall.

'Thank you, I'll see myself out,' he heard her declare, and then the front door closed behind her, leaving heavy silence in Sienna's wake.

CHAPTER TWO

IT TOOK SIENNA a good few minutes after leaving Alejandro's house to realise that she must be in shock. Meeting someone she had imagined would be like Tom, only to find Alejandro so very different, had rattled her to the point where grief for Tom threatened to overwhelm her.

She'd always found it easy to express herself through song, and couldn't get to Soho fast enough. How she got there was another mystery. She was on autopilot, with her thoughts reeling as her feet found the way.

Tom's bequest had left her speechless. She'd had no idea he had so much money. And half an island? Incredible. But why hadn't he said something the last time they'd been together? They'd spoken on the phone, she remembered, thinking back. Tom had given no hint of impending danger. How could he, when the nature of his job meant that everything had to be kept top secret? He'd been upbeat as usual, and had quickly turned the focus on Sienna. As usual. She should have pressed him for more details about his life—

Would the guilt ever stop?

This was all such a mess. The meeting with Alejandro had only made things worse, by going as badly as it could. She didn't like the man and could tell he didn't like her. There was nothing to be done about it. Convincing Alejandro that she had never wanted anything from Tom, except his love, was a lost cause. All she wanted was her brother back.

Why had Tom made it a condition of his will that she had to ask Alejandro for permission each time she wanted to use the money in Tom's bequest? Didn't he trust her? Nothing in their past pointed to that. If the idea hadn't been so preposterous, she might imagine Tom had thrown them together on purpose.

That thought was enough to make her shiver with awareness and dread. Alejandro was like two sides of the same coin. One side rubbed her up the wrong way, while the other held a fatal fascination. She couldn't think of a better reason to keep her distance from him.

Thoughts splintering into a thousand different strands, she dipped her head to barrel through the biting London wind. After the sedate pace of Mayfair, hurrying to the club through such a lively, bustling area was almost a relief. The contrast with Alejandro in his sombre Georgian mansion, located in a silent upmarket street, made her smile. She lived in a bedsit in someone else's house, in a not very fashionable part of London, but at least her room was bright and cheery, and she'd been happy living there, until Tom's death, while Alejandro didn't look the least bit happy.

Catching sight of the club always lifted Sienna's spirits. There was the customary long line of eager patrons, snaking around the building, waiting for the doors to open. Music had always saved her. When she'd lost her parents, she'd turned to music as a way to express her grief. Looking for a way to support herself, she turned to music again. And when Tom died, she found solace in singing.

An appreciative audience was a gift beyond price. They didn't come to the Blue Angel to see long faces. It was an opportunity to leave their troubles behind for an hour or two, and she was happy to join them in that. Losing Tom had been like a light going out of Sienna's life, but during the reading of the will she had realised that Tom had lit the light of possibility. And no one, not even the formidable Alejandro Acosta, was going to stand in the way of that.

Rex, the doorman, ushered her through the waiting queue. Rex didn't wear white gloves. Rex didn't wear any gloves. His knuckles bore many scars, but he was a kindly man, a widower with a heart of gold, who did everything for his two school-aged children. Patrons of the club only knew him as King Rex, a man they wouldn't dare to cross, but if Rex liked them he might ask Sienna if he could bring them to meet her.

'No visitors backstage tonight, Rex,' she said regretfully. 'I'm going to leave as soon as I finish my last set.'

Rex sympathised immediately, because he understood. 'You must be exhausted. Your brother...' Rex shook his head as he shrugged in sympathy.

'You too,' Sienna said gently. 'I hope you know how much we all appreciate you being here, when your life has been turned upside down?'

'You and my children are the ray of light that keeps me going,' he said, making Sienna wish that a ray of light could penetrate Alejandro's dark world. For a moment there, she felt sorry for him.

The following day, while Alejandro was straightening the picture of Tom on his desk, he thought about Sienna. He'd thought of little else. Unused to wealth, she would be vulnerable to predators. He had to find a way to persuade her to come to him for both money and advice.

Don't mess with my sister. The words rang in his head. What had Tom meant by that warning? Tom knew full well that Alejandro's taste ran to sophisticated women who knew the score. You needn't worry, he silently informed his old friend. Your sister is safe from me.

If that were true, why was he still thinking about her?

The challenge in Sienna's eyes was to blame, he concluded. Who knew what she had in mind when it came to Tom's money and land? He'd have to see her again in order to set parameters, and, in truth, he'd like to hear her sing. Anything he could learn about Sienna would help him when it came to interpreting her intentions going forward.

Is that the only reason I want to see her again?

What else could it be?

There weren't many things forbidden to Alejandro Acosta, but Tom Slater's sister was one of them.

He dredged his mind for snippets of information that Tom might have told him about Sienna. His main concern was that Tom had always sounded tense when he talked about his sister. In Tom's opinion, Sienna had left school too soon, in order to pursue a career in music. 'She's headstrong,' Tom had explained, 'and refuses to listen to me.'

Hmm. She would have to listen to Alejandro. Headstrong or not, Sienna wouldn't receive a penny of her inheritance unless she—

Unless she what? Kowtowed to him?

Recalling those fiery green eyes, he knew the road ahead wouldn't be easy, and, strangely, he looked forward to embarking on that journey. Gazing at Tom's photograph again, he had to wonder, how could one sibling become a tortured hero, while the other appeared content to work in a club?

Necessity? his interfering inner critic suggested.

He dismissed this out of hand. Club work was not a safe option for a woman who had recently inherited a fortune in money and land.

Those fiery green eyes should see her through?

Unlikely, he thought as he cleaned the already clean photo frame with his sleeve. The action prompted him to study Tom's face. Tom certainly didn't seem on the surface like a deeply troubled man, which was why the army had deemed him fit for service. He'd shared the island with Tom in the hope that it would give Tom the chance to build a new life away from the battlefield. And now he would build a fitting memorial to the dearest of friends.

The irony of a friendship based on mutual guilt had not escaped him. Neither he nor Tom had ever forgiven themselves for their parents' deaths. *If only we'd done this, or that, we might have stopped them.* That had been a common theme between them. And now Sienna found herself in the middle of that turmoil, which made finding the right way to deal with her twice as hard.

Sienna sang her heart out that night at the club, dedicating each song in her mind to Tom. Jason, her accompanist on the piano, sensing her intense involvement in the music, had played like an angel. The audience couldn't have been more responsive or warmer if they'd tried. She would never be able to thank them enough for the distraction they provided.

The surprises in Tom's will hadn't helped to settle her mind. Nor had the fact that Tom had gone, while Alejandro Acosta was very much here, and very much in her life. That said, however powerful he was, she would not be browbeaten, and whether Alejandro agreed or not she would find a way to turn Tom's bequest into a living memorial for everything her brother had stood for.

The club organised a cab to take her home each night, and once she was safely inside her tiny bedsit she ran through the solicitor's words in her mind, but thoughts of Alejandro proved a constant distraction. Leaning back against the thin padding of a threadbare chair, she wondered what Alejandro thought of her. He was a living symbol of success, but that didn't make him compassionate.

Why, Tom, why? I don't want anything from you. I certainly didn't want to meet up with that awful man. I don't want an island, or your money, I just want you back.

But Tom wasn't coming back, and the only way to handle a man like Alejandro Acosta was with endless patience, and as much diplomacy as she could muster.

On that discomforting thought, she switched off the fire and crawled into bed. The covers were so cold they felt damp, and again, thoughts of Alejandro intruded. What an unlikely friend for Tom. There had to be something she didn't know about her brother that had led to his close friendship with Alejandro. If only she hadn't kept news of her recent professional qualification from Tom. She'd paid for her college course by working at the club, but she'd enjoyed that. Turning her face into the pillow, she tried not to be sad. There was so much to be grateful for. Music was her life, and, thanks to Tom's generosity in his will, she could build a centre in his name, and share music with countless others—

Even Alejandro?

She all but growled when his face came into her head, and all chance of sleep was lost. Reaching for the light, she climbed out of bed. Shrugging on her outdoor coat to fend off the chill, she switched on her heater. Ferreting about in her cluttered tote, she found the will and read it again. Would she ever understand Tom's intentions? A vast tract of land *and* all that money? Half an island off the coast of Spain, for someone who, with her studies and work, had rarely travelled out of London. And her land abutted Alejandro's. At first, when the solicitor had read out the will, she'd imagined building a retreat on the island, but later she'd learned that she would have to ask Alejandro's permission to do anything. Well, whatever he thought, she would visit the island and make her own decision about what to do next.

Did that mean meeting up with Alejandro?

Her heart thundered at the thought. Even here, in a tiny room she could cross in five steps, it was as if he occupied every inch of space.

Putting the will away safely, she got back into bed. The frigid covers couldn't compete with the expression she pictured on Alejandro's face, when she pitched her idea for a therapy centre on the island. She resolutely turned her thoughts to sun-kissed beaches instead. It was just a shame that the last image in her mind before the world of sleep claimed her was of a blisteringly handsome man with a jaw set as firm as her own.

CHAPTER THREE

RAGE AT THE injustice of Tom's will soared inside him as he got ready for a night out that Sienna would not expect. What did she know about farming fertile farm land in Spain? What would she do with her portion of the land? Visions of a glitzy shopping mall, or, worse, a forest of high-rise hotels sprang to mind, with Sienna dressed to the nines, fêted on every side by shallow, grasping individuals, all scheming to take advantage of her. The island was easily big enough to warrant development, but that had never been his plan. The islanders didn't want it, and it was up to him to protect them from some badly thought-out scheme.

Rasping a thumbnail across the fast-growing stubble on his face, he glowered into the mirror. Pocketing his phone, he headed out. Turned out, Sienna was the headline act at the Blue Angel tonight. He had to concede that said something about her ability. He'd learned the club was well thought of, and not by those hoping to see and to be seen. The Blue Angel had built its reputation solely on the quality of its musicians, which drove his curiosity where Sienna was concerned.

Beautiful, intriguing and exasperating, he concluded as he gunned the engine of his favourite car. Rebellion glowed in those green, green eyes; emerald eyes with a mix of intelligence and stubbornness blazing from them. By the time he brought his vehicle to a halt outside the club, he had to remind himself firmly that fantasies about emerald eyes were superfluous to requirements.

His arrival had attracted the doorman's attention. That and a fifty. 'I'd like a word with your singer, Sienna Slater,' he explained to the burly bouncer. To his surprise, the man didn't assure him that anything and everything was possible, and instead returned the fifty as he said solemnly, 'If you give me your name, I'll pass your message on.'

Kudos to the man. 'I'd appreciate that, thank you.'

'I'll see your car's parked safely,' the doorman added as he summoned a younger man to take the keys.

'Am I allowed to tip him?' Alejandro asked with some irony.

'As you see fit,' the doorman told him with dignity.

Good man, he thought, acknowledging this with a nod of his head.

He entered the club to find a more than half-decent jazz band playing. He guessed the musicians were warming up the crowd for the main event, which was Sienna. Just that. Just her first name written in gold on a full-sized billboard showing a young woman with wistful green eyes, and a beautiful, if surprisingly mischievous, face. But what really caught his attention was Sienna's spectacular hourglass figure. Far from the defensive waif in shabby clothes he remembered, this was a confident woman with a warm, friendly smile. Tumbling auburn hair completed the picture. Set free to cascade in gleaming waves down her back, the glossy profusion was styled to cover one naked shoulder.

A single word sprang to mind, and it wasn't for public consumption.

The moment she walked on stage Sienna was aware of a brooding presence. Was that really Alejandro standing by the door? *Why was he here?* Heat and shock raced through her. He was staring at her. And only her.

Everyone was staring at her. That tended to happen when you were on stage.

Maybe, she conceded, but only one stare in the club held erotic menace. And, by some alchemy of his own, Alejandro managed to look even more striking than before. Who knew that dressing down could look this sexy? Snug-fitting jeans secured by a heavy-duty belt, with a dark top that clung to his impressive torso with loving attention to detail, was completed by black loafers, black jacket, thick black stubble, and wildly tumbled, wavy black hair.

Did he ever comb that hair, or did he just rake it in frustration each time they met? A steely billionaire was transformed into what looked more like a pirate of old on the loose. Sienna knew which variation she preferred. Her erotic zones did too. But now she had to concentrate, or she'd never be able to sing.

Tearing her gaze away from Alejandro, she almost wished he'd turn back into the cold man at their first meeting. This primal brute, with barely suppressed energy raging off him, was a threat to her senses, and she didn't have enough experience to know how to deal with that. He'd even managed to silence the jokers at the bar, who, after a couple of drinks, thought they could take on the world. Was this dangerous-looking individual the real Alejandro? A shiver coursed down her spine at the thought.

Propping a hip against the wall, he stared straight back, upping the threat to her senses. Her mouth dried and her throat closed. Would it even be possible to sing? For the first time ever, she missed her musical cue. Thank goodness for Jason at the piano, who took the hitch in his stride, improvising as if his piano solo had been intended all along. Recovering fast, she smiled across at Jason, whose deft touch on the piano reassured Sienna that this was her world, a world where she was comfortable. And this was her music, the same music that had allowed her to pay her way through college with a distinction at the end of her course.

The audience fell quiet as she began to sing. They were attentive throughout and went wild when she finished. Her gaze sought out Alejandro, who nodded his head with approval. She had no idea why his appreciation meant so much to her, just that it did.

Bringing Jason forward to share the applause, she smiled warmly across at her brilliant accompanist, and when the crowd called for more, they were happy to oblige. Once that encore had finished, she refocused to find Alejandro moving towards the stage.

What did he want? Why was he here? She couldn't imagine a club like the Blue Angel would be Señor Acosta's venue of choice. Though tonight, she had to admit, he fitted in perfectly in casual clothes, though he was causing quite a stir. Several people had recognised the famous billionaire, polo-playing Acosta brother from his pictures in the press, and were transfixed by his striking presence as he walked through the club.

What was she supposed to do now? She could hardly invite him into her cupboard-sized dressing room, which she shared with her friend the boiler and a few crates of beer.

'Alejandro,' she said, as pleasantly as she could.

'Sienna.'

He made no attempt at all to sound pleasant, and his shrewd dark eyes pierced her soul with unforgiving intensity. Ignoring the fact that he was holding out a hand to help her down the steps at the side of the stage, she picked up the hem of her gown and made her own way down. 'I didn't expect to see you here tonight,' she admitted, craning her neck to meet his black stare. How could she have forgotten how tall he was, or how big and powerful, and evenly tanned? At least, she imagined he was evenly tanned...

Stop that! she told herself firmly as the man in question began to speak. 'I'm sure you didn't expect to see me here,' he agreed, in the now familiar dark-chocolate voice.

Be polite. Treat him like a welcome guest. Don't avoid his stare. Meet it. And smile. 'I hope you enjoyed the show?'

'Very much,' he said, surprising her by sounding as if he meant this.

Alejandro's sexual charge made it hard to keep focus. He made it impossible to look anywhere but into his eyes. Radiating a force that she found almost hypnotic. It was a struggle to blank thoughts of how it might feel to be in his arms.

'I'm sorry,' she said briskly, 'but I need to get changed. My cab will be arriving to take me home soon.'

'There's no need for you to take a cab.'

There was every need to take a cab, she thought, interpreting the smouldering interest in Alejandro's eyes as something it was safer not to get too close to. 'I have to wash off my stage make-up first.'

'Of course,' he allowed.

'If you'll excuse me—?' She tried to move past, but, just as he'd been at the door in his house, Alejandro took up a lot of space. She was intensely aware that the gown she had chosen to wear that evening was a figure-skimming column of silver silk satin that clung to every curve she possessed, the urge to replace it with baggy jeans and an even baggier top was suddenly a priority. Alejandro's expression was calculating, and if she hadn't promised herself to try and keep things smooth with him, she'd tell him straight out that she'd dressed for her audience, not for him.

Sidling past, she opened the door that led down to her basement dressing room, leaving Alejandro and his smouldering look in her wake. Once she was safely enclosed inside the small space, she stared at her reflection in the fly-blown mirror. Her cheeks were flushed. She looked excited, and that was definitely bad news.

Easing out of her gown, she hung it up on a hanger. Reaching for her cleansing cream, she removed every trace of the siren who had sung on the stage. Girl-next-door restored, she felt confidence returning along with her clean, shiny face, and laughed bitterly at the thought that life could not be transformed quite so easily.

But she'd get through this, Sienna determined as she picked up her things. And if she and Alejandro got the chance to know each other a little better, she felt sure he'd see reason when it came to her scheme for a music facility on the island.

Really? You think he'll go for that?

Tom had said a lot of things about Alejandro. One, that he was the bravest man Tom knew, and also the most loyal, as well as being the fairest, so perhaps there was a chance he'd agree to her scheme.

'Alejandro leads from the front, and never leaves a man behind,' Tom had said. This was true, according to the officers who had broken the terrible news to Sienna. Alejandro hadn't left Tom behind. He'd carried Tom's lifeless body through gunfire and explosion, all the way back to camp, where he'd spent that first long night talking to Tom as if he were still alive. On that basis alone, she had to give Alejandro a second chance. She could only trust he'd give her a second chance too.

Firming her resolve, she went upstairs to find Alejandro in the same place, resting back against the wall. 'We need to talk, Sienna. Are you cold?' he asked with concern when she shivered.

Cold? No. Apprehensive? Yes. What was so important it had brought Alejandro to the club tonight? She would not be rushed into any decision when it came to the island.

'Let's go,' he said. 'We can't speak here. It's far too noisy.'

'Go where?' She hung back. 'My cab's due any minute.'

'I've told you before, you don't need a cab. I'll take you home.'

'Thanks for the offer, but I'm really tired tonight. It's been a long day,' she excused, thinking, no way, I'm not ready for that. 'A long few days, in fact. I doubt I'd be very good company.'

'Whatever suits you.' Alejandro didn't seem bothered as he shrugged and smiled, and for a moment she was tempted to accept his offer. Thankfully, reason prevailed. She'd be in his car, under his control, going who knew where. Alejandro might have been Tom's best friend, but she didn't know him from Adam. Would she break the habit of a lifetime, and climb into a stranger's car?

'Why don't we come to this fresh in the morning?' she suggested. 'We could meet at the café next door. I have a rehearsal at nine with my pianist, Jason. Shall we say eleven o'clock? That would suit me,' she couldn't resist adding with the faintest of edges.

One sweeping ebony brow lifted in acknowledgement of her counter-punch. If Alejandro's firm mouth hadn't been quite so dangerous when it curved like that, or his stare so amused and compelling, she might have turned on her heel and left him right then and there, but this change in him, from the stern individual at the dreadful reading of the will to the Master of the Sexual Universe, lounging in a club, was so surprisingly marked that curiosity got the better of her, and she waited to hear what he had to say next.

'What if I tell you that this can't wait until tomorrow?' he suggested.

'I'd say, you need to learn patience,' she countered levelly.

His brow shot up again, but this time the amusement had died in his eyes. Too bad. She had no intention of becoming anyone's doormat.

'Before you go,' he said, 'I want you to know that I really enjoyed your singing tonight. You are an exceptionally talented singer.'

She said simply, 'Thank you,' just as her singing teacher had advised when praise made Sienna feel awkward.

'Until tomorrow?' Alejandro queried.

She must have looked at him with a blank stare, because he reminded her about their next appointment at the coffee shop. 'Right,' she agreed, wondering with concern what exactly she was agreeing to. 'See you then…'

Dragging greedily on the chill night air, she didn't turn to see Alejandro had followed her out of the club. It was a relief to find her usual cab waiting at the kerb. She remembered very little of the drive home, and must have been in a state of shock, she concluded on her return. What would have happened if she had allowed Alejandro to take her home? Nothing, she reasoned sensibly as she put her key in the front door. She was hardly his type. Coffee the next morning in a bustling café was neutral territory, and that was where they would sort things out.

Over a flat white? Did that seem likely?

A restless night later, concealer was needed under her eyes. She was groggy and under par at rehearsal, and Jason was kind not to mention it. 'See you tonight.' She forced a grin as she hurried away to keep her date with destiny.

Her date with a flat white and a spoonful of sugar, Sienna corrected herself firmly.

* * *

Arriving first, he ordered, then found a table. A basket of pastries, coffee and a jug of hot milk were duly delivered with early-morning speed. Sienna breezed in, stared around—not anxiously, but with a keen eye. He raised a hand in greeting, and she wove her way through the tables towards him. Not for the first time, he wished they'd met under different circumstances, with no restrictions placed on him by her brother, so they could proceed from casual hook-up to bed. He wasn't proud of his attitude towards sex. That was just how it was for him. Sex was as essential as eating and sleeping. No long-term commitment required, either by him or the women he dated.

Sienna sat across the table, her knees a whisper away from his. 'Flat white?' She sounded pleased. 'How did you know?'

'Educated guess. Actually,' he admitted with a shrug, 'Tom told me about your love of strong coffee with just a hint of steamed milk.'

'Tom loved strong coffee, straight up,' she remembered with a wistful smile that drew his attention to her lips. 'Oh, and by the way, good morning, Alejandro,' she added with a smile into his eyes. 'Where would you like to begin your interrogation?'

His mock-warning look made her blush. Where he'd like to begin was better kept to himself, so he confined himself to the blandest of questions, if only to see her kissable mouth form the syllables. 'I hope your rehearsal went well this morning?'

'Very well, thank you.'

'You sang great last night. I trust you got home safely?'

Holding his gaze, she barely missed a beat. 'Of course, I did. I made sure of it, didn't I?'

'I can't imagine what you're suggesting, *señorita*.'

'Can't you?' she said with a teasing sceptical look.

Neither one of them was a pushover, and that pleased him, for some reason. 'Have you had a chance to give any thought to your plans for the land you have inherited?'

'Launch straight in, why don't you?' Her eyes sparkled with amusement, challenge and warning as she stared at him over the rim of her coffee cup.

'You might be relieved to hear I can find a way out of this.'

'And what's that?' Putting her cup down, she frowned.

'I buy the land, and set you free.'

Pulling her head back, she gave him a caustic look. 'Not a chance, *señor*. What makes you think I'd ever want to sell that land? And I certainly don't need to be set free, by you or anyone else.'

'Caring effectively for so much land is a huge responsibility.'

'Here ends today's sermon?' she intoned, clearly not afraid of mocking him, but her expression quickly changed to serious. 'Do you think I don't know that?'

Sitting back, she contemplated the table for a moment or two, before lifting her chin to accuse him of leaping to conclusions. 'By your own admission, you know nothing about me, yet you've decided I'm not capable of handling responsibility.'

'That's not what I said,' he defended. 'But I don't believe you have any experience of land management. I'm quite prepared to discuss this issue in more detail, back at my place—'

'We can discuss it here,' she cut in firmly.

'Where it's noisy and hardly private? I give you my word, you can leave at any time, and I won't pressure you to act one way or another. All I ask is that you hear me out before firming up any decision.'

Going on Sienna's past reaction to his invitations, he fully expected her to say no, but instead she stood and said with a shrug, 'Okay.'

He led the way out of the café, en route to the next chapter in the ongoing saga of Acosta versus Slater, and, for once, he couldn't wait to turn the page.

The last time she'd been to Alejandro's smart London home, she had arrived on foot. This was very different. He kept the sleek red sports car, in which they'd arrived, in an underground garage beneath the house, where it joined a line of similar supercars. Alejandro got out first, and came around to open her door. Good start. An elevator took them up to the main part of the house. Its doors slid open to reveal a subtly lit corridor where the décor was opulent and subdued, and jewel colours predominated. Her feet were instantly encased in deep-pile carpet. Full sensory overload. She dragged deep on the scent of old money. But new ideas, she hoped.

She gave a sharp intake of breath when Alejandro put his hand on her shoulder. 'Apologies,' he murmured. 'I didn't mean to startle you. Just leading you in the right direction.'

She could only hope.

His touch lingered, not in actual fact, but in her muscle memory. It was so compelling. He was so compelling. So, keep your wits about you. But it was hard not to be beguiled by so much hypnotic glamour.

That same glamour was reflected in Alejandro's house. Gilt-framed mirrors and oil paintings of horses lined the corridor, together with impressive bowls and urns with an oriental look about them. No children allowed here, she thought with amusement. How did he cope when the children of his brothers and sister visited, when everything had obviously been curated to impress? But not by Alejandro, Sienna suspected. The *objets d'art* had been placed to impress a man who was clearly oblivious to his surroundings. Alejandro had probably paid someone a fortune to come and mess up his house. If she lived here, there'd be clean lines and no clutter. But she didn't live here, so...

'What are you thinking?' Alejandro asked when she stopped walking to stare around.

'That I've left my world behind and entered yours.'

He remained non-committal. Had he brought her here to try to seduce her? No. Alejandro was far too cool for that. The more pressing question was, if he tried, did she have what it took to resist him?

Thankfully, he gave her no chance to think about it, before opening a polished mahogany door she remembered well, because it led into his study.

CHAPTER FOUR

BLUEBEARD'S LAIR, this was not, though it was the same sombre room she remembered from the reading of Tom's will. In that moment she felt sorry for Alejandro. With all his money, he should have someone to help him brighten up his life. Even a coat of whitewash would be better than these dull grey walls.

'Would you mind if we went somewhere else?' she asked as a shiver of recall crept down her spine.

'The will, of course,' he said, remembering. 'I'm sorry, I should have been more sensitive.'

Was it too much to hope they were getting somewhere at last?

'How about the library?' he suggested.

Just the word lifted her spirits. 'Perfect.'

And it was. Who owned so many books, apart from Alejandro? Some were clearly very old and precious. There was even a beautifully illuminated manuscript in glass case.

'You're a very lucky man...'

For a while, she was so immersed in studying Alejandro's books, she almost forgot the purpose of her visit. There was so much to look at—and he had so much to explain. Halting her avid tour, she turned around to face him. 'What was it you wanted to say to me? I should tell you right away that my half of the island is not for sale.'

'What a relief,' he intoned dryly. 'Why don't you sit down?'

'Will this take long?'

'Why? Do you have another rehearsal?'

It would have been the easiest thing in the world to say yes, but she couldn't lie to him. 'No. I'm free for the rest of the day,' she admitted.

'Then, relax,' he advised. 'Better we get to know each other if we're going to work through this successfully.'

Tipping her chin, she gave him a look. 'I'll tell my lawyer what you said.'

'Your lawyer?'

It had been an off-the-cuff remark, but Alejandro's face had changed completely, from open and easy, to narrow-eyed suspicion. 'That was a joke. Not a very good one,' she conceded, but the storm in his eyes failed to subside. He must think she was a gold-digger with only one thought on her mind—to do as she pleased, when she pleased, and to hell with him. 'I'm sorry. It was an ill-judged remark. If the land's worth that much to you—'

Alejandro shot back with passion. 'Of course, it is. I care deeply about the land and the people who have lived there all their lives. Their livelihoods and future depend on careful management, and I won't see anything stand in the way of that.'

'Are you suggesting I'd do something to harm them?'

'I don't know what you'd do,' he admitted as things grew heated. 'I don't know you.'

'That makes two of us, but, whether you believe me or not, this isn't about money for me.'

'It must be the only thing on God's earth that isn't,' he said with a scowl.

Perhaps suspicion always accompanied great wealth, and

again she felt sorry for Alejandro. Could he trust anyone when so much was at stake? 'I apologise for wasting your time,' she said, standing. 'To be honest, I don't know yet what I'm going to do with Tom's land. But—'

'But you must have some idea,' he cut in.

'All I can promise is that you have my word that I will do everything in my power to protect that land.'

Laying out her hopes and dreams in any more detail, before Alejandro, a man with boundless power, and teams of people to do his bidding, would make her own ideas seem naïve and unformed. She didn't have a business plan, or even an architect's sketch to show him. All she had was a firm conviction that she would build a tribute to Tom. Telling Alejandro that she would make that happen somehow would only make her look foolish. He'd think she was a dreamer, or, worse, he might imagine that she was hoping to lean on him to bring her dreams to fruition.

'I imagine you won't be doing anything in the near future, unless you have the money to proceed,' he said in a clipped tone.

Why didn't he just come right out and say it: before she got her hands on Tom's money? Alejandro had reinforced the fact that she'd have to ask him to release funds from Tom's estate to do anything, and even then he'd be looking over her shoulder every step of the way. They couldn't go on like this, facing each other, daggers drawn like two combatants in a ring. 'You know music's my first love—'

He pounced on that one simple statement. 'Are you planning to open a music school on the island?'

'Is that such a terrible idea?'

To her relief, Alejandro appeared to relax. 'I'd be concerned that you'd find enough pupils on a small island to keep the school afloat, and I'd have to wonder why you didn't open your school in London.'

Sienna had been wondering the very same thing, but the mysterious island that Tom had loved so much beckoned to her. Tom had shouldered the responsibility of bringing her up, and had allowed Sienna to pursue her dreams at music college. It seemed only right to try to repay him, and where better to build a retreat than the sun-kissed land Tom had loved so much, with all the associated health benefits the island could bring to those who needed it?

'Don't forget your bag when you go.'

Jerked back into the present, she remembered that Alejandro had offered to take her home whenever she wanted. 'I won't—and thanks for the lift. It's very kind of you.'

'Under the circumstances?' he suggested.

She found a smile. 'Let's just say, I appreciate the kindness.'

Alejandro Acosta could say more with his eyes than anyone she knew could with words, and his gaze right now said, don't mock me.

I won't, she answered silently on her way to the door.

Everything went well until they brushed against each other when he opened the door, and then, like two magnets that couldn't fend off contact for ever, they exchanged a brief, intense stare. For a moment, she was sure he was going to kiss her.

Should have known better, Sienna ruefully accepted as Alejandro stepped back. He was a seasoned campaigner, while she was very new to the game.

'We'll talk again tomorrow,' he said, 'but, if you'll take some advice, don't make any decisions until you've seen the land.'

'I won't,' she promised on her way across the hall.

'I'm looking forward to hearing you sing again,' Alejandro said, surprising her.

'Glutton for punishment?' she suggested.

'Glutton for pleasure,' he countered with another of his disturbing looks.

Apart from a few civilities, they didn't speak as he drove her home, but Alejandro so close beside her heightened her senses to a painful degree. The instant she closed the door on her bedsit, she touched her lips with her fingertips, imagining the warm pressure of his lips on her mouth. A restless night followed, and it felt as if she'd only just dozed off, but light was streaming through the curtains when the phone rang. 'Hello,' she managed groggily, fumbling the receiver.

'I'm taking you home from the club tonight, okay?'

'Alejandro?' Instantly awake, she shot up in bed. 'Do you always firm up your plans before other people are properly awake?'

'Best time ever,' he countered in an amused drawl. 'How do you think I'm so successful in business?'

'No scruples?' she suggested dryly.

'Harsh,' he said, but his tone was disturbingly intimate, and the smile in his voice warmed her.

Sienna gave a spectacular performance that night. Not wanting to crowd her, he waited at the stage door, mingling with a group of fans for the sheer pleasure of hearing them praise her. Finding time for everyone, Sienna laughed, signed autographs and shared her joy. Her gaze found him right away, but he shook his head, indicating that she should carry on for as long as she needed to.

He took her to a small supper club off Regent Street where the waiters were discreet, the clientele was low-key classy and the crème brulée was spectacular. They laughed when he told her it was something she shouldn't miss.

'Are you trying to bribe me with burned sugar and cream?' she suggested, cocking her head to one side so her eyes sparkled in the candlelight like emeralds.

'I'm recommending something I know you'll enjoy.'

'In that case...' She smiled up at the waiter. 'Two crème brulées, please.'

He never ate pudding, but tonight he'd make an exception.

They talked about everything except the land. It was hard not to enjoy talking about the exceptional childhoods both of them had been lucky enough to experience. They made no mention of the tragedy that had struck both their families, and it seemed as if their mellow surroundings had provided a cocoon, where they could enjoy each other's company without the harsh facts of life intruding. Against all the odds, he realised as Sienna sucked sugar cream from her tiny spoon. Even he couldn't see much wrong with that. 'Coffee?' he suggested.

'No, thanks. I don't like decaf, and I wouldn't be able to sleep if I drank full-strength.'

Her innocence pierced him. He couldn't think of any other woman who'd have sleep at the front of her mind right now. 'Mint tea? Anything at all?'

'No, thank you. I've really enjoyed tonight,' she said, as if she was as surprised as he was. 'I haven't felt so relaxed in ages, even though we've been talking about our child-hoods, which usually makes me sad.'

'But it also drives you on, doesn't it?' he proposed with a frown. 'I mean, we both like to seize the moment, seize life, and squeeze every drop out of it, because of every-thing we've lost.'

'I've never looked at it like that,' she admitted.

'It's hard to see the positives, when they come with so much grief attached.'

'And wariness,' she added with a twisted smile.

'And that,' he conceded as he called for the bill, and stood to pull back her chair.

When she turned their faces were briefly so close, they shared the same breath, the same air. Something changed between them then. Whether it was the adrenalin of performance in her case, or the thrill of the hunt in his, he had no idea, but Sienna's eyes had darkened as she stared into his, tightening his groin to the point of pain. *Behave,* he told himself sternly. He'd take her straight home. That was the right thing to do.

But the right thing to do was never the only option, and without giving it too much thought he turned the vehicle in the direction of Mayfair. Sienna didn't query the route. Tension spiked between them. *Sorry, Tom.* They both knew why they were here, he reflected as he turned the wheel and they parked up in his underground garage.

He called the elevator, and they stepped inside. It stopped suddenly between floors. Had Sienna leaned back against the controls on purpose? Or was fate in charge? It really didn't matter. Neither did who made the first move. Fire raged equally between them.

'Take me to bed,' she whispered.

Was Sienna fulfilling some long-suppressed desire? Was he? Probably. Did it matter? They could have been standing on a beach, or lying on a bed entwined around each other, and there would still be this same, undeniable urge to forget the past and put the future on hold for now.

How she arrived in Alejandro's bedroom would always remain a bit of a blur. She remembered them tearing at each other's clothes as the same erotic force swept them into its embrace. It was only when Alejandro had removed the last vestige of her clothing that she realised how calm he had become, while she was still wild for him. He'd made her feel safe enough to lose all her inhibitions. She was lucky that this man, who so closely resembled a barbarian, quickly proved he could be measured too. It was a surprise to find his control really turned her on.

'Do you want me?' he murmured, knowing what her answer would be. She had no breath to tell him, *So much.*

Answering his every touch with frantic sounds of need, she grabbed at this chance to put the past with all its sadness behind her. They were communicating on the most basic level: touch, taste, scent, and sound. Alejandro's strength and her need combined into one irresistible force. Impossibly attractive, virile and masculine, he made it impossible to hold back, and why should she? Plunging into a powerful release when he'd barely touched her, she screamed out, *'Yes!'* as the pleasure waves consumed her.

'Greedy...' Alejandro murmured, smiling against her mouth when she was calm enough to hear him.

'Are you complaining?'

'Complaining?' he said softly. 'No...'

And then he kissed her again, while she writhed shamelessly in his grasp.

'Slow down,' he advised in the same soothing tone. 'We've got all night.'

But she was trembling with arousal and was soon on the brink again. Alejandro knew exactly how to school her responses, and he made her wait.

'Brute,' she complained, pummelling him with frustration. 'I'm not one of your world-class ponies to be trained in your ways.'

'No,' he agreed. 'You're far more wilful, so your schooling may take a lot longer.'

She could only hope. Loving the way he held her so lightly, yet so firmly, always keeping satisfaction at bay, raising her arousal to a thrilling breaking point. Pinning her wrists above her head, he continued the delicious torture, leaving her whimpering with desire as he laved her nipples until she thrust and bucked with longing. But, once again, he pulled back.

Calling him names she couldn't believe she knew, she gasped with relief when she realised that Alejandro wasn't stopping, he was protecting them both.

Easing her legs apart, he allowed the tip of his erection to brush against her most sensitive core. Placing a hand beneath her buttocks, he lifted her. Slipping a pillow beneath her hips, he positioned her to his liking. Drawing her knees back, she wrapped her legs around his waist. Exposed and vulnerable, she had never felt so safe. Arching her back, she cried out with need, but still he refused to be rushed.

Well, she refused to be kept waiting.

But could she take him? Could she take all of him? She had to. This was the oblivion she needed. Alejandro was everything she needed. And more.

CHAPTER FIVE

SIENNA WAS BEAUTIFUL. Her pleasure was his pleasure. Drawing sensation out was a skill he took seriously. By the time he eased her over the edge again, she had reached another level of consciousness. Denial followed by fulfilment allowed her to experience the ultimate in arousal, and she came with his very first thrust.

They both needed this, he reasoned as he moved rhythmically and firmly. He allowed her to use him, exactly as she wished. Having extracted every last pulse of pleasure, he was careful not to over-stimulate her recovering body, but remained confident that it wouldn't be long before Sienna was desperate for more.

'If you'd like me to stop,' he teased as she clung to him.

She turned a fierce stare on his face. 'Don't you dare!'

'Whatever you say, *señorita—*'

'You'll give me everything I want?' she queried.

In bed? Yes, of course he would. Out of bed remained to be seen.

It was easy to stir her hunger again with shallow, teasing probes. Sienna encouraged him with words he doubted she'd used before. 'I can do that,' he whispered against her ear. 'And I'll keep on doing it, until you ask me to stop.'

'That's never going to happen,' she assured him fiercely.

By rotating his hips, he could massage the little nub that

begged for his attention. Persuasive brushes and nudges were gradually turned into a firmer movement that had her teetering on the edge. He held off for as long as he could, while Sienna gripped his buttocks with fingers turned to steel.

'Relax…let me do this,' he instructed, and once she was limp again he used firm, rhythmical strokes to bring her the pleasure she craved.

It was light when she woke in Alejandro's bed, taking stock of a body well used. He was already out of bed—and dressed. For the office?

'Hey,' he urged, seeing she was awake. 'I've got work to do. Do we need to talk before I go?'

That did it. She was instantly awake. And offended. 'Don't let me keep you.'

'I've got meetings crowding in on me, babe.'

Babe? 'You don't have to explain. Just go.'

Alejandro looked relieved. Throwing back the curtains, he blinded her with light. 'Take as long as you need,' he said. 'There's no point in rushing. The staff won't be back until midday.'

By which time, she must be gone, Sienna gathered, reading between the lines. Hot shame suffused her. Alejandro was treating her like a one-night stand. Not that there was anything wrong with a one-night stand, but she had thought they had more between them.

Wrong. He was clearly having second thoughts about sleeping with her. But at the restaurant last night she'd thought they'd become close. Wrong again. Alejandro was merely being polite. She wasn't his type, and she should never have pushed things until they ended up like this. Her cheeks flared red when she remembered launching herself at him in the elevator—but he'd done quite a bit of launching too. Okay, but she should have resisted.

Seriously?

Whatever their motivation, sex without emotion would never be enough, Sienna realised as Alejandro strode to the door. She'd never really considered what she wanted, or even what she expected, from relationships before. A craving for the closeness her parents had shared, she supposed, biting back emotion, and yet, there was always that fear that caring too much could lead to the most terrible loss. Both she and Alejandro wore armour to protect against that.

So, where did that leave her? Having woken content in the certainty that they'd built on their closeness last night, she now suspected that Alejandro had been having sex, while she had expected too much from him on the emotional front. Like supreme athletes, they'd given an outstanding display, satisfying their most basic needs, but to read anything more than that into what they'd done was foolish. A night that had meant so much to her, a night when she'd fooled herself into believing that concord of mind led to intimacy of body, had ended now, and as abruptly as a safety curtain coming down on a show.

Some show, she mused with an ironic twist of her mouth. 'Don't worry, Alejandro, I'll be leaving soon.'

Quite suddenly, her nakedness became an embarrassment, and she dragged the sheet close around her body before she got out of bed. 'Do you mind if I take a quick shower before I go?'

'Of course. Be my guest.'

That just about summed it up, Sienna thought as Alejandro palmed his keys. She was a chance visitor, no more than that, and, as if to prove it, he didn't look back once as he left the room.

* * *

Had he been too harsh? No. He had no intention of taking things further, and it would be wrong to lead Sienna on. He shouldn't have seduced her in the first place.

Seduced her? Desire had been mutual. Maybe, but nothing lasted for ever, and beneath Sienna's bravado she was vulnerable, and he would not stamp on that.

In spite of this reasoning, on the drive to his office he could think of nothing but Sienna. She'd woken in obvious confusion: where was she? What had they done? When realisation had dawned, her fantasies had taken over: they'd made love. Seeing her so happy, he'd felt an impulse to stay with her. Sleep-rumpled, and flushed, she had never looked more beautiful to him, but his world turned relentlessly, and he had no doubt that, when Sienna thought things through, she'd be glad that he'd gone.

Flashbacks of the previous night plagued him throughout the morning. It was hard not to smile when he remembered the little anecdotes they'd shared during their meal in the restaurant. There was no doubt that, on a personal level, they'd got on really well. As far as sex was concerned, her passion had surprised him. But he should have known better—

It was almost a relief to answer his secretary's call on the intercom, but before he could say a word, there was a knock at the door. 'Come.'

Anticipating the arrival of his morning coffee, he had already turned back to the documents on his desk.

'Sorry—this couldn't wait—'

'Sienna!' He was on his feet immediately. 'Is something wrong?'

'I hope I'm not interrupting anything?'

'Nothing that can't wait,' he assured her. 'Come in. Close the door. I'll ask June to bring us some coffee.'

'Don't.'

His anxiety levels soared when he saw the expression on her face. 'I insist you come in and sit down.' Crossing the room in a couple of strides, he closed the door behind her, and then returned to the desk, where he pulled out a chair. 'Sit down and tell me what's on your mind.'

'You promised we'd talk, and we didn't,' she said.

'That's it?' he queried as he propped one hip against the polished wood surface.

'Should there be more?'

She seemed tense. Wanting to make her feel at ease, he pulled out a chair to face hers. Big mistake. Now he couldn't concentrate on anything but her scent rolling over him: wildflower and soap. She'd twisted up her glorious hair, which revealed the fine line of her cheekbones—a pang hit him when he took in her shabby coat. No one in his office dressed like this. Quite suddenly the luxuries he took for granted seemed both superfluous and meaningless. 'Are you sure you're okay?' he asked with concern.

'I just wanted to talk,' she insisted. 'I promise, it won't take long.'

'Take as long as you want.' Lifting the phone, he issued a brief instruction: 'No calls.'

There was always a degree of awkwardness the day after first-time sex, but this had never happened to him before. He was worried if Sienna was hurt, if she'd had second thoughts. 'Are you hungry?' he asked, hoping to break the tension. 'I can send out for breakfast—or we can find a café—'

'No,' she cut in. 'No more distractions, Alejandro. I'm fine as I am.'

'If it's the land you're worried about, don't be. I'm happy to revise my offer—'

'I'm sorry?' she said quietly, frowning.

'The land,' he repeated, following this with a figure well over the land's value, which would enable Sienna to fulfil all her dreams. He imagined Tom would want this. Withholding Sienna's money just didn't seem right to him.

'I knew I shouldn't have come here,' she murmured, as if speaking her thoughts out loud.

'Why?' Who on this fine earth had access to the amount of money he'd offered? Tom's legacy paled into insignificance by comparison with the sum he'd suggested for Sienna's land.

She studied him thoughtfully. 'I've been wondering, since I woke up this morning, how amazing sex with someone I think I could really care about could leave me with such an empty feeling, but now I know.'

Her words hit him like bullets. Why was she so upset? Sienna had seemed to enjoy last night every bit as much as he had. 'I think you'd better explain.'

'I'm happy to,' she assured him. Lifting her chin, she let him have it straight. 'Having softened me up with fabulous sex, you're now putting forward the most ridiculous pay-off.'

'Is that what you think this is?'

'What else am I supposed to think? You got what you wanted,' she said with a shrug, 'while I got what I thought I wanted.'

'So, you didn't...want it?' he pressed, drawing his head back in bemusement as he remembered Sienna's passionate responses.

'At the time? Absolutely,' she confirmed. 'Now?' Her eyes turned sad.

He understood from this that any thought of sex must be

returned to Pandora's box and safely sealed inside. That left one thing to talk about. 'You'll have total autonomy over the proceeds of the sale. You'll get the money immediately. No coming to me, cap in hand. You can do anything you want with the money. Please,' he said when Sienna didn't seem to take this in, 'tell me what you want.'

She was silent for so long, he wondered if she'd forgotten the question, but then she said in the smallest of voices, 'All I want is my brother back.' *Dios.* Guilt crushed him.

'No amount of money can bring Tom back,' she added in the same faint tone. But then she rallied and pierced him with an accusing stare. 'And your money can't buy my respect.'

'I'm not trying to buy your respect,' he defended.

'Then, don't offer me money. Why can't you understand, Alejandro? If you have children one day, are you going to teach them that money can buy anything and everything? Would you still do that, knowing it's a lie?'

Impassioned, she sprang up. He stood too. 'If this is because of last night, don't you think it's time we were honest with each other, Sienna? We both wanted sex. The decisions we made were entirely mutual.'

'Decisions?' Her laugh sounded ugly in the pristine surroundings of his large, light-filled office. 'Our bodies took all the decisions, leaving you and me out of it. Neither one of us made anything close to a rational decision last night.'

'Are you saying that you regret what happened?'

'Let me think about this,' she flared. 'You left before I was properly awake, as if sex was nothing more to you than a mechanical act.'

'It's only natural, when emotions are heightened, that instinct takes over.'

'Instinct?' she queried. 'That just about sums it up. What about emotion, Alejandro?'

'Says you?' he countered. 'Accusing me of trying to pay you off, you couldn't be further from the truth. I'm offering you a bank draft that will allow you to pay off all your debts, and more besides—'

'What do you know about my debts?' she cut across him angrily.

Did she really think he wouldn't do his homework? How could he make Sienna understand how careful he had to be, with so much at stake? 'I'm not trying to buy you off. I'm making you a more than fair offer for the land that will allow you to do anything you choose to do for the rest of your life.'

Thrusting her face towards him, she exclaimed furiously, 'But isn't buying me off exactly what this is? Or do you make a habit of giving away so much money on a whim?'

'There's no whim involved,' he fired back. 'I'll do anything it takes to get Tom's land under safe management.'

'D'you seriously think I'd do anything to damage Tom's land?'

'That's the whole point. Until you tell me your plans, I don't know what you intend to do.'

'Okay...' She took a deep breath, and a very long moment before admitting, 'Maybe I shouldn't have sounded off, but it takes a lot to come to someone like you and expose my hopes and dreams, when I know I can never compete with your resources.'

'Go on,' he encouraged.

'You and Tom shared an island, and now Tom's share belongs to me. I would never embark on something I don't know anything about without consulting someone who does. That doesn't mean I won't make my own decisions when I have all the information to hand, but what about this—what if I lease the land I don't use to you?'

That was a novel thought, and one that hadn't occurred to him, he was forced to admit, but there were still problems, even with that proposal. 'I need to know what you're going to do with the land you keep.'

'Anything I like, sure—bearing in mind that you have my promise not to do anything that might be to the detriment of the land, or the people living on it.'

'Will you build a music school?'

Lifting her chin, she explained, 'I'm hoping to build a music therapy centre in memory of Tom.'

The fact that they had such similar plans shouldn't have surprised him. They had both loved Tom, and what better to do with the money Tom had left than to create a facility in his name, to help those who were suffering as Tom had?

'Music has the power to heal,' Sienna continued with compelling sincerity. 'That isn't just something I believe. I've seen it in action.'

As had he, he recollected, when he'd heard Sienna sing. For that short time, he had been transported, and uplifted, a state, he was forced to admit, that was entirely new to him.

'I can tell you one thing,' she said with a direct stare. 'That land will never be for sale.'

Pulling his head back, he stared at Sienna. He always took the lead in business and had never known a fair offer to be refused. Nothing like this had ever happened to him before, but, far from angering him, she intrigued him. 'You may change your mind,' he thought it only fair to remind her.

'And I may not,' she said.

'This has nothing to do with last night, does it?' he pressed, frowning.

'Everything between us is, or should be, connected to the

land,' she said with renewed intent that was somehow unconvincing. 'Anything personal shouldn't even be entering our thinking,' she continued in the same vein. 'We wouldn't have met, if it hadn't been for Tom, and you should know by now that I'm not impressed by wealth, or power, or influence. I've managed to jump through quite a few hoops in the past, and I can do so again.'

'Sienna, wait.'

He sprang to his feet as she made for the door, but her step didn't falter and, like their first meeting in London, he was left alone, listening to the sound of her footsteps fading.

For a few moments he did nothing, then he returned to the desk and called his PA to make arrangements to leave the country. He and Sienna needed space from each other. Thanking his control for allowing him to make this decision, he resisted the impulse to go after her.

A woman removing herself from his life was new to him, but it held faint echoes of previous loss, and for that alone he knew he'd made the right decision. But it was hard to cut off Sienna completely, though it seemed incredible that a woman who aggravated and attracted him in equal measure could have this hold over him. Because she lifted him with her singing, he reasoned, and that made him feel light. She made him laugh, when no one else could, and last night he had almost believed that she completed him.

All the more reason not to drag things out. Tom's loss had reminded him that risk never passed, and pain could rarely be eased. Maybe he could have handled things better with Sienna. He hadn't set out to hurt her.

And now a bland and boring world loomed without her?

So, he'd fill that gap with business. They'd meet up eventually, if only to agree on the land. These thoughts were perfectly logical, but that didn't help where his preoccupation with Sienna was concerned. Two strong people, who'd grown accustomed to paddling their own canoe, were probably both wondering right now if a satisfactory resolution between them was even possible.

Was he going to sit around, doing nothing, waiting to find out? No. He would fly to the island, making the break with Sienna, for her sake, as much as for his.

CHAPTER SIX

SHE WAS PREGNANT.

Six weeks had passed since she'd last seen Alejandro, and now she knew for sure.

Expecting a baby changed everything. Absolutely everything. The growing suspicion that she was no longer alone in her body had just received the most amazing proof positive in the form of two horizontal blue lines. She'd done the test three times in the tiny staff bathroom at the club, to make sure. There was no mistake.

How could it be? They'd used protection.

Protection can fail. How many times had she been told that back at school?

How could it not be? Staring into the mirror, she was overwhelmed by feelings of elation: a child, their child, a new life, a new love, an arrow to send flying out into the world.

She was pregnant with Alejandro's baby. By mutual agreement, they'd gone their separate ways for now—at the worst time possible, as it turned out. But nothing could spoil the moment. If she could give their child half the love her own mother had shown her, their baby would be the happiest child on earth. With every fibre of her being, she welcomed this new life. This baby was a living extension of the families they'd lost.

Thinking about her mother always made her pause, and always made tears threaten, but this was such a special moment, if her parents had lived to see it Sienna knew they'd be rejoicing and would surely tell Sienna that regret had no part to play.

Pregnancy tests were so precise they even showed the approximate date of conception. Six-plus weeks. Her cheeks flushed red at the memory. Yes, they'd used protection, but with passion like theirs anything could happen.

Alejandro.

Eyes closed, heart open, she knew for certain, only him... only ever could be him.

'Welcome, little one.' Mapping her still-flat stomach, she smiled gently as happiness flooded through her. 'Sleep and grow strong. You don't have anything to worry about. I'm here for you.'

Sienna felt as if she were walking on air as she crossed the deserted club to join Jason in rehearsal at the piano. Alejandro's baby had brought everything into clearer, brighter focus, making her world spin on a completely different axis. All those years of determinedly feeling nothing had vanished in an instant, as if the most wonderful switch had been turned on.

Would a child change Alejandro in the same way?

How would he react? She was desperate to tell him, but he'd left the country, his PA had informed her when she'd rung. The woman had politely refused to hand over Alejandro's personal details. Would she pass on a message? 'Señor Acosta can always contact you at the club, should he wish to do so.' Those cold words had chilled Sienna—

'Hey, Sienna—daydreaming this morning?'

With a smile of apology, she said hi to Jason.

'I see our friend is back.'

'Our friend?' she queried.

'Alejandro Acosta,' Jason explained. 'His superyacht has returned to the Thames.'

Apprehension, panic and excitement roiled inside her. She could tell him her news. Today! The instant the rehearsal was over, she'd go straight to his yacht, and—

What if his security staff wouldn't allow her on board? She'd sit on the dock and wait until they did.

She turned as the manager of the club shouted to her from the doorway of his office. 'Hey, Sienna, call for you.' Her heart thundered a tattoo. But surely it wouldn't be *him*, would it?

'Take it,' Jason encouraged, seeing how tense she was. 'I'll still be here when you get back.'

Flashing a smile in Jason's direction, she hurried off to take the call.

'Hello?'

'Sienna?'

She almost jumped out of her skin. 'Alejandro? It is you. I was just thinking about you.'

'Good thoughts, or bad?'

His voice rolled over her like melted chocolate, and he sounded amused, not at all like the matter-of-fact business-man prowling his office. 'I'll leave you to decide,' she said, smiling.

'Why don't you come here, and tell me yourself?'

'Where are you?'

'At the coffee shop next door.'

Breath hitched in her throat at the thought of him just a few yards away.

'Are you still there?' he queried in a low, mellifluous drawl.

'I'm still here.' Gathering her wits quickly, she added his private number to the contacts on her phone.

'If you're too busy to join me for coffee…?'

'I'd love to join you.' Major understatement. 'Thank you.'

'See you in ten?'

'I'll have to—' Too late. The line had already cut.

Making her excuses to the manager, and then to Jason, she postponed the rehearsal.

'You don't have to explain to me,' Jason told her with a smile.

Alejandro's striking presence in the everyday surroundings of the local café had drawn everyone's attention, and he took her breath away. He stood as she approached and gave her a quick assessment. 'Good to see you, Sienna. You're looking well. The London drizzle obviously suits you.'

He suited her.

'Flat white? Something to eat? Are you okay? You usually have a lot to say for yourself. Did the cat get your tongue?'

'You're right about London suiting me,' she said, anxious not to give him the impression that she was nervous on this occasion. 'Nothing to eat, thank you,' she added as he pulled out her chair.

'A flat white, please,' he said to the waitress.

'It's good to see you again, Alejandro.' Another major understatement. Couldn't he just look ordinary for once? Must he command every space?

'It's good to be back—'

Her brain scrambled to find a reason for his visit. Why was Alejandro here? They'd made no progress with the land. She couldn't afford the air fare to Spain yet, though she was saving hard.

Don't flatter yourself that you're the reason he's here. He wants the land.

Did he? Well, he hadn't mentioned it yet. And where the baby was concerned, she had nothing to be ashamed of. The promise of new life was a reason for joy. If she would fight for the land Tom had left her, how much harder would she fight for her unborn child? *Their* unborn child, Sienna's ever-present conscience rushed to remind her.

'Don't let your coffee go cold...'

She'd made him suspicious. Alejandro was giving her a long, assessing look. Going through the motions of lifting the cup to her lips, she nursed it for a while, wondering if this was the right time to tell him. Putting the cup down again, she gave him a level stare. 'I'm glad you're here, there's so much I have to tell you.'

'I'm intrigued. But surely you don't want to tell me here?'

As he glanced around, she had to agree that a bustling café was not the somewhere special she'd had in mind for when she told him about their baby.

He glanced at the door. 'Shall we go for a walk?'

'Why not?' she agreed, but even as they walked to the door, doubt crowded in. Could a man like Alejandro with his powerful engines running full tilt all the time, ever be able to slow that pace enough to accommodate a child? Or would he simply dump an obscene amount of money in her bank account and move on?

'I guess I should tell you why I'm really here,' he said as they sheltered beneath the awning.

Hope springs eternal wasn't just a saying, Sienna discovered as her pulse picked up pace. 'Yes?'

'I want you and Jason to perform at my party tomorrow night.'

For a few moments her brain refused to work, and then it computed: Alejandro was only here because he wanted to hire her to sing at his party tomorrow night. Get over it.

'Tomorrow?' she managed vaguely.

Any opportunity to sing was something she usually grabbed with both hands, but right now she felt achingly flat, because it was time to get real. Had she seriously imagined that the great Alejandro Acosta had found her so irresistible that he couldn't wait to see her again? She could see the headline now: *Billionaire Sleeps with Nightclub Singer and Both Live Happily Ever After.* This was just another deal for Alejandro. She and Jason were at the top of their game. It made sense for Alejandro to book them to entertain his guests.

And now doubts crowded in. 'Has someone dropped out last minute?'

Alejandro stared at her, perplexed. 'No,' he protested. 'I'd be very pleased if both you and Jason could perform at my party tomorrow night. You're the only act I want. It's that simple.'

Nothing was ever *that simple*. Whatever Alejandro wants he gets, sprang to mind. Her frown deepened as she remembered Alejandro's brusque PA, giving her the brushoff. Didn't he have a loyal army to arrange things like this?

'Will you do it, Sienna?' he pressed in a voice that was deep and compelling.

'I can't give you my answer until I've spoken to Jason.' But it would be a thrill to peer through the looking glass into another part of Alejandro's life. Plus, this would almost certainly be the best chance she'd get to tell him about their baby.

A more cautious side of Sienna urged her to stamp on the brakes and take a little time to get used to the fact that Alejandro was back. But he'd given her no time to consider at leisure, and caution lost out.

'Good. I'm glad that's settled,' he said with a dip of his head. 'And don't forget your passport.'

'My passport?' she queried with surprise.

'Standard procedure,' he explained. 'You'll have to go through security before either of you can board the yacht, and with time so short I'll need your answer today.'

'Will there be a fee?' she said, thinking of Jason.

Alejandro's outrageous offer made her blink. Was this another opportunity to stun her with his wealth? 'We won't need that much,' she protested, making a very much smaller counter offer.

'Don't you think you should check with Jason, before you turn down my proposed fee?'

Yes, she should, Sienna concluded, firming her jaw as she stared back at Alejandro. And she would, but even as she thought about Jason's likely reaction when he heard the amount they would be splitting between them a shiver of apprehension tracked down her spine. Alejandro had so much wealth and power. How would that affect the future, and their child? Would Alejandro even want to be a part of their lives?

'Jason will receive the same amount, of course.'

'What?' She stared at him blankly.

'You'll each receive—'

She didn't even hear the amount. Her brain had simply switched off. 'That's very generous of you,' she managed to mumble, knowing it would be wrong to rob Jason of the chance to make so much money for a single night's work. 'I'll let you know as soon as I've checked with Jason that we're both free.'

'I've already checked. Both of you are free.'

What else had Alejandro checked. Did he know she was pregnant? No. He'd have said something by now. Why hadn't she said something? And now it was too late. Alejandro was already lifting the collar of his jacket as he got ready to leave the shelter of the awning.

'Why don't you call Jason now?' he suggested.

'Good idea.' Fumbling for her phone, she almost dropped it, and gasped as he retrieved it and placed it back in her hand. Bare skin on bare skin was too, too much. 'Your yacht's at Tower Bridge?' she confirmed in an attempt to swerve her thoughts from skin-to-skin contact.

'Correct.'

There was only one notable yacht capable of stealing everyone's attention away from the historic bridge, and it was more of a floating palace than a boat.

'The *Acosta Dragon* is a convenient mode of transport.'

Laughter found its way through her concern. 'So's a bus,' she pointed out.

'Buses don't generally house Biedermeier pianos.'

That was a carrot Jason would find impossible to refuse, and Alejandro knew that. 'You have a Biedermeier piano on board?' she confirmed.

'Jason will love to play it, don't you think?'

'I'm sure he would, but he's not picking up the phone right now.'

'Then, try him later. And when you do speak to him, tell him that the piano used to belong to Clara Schumann, and that I've had it restored. It's such a beautiful instrument, it deserves to have someone like Jason at the keyboard.'

'Do you play?'

'A little. I find music both stimulating and relaxing, depending on my mood.'

What was Alejandro's mood now? she wondered, trying to read his eyes.

Braving the persistent drizzle, they started walking side

by side. So close, and yet so far. No one seeing them would imagine they'd shared the most exciting passion, or that now they were expecting a child together. Seeing Alejandro again had reignited so many feelings. For such a long time, she'd believed it was easier not to feel, but now she longed for closeness, and for more openness in her life. She was the last of her family left, but soon there'd be one more. The tribe was coming back from the brink of extinction, and she owed it to her child to feel fully and experience everything keenly, both to honour her parents, and to live by her pledge that her child would be loved deeply and always, whatever the future held for Sienna and Alejandro.

'If you could perform around ten o'clock, that would be great,' Alejandro informed her as they prepared to cross the street and go their separate ways.

'*If* Jason can make it,' she reminded him.

'Jason will make it,' Alejandro said with confidence. 'Just tell him about the piano. A man like Jason doesn't play for money—or, at least, not just for money.'

'You're right,' she admitted. 'Jason would play for nothing, or even to an empty room. Same goes for me, which is probably why we're not rich and famous—'

'Like me?' Alejandro cut in.

'I didn't say that.' She glanced up into his harsh face, wondering what it would take to soften him.

'You didn't need to say it,' he assured her. 'Don't look so worried, Sienna. If I took offence that easily, I'd be reeling from verbal punches all the time.'

She pulled a face. 'I can't see you reeling any time, anywhere.'

'Thanks for the vote of confidence.'

'You're welcome,' she replied in the same dry tone, thinking that maybe, just maybe, they were reaching an accommodation where they could be friends, without the sex that had consumed them getting in the way. They'd reached the river and, like so many others before them, they stopped to take in the dazzling view. Even under a grey sky, the land-scape of London was spectacular.

'Well, I'd better get going,' Alejandro said, turning in the direction of Tower Bridge.

'Wait—' She put a hand on his arm, which she quickly withdrew when he turned back to face her.

'Yes? Oh, yes, you had something you wanted to tell me.' Dipping his chin, he stared her in the eyes.

Suddenly, she was lost for words. She had intended to tell him about the baby, here, with this wonderful backdrop, but he was in a rush, and what she had to say couldn't be rushed.

'Sienna?'

Another question entirely forced its way through her lips. 'Can I ask you—about Tom?'

'Tom?'

'Yes,' she lied. How could she talk about a baby when even the sky was crying? But it was the perfect opportunity to talk about her brother—'If you've got time?'

'I'll make time.'

'It's just a question that's been plaguing me ever since the officers gave me the news of Tom's death. They said you brought him back from the battlefield. It meant so much to know he wasn't alone.' She could see that Alejandro nei-ther sought praise, nor wanted it, and that he'd grown dis-tant again.

'I've never left a comrade behind,' he admitted stiffly.

'I'm sure not.' She believed him absolutely.

'Tom,' he murmured, as if thinking back. 'There was no one like him. He could make us all laugh...'

There was something in Alejandro's eyes that said that wasn't the whole story. 'Go on,' she begged.

'Tom was the joker in the pack...'

'The troublemaker?' she asked with a frown.

'No,' Alejandro stated categorically, 'but Tom had his demons.'

After saying this, he pressed his lips together, as if he'd already said too much.

'I guess he covered any problems he had with humour?'

'Always,' Alejandro agreed.

'It can't have been easy for any of you,' she said with feeling.

'Which is why, when we were on leave, we played polo. Tom became quite the star.'

'I'm glad you had some good times together,' she said gently.

'We did.'

Alejandro's tone of voice said he didn't want to talk about it any more.

'You're drenched,' she said, thinking it would be a good time to part.

'And you need to take care of your voice. I need you in good shape tomorrow.'

'You're right.' She laughed as she huddled into her coat. 'I hope that both Jason and I can make it.'

'You will,' Alejandro stated with confidence.

With a wry smile, she hurried off.

Glancing over his shoulder at Sienna's fast-retreating back, he made a promise to himself that Tom would be cloaked in sunlight for ever, as far as Sienna was concerned. It would crush her to know that her brother had been killed because he'd been reckless one time too many. Or that he'd put the lives of his comrades in terrible danger on that last night. Sienna had enough grief to deal with already.

He replayed their conversation over and over once he was back on the yacht, and knew, if he had needed further proof, that Tom's last few hours had impacted heavily on Sienna. Her eyes had filled with tears as she'd repeated what she'd been told, that Alejandro had held her brother in his arms, and spent that first long night with him, talking to Tom even though he'd gone. She'd been spared the disturbing details, and he was glad about that, but by the end of the telling something had changed in her voice, almost as if she found herself wishing for a different outcome. As if she'd never forget what he'd done for Tom, but would never forgive him for being the one who had lived.

Hearing Sienna praise his role in a nightmare when she only knew half the story cut him deep. Tom had been in one of his manic phases that night, convinced he could conquer the world, and had put the entire regiment in danger, several men being injured in the attempt to bring Tom back. Alejandro had succeeded with determination driving him on, and stayed by Tom's side. But he hadn't been able to save him, and that fact would stay with him for ever.

Wrenching his thoughts onto a lighter path, he was confident Sienna would delight his guests, even if, for once in his well-ordered life, his own thoughts regarding Sienna were in turmoil. Having decided to avoid her, he hadn't reckoned with Sienna lodging in his mind. At the forefront of his mind, in fact. He just couldn't get her out of his head. Perhaps her performance on his yacht would set things straight, proving once and for all that Sienna was nothing more than his last, fleeting connection with Tom.

Remembering her comment on the fee, he was glad to pay both Sienna and Jason a decent amount. For people who brought such enjoyment and peace of mind, it niggled him that musicians were always undervalued. Whatever Sienna imagined about coming to him cap in hand to ask for Tom's money, that situation would never sit easily with him. As far as he was concerned, Sienna and Jason were worth every penny of their fee.

Back in his stateroom, legs crossed, whisky in hand, he ruminated on the past few hours. Sienna didn't know what to make of him. That made two of them. With siblings, landholdings, and a business to protect, grief would have been a self-indulgent luxury when his parents were killed, and he had come to believe that he was impervious to pain. Like a wolf that depended on its strength, or the appearance of strength, for its survival, he had buried every vestige of emotion beneath a blizzard of activity that had made him richer than Croesus, but not as happy as his brothers and sister with their sometimes chaotic, but so obviously contented family lives.

He smiled as he glanced at the family photograph, and then grimaced as he thought about Tom. His friend's loss reminded him of how much pain it was possible to feel. For a man who valued control and self-control above everything else, he could not let that pain back in. Controlling both his experiences and his environment had always been his shield against pain. He was responsible for the livelihoods of many, many people, so taking himself off to grieve, or dwelling on anything overlong, would be an unforgivable self-indulgence—

The trilling of his phone jolted him back into the present. Glancing at the number, he allowed himself a smile. 'That's great news,' he told Sienna. 'I look forward to seeing you both tomorrow night.'

By the time he put the phone down, he knew she'd broken through his reserve. His capacity for feeling was back full force. There was no other way to explain his anticipation of their next meeting.

CHAPTER SEVEN

THIS MUST BE a dream, Sienna concluded as she struggled to take in the alternate, floating universe she was about to walk into with Jason. If her friend hadn't been at her side, she might have needed to pinch herself at the sight of so much unrestrained luxury.

Alejandro's sleek white yacht was enormous, easily the size of a low-rise upmarket building. It seemed incredible that, a few feet behind them, life went on as normal: pedestrians huddled in heavy coats as they hurried down the rain-slicked pavement, horns blared and engines revved, while ahead lay ordered calm. The soft strains of a jazz band filtered through the drizzle towards them, white lights twinkled with promise up on deck.

They were waiting to be checked off a guest list at the foot of the gangplank. Alejandro was right. They had to show their passports. His security guard loomed over them with a two-way radio in hand, checking their details. The guard's voice was curt, while his black-clad appearance was unrelentingly grim. After a few tense moments, he handed their passports back, and indicated that they were free to pass.

She had to tell herself that this was the adventure of a lifetime, before lifting her chin to walk the length of the sloping gangplank. Part of her was terrified, while another part was desperately eager to discover what type of world Alejandro inhabited when he wasn't residing in his sombre London house.

This is for you, Tom. This is me thanking your friend Alejandro for being with you at the end, and then all my debts to Alejandro are paid in full.

If only it were that easy, she reflected as her hand moved instinctively to map her still-flat stomach. Years of trying her hardest to feel nothing, because emotion hurt, and grief was corrosive, had to be put aside now because there was a new life inside her, and that child deserved a mother who confronted life with all its problems head-on.

A uniformed steward appeared seemingly out of nowhere with the offer to escort them to their quarters. There was no turning back now, Sienna concluded wryly as Jason murmured, 'Here we go,' adding discreetly, 'I don't know about you, Sienna, but I've no intention of missing a single second of this experience.'

Neither had she.

She was here.

Now he could relax.

Exhaling steadily, he pulled back from the rail. He'd sensed Sienna's arrival long before he'd caught sight of her. Call it intuition. Call it what the hell you liked. Almost an entire adult lifetime of suppressing feelings had been overturned by one infuriatingly unique woman. *Don't mess with my sister* was long in the past. He would never *mess* with Sienna. She wasn't any type of one-night stand, but a woman he was starting to admire for so many reasons, the way she stood up to him being just one. Sienna was also an outstanding musician, and he got the sense that there was so much more to learn about her.

And then there was lust.

He could think of little else but holding her in his arms again. Vulnerable, maybe, but she had her brother's stubborn side too. There was more steel in Sienna's character than even he had suspected. Not knowing her plans for the land was his main concern, but tonight was an opportunity to find out more. He had his own project planned for the island and would tolerate neither interference nor delay. She'd see reason when he explained. They'd come to an agreement soon.

And then?

Who knew what the future held? Once the deal was done, anything was possible. He'd miss the challenge of Sienna if she took his money, left and never came back. He'd miss the passion she brought to his bed. She was uniquely complex and endlessly intriguing—it was fair to say that Señorita Slater had turned his well-ordered world upside down.

Alejandro's yacht was like the most luxurious residence imaginable, as well as the most surprising. The first thing she noticed was how bright it was, and how full of colour. The overall impression of vitality and purpose was as different as could be from his austere London home.

The yacht was packed with elegant people, and she was surprised at how many smiled as she and Jason passed. There was a great atmosphere of ease and interest, and it was quite reassuring to notice that even these obviously well-heeled people were as awe-struck by their surroundings as Sienna.

There were new surprises around every corner, from the crystal staircase to the ice-topped bar, and she was agog at all the fabulous fashion and flashing jewels. She'd pitched her outfit about right, thank goodness. The understated floor-length column of emerald-green silk was a piece she'd been lucky enough to pick up for next to nothing in a trunk sale. Maybe it had been reduced, because it veered towards subtle, rather than obvious, but, whatever the case, she felt good.

The jazz band she'd caught a waft of on shore was even more impressive close up. As she'd suspected, when Alejandro mentioned that he played the piano, he was a cultured man who appreciated good music. Now she noticed the air of anticipation. She guessed it had nothing to do with the entertainment tonight, and everything to do with Alejandro. Everyone was waiting for him to appear, like the star of a show.

Thankfully, the rain had stopped falling, which allowed everyone to mingle on deck, but Sienna and Jason had no time to linger, as the officer escorting them was keen to show them to their rooms. He had explained that they would both have a stateroom for the night, where they could get ready for their performance. Refreshments would be provided, and they could call on the house phone for anything else they might need.

'How the other half live,' Jason murmured as they crossed the tastefully decorated reception lobby. Furnished in clean Scandi style, it was decorated with vibrant flower displays that gave the air a faint perfume. Modern art lent pops of colour to an already tasteful décor, and it was almost a letdown to step out onto the open deck, even in the shadow of the magnificent Tower Bridge.

'Welcome to the *Acosta Dragon*.'

She froze, then gazed up to see Alejandro watching them from an upper deck. Her entire body thrilled. Everything else faded into the background as Alejandro's potent charisma took over her world. Whatever they were, or weren't, to each other, his magnetism had enveloped her in a warm, erotic cloak.

'Thank you for inviting us,' she called up, trying to sound as if visiting a billionaire on his incredible yacht were something she did every day.

It was almost a relief when the officer invited them to follow him to their staterooms. She could do with a moment to accustom herself to the fact that Alejandro would be close for the rest of the night. Was he pleased to see her? It was hard to tell. His face had been in shadow. She replayed his voice in her mind. His tone had been warm, but he'd been greeting Jason too.

'Courage, mon brave,' Jason whispered, as if he read her uncertainty. 'You've got this.'

Had she? There was no doubt she could fulfil the terms of her contract to sing tonight, but just being here, on board Alejandro's mega-yacht, was a stark reminder of the power and wealth he wielded. Could she deal with Alejandro?

She had to, Sienna determined, for the sake of their child. He must agree to sharing the care of their baby. Surely, he would...

Snug in what turned out to be a gloriously opulent stateroom, she instructed herself firmly not to lose confidence, and to enjoy every moment of her time on board. The enormous fee she'd been paid was already safely stowed in her savings account, marked 'Tom's school', so she had every reason to be optimistic.

But...

But telling Alejandro about their child wouldn't be easy. How would he take the news? She allowed herself a moment of contemplation. Even the air smelled expensive, and although she lived more comfortably than many, Sienna couldn't change who she was. 'A nightclub singer?' had been directed at her more times than once, and not in a nice way. Could she bear it if Alejandro chose to dismiss her in the same way?

She'd have to. Toughing it out was her stock-in-trade. She and Alejandro had a child's future to consider, and anything else would be banished from her mind.

When she'd saved enough, she would visit the island— to find out what it had meant to Tom, if nothing else. The opportunity to build something exciting in his name filled her with enthusiasm for the future. How many times had she walked through the corridors of Tom's music centre in her mind? Airy classrooms, spacious practice rooms, and, of course, the Tom Slater Concert Hall had all come one step closer thanks to the massive fee she was earning tonight.

I won't let you down, she silently promised her brother.

With her confidence restored, Sienna sprang up from her stool at the spacious dressing table with the intention of exploring her accommodation. It was at least twice the size of her bedsit in London, with a dressing room, a glorious pink marble bathroom full to the brim with expensive products, and a sitting room made comfy with a plump sofa and two easy chairs. And then there was the bed. The size of her bedsit. It took all she'd got not to bounce on it. All in all, this was quite an improvement on her usual changing room at the club. Could she get used to this? You bet, she concluded, turning full circle. It was a shame she wouldn't get the chance.

Having done her research, Sienna had learned quite a bit about the *Acosta Dragon*, but nothing had prepared her for intimate contact with a yacht built to Alejandro's precise specifications. In excess of three hundred feet long, the *Acosta Dragon* was as close to a palace on water as she could imagine. Boasting a nightclub, a cinema, a full gym, several swimming pools, both inside and out, as well as a full spa, there were two helicopters perched like huge black birds on an uppermost deck, as well as a number of small speedboats stored in the hull, for those snap decisions any billionaire might make to spend a day on the beach, she supposed.

Ah, well, enough of that, she concluded as she checked her hair and added a dab of lip gloss. It was time to knock on Jason's door.

'How great is this?' Jason exclaimed the moment he joined her in the corridor.

'I hope my performance lives up to it,' Sienna replied.

'Of course, it will,' Jason assured her. 'Are you sure you're okay?' he added, taking a close look at Sienna.

Musicians were nothing if not speedy at picking up mood. *Alejandro is a musician...*

Allegedly. She'd never heard him play. Never seen him play polo, for that matter. She had no idea how he operated in business, apart from market reports saying everything Alejandro Acosta touched turned to gold. Her thighs tingled inconveniently at that thought.

Willing her mind to remain on track as they approached the grand salon, she was only half listening to the officer escorting them, and was wondering what Tom would say if he could see her on Alejandro's superyacht.

Never mind that—what about the fact that her hand was wrapped like a vice around an evening purse containing yet another positive pregnancy test? She'd done one last minute to be absolutely sure, and had taken it with her to show Alejandro at an appropriately discreet moment. Alongside her usual pre-concert nerves, there was another reason for her pulse to race.

CHAPTER EIGHT

SHE WAS AWARE of Alejandro watching her intently through-out her performance. Was he judging her singing, or was it something else causing that disturbingly focused interest?

What was she doing here, anyway? With a world of per-formers to choose from, why had Alejandro Acosta invited Sienna to sing at his party? It was a strange feeling to sense he wanted her in his bed, yet not to have an inkling of what he was thinking. Being hired as his entertainer tonight made her feel that she was straddling two worlds without a secure foothold in either.

It was a relief to lose herself in music. The atmosphere on board the yacht was very different from the club, but equally warm. One song had led effortlessly into the next, and only one partygoer appeared restless. Alejandro's fierce black gaze had never left her face, and once the applause died down, he came over to speak to her. 'Thank you, Si-enna—thank you, Jason. My guests adored you. You've been everything I expected and more.'

As his brooding look rested on her face, tremors of ex-citement raced through her body. She had to remind herself that Alejandro was talking about her singing.

'Will you perform again for us tonight?' he asked as a general question to both Jason and Sienna.

'We'd love to,' Jason said.

'If you want me to, of course I will,' Sienna agreed, feeling a glow of pleasure that the evening was going so well.

Would this be a good time to tell him, she wondered as Jason was waylaid by some of the guests. Everywhere she looked there were friendly faces waiting to talk to her too, but she had to take this chance. 'Could we talk in private?' she asked Alejandro.

His brow furrowed, as if he couldn't imagine what she wanted to say. 'It's not about money,' she said quickly.

'What do you want to tell me?' he asked, remaining resolutely in place.

Guests were hovering close by, waiting to talk to Sienna. How could she tell him here? But she had to say something, to remove that suspicious look from his face. 'Do you have a favourite song?'

Alejandro's expression changed enough for her to know that he realised she was swerving his question. 'I'm happy to sing requests,' she added out of sheer desperation.

'Are you changing the subject on purpose? You seem overly anxious to me,' he observed, staring down at her with a frown. 'I'd like to know why.'

'I'm not anxious,' she said too fast. 'What you're seeing is nervous energy.'

Alejandro hummed, as if he didn't believe a word. 'We'll talk later,' he said, making this sound more like a threat than a promise, before moving away to give his guests their chance to meet Sienna.

He had to get away from her or remain at the party with a hard-on. She looked amazing, had sung like an angel, and lied like a demon. What was he to make of that? Apart from the fact that challenge always turned him on, the fact that she was hiding something would plague him for the rest of the night.

Even enjoying the company of his guests couldn't distract him from Sienna. This was another first. How was he supposed to forget how she felt in his arms, or how it felt to make love to her? Was he supposed to concentrate on anything else with Sienna hammering at his mind? To aggravate him all the more, she was currently in conversation with his friend. Sheikh Shahin, the Sheikh of Qabama, was talking animatedly to Sienna. She was listening intently, and occasionally sharing something that amused them both. Were they discussing a song? He doubted that. Shahin was a notorious player. And Sienna appeared to be enjoying the sheikh's company. Was she so easily beguiled, or simply attracted to great wealth?

Was he jealous?

Fortunately, he wasn't required to answer that question, as one of his guests, an elderly senator from the States, stopped by with his very elegant wife to ask Alejandro if Sienna might agree to perform at their anniversary party in Florida.

'I don't speak for Sienna,' he told the senator politely, 'but I'm sure she'd be flattered that you asked.'

'I don't mean to flatter the woman. She's a very talented artiste. We'd send the jet, of course, and she can name her own fee.'

Sienna as paid entertainer didn't sit well with him, and the senator's question had forced him to ask himself what he was doing tonight but paying Sienna for her services. Biting back impatience at his own crass lack of judgement, he promised the senator that he'd pass on his message—just as soon as Sienna finished chatting to the sheikh.

He was glad of a reason to do so. His main concern was that Sienna had some sort of plan going forward. The last ten minutes had brought home to him the fact that she could so easily end up flitting around the world, singing for people like him and the senator, but would she make enough to sustain her career? Having promised Tom that he'd take care of Sienna, that was exactly what he intended to do.

Interrupting her conversation with Shahin, he drew her aside. 'You were stunning tonight. Thank you again.'

'But?' she said, flashing a glance at his friend the sheikh, who'd had enough good sense to step back, but who was now watching them with his dark, hawkish stare.

'I worry about you,' he said as he steered her away. 'You're a beautiful woman, and a talented singer, and I'm concerned that you don't have a plan in place to see you go on to greater success after tonight.'

'As a matter of fact, I do,' she said. 'I'm planning to do what I love. I'm going to teach. I can't think of anything better than sharing the happiness I feel when I'm wrapped up in music, and with as many people as I can.'

'That is a good plan,' he agreed, 'and I'd like to hear more.'

'Can we talk now?' she asked with a degree of urgency that surprised him.

In the middle of his party? But now he noticed that Sienna's hand had tightened around her evening purse, turning her knuckles white. What was so vital that she had to tell him now? Glancing around, he concluded that his guests, still high on their enjoyment of Sienna's performance, were unlikely to miss them. Ushering her inside, he took her to his suite. 'Tell me what's worrying you,' he said as he closed the door. 'Sienna?' he pressed as her eyes filled with tears.

'I don't know how to tell you this…'

'Just make a start,' he encouraged, and, because it felt right in that moment, he brought her into his arms.

'I don't want to make it all about me,' she blurted, staring up with wounded eyes.

Why shouldn't it be about Sienna for once? He hated seeing her like this. Drawing her close, he cupped the back of her head to kiss her, tenderly at first, and then with increasing passion.

Erotic fever blanked her mind. The moment to tell Alejandro about their child vanished in a frantic need to be one with him. Knowing they had to get back to the party only added urgency to their actions. There was no time for finesse. Turning her against the wall, he cupped her buttocks with one hand and freed himself with the other. Urging him on, she exhaled noisily with relief as he tossed her thong aside and plunged deep. She bucked greedily against him, with only one thought in mind, and it was only seconds later that she screamed out her release.

'More,' she gasped as he planted one fist against the wall above her head. Supporting her with his other hand, Alejandro began to move deeply, rhythmically, rotating his hips to add to her pleasure. The outcome was as swift as it was inevitable. Was his suite soundproof? She could only hope.

'Relax,' he said with a smile in his voice as he caressed her back with long, even strokes. 'Just concentrate on what I'm doing to you and let me do the rest.'

With pleasure. With immense pleasure—

Not taking this chance to tell Alejandro about their baby was foolish, but she couldn't think while he was plunging her into pleasure again.

He cared for this woman. The realisation swamped him as Sienna collapsed, sated, in his arms. He'd never known a woman like her. There'd been a desperation to her lovemaking that left her vulnerable, and yet she was so strong. The contrast perplexed him. She was self-willed, he reflected as he watched her drift off to a level of consciousness that was only just above sleep. She had wanted to tell him something, but there wasn't time now.

Carrying her into his bedroom, he laid her down carefully on the bed. There was no reason why she had to rush back to the party. She'd given her all when she sang to his guests. It was time for her to sleep now.

A fast shower later, and he was dressed, ready to return to the party. Pausing at the door, he glanced across his bedroom at Sienna. Deeply asleep, she looked so calm and contented. There was no reason to disturb her. Whatever she had wanted to tell him could wait.

He was about to leave the room when he noticed her evening purse had fallen onto the floor, strewing its contents across the carpet. Returning, he hunkered down to retrieve it, doing the best he could to stuff everything safely back inside. He was about to put the purse on the nightstand, where she'd see it as soon as she woke, when he realised what he was looking at. Cursing softly, he examined the pregnancy test sticking out of the top. The torch on his cell revealed two distinct blue lines.

Sienna was pregnant?

With his child?

Of course, with his child. Everything made sense now. She was expecting his child. Far from feeling nothing, he was finding it a struggle to balance control and his undeniable emotional reaction to the fact that they were expecting a child.

Why hadn't she told him? Didn't she trust him? He glanced down at Sienna. Was he to blame for her lack of trust? Realising that she was probably frightened to tell him, because he'd always been so emotionally restrained, cut through him like a knife. But any discussion would have to wait. His guests had been neglected long enough. The party was due to end soon. He had to be on hand to thank everyone for accepting his invitation. After which, he would instruct the captain to prepare for immediate departure.

With Sienna still on board?

Fear of losing those he loved was nothing compared to the thought of losing touch with his unborn child. By the time Sienna woke, they'd be at sea. No longer was she simply Tom's sister, or the woman Tom had left half an island to, Sienna was the mother of his child. *His* daughter or son.

Their child.

He frowned at the thought of a new life connecting them for ever, uncertain as to how he felt about that. There was a lot he would have to get used to, he accepted as a discreet tap sounded on the door.

His purser was waiting to speak to him.

'The ambassador and his wife are about to leave, sir. I thought you would want to know.'

'Thank you. Yes. I'm coming now.' With one final glance at Sienna, he left her to sleep.

CHAPTER NINE

WAKING TO MEMORIES of being naked in Alejandro's arms, Sienna concluded that she'd had the best sleep ever. But now she must hurry to get back to the party. Alejandro had already left, she realised as she traced the indentation left by his powerful body on the crisp white sheets. Remembering everything, she stretched her limbs with a sigh of contentment. Swinging out of bed on a wave of optimism, she felt confident that it would be easy now to tell him about their baby.

Sex brings people closer...

It must go some way to doing that, she mused as doubt set in.

How would Alejandro handle her news? With a bank draft, or with his heart?

If he felt the same way she did, there was nothing to worry about, she determined as she felt her way around the stateroom. It was pitch black inside Alejandro's bedroom, and she wasn't sure where the light was. The torch on her phone lit the way—and then she saw her evening purse open on the nightstand, with the positive pregnancy test sticking out of the top.

Panic ripped through her at the thought that Alejandro knew she was pregnant. What must he think about her leaving him to find out, rather than telling him straight? As soon as she'd discovered the test was positive, he should have been the first to know.

Calm down. It's not too late.

If her hectic pulse would only slow down, she would go to find him, and explain.

Rushing into the bathroom, she took the fastest shower ever, and barely dried herself, before shoehorning her still-damp body back into her gown. Squeezing her feet into shoes that suddenly seemed several sizes too small, she steadied herself against the wall—

She steadied herself...

The River Thames was tidal, but—

Rushing across the room, she dragged back the drapes. The meagre sunlight of early morning sifted through the clouds, revealing a ragged ocean, and not much else besides.

'Jason!' Frantic to find him, she exploded out of the room. Hammering on Jason's door, she yelled at the top of her voice, 'Jason! Are you there?'

'Can I help you, ma'am?'

Only now did she refocus to see the uniformed steward standing patiently by. Composing herself, she battled to keep her voice steady enough to ask, 'I'm looking for my friend Mr Mullings? The pianist who accompanied me last night?'

With a smile, the steward relaxed. 'What a wonderful musician he is—'

'Have you seen him?' Politeness was lost in the panic of the moment.

'Yes, ma'am,' the steward confirmed, obviously concerned now he realised how upset she was. 'Mr Mullings left the yacht with the rest of the guests, shortly before we sailed last night—'

'We sailed? Last night?' Her voice had turned mouse

small. How could Alejandro allow his yacht to sail without warning her first?

Why wouldn't he, when he knew she was pregnant? His shock must have been at least equal to hers.

'Mr Mullings asked me to tell you how much he'd enjoyed the evening, and that he hoped to see you very soon.'

Very soon? That was a vain hope, Sienna suspected. Her brain began to whirl as she struggled to find answers. Jason must have known she was still onboard. Why hadn't he warned her what was happening? She had to speak to him right away—

Jason would hardly call by Alejandro's stateroom to find out what was going on. And wasn't it more important to confront Alejandro right now? Yes, she should have told him that she was pregnant, but that didn't give Alejandro the right to keep her onboard while the *Acosta Dragon* sailed out of London.

Realising that the steward was still waiting patiently, she took a deep, steadying breath before asking, 'Could you please tell me where to find Señor Acosta?'

'He's in the breakfast room, *señorita*. Would you like to join him? Or I could arrange for food to be sent to your room?'

And seem afraid to show her face? 'I don't want to put you to any extra trouble, so if it's all right with you, I'd prefer to join Señor Acosta.'

'Of course. As soon as you're ready, just call me.'

The steward kept his eyeline commendably high, sparing Sienna the embarrassment of wearing last night's clothes. 'That's very kind of you,' she said, adding with a tight smile, 'Also, would you happen to have a phone charger?'

'Certainly, ma'am.'

Going back inside the stateroom, she shut the door and leaned against it. There was no point panicking. She was stranded at sea with a billionaire who'd just learned he was the father of her child. She'd handle it, as she handled everything else, with calm reason. Fairly calmly—maybe not calmly at all, she accepted as a knock sounded on the door.

'Your phone charger, ma'am.'

She breathed a sigh of relief. 'Thank you so much.' At least she now had the means to contact the outside world.

'Kidnapped?' Alejandro barely glanced up from his phone when she confronted him in the dining room. 'Don't you think that's overly dramatic?'

His gaze pierced her. Okay, guilty as charged, but she was going to become a mother, and that required strength and resolve. 'What would you call leaving London without informing the only remaining guest on board that the *Acosta Dragon* was sailing?'

'Hospitality?'

She wasn't fooled by Alejandro's relaxed manner. That wasn't a joke. Tension radiated from him in suffocating waves. 'Just tell me why you've done this, Alejandro.'

'I would have thought that was obvious.' Lifting his head, he studied her without warmth. 'Why did you hide the fact that you're pregnant?'

'I didn't hide it—'

'You just didn't get around to telling me?'

The chilling timbre of his voice made it sound as if they were two strangers who had never shared a moment's intimacy, and all that had ever been between them was sex.

'I only just found out myself.'

'And there hasn't been a single chance to tell me?' he suggested with a sceptical stare.

'I can only tell you the truth, Alejandro. I would never leave you out of such an important fact on purpose.'

'No,' he drawled. 'So, instead you decide to spend one more night in my bed.'

'That's not how it was!' she shot back. 'You make it sound so—'

'Tawdry?' he supplied.

'No! How can you even think that?'

'I'm supposed to believe you forgot that you were carrying my child?'

A desperate, sinking feeling told Sienna there was no coming back from this. Alejandro had retreated into his old, cold ways, but she would not be blamed for something they had both wanted, and told him straight. 'I forgot everything last night. You did too.'

With a shake of his head, he dismissed her, but the *Acosta Dragon* had other ideas, and chose that moment to lurch. Staggering, she flailed around for something to cling onto. Alejandro was on his feet in an instant. Taking firm hold of her, he guided her to a chair. 'Sit down before you fall down,' he commanded, but concern had returned to his voice.

'I was going to tell you last night,' she explained, seeking his gaze and holding it.

'But you didn't,' he said.

Sensing once again that he was withdrawing emotionally, she refused to let him stay in that ivory tower. 'I didn't tell you because we were making love,' she insisted. 'Or, at least, I was.'

'You trusted me with your body, to the point that you were happy to fall asleep in my arms, but you couldn't trust me enough to tell me about our child,' Alejandro said with a disbelieving shake of his head.

They had briefly shared something special, and she had trusted Alejandro absolutely, but that only made his cynical reading of the situation harder to take. 'If you'd only woken me before we sailed—'

'You would have told me then?' he queried in a cold tone.

Something inside her snapped. 'What's wrong with you, Alejandro? Are you frightened you might come to care too much for a child?'

'Frightened of releasing my emotions, as you are?' he suggested bitterly.

'I didn't have much trouble last night,' she fired back in full warrior mode.

Turning his back on her, he began to pace the room, but she refused to leave it there.

'Is this attack your way of avoiding how you'll feel when you hold our child in your arms?'

Stopping dead, he wheeled around. 'The consequence of bringing another innocent life into the world has always been glaringly apparent to me.'

'But not to me?' she suggested. 'Why are we attacking each other, Alejandro? Shouldn't we be rejoicing? I'll make no excuse for being pregnant. If you must know, I'm glad. I didn't even realise how much I wanted this baby until I re-membered the relationship I was lucky enough to have with my own mother. It was then I realised that I had a chance to recreate all those precious moments with my own child. The moment I saw those two blue lines, I was in love, and I can't wait for our baby to be born. Whether that's conve-nient for you, or not,' she added, with a direct but compas-sionate stare into Alejandro's hooded eyes.

Reaching out, she touched his arm, but Alejandro had gone beyond her reach, and he felt stiff and unyielding. If only she could read that inscrutable mind. She guessed that he was hurt that she'd excluded him, even for a short time, but she couldn't repair that now, and it was vital they both moved forward. 'Alejandro...' She spoke softly, gently. 'I'm so sorry I didn't tell you right away.'

'Where are you going?' he asked as she got up to leave the breakfast table. Standing, he barred her way. 'It isn't safe for you to go anywhere, until the wind drops—'

The words had barely left his mouth when the deck bucked again. And again, he saved her. Being safe in Alejandro's arms felt better than anything else on earth, and tears began to spill down her cheeks. If only things had been different, less complicated, they should have been celebrating this news, rather than confronting each other.

Allowing him to steer her back to a chair, she sat down and admitted, 'I wanted the news to be as special for you, as it has been for me. As soon as I knew, everything changed—my horizons, my hopes and dreams. Don't worry,' she added with a faint smile. 'I'm not about to ask you for anything. I can handle this by myself.'

'I don't understand,' Alejandro protested. 'You're speaking as if you're on your own. Is it your intention to cut me out?'

'I would never do that. I'm trying to reassure you that I don't plan to be a—'

'A drag on me?' Alejandro suggested. 'What are you imagining, Sienna? Do you seriously think I'd wash my hands of a woman who is carrying my child? What sort of man do you take me for?'

'I don't really know,' she admitted. As long as she'd known him, which, admittedly, wasn't long, Alejandro had steered clear of emotional involvement, and she wasn't much better. Craving the closeness of the family she'd lost had left Sienna believing that she'd never find that certainty again. Getting close to anyone was scary. The closer you got, the more you stood to lose. Desperation filled her. How could

the two of them, with all their hang-ups, hope to successfully raise a child?

Pregnancy hormones had a lot to answer for, Sienna told
herself sensibly. Closing her eyes, she settled her thoughts.
Her first thought was for Tom, and why he'd put her in the
way of this man, only to drive them apart. 'It would have
been better if we'd never met,' she mused out loud on the
heels of this thought.

'But we have met,' Alejandro pointed out bluntly, 'And
now you're expecting my child.'

Trying to imagine such a formidable man playing father
to his children, and giving them the great life Sienna's father had made sure she'd had, proved a hard ask. Protecting
her stomach with one hand, she voiced her innermost fears.
'This baby isn't *your* child, Alejandro, it's *ours*.'

'If you think for one moment that I don't take responsibility seriously,' he replied in a voice of menacing quiet, 'you'll
find out how wrong you are. When it comes to my brothers' and sister's children, I would do anything for them.'

The fire in his eyes, and the resolve in the set of his chin,
said everything about money, control, and power. What
chance did she have against that?

Every chance. She was a mother.

'Sharing a child is nothing like sharing an island,' she
said, firming her jaw.

'You think I don't know that?'

Now she saw that his face was strained as he spoke, and
compassion rose inside her as Alejandro continued, 'I will
play a full part in the raising of my child. Anything less
would be an insult to my father, who was the most wonderful
man. I won't deny my child the same chance to know me.'

Of everything he'd said, she found this the most poi-
gnant. Locked away in his tightly controlled world, Ale-

jandro didn't realise how isolated he'd made himself, and as she spoke her heart reached out to his. 'You can see our baby at any time—'

'Obviously.'

His expression chilled her even more as he continued, 'I doubt you could stop me.'

'Why would I want to stop you?'

'Will the visits be at a time to suit you?' he fired back.

Alejandro was referring to the reading of Tom's will, where everything had been done to suit him. 'I wouldn't be so inconsiderate. Any arrangement I make must suit both of us.'

'Don't worry,' Alejandro told her with a long, assessing look. 'I will make sure that they do.'

Did that mean he intended to keep her close until their baby was born, when she would become superfluous to requirements and dismissed? Alejandro could easily afford an army of nannies. With the power he wielded, Alejandro Acosta could do anything he damn well liked. All of this overwhelmed her, and it took a moment to grind her brain into gear again. 'I'd like to disembark at the next port,' she said once she'd got her thoughts straight. 'I'll return home, make a plan, see a doctor—'

'The next port is the island,' Alejandro said, cutting her off.

'*The* island?' It was a surprise to feel how excited she was, at finally arriving at a place that had meant so much to Tom.

'That's right,' Alejandro confirmed. 'I was heading back, and thought this would be the ideal opportunity for you to view your inheritance.'

She'd inherited a lot more than an island, judging by that suspicion in Alejandro's eyes. Did he really think she was a gold-digger, only interested in what Tom had left in the monetary sense? That hurt. After everything they'd been to each other, everything she'd thought they'd meant to each other, while she was confiding in Alejandro, how could he think such a thing?

And now the doubts really set in. When she'd boarded his yacht, she'd got the sense of leaving her world behind and entering his. How much more would that apply when they landed on an island that was as good as Alejandro's private fiefdom, from where there might be no escape? 'I really need to make some calls before we reach the island,' she said as her panic rose.

'Of course,' Alejandro said calmly.

Was she guilty of overreacting? It was impossible to tell from his face. Finding yourself at sea on a billionaire's yacht tended to muddle a brain, she concluded, and all that really mattered was putting the interests of their baby first.

'We're both angry,' she said in an attempt to smooth things over. 'And that's not good for our baby. I'd like to start over.'

Alejandro was not so easily persuaded. 'Start over?' he asked, staring at her from beneath a lowered brow. 'Would that be from before or after you joined me in bed?'

'For the first or second time?' she shot back.

Like two combatants in a ring, facing each other un-blinking, neither of them was prepared to look away first. It was a relief when Alejandro broke the silence, but he did so with the most surprising question yet. 'Have you eaten since yesterday?'

'Some nibbles at the party,' she said, thinking back.

'And do you think that's sensible, for a pregnant woman?'

'Do you intend to monitor my behaviour throughout this pregnancy?'

'Someone should.'

They were in danger of returning to the silent stand-off, and once again Alejandro spoke first. 'There is a difference between control and caring.'

And nothing to be gained by remaining stubborn, Sienna accepted, though she could have used a handy manual to teach her how to deal with a billionaire she barely knew, whose child she was expecting.

'Choose something and eat,' Alejandro encouraged.

As he lifted up a basket of flaky treats, Sienna was reminded that she was ravenous. 'Good,' he said as she began to eat. 'I'm sure you feel better now.'

She almost laughed, he sounded so much like Tom. Both Alejandro and Tom had been forced to take on the role of both parents. Tom's care and concern had sometimes felt smothering. Now she realised that love had driven her brother's actions, and that Alejandro must have done the same for his siblings. Similarities between the two men had never occurred to her before. Alejandro was accustomed to taking responsibility for his family, and would find it hard to relinquish that role. Understanding this made it easier to open up. 'I need something from you.'

'Butter? Or jam?'

Pressing her lips together, to avoid laughing out loud, she said, 'Clothes? I can't wear this gown the entire time. And I need to call Jason.' She frowned as she remembered. 'People need to know where I am.'

'And the manager of your club,' Alejandro reminded her. 'He'll be concerned about your safety too. You'll have to tell him that you won't be coming in for a while. Relax. Eat. We'll sort everything out later.'

They'd sort everything out now, Sienna determined. 'You have helicopters on board, don't you? Why can't I fly back to London?'

'In this weather?'

Her heart sank as she followed Alejandro's gaze outside the window, to where rain mercilessly lashed the deck. Quickly recalculating, she said, 'So, Tom's island is our next port of call?'

'Correct,' Alejandro confirmed. 'The island you now own half of.'

The warmth that had flared briefly between them was instantly gone. It was obvious to Sienna that Alejandro was still furious at the way Tom had written his will. But the fact remained that the half she owned was Sienna's to do with as she wished. If only Alejandro could see that she would never ride roughshod over anyone. Of course, she'd consult with him first. She'd always keep him in the loop. Would *he* agree to her raising their child?

Her hand flew instinctively to her stomach, where their baby, in its innocence, was growing stronger every day, vulnerable to the decisions they made.

CHAPTER TEN

He was going to be a father.

NOTHING ELSE MATTERED. Staring out over the starboard rail, he realised how much he loved wild, elemental weather. It suited his nature, he supposed. He loved anything with a challenge attached—except for one, infuriating woman. 'Sienna!' He whirled around. 'What are you doing out here? Can't you see how dangerous it is?'

'But safe for you?' she suggested.

He wasn't a pregnant woman. Taking hold of her, he steadied her, to keep her safe.

She felt so warm and soft in his arms. It would be easy to forget how strong Sienna was. 'This weather is dangerous.'

'And you're not?' she said with a lift of her chin. 'Lucky you don't frighten me.'

'Evidently,' he agreed.

Guiding her back inside, he took her to his study. 'Can we talk now?' she asked as he closed the door.

'Of course.'

'What were you thinking out there?'

'How to kidnap my next victim,' he suggested, tongue in cheek.

She almost smiled, and then said, 'Truce?'

'Coming from you, I take that as a compliment.'

'Don't,' she warned, turning serious. 'I'm only suggesting a truce between us because, very soon, there will be a very important addition to you and me.'

'For once, I agree with you,' he confirmed, surprising himself by how relieved he was that they were talking again. Life without Sienna was something he was finding increasingly hard to imagine. Everything he'd once thought important had been relegated to a distant second place. Nothing mattered more to him than the welfare of mother and baby. It was because of that that he'd keep her close, as his father had cared for his mother throughout all her pregnancies. Except, unlike his own mother, Sienna would never have to work another day in her life if she didn't want to. Remembering this, he smiled. Sienna would be right up there with the best of mothers. Her warmth, strength and resilience would make sure of that. She'd be the bedrock of any family.

His family?

He shifted in his seat. Love was the final taboo. Like a distant promise he didn't deserve, it was a reality for so many, but not for him. Until he could forgive himself for allowing his parents to take that flight, he could never rejoice about anything fully, because that only brought on crushing guilt. Destined to go through life wondering, if he'd called his parents, could he have stopped them taking that flight had left him incapable of relaxing his hold on anything it was possible to control. Only by concentrating on the practical could he blank out the emotion.

'Alejandro?' Sienna prompted with concern. 'You okay?'

'Yes,' he said in a distracted monotone.

'Come and look,' she said, grabbing his hand briefly in her excitement to look out of the window. 'I can't believe this. The rain has stopped, the wind has dropped, and the sea is as flat as a pancake.'

'That's the magic pull of the island.' In spite of his doubts about Sienna, she'd been through a lot, and he couldn't deny that it felt good to see her smile.

'Is that grey smudge on the horizon the island?' she asked in a voice tense with pent-up excitement.

'Yes, it is,' he confirmed.

He allowed himself an indulgent moment, during which he imagined raising a child on the island. It was the perfect place to bring up children, and Sienna's news had supercharged his plans. When his child was old enough, they could ski together in the morning, and bathe in the warm surf during late afternoon. That happy combination was just one of the reasons that had led him and Tom to the same conclusion, that there was nowhere better to build a rehabilitation centre for injured vets. Nothing could be allowed to stand in the way of that.

'Is it safe to go up on deck now?'

He turned to look at Sienna. 'Of course—' She was already heading for the door. That was the magic of the island. There was still so much to talk about: the island, their baby, the future, but as land grew slowly closer and more distinct, and their destination revealed itself in all its summer glory, he knew that questions could wait, because they would unfold organically onshore, without the past or preconceived ideas getting in the way.

He found her leaning over the rail. 'I can't wait to explore,' she enthused.

He couldn't remain immune to Sienna's enthusiasm, which was only increased by the crowd on the dock, waiting to greet them. 'Look at this, Alejandro! *Look at this!*'

His fellow islanders were naturally curious to see Sienna.

Tom's sister was a draw in herself, because Tom had been a huge favourite on the island. Today, she would stand at his side, and, very soon, their child would join him.

'I can't believe how many people have come to see you,' she exclaimed as she waved to the crowd. 'I had no idea how friendly the people here would be, or how incredibly beautiful this island could be.'

Seeing the land through Sienna's eyes was a revelation. The dock was neat and clean, and everything looked prosperous. The road beyond the dock was well maintained, like all the roads on the island, but it was the spectacular countryside that really captured his attention. Framed by it, Sienna had never looked more beautiful to him.

'Tom never got the chance to show me any photographs,' she explained with a wistful note in her voice. 'I had no idea he owned something like this.'

'Half of this,' he felt it only fair to remind her.

Troubled questions clouded her eyes when she turned to look at him. 'Of course,' she said softly. 'I hadn't forgotten.'

He hadn't mentioned buying back Sienna's half of the island for some time now, which had maybe given her the wrong idea—that he'd given up. This was not the case. Her idea to lease any part of the island she didn't use back to him wouldn't fly, so he'd ignored the suggestion. Parcelling up this land into even smaller plots would be an insult to the islanders, and he would never agree to anything that might upset them.

He watched as ropes were tossed to shore, and raised a hand to acknowledge the cheers from countless voices. 'It will be my pleasure to show you around,' he told Sienna. She had to see, in order to understand.

'What will everyone think when I disembark in my evening dress?' she asked with sudden concern.

'That's not going to happen. See over there...' He pointed to where a team of men were carrying a number of suit-cases on board.

'I don't understand. What's happening?' Sienna asked.

'I've arranged—or rather, my PA has arranged—for clothes to be delivered this morning for you.'

'Now I've seen everything,' Sienna admitted, standing back with a sigh. 'Is there anything your magic wand can't conjure up?'

He shrugged. 'Not much.'

'Well, thank you for thinking about me. And don't worry, I'll pay you back for anything I choose.'

'There's no need,' he said, not wanting to talk about money. He didn't want anything to spoil their arrival on the island. 'Why don't you go and choose something to wear?'

'There's every need to talk about money,' Sienna insisted.

'Later, then,' he agreed as she hurried off.

It was good to see Sienna return in a casual outfit of jeans and a loose blouse. Good? She looked hot. Distrac-tion was needed fast. 'If there's anything else you need, my housekeeper, Maria, will be glad to source it for you. Prac-tically anything can be couriered over to the ranch house, and Maria is a dab hand with alterations, or she could even run up a dress for you herself.'

'You are a very lucky man,' Sienna observed, frowning a little at his burst of information.

'I'm extremely lucky to have Maria care for my home,' he agreed as they made their way through the crowd. This took some considerable time, as Sienna, who was warmly received, was making it her business to chat with everyone she could. He did too. It was a great start, and they were both reluctant to leave when he finally led the way to an open-topped Jeep. 'In her youth, Maria was a seamstress for a top Spanish couturier,' he explained as he opened the door for Sienna.

'This is the most you've ever told me about anything,' she said as he climbed in beside her. 'I'm in real danger of getting to know you.'

'Impossible,' he returned dryly.

'Well, I can't wait to meet Maria, but please tell Maria that I don't need any fuss.'

He laughed to himself. That wouldn't work. Maria's life was all about caring for others. 'I will,' he promised, keeping those doubts to himself.

Alejandro had taken time to speak to everyone on the dock, and he'd introduced her around, Sienna remembered. Their warm reception had been such a thrill. And now this beautiful island. She could almost forget that Alejandro had brought her here in the most unconventional way, because this was the perfect place to launch the Tom Slater trust.

'I used to come here on holiday with my parents,' he revealed as they drove through sun-kissed vistas of rolling green hills and blue, blue skies.

She stared at him with interest. 'And then you bought the island.'

'It seemed a fitting memorial.'

After he said this, Alejandro's face closed down, as if he'd said too much. Remembering the past would always be painful, until he built on the loving memories he shared with his parents, instead of blaming himself for the fact they were no longer here.

To reinforce this thought, he gunned the engine and they took off at speed. She refused to be nervous. Responsibility meant everything to Alejandro, and he had the mother of his baby sitting next to him. He wouldn't take any chances.

'How could you not fall in love with this island?' she exclaimed as they reached the summit of a hill to find the calm azure ocean spread out in front of them. 'Paradise doesn't even come close.'

I understand you better now, Tom. No wonder you loved this special place and wanted me to discover it for myself. I only have one regret, and that is that we can't explore together—

'Do you like what you see?'

Alejandro distracted her. 'I certainly do,' she said with feeling. And it wasn't just the island she admired, but Alejandro. There was such strength in him, and as they drove on she noticed he was becoming more relaxed. She'd never seen him like this before, and it warmed her to see him happy here.

Settling back in her seat, she enjoyed the rest of the drive. Tom's dream had been to build a home on the island and settle down, and now it was as if Tom had passed that dream on. The more she saw of the magical island, the calmer she felt. This was the place where Tom's dream would become a reality.

Alejandro's sprawling ranch house was beyond impressive. She might have known. Of all his dwellings, this was the one that spoke to her the most, maybe because it was rustic, rather than grand, but she could see the care in every inch of the sprawling wooden structure. The grounds surrounding it were immaculately groomed, and it stood at the end of a very long drive. There were no gates to that drive, none needed for a man who owned the island.

Half an island, she amended with the same spear of surprise that always hit her when she realised that the other half belonged to her.

Alejandro had brought the Jeep to a halt in front of a large, arched front door, in front of which an older woman stood waiting to greet them.

'My housekeeper, Maria,' Alejandro explained.

Sienna was immediately drawn to the warmth on Maria's face. His housekeeper couldn't have appeared more welcoming if she'd tried. The moment Sienna was out of the Jeep, she advanced, arms opened wide. 'Welcome—come in. We've been so excited since we knew you were coming. Tom's sister,' Maria exclaimed, studying Sienna's face with shrewd, raisin-black eyes. 'Yes. I can see your brother in you.' She smiled. 'And you in him,' she added warmly. 'I hope your journey has been smooth?'

Fortunately, Sienna didn't get chance to answer. What was the point in telling this lovely woman that her boss was an unscrupulous rogue who stopped at nothing to get his own way? As she worked for him, Maria probably knew that already, Sienna reasoned as she revealed, 'We did have some choppy water…' She stared pointedly at Alejandro. 'But as soon as we arrived here, the sun began to shine again.'

'Perfect,' Maria remarked as she led Sienna into the house.

'It's wonderful to be in a place that meant so much to my brother,' Sienna said quietly as they stood in the hall.

Taking both Sienna's hands in hers, Maria told her, 'We're so very glad to see you.'

'As I am to be here.'

'Before I take you to your room, there's something I'd like to ask you.'

'Yes?'

'I'm sorry to throw this at you the minute you arrive, but we always have a fiesta when Señor Acosta comes home, and this time I wondered if we could dedicate the celebration to your brother?'

'I'd love that, and I know Tom would too.' As Alejandro was right behind them, she felt it only right to check with him.

'If it makes you happy...?'

'It does.' It would make her happier still to put a smile on Alejandro's face. Coming back to the island had made him briefly glad, and had obviously made him relax. Now, she suspected that thoughts about a party for Tom had plunged him back into the past. She looked from him to Maria. Were they keeping something from her? Something about Tom they thought might upset her, perhaps?

'If it's all right with you, Alejandro,' she said carefully, 'I think that's a lovely idea. Tom loved a party.' For some reason, she found herself thinking back to how wild Tom could become at a celebration. 'He wouldn't have wanted any of us to be sad,' she said with more determination.

Another glance at Alejandro was enough to tell her that the shutters were well and truly down. 'I'm sure Tom will be cheering us on,' she said to reassure Maria, who, Sienna now noticed, was also staring with concern at her boss.

Maria turned out to be a dab hand at diplomacy. 'With your permission, *señorita*—and, of course, with Señor Acosta's permission...' Alejandro gave a curt nod. 'That is what we shall do,' Maria decreed. 'And I will arrange everything for you.'

'Thank you, Maria.' She gave the older woman a hug. With people like Maria around, Sienna's plans for her share of the island didn't seem quite so out of reach.

And Alejandro? What will he have to say about your plans?

She would have to hope that a deeper understanding grew between them. Give it time.

An understanding? Is that enough for you?

It would have to be, Sienna concluded as she followed Maria deeper into the house.

It was impossible to remain under the same roof as Sienna without lust plaguing him. And he wanted to show her the island. He wanted so much, too much. Leaving her in Maria's capable hands, he left the house to drive about a mile or so; anywhere to give him distance. Halting the vehicle beside one of the vast paddocks, he climbed out to whistle up one of his ponies. Riding bareback, he headed out at the gallop without any clear destination in mind. Just not back to the ranch was currently enough for him.

So much had happened between him and Sienna, he needed mind space to think. How much did she know about Tom? Did she know that when the darkness came, Tom could be violent and unpredictable? That same darkness had claimed Tom on the night he was killed. Having defied Alejandro's orders, Tom had placed their entire group in danger, and had paid the ultimate price. Should he tell Sienna that?

As soon as he reached the long, flat shoreline, he urged his horse into the surf. Pounding through the waves was exhilarating. His earliest memories had been forged here. Happy family events, too numerous to count, so when the island had come up for sale, it had seemed obvious to seize the opportunity to make more memories. But he would not forget the past. Reining in, he stared out to sea, recalling his belief that men like Tom could be healed if they were this close to nature. It hadn't taken him long to persuade Tom to believe it too, and a project they could both work on had come out of that. He had hoped Tom would be one of the first to be cured here.

Alejandro Acosta, known in the forces as the Master of Control, had never been able to explain his close friendship with Wild Tom, as others in their platoon had called Tom. He didn't need to explain their friendship. They were firm friends, and that had always been enough. Occasionally, Alejandro saw the same wildness in himself, and they had definitely shared a vision. Care for all living creatures, and a deep appreciation of the natural world, added to the fact that Tom could always make him laugh, which was a small thing, but a rare and beautiful thing.

Turning his horse, he allowed it to amble along the lacy fringes of the surf. Tom had been a dreamer, not a doer, hence the broken-down ranch house Sienna had inherited. She was cut from a very different cloth from her brother. Determination could have been her middle name. He could imagine her, spade in her hand, digging the foundations her-self, and probably singing an aria as she did so.

Smiling as he thought about Sienna, he realised he was growing dangerously fond of her. She lightened him, as Tom had, and lifted him, but could he commit fully, knowing how he'd pulled back in the past? And would she want that, or were all her thoughts for the island and Tom?

It was late afternoon by the time he arrived back at the house. He walked in at the very moment Sienna came down-stairs. The luminosity of her beauty hit him like a punch in the gut. Memories of how abandoned she'd been in his arms, in his bed, instantly flooded his mind, but Sienna had on a businesslike expression, and lost no time in telling him what her future plans involved.

'Alejandro, we need to talk.'

'No problem. I'll get cleaned up, then we'll meet in my study downstairs, okay?'

Her wildflower scent assailed him as he jogged up the stairs. Thanks to his PA, Sienna had a whole world of designer clothes to choose from, but had picked out fresh jeans and a simple white top. No make-up, and with her hair drawn back, she looked effortlessly beautiful, beautifully understated. And keen to talk.

He found her in the kitchen, chatting to Maria, and suggested they go to his orangery, which was one of his favourite rooms in the house. The huge glass structure overlooked his ponies, grazing contentedly in the paddocks beyond. The ambience was restful, and he thought it perfect for their talks. Simply decorated, with plants and rugs and ethnic throws, this was his choice, rather than an interior designer's. He always found it a toss-up between staring out at the mesmerising view or simply contemplating the interior of a most attractive space.

'You have a beautiful home,' Sienna observed. 'Each time I think I've seen perfection, I discover more here, and it tells me a lot about you.'

'I think you'd better explain that,' he said.

'My guess is this is all you.'

He laughed. 'You found me out.' He was glad that it pleased her.

'It isn't dreary,' she said thoughtfully.

He laughed again and held up his hand. 'I'd stop there, if I were you. I built this house with the help of my friends on the island. Something else bothering you?' he asked as she frowned.

'Two things,' she admitted.

'Start with the first,' he advised, settling back.

'Okay.' She launched straight in. 'I'm going to build a

music facility here on my part of the island. I dreamed of doing something like this for years, and now I can. I'm planning to build a music therapy centre, to be exact.'

'That's the first thing. What's the second?'

'Sounds silly after that, but the clothes your PA sent are a bit confusing. Do you expect me to sing while I'm here?'

'No,' he said with surprise. 'Why?'

'Just that evening clothes don't seem appropriate wear for a ranch?'

'Perhaps my PA imagined I might fly you to the Ritz for a meal.'

Sienna hummed. 'Do you do that often?'

'Why? Are you jealous?'

'No,' she protested, rather too fast and too loud.

'I don't expect you to do anything while you're here, but take a view of your land,' he said.

'Do the deal and leave?' she suggested.

'I didn't say that.'

'So, what do you think of my plan?'

'I'm reserving judgement for now. On the face of it, it sounds interesting.'

'You could sound more enthusiastic.'

'You want the truth—you'll soon be having my child, and I don't understand how you're going to handle becoming a first-time mother while you run such an important institution.'

'First off, I doubt it will be built in a few months.'

'But you might need to rest during your pregnancy, and then what?'

'There's a third question.'

'Go on,' he invited.

'Why are there so many business suits amongst those new clothes, when I've never owned a suit in my life?'

'I thought you'd be more comfortable if you were formally dressed for any meetings with lawyers.'

'Lawyers?' Sienna sounded shocked. 'Should I appoint someone?'

'I can advise—'

'Thank you,' she interrupted. 'I'm sure you can, but legal advice is something I prefer to handle myself.'

'As you wish.'

I do wish, her glance told him. He put his hands up, palms flat. 'This doesn't need to become a confrontation. I only meant to suggest that when we firm things up for the transfer of the land from Tom's name to yours, you should have independent legal advice.'

'Oh.' She seemed lost for a moment. 'I just thought with us being as close as two people can be, and the fact that we've confided in each other, and discussed so many things, you have previously seemed evasive when it comes to the land or our baby.'

'Is that what you think? I don't.'

'Okay, so maybe we're both guilty of not explaining our feelings clearly. Can you even remember the last time you admitted how you felt about anything?'

'Can you?' he asked.

They were both haunted by the past, but must not allow that to impact the future of an innocent child. They sat in silence for a while, until Sienna prompted, 'So, where does that leave us, Alejandro?'

'More than two people thrown together because of Tom, I hope,' he admitted.

He could tell she was surprised by his candour, and her next words proved it. 'You promised me a tour of the land,' she reminded him, giving the impression that the wealth of feeling pent-up inside her needed a far bigger space if it was ever to run free. 'Do you think we could talk as we tour?'

'The Jeep?'

She frowned. 'Horseback?'

'You ride?'

'Tom taught me,' Sienna explained with a wistful smile as she thought back.

He could have kicked himself. Of course, Tom had taught her to ride. 'Your brother was an excellent rider. He often used to sub for our polo team. Why don't we go to the stable, and I'll match you with a suitable mount?'

'High-spirited and temperamental?' Sienna suggested deadpan.

It was the smallest spark of humour, but he'd take it. 'I'll find you something gentle and biddable.'

'You wish,' Sienna replied.

CHAPTER ELEVEN

SIENNA WAS AN accomplished rider, and formed an immediate bond with the pony he'd chosen. 'But you should slow down,' he objected when they eventually reined in at a spectacular viewing point that could never have been reached by Jeep.

'Do you mean because of the baby? Relax. I'm pregnant, not sick,' she said, dismounting. 'What a view! What a place. No wonder you and Tom loved the island so much. My brother was always a romantic, but I can't think of anyone who'd remain unmoved by this. Oh, wait,' she said with a teasing glance at him.

'Okay. You got me,' he said as he sprang down to join her. 'I love this island.'

'You can't hide it,' she said.

'I don't want to hide it,' he admitted to his own surprise. If Sienna stayed on the island, he hoped she'd come to love it as much as he did. 'Do you know what I'd like to hear about?' he said as he leaned back against a tree.

'Is this a guessing game?'

Responding to her sideways smile, he said, 'No. I'd like you to tell me more about the Tom I didn't know—your big brother.'

'He was the best—the most fun, the most caring, the most adorable, loving big brother anyone could have. Tom always threw the best parties too. I guess he was trying to make up for the fact that our parents weren't there to do things like that for either of us. He did get a little wild at times,' she remembered with a frown. 'One time Tom hired circus performers and insisted on going up on the trapeze with them. He used to terrify me with some of his stunts, but, being Tom, he somehow got away with it.'

Not that last time, he thought.

'And you?' she pressed, turning to stare at him. 'What about you, Alejandro? You used to come here with your family before...' Her voice tailed away as she stopped short of reminding him that everything had changed when his parents were killed.

'We used to have great times here,' he admitted. 'We stayed in a simple ranch house—the same one Tom left you. Boys slept in the attic, while Sofia, often as not, slept in the stable with the kittens. We'd ride bareback for hours, and tumble off exhausted at the end of the day. As the oldest I had to keep everyone in check, and that was no easy task, I can tell you, but somehow we managed to survive: riding, swimming and skiing until we dropped, in between picnicking, thanks to Maria, to our hearts' content.'

'You make it sound like paradise.'

'It was.' But now it was time to return to practicalities. Exposing his innermost feelings like this was new to him and took some getting used to. 'The river divides our land,' he explained. 'Your land is on the left, as we look at the river, with mine on the right.'

'With nary a bridge in between?' Sienna suggested, raising a brow as she looked at him.

He refused to be drawn, and, remounting his horse, he informed her that they would be riding home at a sedate pace.

'If you need a gentle ride,' she said as she mounted her pony, 'I'm fine with that.'

Ignoring her light, mocking tone, he urged his horse into a steady canter. Sienna rode up alongside. 'Don't worry,' she reassured him. 'Tom taught me to always ride within my capability.'

'Did Tom also mention that horses are unpredictable?'

'Anyone would think you were concerned about me,' she remarked with an amused grin.

'Of course, I'm concerned about you,' he said with a frown. 'If you think for one moment I take responsibility lightly, you really don't know me at all.'

'That's just it, isn't it?' Sienna replied. 'We don't know each other, and we should have discussed our plans for the future long before this. But—if I'm allowed to make an observation—I'd say things are improving, and we're both opening up.'

'One step at a time?' he suggested.

'Something like that,' she agreed, turning her face to the sun. Opening her eyes again, she stared him square in the face. 'Whether you accept what I'm going to say next, or not, you have shown concern for me. You chose a very kind pony, and you're in danger of relaxing. You just don't like anyone to imagine you've got a heart.'

'Concentrate on riding,' he advised. Just in time, as it turned out.

A snake hissed and Sienna's pony shied.

Reacting on instinct, he whipped her out of the saddle and seated her in front of him before she had chance to protest.

'There—that proves I'm right,' she insisted as he snapped a lead rein on her pony. 'Caring is second nature to you, so, however harsh you try to appear, you can never quite bring it off.'

'With a baby to think about, of course I care.'

'Our baby will always come first,' she agreed.

'It will,' he confirmed, riding on.

Had she made a breakthrough? Sienna wondered as they rode on. Whatever had happened, or not happened, between them since they'd first met, Alejandro made her feel safe. Sex alone would never be enough for her. For Sienna, the intimacy of closeness meant everything. It was like a tiny green shoot she had to nurture and see grow. Both she and Alejandro were stubborn, and they had been unyielding, but maybe in time that could change. The challenge that was Alejandro was what she found so attractive about him, but if only he could extend the care he showed others to himself.

He reined in beside the river that divided their land. Could anything bridge that span? she wondered as she stared at the rushing water. Alejandro and Tom had been happy to share the island, so why couldn't she? 'Is that Tom's farmhouse?' she asked with interest.

'It was going to be,' Alejandro confirmed as they surveyed the caved-in roof and broken-down walls. Dismounting, he held out his arms to help her down. 'We had intended to rebuild it together.'

'Together?' she said, staring up as he lifted her down. 'Don't you mean that you would do the grunt work, while Tom lay on the grass dreaming, when he wasn't issuing the occasional order?'

'Is that any way to speak about your brother?' Alejandro asked in a disturbing, teasing murmur as he held her a hair's breadth away from his mouth.

'I speak the truth,' she whispered back. 'You know I do.'

He'd paused in the act of lifting her down, which resulted

in a slow slide down the length of his hard body. By the time she was steady on her feet again, she was lost to reason, but Alejandro stepped back. 'I promised to help Tom with all the repairs, and as far as I'm concerned nothing has changed. I'll do the same for you.'

They were both sad that Tom hadn't lived to see his dream come to fruition, but they still had time to make things right. She said so.

'I hope you're right,' Alejandro admitted. 'One thing's certain,' he added as they each mounted their own horse. 'I'm glad about the baby. You need to hear that.'

'Yes, I do.'

One step at a time, Sienna thought as she settled back into the saddle. 'This has been a lot for both of us—Tom's death, me inheriting his land, and now we're having a baby. I just want you to know, I won't hold you to anything—'

'Stop,' Alejandro advised. 'Good news has the power to heal grief, and we have great news. Give that chance to sink in.'

'Chance to heal?' she suggested with both longing and hope.

Alejandro's long stare confirmed her belief that they'd grown closer during the ride. One step at a time, indeed, she thought, smiling back.

When they had dismounted in the yard, Alejandro explained that there was a new horse he wanted to trial. 'Leaving you free to do as you like for the rest of the evening.'

With a smile, she left him. Walking into the kitchen to see Maria's cheerful face turned her growing optimism into certainty. How could anything go wrong with Maria around? They chatted for a while, and then Sienna excused herself to go upstairs to her bedroom. Her room overlooked what

Maria described as the home paddock, explaining this was where Alejandro trained his horses.

A quick shower later, Sienna was standing by the window, on the pretext of drying her hair with a towel, when actually she was staring at Alejandro. Could there be a better sight than this man in snug-fitting breeches? Calf-length, close-fitting riding boots teamed with a form-fitting black top completed the picture of male perfection. A red bandana held his wild black hair out of his eyes, and the stubble on his cheeks had grown so thick, he looked more like a marauding barbarian than a smooth tech billionaire. A glint of gold in his ear made her smile. If Alejandro had needed anything more to convince her that he was exactly the type of man any sensible woman should avoid, that earring said it all. He was unconventional. And exciting.

Now she realised something else. When it came to dealing with animals, Alejandro appeared to be transformed. He was patient and measured, endlessly gentle and kind. It was hard to believe that this was the same man she'd first met in London. Soothing his horse with long sweeping strokes down the length of its neck resulted in the half-wild stallion resting its head on his shoulder. It was at this point he looked up. Had he sensed her watching him? She shouldn't forget that working with animals tuned people's senses to an acute degree.

None of that would have mattered if she hadn't been wearing sexy silk pyjamas. Who could resist plundering that new supply of clothes? She'd ended up selecting something totally inappropriate to wear for a long, solo night on a rural ranch, but they felt so amazing next to her skin.

Turning away from the window, she stared at her reflection in the mirror. It was like staring at a stranger. The sensual slither of silk against her shower-warm skin reminded her of Alejandro's feathering touches. Turning her head, she looked at him again, only to find him looking back at her. She held his gaze boldly with a question in her eyes. Was this the sort of bedroom attire he was accustomed to women wearing? Was that why his PA had chosen such provocative nightwear?

Resisting the temptation to shred the glorious garments at the thought of other women flaunting themselves in front of Alejandro, she accepted the harsh truth: she wanted him to see her like this. She wanted him to find her irresistible. Playing with fire was dangerous, but it was also dangerously appealing.

The sight of Sienna in upmarket lingerie took him completely by surprise. Framed in an upstairs window, she looked like a goddess with her glorious auburn hair cascading in gleaming waves to her waist. The colour of the silk against her skin looked amazing. The soft cream and gold enhanced her luminous beauty, making it dangerously easy to imagine the flimsy fabric brushing intimately against every part of her.

Aroused? He was in agony.

Sheer effort of will allowed him to return his attention to the horse. Control was everything, but training would soon be over, and then it would be time to set the horse free. There was always a balance to be struck between managing and spoiling the spirit of a beautiful animal. Respect on both sides was vital. Trust equally so. Would it ever be possible to achieve that same fine balance with Sienna? Could he commit to a relationship without losing control of his heart?

'Hey,' he murmured to the horse as he removed its head collar. 'It's time for you to run free.'

* * *

She rang down to let Maria know that she wouldn't be joining Alejandro for dinner.

'Relax,' Maria insisted. 'If you're changed and ready for bed, snuggle up and let your cares float away.'

If only it were that easy, Sienna thought ruefully as images of Alejandro in the saddle, where he belonged, made her mouth dry and her body yearn. 'It's been so long since I rode a horse, my muscles are screaming,' she explained. 'I'm not sure I could even make it down the stairs.'

'Well, you don't have to try.'

There was something in Maria's voice that said she didn't believe a word of Sienna's excuse, but, with her usual diplomacy, she let it pass.

Missing dinner led to brooding on her own. Switching off the light allowed moonlight to flood the room. The setting was painfully romantic, but without a romantic hero it was a waste. As her mood took a downturn, it wasn't long before the plans she'd made in London, to build a treatment facility on the island, seemed over-ambitious, even reckless. What made her think she could take half an island, build on it, live on it, run a business *and* bring up a child, and do all of that successfully? What was her track record in the commercial world? Tom had paid for her singing lessons, and Jason had been at her side during every professional gig.

Why don't you give up right now? Sienna's inner critic suggested.

The only sure path to failure was giving up. She had to reason things out. Her biggest hurdle was Alejandro and the way he made her feel. Did he still want her? Was he only keeping her here because of their child? Business challenges turned out to be the least of her worries.

So, what are you going to do about it?

'Me?' She actually spoke the word out loud.

I don't see anyone else sitting on the bed, feeling sorry for themself.

It was a relief to hear a tap on the door as Maria arrived with a tray of food. 'I can't let you go hungry,' the housekeeper insisted, adding a stern instruction for Sienna to eat.

What was she hiding away from? What did she hope to achieve? She picked at her food. It was delicious, of course, but she had no appetite. Pushing the tray to one side, she climbed into bed. The irony of wearing silk pyjamas wasn't lost on her. They might feel amazing, but who would see them, touch them, peel them off?

Thoughts continued to whirl in her head, expanding like ripples on a pond. Being pregnant with Alejandro's baby was the most wonderful gift, and he'd been right to say that the island was the perfect place to raise a child. Maria's smiling face came into her mind. There'd be so much support here...

Inhaling deeply on the scent of freshly picked flowers, she felt their soothing presence on the dressing table like a warm hug, and, with the first sigh of contentment she'd uttered in a very long time, she snuggled down beneath the covers, and quickly fell asleep.

She dreamed about Tom. Her brother was talking to her, and encouraging her to give the island a chance, and stay. He didn't seem at all alarmed she'd arrived by such unconventional means. Quite the opposite, in fact; he seemed thrilled and happy that she was pregnant with Alejandro's child.

Did you plan this? Is that why I'm here?

But the dream was already fading, and, as hard as she tried to hold onto it, Tom vanished. For the first time since the officers had brought her the terrible news, she woke up and cried for her brother. It was a long time before she fell silent again, but when she did it was with the certainty that Tom would always be safe in her memory, while Alejandro was safe in her heart.

He heard Sienna crying as he passed her room on his way to bed. He wouldn't intrude on private grief, though her sadness moved something deep inside him. The loss of a friend like Tom would stay with him for ever. He knew there were strategies to help deal with loss, but had chosen to distance himself from all relief. He was too busy—there were too many calls on his time for him to sit around grieving. But Sienna's tears could not be ignored. He found it impossible to distance himself from that.

Alone in bed, he turned out the light, but he couldn't sleep, and he couldn't relax. It was back to the old dilemma. Could he give Sienna everything she needed? The thought of anyone else trying to made him more restless still. What did she want out of life? They'd already established that she didn't want his money, his power, or any of the more obvious things.

She needs love.

Was he the man to give her the love she craved, or would he back away when things got heavy, as he always had before? Remaining remote had allowed him to skirt around meaningful involvement, but Sienna was different, she was unique, but that didn't make the problem go away, it only made it worse. Staring at the ceiling, he eventually fell into a restless, troubled sleep.

They sat in silence over breakfast the next day. The chat she'd planned didn't happen. It was impossible to start a conversation with Alejandro in this mood. Closed off didn't even begin to describe how he was this morning. He barely acknowledged her presence at the table, and ate with studied concentration, as if breakfast was a chore to get through before the real business of the day could begin.

'Ready?' he demanded, startling her into full attention.

'For...?'

'Settling our affairs, of course. The land?' he prompted.

She didn't move as he left the table. 'As far as I'm concerned, the land is a secondary consideration.'

'For you, perhaps.' He stood, waiting by the door. 'We can talk on the way,' he insisted.

'On the way to where?'

'To show you your boundaries, of course.'

Someone had got out of bed the wrong side. 'The land can wait,' she said calmly. 'It isn't going anywhere, while our child—'

'What about our child?' he said, coming back to plant his fists on the table. 'I don't see there's anything to discuss where the baby's concerned. You'll live here. Maria will help you. What more could you ask? When the child's older, Maria's daughter runs an excellent play scheme, and there are several excellent schools on the island—'

'Do you intend to live here too?'

'Well, I—'

'Exactly,' she said, standing to confront him. 'You haven't decided. You'll do as you please, as always, I imagine. And, as for education, don't you think it's a little soon to be discussing our child's schooling?'

'Never,' Alejandro countered with passion. 'Education is the most important element in a child's life.'

'So is love, care, support, and happiness,' Sienna argued fiercely.

'I don't understand your problem,' Alejandro admitted as they fired angry looks at each other.

'I'll tell you what my problem is. I feel as if you've made a decree, and I have to fall into line. I thought we were getting somewhere yesterday. I thought we were close. But that's just it, isn't it, Alejandro? You can't bear to get too close to anyone, so you've stepped away before that can happen. You're allowed to talk and express opinions, but you expect me to listen without comment. I'm not allowed to interfere, because you've taken over something we should be planning together. Control is great sometimes, but you can't control me, or use control as an excuse to ignore your emotions.'

'That has never been my intention,' he said stiffly.

'Then, bend a little,' she begged. 'Look to the future, as I do, to when we have a new life to consider.'

'I have many businesses to run, and endless calls on my time—'

'So, you'll be too busy to take an interest in your child?'

Alejandro made a sound of exasperation as he raked his hair.

'Sit, talk, discuss the future with me. Give some of your time, Alejandro. Our baby deserves that much, at least. Think of the benefits if we work together. Two people at war can't hope to achieve anything. I'm not saying we have to live together, but we must raise our child together.'

'Continents apart?'

'Even then,' she said steadily.

Several long, tense moments passed as they stared at each other unblinking, until finally Sienna broke the silence. It wasn't the conversation she's planned, but at least seeing the island would be better than this tension. 'When you're ready, I actually would like to take another look at the land. We've both got a lot to think about, and I don't want to rush into an uninformed decision.'

'Are you planning to leave the island?'

There was real concern in his voice.

'I don't know yet,' she said honestly.

Whatever the outcome between them, she would go it alone, if she had to. She'd raise her child with love and live happily, while somehow finding a way to bring Tom's dream to fruition.

CHAPTER TWELVE

THEY HAD ACHIEVED a truce of sorts, and that had to be
enough for now. At least they could talk without trying to
score points or remain stubbornly standing on their dignity. They were as bad as one another, Sienna mused as
she accompanied Alejandro outside again. Butting heads
was putting it mildly. 'The solicitor gave me a map,' she reminded him as they crossed the stable yard. 'I've marked a
few places in red—places I'm particularly interested in…'

He paused mid-stride.

'Before you take me to see them, please accept that this
isn't about money for me. It's more about building a life.'

'Everything's about money,' he said with a frown.

'If you believe that, I feel sorry for you,' she called after
him. 'You can't just make the rules and expect everyone
else to live by them. I might be in your world right now, but
I insist on having a say.'

'You insist?' he called over his shoulder.

'Yes, I do. Did your father put money before love?' she
demanded, catching him up. 'You told me about your wonderful childhood with loving parents, who always wanted
the best for their children. Has something changed since
then? Are you concerned that you will never be able to live
up to your parents' example?'

'My child will lack for nothing,' he barked, increasing his stride and the distance between them. 'I promise you that.'

'If you give your children everything,' she said, jogging alongside, 'what will they have to strive for?'

'Children? Do you intend to have more?'

His gaze was harsh, but she held it steadily. 'Who knows what the future holds?'

'You apparently know more than me. Well?' he queried in the same harsh tone. 'Do you want to see this land, or not?'

'I do,' she confirmed.

'We'll take the Jeep to save time.'

She didn't argue, having sensed that Alejandro's mood was already easing. He wasn't a bad man, he was a man coming face to face with an argumentative nemesis, and for that she could only feel glad. Alejandro had always taken charge of everything, but now he had a helpmate in the mother of his child.

'Would you be interested to hear about my plans?'

'Very much so.'

Her spirits lifted at Alejandro's suggestion. This wasn't a small step. It was a giant leap in the right direction. *'Vamos!'* she said, smiling as he leaned in front of her to open the passenger door of the Jeep.

'One proviso…'

'Which is?' she asked, turning to face him.

'We can't be late for Tom's party.'

Her heart beat a furious tattoo at Alejandro's use of the word *we*. She didn't want to read too much into it, but it felt good. 'Maria's gone to a lot of trouble,' she agreed. 'We won't be late. I'm sure you'll see to that.'

Before they left Maria caught sight of them, and as always his housekeeper was fully prepared. 'Here's some food for your picnic,' she said, racing up to the Jeep.

'That's very kind of you,' Sienna said, leaning across him, delivering warmth and scent and womanliness to his starving senses. 'We won't be late back,' she promised with a smile.

He parked up on the riverbank, where they had a good view of both parcels of land.

'This is perfect,' Sienna said when they'd laid out the picnic.

'It's the exact spot where I used to come with my family,' he revealed. 'My parents used to set out a picnic beneath this very tree. If you look over there,' he said, pointing to where building work had already started, 'you can see where I'm building Tom's retreat for veterans.'

'You're building Tom's retreat,' Sienna echoed thoughtfully.

'It's been a long time in the planning. It will overlook the river on one side and the mountains on the other.'

'Which sounds perfect,' she agreed.

He could see her thinking, how could one small island house two similar facilities? The answer was, it couldn't, but, being Sienna, she put her own hopes and dreams to one side and thought only of the benefits for others.

'It's going to be wonderful,' she said, smiling with sincerity into his eyes.

Her hair was loose and blowing free, and her cheeks were already pinking up in the sun. Understated appeal had truthfully never interested him before, but that was before he met Sienna.

'I wonder,' she said as she brought a cup of juice to her lips.

'You wonder what?' he pressed.

'Could we work together? It makes sense, doesn't it? You're building a retreat, and I want to build a music therapy centre. Why can't we combine the two? I'd have to renovate Tom's house first, of course,' she said, frowning as she developed her plan, 'but once that was habitable and I moved in, we could allocate some of the rooms in your facility for music therapy. Couldn't we?' she added hopefully.

He wondered if she knew how appealing she was, but had she really considered everything in detail as he had? 'Do you intend to keep on working when you have the baby?'

'Of course. Why not?'

'Because I imagine you'll be fully occupied bringing up our child.'

'I won't stop being me when our baby's born,' she protested. 'I'm a qualified music therapist. I can help people. I won't allow my studies to go to waste.'

Alejandro was frowning but she could tell he was listening. 'Tom taught me the importance of independence when our parents were killed, and that's a lesson I've never forgotten.'

But it was more than that, Sienna realised. She had to work. She would always work, because love could be ripped away, while music was something that no one could take away from her. Her insecurities were showing, she accepted, but Tom had sacrificed so much to pay for Sienna to advance her studies. She couldn't imagine he'd be pleased if she gave up both her career and her self-determination the moment Alejandro came into her life.

She continued, 'Didn't you admit that playing the piano offered you a form of escape? Music heals, Alejandro. We both know that. Why shouldn't our child grow up knowing that too? I plan for our baby to accompany me. The first thing I'm going to do is create a crèche within the facility, so that mothers can be close to their children.'

Alejandro's hum suggested he liked the idea, but he was

still frowning. 'As the child's father, I can promise you that you'll never have to work another day in your life.'

'Is that supposed to make me happy?' she asked with a sad smile. 'I'm sure it would sound attractive to some, but I want to work. I don't want to be treated like one of your brood mares, pampered and cared for until the day our baby is born, at which point, according to your reasoning, I'll be superfluous to requirements, and likely dismissed.'

'Your reasoning is wrong.'

'A woman defending her child is wrong? Why can't we both work, and still give our child all the love in the world? Alejandro?' she pressed. 'What's really behind your concern? Are you afraid you'll never be able to replicate your own happy childhood? Honestly, I sometimes think I have more faith in you than you have in yourself.'

'Replicating my childhood is a big ask.'

'Mine too, but I'm determined to do it. Will you join me?'

He said nothing for a long while, and then admitted, 'If you met my sister and brothers, you might realise that the great wealth you fear so much isn't necessarily a burden, but an opportunity to do good.'

'I'd really like that, and I hope I get the chance. I only have to see your face light up when you talk about your family to know you must have deep feelings locked away somewhere. You have to set those feelings free. I'm the first to admit that isn't easy, but it's possible, and the next step is to learn to care about yourself.'

Alejandro Acosta, forced to climb down by an outstanding woman? Guilty as charged. If he lost her—if he lost Sienna's trust—that was the worst he could imagine.

'Let's toss ideas around,' she suggested. 'We can argue and reason, until finally you accept that—'

'You know best?' he suggested with the hint of a smile.

'Until you accept that I can be a good mother, and do other things too,' she said, smiling warmly into his eyes.

All he wanted was to be close to this woman. He wanted them to understand each other, and to trust each other, and for Sienna to realise that his wealth was no barrier to happiness. To convince her, he would first have to prove to her that the power he wielded would never be used to control her.

As if reading his mind, she smiled and touched his arm. 'I've never doubted your sense of responsibility, Alejandro. I just don't want to be crushed by it.'

Their stares locked and held in mutual understanding. They'd got a lot off their chests, opening the door to more discussion. By the time they swapped conversation for food, great strides had been made. 'After you,' he insisted.

'Oh, no, after you,' Sienna countered with a grin. 'I can wait.'

To hell with that!

'I can't,' he said, dragging her close.

It was like a first kiss, intense, searching, and beautiful. When they eventually parted, it was as if they couldn't bear to move more than a breath away. Alejandro's fierce gaze warm and reassuring. Was she still hoping for too much?

Kissing her again, he made it easy to stay in his arms. Maybe she didn't pull back as soon as she should, but there was still a moment, even at the point of no return, when questions forced their way into her mind. 'You want to ask me about Tom,' Alejandro guessed, when she failed to put her thoughts into words.

'Only because I can sense when you're holding back,' she said. 'I know you want to protect me, but I'm stronger than you know, and I'm asking you not to. I want to see Tom as you knew him.'

Alejandro paused, and countless expressions flashed behind his eyes, as if he was battling his own demons. 'We were similar in some ways,' he said at last. 'Neither of us could forgive ourselves for our parents' deaths. The fact that Tom, like me, had nothing to do with it has never counted, because guilt is a strange animal. It can drive you to believe that you could have done something, or that you *should* have done something, and that if you had, you might have saved them. Tom once told me that the only reason he carried on living was to protect you.'

'I wish Tom had tried harder to stay alive.'

'So do I.'

As Alejandro fell silent she felt guilty for pressing him.

'Thinking back isn't easy,' he said at last.

'I'm sure not,' she agreed softly. 'I'm guessing you won't give me the detail, but I can still work it out. Tom tempted fate once too often. He liked to taunt fate.'

'Because Tom saw fate as being unfair to him,' Alejandro said, quick to excuse his friend. 'You're right, he took a risk that night that cost him his life. As for telling you more? I don't see there's anything to be gained by that. I'm not even sure there is more—at least, nothing that would help you.'

'You don't like to lie, and you don't like to pile on the pain,' she observed with a wry twist of her mouth.

'Why would I do either of those things?'

Leave it. They'd both suffered the most terrible grief. Who would want to revisit that? She started to clear up their picnic as a cover for threatening tears. 'I don't want to upset you. I'll just say that, whenever you remember something you can tell me about Tom—happy times, playing polo, maybe—you tell me more about the Tom I didn't know.'

'Tom was brave—the bravest man in the regiment.'

After his reticence on the subject of Tom, Alejandro's words shocked her. 'Brave, or foolhardy?'

He turned his head away briefly, as if to acknowledge the distinction, then turned back to her, to state firmly, 'Tom was brave in so many ways.'

That told Sienna more about her brother than a thousand words. Tom's impulsive phases, back when they were living together, his countless reckless actions. It had all been there under her nose, but she hadn't seen it—

'Don't feel guilty, Sienna. I can read you. You've seen what guilt does. It's corrosive. Fight it off. Move on. Move forward. You know that's what Tom would want.'

'You're right,' she conceded, firming her jaw. 'I guess this is why Tom talked about you all the time. He relied on your judgement.'

A faint sad smile touched Alejandro's mouth. 'Your brother talked about you all the time. He was so proud of you and your beautiful voice.'

'Yet now, I wonder if I even knew him.'

Alejandro shrugged. 'Did anyone know Tom? Like the rest of us, your brother was a complex character.'

'Which is why you tiptoe around the truth.'

She was right. No one had truly known Tom; not the psychiatrist who treated him, his sister, Sienna, not even Alejandro. The light-hearted man Sienna described was a front Tom adopted when it suited him. Guilt had ruled Tom to the point where he took far too many risks, as if inviting fate to notice *him*. 'If you're asking me, did your brother have mental health issues? Yes, he did.'

'And you covered for him,' she suggested.

They had all covered for Tom. Believing him when he said he was getting better. Not realising how ill he was until it was far too late. It was something Alejandro would never forgive himself for. When breakdowns happened in the heat of battle, there were no convenient committees to decide if someone needed to be medevacced out.

Seeing the pain in her eyes, he couldn't tell Sienna that. She'd lost a brother, which was bad enough, and was pregnant, which was another life-changing event. The last thing he wanted was to add to her pain. 'Tom meant a lot to me. We were as close as brothers. I'd have done anything for him, which is why I know Tom would want you to enjoy this pregnancy, and not feel guilty for being happy.'

'He would have been a fun uncle, don't you think?'

'Yes, I do,' he agreed. It might even have been the saving of him. They'd never know. 'The best way to honour Tom's memory is to embrace every moment, as he would, with optimism and energy.'

'That's such a lovely thing to say.'

Drawing her into his arms, he kissed her brow. 'Tom's probably looking down right now, and agreeing with me that you will be a great mother.'

'He was certainly a great brother. He never missed a parents' evening, and somehow found time to teach to me to ride, to drive, and so many other things.' Lifting her head, she searched his eyes with distress. 'And all that, while he was sick. I wish he'd been more open. I'd have found help. There are so many people waiting to offer support.'

'You, for instance.'

'Me?'

'Now you're a fully trained music therapist,' Alejandro reminded her.

She had to turn away. The irony of her vocation had never struck Sienna before, but now it did, and forcefully. 'I could have helped Tom.'

'You did help Tom,' Alejandro insisted. 'You gave him

unconditional love, and now Tom's legacy will live on through you. No one should feel alone, and we can all play a small part in letting people know that support is available.'

'You're so wise,' she said quietly, then, turning to him, she added, 'Do you think Tom planned this all along?'

'Planned what? Throwing us together?' Alejandro smiled as he shrugged. 'Maybe he threw the dice, but he couldn't know where it would land.'

That made three of them, Sienna guessed as Alejandro picked up the picnic basket and they headed back to the car.

CHAPTER THIRTEEN

ALEJANDRO HAD MADE a lot of things clearer, Sienna reflected as they drove back to the ranch, but one thing still troubled her. If Alejandro had known Tom was sick, had he allowed Tom to go forward into danger? Was Alejandro responsible for Tom's death?

If she could be reasonable for ten seconds together, she might accept that this was an overreaction, produced by raging pregnancy hormones, all mixed up with her old friend doubt.

She needed to be alone to think things through, and the moment they reached the ranch house, she leapt out of the vehicle before Alejandro had chance to help her down. The sight of Maria arranging trestle tables for the party brought her up short in the yard. How could she take herself off when Maria was working so hard to make Tom's party a success?

Holding out her arms to Sienna, Maria welcomed her back. 'I hope you had a good picnic?'

'Wonderful, thanks to you.' The food had been great, the company too, it was just those unanswered questions plaguing her. All the more so because Alejandro was still close by.

But not for long.

'You'll excuse me,' he said.

'Of course,' Sienna chorused with Maria.

'I've saved the vital final touches for you—' Maria broke off, to take a closer look at Sienna. 'Is something wrong?'

Maria could never be fooled. 'Nothing,' Sienna insisted with an unconvincing laugh.

'Go back to the house,' Maria instructed gently. 'You've had a long, hot morning, and should take a shower and have a rest.'

'And your morning has been cool and easy?' Sienna said.

'This is what I do,' Maria exclaimed with a happy gesture that encompassed the entire yard. 'Go,' she encouraged warmly.

The cool of the house was a relief. Sienna's thoughts were in such a muddle that a shower seemed like the best idea. A quick change of clothes later, and she hurried back to the vast cobbled yard to join Maria. If there was anyone who could tell her more about Tom, Alejandro's warm-hearted housekeeper was that person.

Maria's face softened the moment Sienna mentioned Tom's name. 'He was such a lovely young man,' she reminisced with a wistful look on her face. 'Always helpful, always smiling—' She paused there, to look at Sienna with concern. 'I was surprised when Alejandro explained that he had brought Tom to the island, to help him…recover.'

'Recover?' Sienna pressed carefully.

Maria gave a heavy sigh. 'There were two sides to your brother: the charming, happy man who couldn't do enough for you, and the tormented soul who troubled us all. Seeing those contrasts in action gave me some insight into how badly Tom had been damaged in battle.'

'You're not talking about physical injuries, are you?'

'No,' Maria confirmed. Compassion filled her eyes. 'I'm sorry, Sienna, didn't you know about this?'

'Alejandro has told me a few things, but he always draws back. I think he's frightened of upsetting me.'

'Of course, he is, and he doesn't want to add to the needless guilt you're suffering. Alejandro knows how you feel, because he suffers in exactly the same way. You have to stop punishing yourself, Sienna, just as he does. Survivor's guilt is normal. Once you've accepted that, you're halfway to learning strategies that will allow you to move on.'

There was a long pause, and then Sienna asked the question pressing on her mind. 'Can you tell me anything more about Tom?'

Maria paused in putting a tray down on the table. Turning to face Sienna, she admitted, 'He was very good at hiding his illness. Some scars are invisible, some are not, but Alejandro sees everything. I believe that's why he gave your brother half this island—'

'Alejandro *gave* Tom half the island?' Shock ripped through Sienna. 'Do you mean, there was no payment involved?'

'None at all.' Maria's dark eyes searched Sienna's face. 'I don't suppose Alejandro told you that?'

'He certainly didn't,' Sienna confirmed. 'My understanding was that they bought the island together.' She frowned. 'Or that maybe Alejandro bought it, and then agreed to sell half the land to Tom.'

'I can understand how you might think that,' Maria admitted. 'Who else on earth has Alejandro's level of wealth? I realise it's hard to imagine. It's hard for me, and I live in the same house as him. *Buying* an island. *Giving* half an island away. These are regular kindnesses for Alejandro. But I think it was more than that, because Alejandro was always convinced this land possessed healing properties, and if your brother spent enough time here, it would heal him. I do know he begged Tom to find help. He thought he was getting better.'

Alejandro had tried to protect her brother, as he was now offering his protection to Sienna.

Seeing the turmoil in her eyes, Maria advised, 'You must try to remember the good times with your brother, because that's what Tom would want you to do.'

'I wish I could, but I've had terrible thoughts about Alejandro—'

'Haven't we all?' Maria interrupted with a rueful laugh. 'But know this,' she said. 'Alejandro has never backed down from a challenge. He's the best and most loyal of men, which is why he is everyone's hero, and why he's so loved on this island. Tonight's celebration of Tom will mean a great deal to Alejandro, as it does to all of us who knew your brother, and I know it means everything to you.'

'More than you know,' Sienna agreed.

'And the best way to honour Tom is to laugh and sing and dance,' Maria said, giving Sienna a hug. 'Live your life to the full,' she instructed, pulling back. 'Celebrate the brother you remember, as we all will.'

'Tom did love a good party,' Sienna admitted.

'Well, then…' Maria jerked her chin in the direction of the house. 'We're finished here. Go and get ready for the party.'

'I'll be back as soon as I can.'

'No hurry. Everything's under control,' Maria assured her. 'Why don't you go for a relaxing swim? Give your emotions chance to settle down. I promise to leave the finishing touches to you.'

In a very different mood, Sienna turned to go, and missed the shrewd expression sparking in Maria's eyes.

Space from Sienna had allowed him to sort out his thoughts. Seeing her eyes so full of concern had proved that, in trying to avoid hurting her, by editing the truth about Tom, he'd only succeeded in hurting her more. What good would it do to add to her pain by telling her that by disobeying his order to remain in camp until further instruction Tom had risked, not only his own life on that dreadful night, but the lives of all his comrades too?

By the time he reached the gym he was wound up tight. Binding his fists, he took out his frustration on the heavy bag. The only thought that saved him was that Sienna was pregnant with his child. A few weeks ago, he would have thought it impossible for that to take precedence over everything else. He'd come a long way since Sienna had kick-started his emotions. One thing was very clear in his mind, as he slammed his fist into the bag: the role of part-time parent would never be enough for him.

And Sienna?

She was the first person ever to interfere with his plans and scheduling. Unleashing a fresh flurry of blows, he hammered the bag until it almost swung off the hook. Finishing with a couple of punishing roundhouse kicks, he stood back panting, fists clenched, brow lowered. And still the fire inside him refused to go out.

Stripping off his wrist bands and clothes in the changing room, he took a cold shower. No water was cold enough to refresh both body and mind when he was in this mindset. Towelling down roughly, he dragged on a pair of swimming shorts before bulldozing his way through the doors to the pool. He stopped dead. Sienna was there before him.

'I hope you don't mind,' she called out as she pulled herself onto the side.

'Not at all,' he snapped, turning to go.

Too late. She somehow waylaid him, and now she stood, looking like an improvement on Botticelli's Venus. How was it possible for Sienna to be even more beautiful each time he saw her?

She launched straight in. 'Maria told me about the island—about the arrangement you made with Tom. Seems I owe you an apology.'

'Oh?'

'Maria explained that you hoped your gift would heal my brother, which makes me guilty of misunderstanding you, and I'm sorry for that. Turns out there's a lot I don't know about Tom.'

'Save the guilt. There's been too much of that. Any questions you have, I'll try to answer.'

'I'm guessing you won't try too hard.'

'You might be right,' he said bluntly.

What was Maria up to? She'd known where he'd be. Best guess? His wily housekeeper had sent Sienna on ahead. But why? To soothe him? To put things straight? Or was this straightforward matchmaking, by a lovely, if rather misguided woman?

That thought was enough to force him to turn his back on the sight of Señorita Slater, half naked in a provocative swimming costume, no doubt chosen by his PA. 'You don't have to leave just because I'm going,' he said.

'But I do,' Sienna protested. 'I promised Maria I'd help her with the final touches.'

Reasonably content that his body was back under control, he swung around in time to see Sienna styling her hair into a messy up-do. The action pressed her breasts together. There was only so much torture he could take in one day. Taking evasive action, he plunged into the pool with relief.

To be continued, he reflected as he powered through the water. They weren't anywhere near done. He wanted Sienna, in every way there was. He'd even marry her, if that was what it took to keep both Sienna and their child close.

Would that be such a bad thing?

What to wear for the party, when all she could think about was the touch of Alejandro's lips on her mouth—and, of course, would he ever kiss her again?

Come on, hurry up! Maria's waiting.

Choosing a simple, knee-length fit and flare, in a vivid shade of fuchsia pink, she left her hair to flow wild and free around her shoulders.

Was wild and free the look she should be aiming for?

Why not? Mother-to-be, soon-to-be businesswoman, musician, and Tom's very proud sister would definitely choose provocative pink. Slipping her feet into flat, strappy sandals, she added a touch of lip gloss and a spritz of scent before hurrying out of the room.

She worked well with Maria, and they'd soon finished the final decoration of the tables, adding white flowers and a sprinkle of silver glitter to each centrepiece. 'I think we can call that a success,' Sienna declared, standing back with her friend to admire their handiwork.

'I couldn't agree more.'

Sienna's body tingled at the sound of Alejandro's voice. He was standing right behind her. All the tiny hairs on the back of her neck lifted, and, as if by magic, Maria took the hint, and left them to it.

'You okay?' Alejandro probed, when she remained with her back turned.

Apart from a bad case of Alejandro fever, yes, she was fine. 'Yes, thank you,' she said with a smile, turning to face him. This man was Tom's best friend, and Maria trusted Alejandro. Why couldn't she just come out with it, and say how she felt about him? Was she still frightened she might get hurt?

'Tables look great,' Alejandro observed. She and Maria had lit candles, and everything was sparkling.

'I'm surprised you noticed,' she said dryly, since Alejandro's gaze hadn't swerved from her face.

'Maria tells me we have to open the dancing,' he said. 'Is that okay with you?'

He smiled darkly. 'I might ask you the same question.'

'I think we should set a good example to your guests.' Who were beginning to arrive in droves, Sienna noticed as Alejandro steered her towards the dance floor with his hand in the small of her back. If she closed her eyes, she could lose herself in this moment, and want nothing more out of life.

She shouldn't have been surprised to discover that Alejandro danced in the same way he made love, with flawless rhythm and perfect anticipation. When the band took a break, he suggested they head for the house, to continue their conversation.

He wouldn't give her any more detail about Tom, so she couldn't see they had anything more to talk about, but still she agreed to go with him into the house. There was a particular energy about Alejandro that she recognised. It aroused her, and explained exactly why they were leaving the party. Conversation was redundant by the time he led the way across the hall. Linking their fingers, he headed straight for the stairs. They didn't make it halfway up. 'The house is empty.' And his breath was warm on her mouth. He sounded calm, while she was not.

Those eyes. His eyes. She was lost.

In moments the dress she was wearing dropped to her

feet. 'Why stand when you can sit?' Alejandro suggested as he settled her on the stairs.

Where was her next breath supposed to come from? she wondered as her remaining scraps of underwear joined her dress. 'What if Maria comes back?'

'I locked the door,' Alejandro explained with a wicked smile as he began to stroke and kiss, until, freeing himself, he brought her on top of him.

Memories didn't just stir, they roared into life. How could she have forgotten how much she needed this?

'Do you trust me?' he asked, positioning her.

'Yes.'

He filled her completely, but took his time. When she relaxed, he filled her to the hilt. Rotating his hips, he reminded her again how much she'd been missing.

Resting her head on his shoulder, she grabbed the occasional noisy breath as Alejandro brought her the pleasure she craved.

'You don't have to do anything, no need to force. Let everything happen naturally.'

She did. And lost control immediately. Tightening convulsively around him, she screamed with relief as Alejandro held her firmly in place. It took the longest time to recover, and while she was still attempting to catch enough breath he swung her into his arms. 'Bed,' he said. 'This requires my full concentration.'

That was enough to make her almost lose it again, but then she remembered the party.

'The party will go on all night,' Alejandro reassured her as he jogged up the stairs. 'Everyone's having such a good time, I doubt they'll even know we've gone.'

CHAPTER FOURTEEN

HE'D NEVER NEEDED Sienna like this. He'd never been so aroused. Stripping off the clothes she hadn't already ripped off, he stretched out beside her on the bed. Bringing her into his arms, he kissed her. Cupping her buttocks, he brought her beneath him. Moving firmly and rhythmically, he took her to the edge again. The clutch of her fingers on his shoulders, the cries from her throat, all aroused him, and she lost no opportunity to tell him exactly what she needed. 'Now,' he murmured, close to her ear when he judged the time was right.

He held her in place as she let go and didn't stop moving until he was sure she was spent. Only then did he think about claiming his own pleasure.

'That was amazing. You're amazing,' Sienna whispered. 'After so long, I never thought I'd be able to trust enough to be as uninhibited as I am with you.'

'I'm glad I make you feel safe,' he said, and, wrapping his arms around her, he kissed her again, until even he had to recognise that what had started out as savage passion had turned to something more. Sienna was the mother of his child, he reasoned. Hence his deeper feelings.

'We should get back,' she said, reminding him about the party.

Reluctantly, he agreed.

* * *

When they returned to the party, she felt frustrated that she hadn't taken the chance to have a meaningful talk about the future with Alejandro. There had been a moment when something in his eyes said he did want her for herself, not just for the moment, but she had to know that. She had to hear that. Doubts and guilt from the past could not be purged quickly, or all at once.

But even Alejandro didn't have sex out of a sense of responsibility, she reasoned as he drew her back onto the dance floor. Sex was an animal impulse that could be so much more. She wanted that 'so much more'.

Eventually, they had to leave the dance floor and circulate amongst the guests. Everyone was having such a good time, and it didn't take long to realise that Alejandro was the energy of the party, the hub around which the fun revolved. He was very different here, from that cold, austere man she'd first met in London, and all the more attractive for it. Taking everything in, she smiled. Tom would have loved this. She loved this. She loved the island, the party, the bonfire roaring, Maria conducting everything like the most polished maestro. Was this as close to paradise as anyone could hope to get?

As Alejandro peeled away she went to help Maria refill the platters on the table. Alejandro was so easy with everyone, and he looked so relaxed and happy. He didn't seem to care what job he took on. Opening champagne gave him the chance to chat. When he passed around canapés, it gave him yet another opportunity to interact with his friends. No wonder he was so popular on the island. It quite literally transformed him. She could only hope that it would have the same effect on those who attended Tom's healing facility.

Everyone wanted a piece of Alejandro, and no wonder.

Sienna did too, but she'd have to wait for more interaction with a man who looked several degrees hotter than hell in his snug-fitting jeans. An easy smile and open-hearted manner gave him the magic that other people lacked.

Her cheeks fired up when she realised Alejandro had caught her staring at him and was looking back. Lust flared between them in those few seconds. Who else had noticed? Everyone? Maybe, and what was wrong with that?

Doubt didn't take long to set in.

Everyone noticed what? That you and Alejandro are an item? That you're staying on the island in his house?

What should people make of that? Was it even that unusual? And before she could commit herself fully to more than lust, she needed to hear from Alejandro that what he felt for her was a lot more than just a sense of responsibility, or pure lust. He had to want her for herself.

Well, here's your chance, he's coming over...

He took her in, in a sweeping glance that nearly knocked her off her feet. 'You look good,' he remarked with a lift of his brow. 'Sex suits you.'

'You too,' she replied calmly.

'I'm going to make an announcement,' he said, 'and for that, you need to be at my side.'

'Why?'

He didn't answer and had already left her side to mount the temporary stage. It must have something to do with them working together on the facility, she guessed as Alejandro beckoned her over.

She stood quietly by as he tapped the microphone, and was surprised when he reached for her hand. 'I've got a really special announcement,' he said. The crowd fell quiet. 'I know you'll all be thrilled to learn that Sienna, Tom Slater's sister, will be joining us here on the island.'

The cheers rang out, and he had to wait until they subsided. 'And that's not all,' he said.

As the crowd waited with bated breath, Alejandro's manner alarmed Sienna. It was as if he had returned briefly to being the cold, aloof man she remembered from their first meeting in London. He'd decided something, and nothing would sway him from his course.

What could it be? She wracked her brains for an answer. Nothing had been finalised for the music therapy centre, which, she hoped, would now be housed in the facility Alejandro was building. They hadn't even discussed working together on the project—

Forced to curtail her thoughts, she listened intently as he began, 'I've heard it said that lightning can strike, and change everything in an instant. I've never had reason to believe that before...' He turned a piercing look on her face, but instead of thrilling her, it chilled her as he added, 'I guess that lightning bolt was bound to find me eventually.'

She wasn't the only one wondering where this was leading, judging by the occasional awkward laugh.

'I won't keep you in suspense any longer,' Alejandro assured his audience. 'I'm going to ask this incredible woman to marry me.'

Somewhere in her peripheral vision, she saw Maria in shock, with her hand to her mouth. Maria wasn't the only one. Shock was pounding at Sienna's temples. Alejandro was proposing marriage in front of everyone at Tom's party, and without even asking her first?

'A few words, Sienna,' he prompted as he handed over the microphone.

Still reeling with disbelief and confusion, she had to think of her audience, all these lovely people, who only wished her well. She could do this. She had to do this.

'Thank you all for making me feel so welcome here. My brother loved a good party, and I know Tom would want us to remember him with a smile.' Love surged from the crowd, emboldening her to carry on. Careful not to make any mention of Alejandro's proposal, she said, 'I must thank Maria and Alejandro for making tonight possible, and I thank you, for your support.'

Removing the mic from her hand, Alejandro called out, 'Enjoy the party!' before he led her away.

The instant they were alone, she challenged him. 'For goodness' sake, Alejandro, what on earth was that about?'

'My proposal of marriage?' he queried with a surprised look on his face. 'I'm being practical.'

Each of his words wounded her. But, *practical*? That was as bad as being his responsibility, if not worse. He made her feel as if that was the sum total of everything they'd been to each other—everything she had *believed* they'd been to each other, while they were making love, or when they were talking easily together, like people who trusted each other. He'd destroyed that in a few short words.

'It was as good an opportunity as any to state my intentions,' Alejandro explained with a shrug.

'It didn't occur to you, that I might like to be involved?'

'I was being spontaneous.'

'I see.'

'You don't believe me?' he said with a frown.

Actually, she did, though having allowed herself to believe Alejandro was a much-changed man, being proven wrong in the most hurtful way, had come as a shock. 'What century are you living in?' she said sadly, thinking his proposal more a tick in a box than a romantic offer.

Alejandro appeared affronted. 'I thought you'd be pleased. It's a question of security. Surely you understand that, as the mother of my child, both you and the baby are at risk? Marrying me will give you unprecedented levels of security, as well as certainty for the future. Forgive me if I'm wrong, but I thought that was what every mother wanted?'

What about love? Where did love fit into Alejandro's grand scheme? Perhaps it didn't, Sienna concluded, too low to find the words to counter his undeniably logical explanation.

'If it's a question of money,' he said, making her start.

'That's the last thing on my mind,' she assured him with passion.

'I know. We've been through this before. I just don't want you to worry. Finances can be worked on—'

'Finances?' she repeated, as if the word tasted bitter on her tongue.

'Money, your money,' he patiently explained. 'You'll have funds from Tom's estate, as well as an allowance from me, to do with as you please.'

The word *allowance* grated. It suggested a degree of helplessness that Sienna hadn't experienced since the days before she found a way to make a living with her voice. Tom had been only too glad to support her financially, but that didn't mean she'd wanted him to, and as soon as she could be independent, she was.

'I find it hard to believe you're saying no,' Alejandro admitted with a shake of his head.

Why did people get married? Because they were better together than apart? Because everything came into clearer focus when you could see life through someone else's eyes? Shouldn't emotion be involved at some point? 'Just because you're a high-flying CEO with countless companies under your sway, doesn't mean everything has to be a deal, Alejandro. Until you change your approach—adapt it to difference circumstances—you're never going to be happy—'

'A deal?' he repeated, as if this was the only phrase that had registered.

'Yes,' Sienna insisted. 'You thought you were making a decent proposal, and so you went ahead, regardless of my opinion. Marriage means spending the rest of our lives together—agreeing, compromising, disagreeing, but finding a solution that suits us both. It isn't a company you can buy and sell when it suits you. If you go into marriage in that frame of mind, there's no certainty, and no secure foundation on which to build anything.'

'We'll have to agree to disagree,' he said, adding, 'I'll leave you to think my proposal over,' as if he was certain she'd see sense soon.

Deep, wounding hurt swept over Sienna in successive waves as Alejandro walked away. How could she be so wrong about him? Had he never really changed from that autocratic man in London? Was she guilty of fantasising that he had, or that he would?

How could she stay here now? Tom's facility would still be built, just not here. Alejandro had so much power and money, he could create something far bigger and better on the island than Sienna could ever hope to achieve. If she had an ounce of decency in her, she'd stand back and leave him to it.

When it came to their child, there'd be no standing back. They had to come to an agreement. Placing a protective hand over her stomach, she felt with tender certainty that motherhood was a gift, and only had to think back to the happy years she'd spent with her own mother to know she was right.

She couldn't leave the party without speaking to Maria first. And there was something else she wanted to say to Alejandro—She jumped to find him behind her.

'There isn't a problem with the baby, is there?' he asked. 'Is that why you're so upset?'

'There's no problem at all,' she said levelly.

A wealth of feeling flashed behind Alejandro's eyes, to the point where she almost felt sorry for him, but he was quickly distant again. Was she any better at showing her true feelings? Noticing Maria glancing over with concern, she made her excuses to Alejandro, and hurried over to re-assure Maria.

CHAPTER FIFTEEN

SIENNA'S REFUSAL HAD shocked him. It was some distraction to mingle with his guests, but he did so like an automaton—cheery here, concerned there, without registering half the conversations. All he could think of was Sienna. All the time he looked for her, he knew he could have expressed himself better, but pretty speeches, however sincere, couldn't be learned in one night.

There had been more attempts to lure him into wedlock than he could count, and that didn't include his sister's machinations. Sofia longed for more women in the family, she'd told him. Up to meeting Sienna, he'd felt no inclination to please his sister by sharing his life with anyone. The fact that Sienna would never be a compliant wife had only added to her allure. He didn't want compliance. He wanted challenge, spark, and energy, and Sienna had those in plenty.

The odds on him recovering the situation were poor, he conceded. Wanting the one woman he couldn't have, because she had refused him, was a problem he had never thought to encounter. He should have been more open with Sienna from the start, but the day his parents were killed he'd seen how happiness could be snatched away in an instant, and he'd locked down. Trying to fill that emotional chasm with work had only proved that work wasn't enough.

At family gatherings, he watched and yearned, hoping no one would guess that *Uncle* Alejandro ached for a kickabout that included his own children.

He hoped Sienna would survive his blunder. Was marriage so terrible, or just marriage to him? The irony of his heart finally opening up, only to find there was nothing to fill the gap, was brutal.

There was no point in staying on the island, so she made plans to leave. Marrying Alejandro would make them both unhappy, if he couldn't fully unlock the feelings inside him. Goodness knew, she'd found it hard enough, but had concluded that life without love was empty. Better to risk everything than remain alone. That was her mantra, anyway. And how could warring parents raise a happy child? Better to leave now, before it came to that.

Maria was concerned about her. 'Has something happened?' she asked with a frown.

'Nothing serious,' Sienna said lightly. 'Something's come up that means I have to go back to London right away.'

Maria didn't look convinced. 'Are you sure it's nothing serious?'

'Don't worry. I'd tell you if it was.' She hated lying to Maria, but time was short, and Alejandro could walk into the kitchen at any moment. 'Travel arrangements—timing,' she murmured tensely, glancing at the clock.

'If you hurry, you might catch the last ferry,' Maria said hesitantly, as if she didn't want Sienna to leave. 'Are you sure there's nothing I can do to help?'

'Nothing, honestly.'

Seeing her resolve, Maria suggested, 'A suitcase, maybe?'

Having arrived without anything, she thought that

sounded like a very good idea. 'That would be wonderful. Thank you, Maria.'

Maria missed nothing, and had probably already guessed the reason for Sienna leaving. Like everyone else, Maria must have been shocked by Alejandro's proposal. As if to confirm this, she reached out, and they hugged each other tight.

'Please don't say anything to Alejandro until the morning,' Sienna begged when they pulled apart. 'I don't want anything to spoil Tom's party. You've both gone to so much trouble to make it a success. I'll never be able to thank you enough. Tom would have loved this,' she added wistfully, glancing out of the window where the party was still in full swing.

'Tom does love it. I'm sure of that,' Maria declared with touching certainty.

A moment passed where Sienna guessed they were both thinking back to happier times with Tom, but she had to be quick if she was going to catch that ferry.

'If Alejandro asks where I am, could you say you don't know, or that you think I've gone to bed? Or, maybe say nothing at all,' she amended when Maria gave her a look.

'I'll get that suitcase for you,' Maria said, keeping whatever she thought to herself.

'Just a small one—'

Maria wheeled around, and, with a look of pure distress, pulled Sienna back into a hug. 'Just stay safe. And please stay in touch. I'll be worried about you.'

There were tears in Maria's eyes when they parted, and Sienna knew for sure that what Maria offered was friendship in its truest form, which meant unquestioning support.

'A bird thrives best when it flies free,' Maria said.

If only Alejandro could see that too, Sienna thought as they shared one last, tight embrace.

Packing a few essentials into the suitcase Maria had delivered to her room, Sienna stowed her passport and wallet in the pocket of a riding jacket she'd borrowed from the tack room. Leaving the house, she joined a group of guests heading back to the small port town. It was a short trip from the harbour to the mainland, and from there to the airport and home.

Had she just made the biggest mistake of her life? Sienna wondered as the ferry pulled away from the dock. Refusing Alejandro's proposal was the last thing she'd do if he had shown the slightest intention of marrying for love. Tears stung her eyes as the ferry began to sway as it hit the open sea. Seeking shelter inside, she chose a row of seats at random, and sat down. It would have been better, neater for all concerned, if she had agreed to marry Alejandro.

Neater? Better? Better than what? Better than loving parents who adored their child and made it feel safe? Wasn't that worth all the money in the world, and a great deal more than a piece of paper?

She continued to argue with herself throughout the journey. Marriage to Alejandro made sense. Leaving for the unknown made no sense at all, and as a general rule Sienna was a great fan of common sense. A secure future for her baby wasn't something to dismiss lightly, but she had always been able to support herself, and why should that change now? Exchanging that sort of freedom for a life of always having to ask permission held no appeal at all, but she would have to reach an accommodation with Alejandro eventually. It would probably mean meeting face to face.

This wasn't running away, Sienna told herself firmly as

the ferry picked up speed. She was running towards a new life. How could she settle for anything less than a love so powerful nothing could make it fail? A cold-blooded contract with Alejandro came nowhere near that goal. What he was proposing was worse than no love at all.

CHAPTER SIXTEEN

HAD HE ASKED too much of Sienna? A growing feeling that he had propelled him to the kitchen, where he thought she might be with Maria. He'd said goodnight to the last of their guests and wanted to share with Sienna the kind things so many had said about Tom.

That wasn't all, of course. He had to set things straight. She'd flayed the mask from his eyes, forcing him to admit, if only to himself, that he did want love, and he did want to be loved. He wanted to trust and to be trusted. He wanted children and a family, together with the chance to instil the same values in his children that his parents had instilled in him. But would any declaration of love sound false now? Sienna might think his only aim was to claim their child, and have the entire island back under his control. If he wanted her, he'd have to find a way to convince her that his feelings were genuine.

Shock slammed into him when Maria told him she'd gone.

'Gone? What do you mean, she's gone?'

'Señorita Sienna has been forced to return to England,' Maria informed him in a tone he'd never heard his loyal housekeeper use before. It was as if Maria was struggling to deliver each word with no emotion at all.

'She didn't tell you why?' he pressed with growing desperation.

'There wasn't time,' Maria intoned in the same dull voice. 'She was in a rush to catch the last ferry.'

He exhaled with disbelief. 'And didn't think to tell me this herself?'

'She didn't want to spoil the party.'

'Ha!' Shaking his head, he grimaced. Sienna had spoiled the party. He'd searched for her with growing concern until, finally, he'd convinced himself that she'd taken herself off, to be alone, or to discuss his proposal with Maria, to whom she had become increasingly close. He understood that need for space to think things through.

But not this much space.

Reining in his frustration, he held back on exposing his feelings to Maria. How would that be fair? Torment must have shown in his eyes, because Maria put a comforting hand on his arm, which was something she'd never done before.

'I thought, if she wasn't with you, she'd have gone to bed,' he admitted.

'Sienna would never leave here, until she was certain Tom's celebration was a success. She made a point of coming to thank me, and she thanked you too. I feel sure she'll be back.'

'I wish I had your certainty,' he confessed.

'If Sienna means so much to you, why are you still standing here, Alejandro? This isn't like you.'

He was thinking. Piloting his private jet would allow him to touch down in London, maybe even before Sienna, and where else would she go? 'You're right, Maria. I'll leave right away.'

Going to his study, he went through the mechanics of filing a flight plan, but by the time he replaced the receiver, he'd changed his mind. He needed to prove to Sienna that this wasn't about control, or that he was fulfilling a duty, but that she was an exceptional woman, who meant the world to him.

With a growl of frustration, he cancelled his plans. Micromanaging Sienna would never work. It might be effective in business, but exerting control over every element of such a deeply personal situation was hardly likely to convince Sienna that he was a changed man. If Sienna returned to the island, as Maria had hinted she might, it had to be because Sienna wanted to come back, and not because he could find a million different ways to persuade her.

'Yes?' he snapped, thrown by the sound of a soft tap on the door.

'I've heard from Sienna,' Maria said as she entered the room. 'She's safely back in London.'

He threw himself back in his chair with relief. There was a momentary sting in Maria's words, at the thought that Sienna had confided in Maria before him, but the most important thing was that Sienna was safe. 'Can you tell me what she said?'

As a general rule, he only had to ask and Maria would tell him anything he wanted to know, but this time she held back, and in all conscience he couldn't ask her for more. An ironic smile tipped the edges of his lips. Was it possible he was changing already?

'She sounded so excited, Alejandro, and asked us not to worry.'

'Not to worry?' Was that a joke? How was he supposed not to worry, when he cared so much?

Going to his study, he placed a call to the Blue Angel club. The manager was only too eager to tell him that he'd heard from Sienna, and they'd made plans to hold a testimonial for Tom. Sienna would be the headline act. Desperate for her to run free, and yet in safety, Alejandro thought of other men staring at Sienna as she worked her musical magic on an audience and it hit him like a punch in the gut.

His flight to London was back on.

It was nearly time to go on stage. Mapping her still-flat stomach as she stared into the fly-blown mirror, she could only hope that, after all Maria's good food, she could still fit into one of her gowns. She wanted to look and sing her best tonight, to raise as much money as possible for the newly established Tom Slater Fund. A knock on the door of her cupboard-sized room heralded the worst possible news.

'Jason's sick?' Sienna's stomach lurched. 'Can we get another pianist in time?'

'You'll be fine. You're a professional.' The club manager told her this with the confidence of someone who had never been on stage. 'You've got backing tapes, haven't you? I've heard you use them in rehearsal.'

'In rehearsal, yes.' But tonight's performance was vital for Tom's fund.

When the going got tough... If she had to sing unaccompanied, she'd do it. She had to make this work. It was vital that tonight was a success.

She was blinded momentarily by the footlights when she walked on stage, but the wave of warm affection that greeted her reinforced her determination not to let the audience down.

She had arranged for her backing tapes to be played over the club's loudspeakers, and, even without Jason at the piano to build her confidence, she'd be fine.

Taking centre stage, she wrapped her hand around the microphone, or her comfort wand, as she often thought of it. 'Thank you all for coming tonight, and for supporting the

Tom Slater Fund—' She couldn't help searching the crowd for that one special face, but, of course, Alejandro wasn't there. He was back on the island, and almost certainly furious with her for walking out.

'You don't know what this means to me,' she said. And only then noticed one particular photograph of Tom, amongst the many that the club had thoughtfully arranged on a large display. This one showed Tom and his comrades in the army. She hadn't supplied it, so who had? The last time she'd seen that photograph, it had been on Alejandro's desk.

There was no time to think about it now. Her piano introduction had started. Gathering herself, she closed her eyes, and felt the music wash over her, restoring her confidence as it flowed effortlessly from the pianist's fingertips.

The club's sound system sounded even better tonight. It was almost as if Jason were seated at the piano. And yet there were subtle differences that only a musician would register. And then a spotlight hit the piano.

'Alejandro?'

He turned briefly to face her, and dipped his chin to indicate that the introduction was over, and it was time for her to sing. By some miraculous alchemy, the power of music took her over, and, inhaling steadily, she began to sing.

The piano keys felt like old friends beneath his fingers. Jason had worked from chords, augmented by his own improvised melody, as and when required. That suited Alejandro's style of playing, and Sienna was easy to accompany. Her voice was honey sweet, with more than a hint of sultry about it, and it came as no surprise to him that when the first song had ended the audience went wild.

She glanced at him as she mentioned the name of her second song. He already had a playlist up on the piano, so he began. They were in complete union as the song progressed, until it was almost as if they were alone in the club. If only everything could be that simple, he reflected wryly as they ended the final piece in perfect harmony.

Sienna was clearly thrown when her set ended and they were finally brought face to face. She didn't know how he would react, or how he felt about the way she'd left the island. 'You were amazing,' he said to reassure her.

'You were amazing too,' she insisted. 'I've never heard you play the piano. I didn't realise you were so good. You could have been a professional musician...'

'Never mind that. I've got an idea.'

'Tell me...'

Her eyes worked their magic on his cold, unfeeling heart. Cold and unfeeling before Sienna, he amended as she continued to plumb deep. 'Why don't you do a few encores, with donations for each song?'

Her reply was to grab his hand and lead him back onto the stage.

'I think you all recognise my pianist tonight.' She had to pause for prolonged applause, while he took the chance to settle himself back at the piano. 'Alejandro has suggested that I ask you for requests, with a donation for the fund with each song. Would you do that?'

A great roar of approval greeted her suggestion.

'All in a good cause,' he added into the mic.

'The very best,' Sienna agreed, shooting him a grateful glance.

It was after midnight when they finally left the stage, but the amount of money raised was impressive, and he doubled it. 'Please,' he said, when Sienna begged him not to. 'I don't even know how you're going to pay for all this.

My contribution is small by comparison with what you're going to need.'

'I'll find a way,' she said determinedly, and when her gaze switched to him, her expression softened. 'Seriously, Alejandro, thank you for tonight. I can't believe you saved the day—night—and I'm sorry I had to leave the way I did.'

'You don't have to explain,' he insisted.

'I think I do,' she argued.

'As for the playing, I enjoyed myself. It isn't every day I get the chance to play the piano at such a prestigious club.'

She smiled at that. 'Well, thank you, anyway.'

'Your thanks is all that's required.'

'Is it? Alejandro, I—'

'Don't,' he cut in. 'I won't ask you again,' he promised.

Sienna appeared suddenly diminished. They were their own worst enemies, he realised. Sienna could fill any space with the force of her will alone, but when it came to personal feelings, she was vulnerable. And what he'd proposed was a marriage of convenience. She would never accept that.

'I should go and get changed,' she said with a rueful smile as she turned in the direction of what he couldn't help but think of as her dungeon at the club. Was this how it was going to be between them now? Two sides of an island without a bridge?

'I'll wait for you,' he said.

Awareness fizzed up and down her body, making it hard to breathe. Alejandro had come to the club—to London—he'd accompanied her at the piano. It was almost too much to take in. But why was he here? Because she'd refused his proposal, or because he wanted to hear her sing, and, like her, wanted to support Tom in any way he could?

She was excited and confused as she took off her make-up. Pleased to see him didn't even begin to cover it. Being close to Alejandro again was enough—maybe had to be enough. If only they could break down all the barriers between them, to see what happened then—

'Are you ready?'

She froze, tissue suspended between her fingertips as Alejandro called to her from the other side of the door. 'Soon,' she promised, sitting back. She had to calm down before she saw him again. Calm down? Was that even possible?

Giving her hair the most perfunctory attention, she hurried to dress in her everyday clothes, relieved that she'd made a special effort tonight, for Tom's sake.

'Quite a transformation,' Alejandro observed, when she finally made it out of the boiler room. Simple trousers and a woolly sweater, to combat the London cold, together with a warm jacket she'd treated herself to a few years ago, which completed the sensible, if smart, look.

His interest scorched its way through her body. 'My car's at the front,' he informed her.

'So is my cab,' she reminded him. 'I usually time it just right, so I emerge from the club as it pulls up at the kerb. I jump in. It drives away—'

'Sounds eminently sensible to me. Why don't you take the cab, and we meet up tomorrow?'

Now she was disappointed, and her mouth dried as she suggested, 'Café next door?' Well, she'd asked for this, hadn't she? He'd proposed. She'd walked out.

'Eleven o'clock tomorrow?'

If she wanted to see him again, she had no option, but to smile and say, 'Suits me. Goodnight, Alejandro...' She watched him walk away, knowing that if they could only keep a friendship between them, that would have to be enough.

Sienna's hand strayed to her stomach, where a tiny life depended on both of them to do the right thing. They would have to keep in touch, because of their baby. 'Thank you again for tonight.'

Alejandro turned around and stared at her for a long moment. And then he smiled. 'Thank *you*, Sienna. See you tomorrow at eleven.'

And then he was gone.

CHAPTER SEVENTEEN

HE GLANCED AT the clock. Four a.m.? Another seven hours before he set eyes on Sienna?

Unacceptable.

Swinging out of bed, he tugged on his jeans. Palming his keys, he quit his elegant Georgian town house to drive to an area of North London where Sienna rented a room in someone's house. Wanting to be with her clawed at his soul. Was she awake, thinking of him? Would she be alarmed when he turned up unannounced? Too bad. This was one occasion when being close to Sienna took precedence over everything. How the occupants of the house where she lived would feel when an unshaven brute banged on their door in the middle of the night remained to be seen—

Okay. Calm down. Cool off.

The streets were empty. The drive there was smooth and fast. Placing a call to Sienna, he waited. She answered on the second ring. 'Hello…?' Her voice sounded croaky and sleep-fogged.

'Did I wake you?'

He barely had chance to ask the question before Sienna exclaimed with real alarm, 'Alejandro? Are you okay? Is something wrong?'

'You could say that,' he admitted.

'Are you still there?' she pressed. Anxiety raised the pitch of her voice.

'I soon will be,' he confirmed.

'What do you mean?' She sounded confused.

'I'm driving down your street as we speak.'

'What—?'

'Put your clothes on. Let's talk. I can't wait for coffee in the morning. Okay with you?'

He sounded impatient, which was the last thing he'd intended. No control. Everything to unfold naturally. These were the rules he had given himself. If he went back to being the man who refused to wait for anything, and who never relaxed the reins of his life, he'd stand no chance with Sienna. 'Sorry, I don't mean to rush you,' he added with a frown.

She laughed, and it was such a welcome sound. 'You're sorry?' she repeated. He could hear her smiling. 'Give me five,' she added before the line cut.

Alejandro was actually outside her door. He didn't get the chance to get out of the car before she slid in beside him. 'Hi, stranger,' she teased as she climbed in.

'I missed you,' he admitted.

'You couldn't sleep?' she suggested. 'Neither could I.' She laughed, she couldn't stop the happiness bubbling out of her—or the disbelief. 'How long has it been? Five hours?'

'A lifetime,' he growled.

Firing up the engine, Alejandro checked his blind spot, and prepared to pull away. But then he stopped and shrugged as he looked at her. 'We have to come clean with each other at some point.'

However hard he tried to be serious, Alejandro's expression suggested that the next stop he'd like to make would be his bed. 'Is that what you really want? To talk?'

His lips pressed down. 'Eventually, yes.'

'Well, at least you're honest.' Was it possible to contain so much happiness? Just seeing him again, would have been enough—No, it wouldn't.

Her attention was drawn to his mouth. Alejandro was smiling.

'Just call me spontaneous.'

'Don't you mean impatient?' she suggested dryly.

He gunned the engine. 'Do you care which it is?'

'Not really. Not at all,' she confessed as he pulled away from the kerb. Pressing back against her seat, she did ask the obvious question. 'Where are you taking me?'

'To my place?

'Sounds good to me.'

But before they had sex again, which would be the easiest thing in the world with Alejandro, she had to *know* that his sleepless night and rush to her home had less to do with sex, and *everything* to do with the fact that he had to be with her, for no other reason than he must—not that she was a responsibility, or a duty, or even that he couldn't resist taking her to bed; not even that she was the mother of his child. He must want her for herself. She wanted to be the missing part of him, as Alejandro was for her.

The elegant London square where Alejandro's imposing Georgian home was located wrapped around a small, gated park exclusive to residents. Old-fashioned gas lamps had been converted to new-fangled electricity in the latter part of the nineteenth century, adding to ambience of style and old money. It was still eerily quiet this early in the morning, and the house, when they entered, felt deserted.

'Everyone's day off,' Alejandro explained when she asked him if they were alone.

'I'd like to talk,' she said.

He shrugged. 'Whatever pleases you, Sienna.'

You please me, she thought. *That's half the problem. I've been so distracted in the past by your heart-shatteringly fabulous good looks, your air of confidence and experience, that I've barely paused to think before leaping into bed with you. But this time it's going to be different, because this time our future, and that of our child, depends on what I do next...*

It would have been the easiest thing in the world to head upstairs to Alejandro's bedroom, but when he admitted with a rueful smile, 'Trouble is, I can't think straight when you're around,' she had to laugh, because she felt the same.

'That makes two of us.'

It was only when they were inside his study that she realised how tired he looked. There was more than one night's missing sleep in Alejandro's dark, heavily fringed eyes. 'Have you slept at all recently?'

'Thanks to you?' He smiled a crooked smile. 'Not much. You?'

'Same,' she admitted.

'Because?'

'No, you go first,' she insisted.

'Because I've been a selfish—'

'Don't need to say that word.' She put a finger over his lips. 'And don't beat yourself up. I'm just as guilty as you are, of allowing the past to rule me.'

'Survivor's guilt's no fun, is it?'

'No,' she agreed. 'But we can do something about it, you and me. Maybe not together, as I'd hoped, but—'

'What do you mean, not together?' he interrupted.

'My facility in Tom's name will be here in London, while yours will be on the island.'

'I have a better idea—'

'Trust you,' she said with a small smile.

'It was *your* idea really. *Our* facility on the island. The Tom Slater rehabilitation centre can only benefit if we combine our ideas. Your energy and mine will allow us to achieve so much more.'

She paused and frowned. 'Does that mean you accept my intention to become a working mother?'

'My mother worked, breaking horses, raising rare breeds. She worked on the ranch all her life. I don't remember anything stopping her. If I'm guilty—and I know I am—it's because I saw my mother working so hard, and I wanted something easier for my own wife.'

'Your wife?' she queried.

'Okay, I made a hash of this last time, but I never promised not to try again. And yes, Tom asked me to always look after you, but the way I feel about you has nothing to do with Tom. This is all me. And all you, I hope. I love you, Sienna, and my sense of duty has nothing to do with that. I love you as I have never loved in all my life. I hope you can believe me now?'

She did believe him, and a great well of happiness opened inside her when Alejandro drew her close for a tender kiss. This was swiftly followed by concern for him. Was she really responsible for those deep black circles beneath his eyes?

'I know you said we'd go to bed after we talked, but, honestly, Alejandro, I really think you need to sleep.'

'I will,' he promised with a look that melted her from the inside out.

'I do have one stipulation,' he said.

'Which is?' she queried.

'We sleep in the same bed.'

'Are you short of bedrooms here?' she teased.

He shrugged. 'I'm short of affection.'

Her heart went out to him. 'There's only one thing we can do about this...'

'Which is?'

'We sleep together,' she said.

Sleeping together wouldn't be easy, but did she want to change things up, or not? There had to be more than sex between them.

'Is sleep enough for you?' he asked with a wicked glint in his tired eyes.

She told him straight. 'Your love is enough for me.'

She'd borrowed one of Alejandro's tee shirts, which was around ten sizes too large. And kept her underwear on. Alejandro had no such reservations and stripped off completely. As torture went, that was extreme. And did he have to lie there like Adonis, with his hands tucked behind his head, displaying his ridiculously impressive torso, as if this were just another night for him?

'You don't have to hang onto the edge of the bed,' he advised. 'I don't bite—unless you want me to?'

'That won't be necessary, thank you,' she replied primly, not daring to move an inch.

'Come over here,' he said in a very different tone. 'Don't you know by now that you can trust me?'

She did.

Feeling Alejandro, warm and strong, pressed up against her, was the most extreme and wonderful feeling in the world. Everything they had between them was based on trust. And wasn't that the crux of it all?

He didn't sleep for what remained of that night. He preferred to watch Sienna sleep. Breathing steadily, with all her muscles relaxed. It was a privilege to guard her and their child.

Before the early morning light could wake her, he carefully disentangled himself and left the bed. His alarming erection would just have to alarm itself. He took a shower, eyes closed, face turned up to the icy spray.

And then she joined him.

'Could you turn the heat up?' she asked.

He certainly could.

'You can't hide how you feel about me,' she said.

'Full disclosure?' he agreed as he swept an arm around her waist. Cupping the back of her head, he brought her close. He did wonder for a moment if he was rushing things, when Sienna put her hands palms flat against his chest, but it was the weakest push ever, and her fingers soon closed around his.

Dipping her head, she nipped each of his nipples in turn, before telling him, 'Why should you have all the fun?'

Why, indeed?

Standing on tiptoe, she brushed a kiss against his lips. Being bathed in steam added an edge to sensation. Parting her lips with his tongue, he kissed her. She swayed against him. Closing his teeth lightly over Sienna's kiss-swollen bottom lip, he made her whimper. She clung to him tightly, until, nudging his erection with the lightest brushes of her body, she finally thrust her hips towards him.

If Alejandro continued to stroke the curve of her buttocks as he was doing right now, she refused to be accountable for her actions. Every erotic zone she possessed was screaming for attention. Arching her back, she offered herself shamelessly, only to pull away the moment Alejandro wanted to take her, knowing that when she rubbed her breasts against his muscular chest, it was torture for both of them.

'I want you,' she said, reaching up. Weaving her fingers through his thick black hair, she kept him close. 'Kiss me, and don't pull away this time,' she warned.

'Who's pulling away?' Alejandro gave a deep, sexy laugh. 'Who's teasing me, and torturing themselves into the bargain?'

'If you dare make me wait—' She gasped with relief as Alejandro took over.

Dismissing the last rational thought from her head, he rasped his early-morning stubble against her neck, increasing her arousal. She wanted to feel that friction against every part of her—Well, maybe not *every* part of her, but she'd tell him when and where to stop.

Turned out, she didn't need to give Alejandro any advice, as his touch, as always, was both exquisite and exquisitely intuitive. Running a thumb pad over her bottom lip, he traced the line of her mouth where his stubble had abraded her. 'Did I hurt you with my kisses?'

'No,' was all she could manage to gasp before drawing him back for more kisses.

Warm water continued to tumble down, enveloping them, caressing them, adding to their mutual arousal. Alejandro's eyelashes were clotted together, while his mouth and strong white teeth, and that wicked smile, became yet another aphrodisiac, and one she hardly needed. Closing her eyes, she suggested, 'Why don't you kiss it better?'

'Your poor sore mouth, or somewhere else?'

'Make a start and I'll let you know.'

His smile was long and lazy. 'I'm going to start by soaping you down, and then we'll see what happens...'

'Start anywhere you like. Just don't keep me waiting.'

Some gorgeous-smelling shower gel later—'Vanilla and rosemary,' Alejandro revealed—and she was suspended on a plateau of erotic pleasure.

'I think you like this,' he said.

'I like everything you do to me, she admitted.

Soaping the length of her spine made her arch her back in an attempt to draw Alejandro's attention to the one place that needed him most. And at last, *at last*, he responded as she'd desperately hoped he would.

'Better?' he asked straight-faced.

'Not nearly,' she warned. Was she going to waste that formidable erection? Even with Sienna's determination, she had to bury her face against Alejandro's chest to remind herself that she could take him and that she'd done so before. But he continued to soap her, denying her the satisfaction she craved. Admittedly, being brushed intimately with a sponge controlled by Alejandro was quite a sensory experience, but she'd had enough of teasing and took him in hand.

Lifting her, Alejandro pressed her against the cool wall tiles. Wrapping her legs around his waist, she groaned in ecstasy as he took her with infinite care. He knew just how to move slowly, rotating his hips until she couldn't hold on.

'Okay?' he asked, plunging deeper still. 'And now?'

A wail of intense pleasure pealed from her throat as he

massaged her beyond the point of control. When she lost it, he captured her wrists in one big fist, pinning them against the wall, while he supported and directed her buttocks with his other hand.

'Yes! *Yes!*' Oblivion. Blissful oblivion, filled with pleasure that went on and on.

'Better now,' he said with confidence.

She smiled up into his laughing eyes. 'What do you think, Alejandro?'

'I think I want to kiss you.' Tipping her chin up, he kissed her with surprising gentleness. She sensed a real change in him. It was as if Alejandro knew all her fears, and how to banish them. 'Do you trust me totally now?' he whispered against her mouth.

'You know I do.'

It seemed incredible that they were being so intimate in the shower, sharing their innermost feelings while warm water pounded down. She could marry this man, Sienna realised, but he would have to do a lot better with his proposal.

'Why are you laughing?' he asked.

'I'm laughing with happiness, because of who we are, and how we've stupidly allowed the past to influence our actions and thinking for so long. We're as bad as one another, allowing suspicion and lack of trust to rule us. Fear of loving too much, in case that love is cruelly ripped away, is just another way of punishing ourselves. And it's time to stop,' she said with feeling, staring directly into his eyes.

Switching off the shower, Alejandro reached for a towel, and swaddled her. 'Is this leading up to you proposing to me?' he suggested. 'Or are you giving me a second chance?'

'If I do, it has to be because you don't want to share your life with anyone else. It can't have anything to do with your loyalty to Tom, or the fact that I'm expecting your child. It has to be as necessary as breathing, and as right in your eyes as the sun rising on each new day.'

'Someone should have warned me that you're a romantic,' he teased, pulling her in front of him to drop a kiss on her lips. 'But I'm sorry for being clumsy. Out of practice on the proposal front, I guess.'

'You make a habit of proposing to random women?' They were both smiling, and something told Sienna that this time Alejandro would get it absolutely right.

'I'm better at giving instructions than expressing myself—'

'No way,' she said, pretending surprise.

'That doesn't mean I can't change,' Alejandro insisted, turning serious now. 'And, if I've got it hopelessly wrong in the past, I hope you believe me now, when I tell you how much I love you—that I can't live without you—and if you'll marry me, you'll make me the happiest man on earth.'

'Because?' she probed, quivering on the edge of happiness.

'Because your love has saved me,' Alejandro explained with an honest shrug. 'You, Sienna Slater, have managed the impossible. You've saved me from myself.'

'Well, now we're into true confessions, you helped me find myself again. I'm no one's little sister, but I could be someone's wife.'

'My wife,' Alejandro husked against her mouth.

'You don't find me too challenging?'

'Of course, but that's the wake-up call I need. I realise now that I've been waiting for you, and that a perfectly imperfect woman suits perfectly imperfect me. Besides,' he said as he drew her back into his arms, 'I'm sure I can tame you out of all those challenges in time.'

'Lucky for you, I'm happy to let you believe that,' Sienna teased back.

'Seriously, Sienna. You lifted me when I was down. You raised me up, forcing me to confront emotion head-on. Without it, what would we be? Cardboard cut-outs? Cartoons? Emotion is a gift I'm happy to embrace. Where you're concerned, I can't imagine life without it. I love you, Sienna, with all my heart, and I can't imagine life without you. Admittedly, that wasn't how I felt to begin with.'

'Nor me,' Sienna agreed with a wry smile.

'But it's how you make me feel now that matters,' Alejandro insisted with a long, steady look into her eyes. 'Let's always look forward. You're irreplaceable and unique, and if you won't agree to live with me, I'll have no option but to live with you.'

'In my bedsit in North London?'

'Willingly,' Alejandro exclaimed.

'Now I do know you're joking.'

'I'm being absolutely serious. I'd do anything for you. Not just because I want children, or want to have those children with you. And this has nothing to do with our joint ambition to build something in Tom's name that will benefit countless people who suffered as he did. This is purely about you and me.'

'And our joint ambition,' she said with love.

Securing a towel around his waist, Alejandro laughed. 'You don't think I'd allow you to embark on some crazy project without me, do you?'

She swiped at him with a towel. 'You'd better be joking.'

Binding her arms with his, Alejandro kissed her and teased her until she was crying with laughter. 'Combining our talents will make everything so much better, and we'll reach our goal faster in the end.'

'I'm not sure what your goal is right now,' she admitted, feeling Alejandro growing hard again.

'We'll discuss that too,' he promised.

There was something different in Alejandro's eyes, a gentle truth she'd never seen before. 'A joint project?' she confirmed.

'Two joint projects,' he said, reminding her with many kisses about their baby. 'And a wedding to arrange—if the only woman I could ever love will have me?'

Was it possible for a heart to explode with love?

'Well, what do you think?' Alejandro pressed.

'I think we take it one thing at a time.'

CHAPTER EIGHTEEN

'OKAY, SO THIS is a proposal in three parts,' Alejandro informed her. 'Part one—'

'Alejandro, what are you doing?'

Freshly showered, jeans, shirt with the sleeves rolled up, barefoot, *and* on his knees? While she was still snuggled up in bed.

'Will you marry me?' he said, all humour stripped from his face. Replacing the humour was a steady beam of love.

'Will I—? Seriously, Alejandro—'

'Seriously. I don't have a ring yet, so will this do?'

The flowers his London housekeeper loved to leave around the house had been called into use, Sienna noticed. Having woven one of the vines into a ring—with not such surprising dexterity—Alejandro slipped the green circle onto Sienna's wedding finger.

'I haven't said yes yet,' she pointed out. But snatching his hand back, she kissed his palm. 'But I love you.'

'You will say yes,' he told her confidently. 'You'll say yes here in London, where it's my aim to dispel every shadow you first found in this house. And you'll say yes in Spain, when you're in my bed—'

'I'll say yes more than once when I'm in your bed,' she observed with a happy frown. 'You're serious about this, aren't you?'

'Never more so,' Alejandro assured her as he joined her on the bed. 'Anyway, get up now, and don't bother packing. We'll pick up what you need when we're there.'

'Where?'

'Oh, I don't know—Rome, Paris, Milan, Monte Carlo— wherever the whim takes us.'

'Alejandro,' she mock scolded, shaking her head. 'Tell me where we're going, so I know what clothes to wear.'

'Come as you are.'

'Naked?'

'There aren't too many paparazzi outside—'

'You're impossible,' she protested with a happy growl.

'Yes, I am, and so are you, which is why we get on so well.'

'Do we?'

'You know we do.' Cupping her face in his hands, he kissed her with lingering devotion. 'Be quick,' he whispered against her mouth when he released her.

Alejandro's butler opened the door to his home in May-fair when they returned after a short, passionate break. All the curtains were open, and light was flooding in as they crossed the hall.

'Is everything ready?' Alejandro asked his assembled staff.

'Ready,' they chorused, welcoming Sienna with the warmest of smiles.

'What's ready?' she asked, excitement rising as Alejandro led her into his library.

She gasped. 'I've never seen so many flowers in my life.' The entire room was full of the most glorious floral displays, the scent and sight of which completely dazzled her.

'Have you ever seen so many diamonds before?' Alejandro enquired, as if he were asking her about snowflakes on a lawn. He was standing at his library table where the most fabulous selection of diamond rings was displayed. 'Choose,' he insisted. 'Have them all, if you want.'

If she'd been dazzled by flowers, she needed eye protection to study the gems on display. 'But I'm happy with this one,' she said, staring at the vine band on her finger. She was marrying Alejandro for love, not for diamonds.

'But it wouldn't hurt to wear my ring for the rest of your life, would it? So, choose one...' Taking hold of her hand, he knelt on one knee. She dropped to her knees in front of him.

'Yes,' she whispered, staring into the eyes of the man she loved with all her heart. 'Yes, I will marry you, but not because of diamond rings. I choose you. I choose this.' Raising her hand with its band of green vine still intact, she explained with a shrug. 'I don't need anything else. I never have. I only need you.'

Alejandro groaned as he stood up. 'Don't tell me, you're going to take as long to accept my ring as you've taken to accept me?'

'I won't have to train a ring,' she pointed out, tongue in cheek.

'Have you trained me sufficiently now?'

She frowned. 'I think it might be a lifetime commitment.'

'I can be very persuasive,' he said, taking her back to the rings.

'And I can be stubborn,' she admitted, 'but not when it comes to telling the man I love that I appreciate everything he does for me.'

Alejandro swung her into his arms, making sure that their lips met in the first kiss of a whole new story.

It would have been the wedding of the century, if she'd allowed Alejandro to have his way. They didn't need to show the world how much they loved each other, when that was self-evident. To Sienna's surprise, Maria disagreed. They were back at the ranch house in Spain, where the wedding was due to take place the following month.

'What would your mother want for you?' Maria asked in her usual forthright manner.

'A fairy-tale wedding,' Sienna admitted. They'd always talked about it when they played dress-up. Her mother would take the part of queen, while Sienna played the role of feisty princess in need of a suitable prince. They'd ride off on their snowy white ponies, to find a man 'to bring home the bacon', as her mother so colourfully put it—Or a suitable vegan substitute, Sienna thought now with a happy laugh. Either way, women always took the lead role in their fantasies.

'Then a fairy-tale wedding is what you shall have,' Maria decreed. 'You and Alejandro have hidden your feelings away long enough. It's time to show the world how you feel about each other. It's time to inspire and lead,' Maria finished with a decisive gesture.

Sienna was outnumbered when Alejandro agreed. 'Don't I have any say in this?' she pleaded.

'Yes, you can decide whether to travel to Rome, Paris, or Milan to choose your gown,' Alejandro conceded. 'If you don't like anything there, you can return to London, to visit the couturier favoured by the royal family.'

'Oh, can I?' Sienna said, rallying fast. 'How about this—Maria, will you make my gown?'

'Well, I—'

Maria glanced anxiously at Alejandro, who gave an accepting shrug. 'Maria?' he pressed. 'Would you do that for us?'

'With the greatest of pleasure,' Maria enthused as she

enveloped Sienna in a bear hug. 'It will be both my pride and my pleasure.'

Sienna's wedding gown *was* the most beautiful gown she'd ever seen. A simple sheath of ivory silk, it skimmed her body like a dream, whispering over her skin like the lightest touch of Alejandro's fingers. With her hair flowing free, and a coronet of fresh flowers, she carried a bouquet of glorious white peonies.

The wedding was held in a marquee on Alejandro's estancia on the island, on the banks of the sparkling river, where very soon the Tom Slater Concert Hall would be built. A floral arch marked the exact spot where the stage would be located, and Jason supplied the music on Clara Schumann's Biedermeier piano as Sienna walked down the petal-strewn aisle—on no one's arm, because there was only one man, one heart, one love she would allow to lead her anywhere, and then, only when they agreed he could, she reflected wryly with a heart full of love as Alejandro reached out to take her hand in his.

But they did have one addition to Alejandro's security team. Rex from the club, and if he and Maria were occasionally seen out together, strolling along the banks of the beautiful river, well, that was fate, Sienna concluded, and fate could be kinder than you expected sometimes.

Alejandro's eyes filled with tears at the sight of his beautiful wife. He wasn't ashamed of that emotion, and could only thank the fates for bringing them together.

'Our future will be, oh, so worthwhile,' Sienna whispered when he placed the simple diamond band she'd chosen on her wedding finger.

This was what it meant to have a family, he reflected after they kissed; this was what it meant to come home.

Turning to face their guests, he smiled. His brothers and

sister were smiling back at him, with an expression on his brothers' faces that suggested, why did you take so long? They were right, no more waiting. Bringing Sienna into his arms, he whispered, 'Thank you for saving me.' From what might have been such an arid life, but which was now full of boundless possibility.

'I love you,' she whispered, staring her truth into his eyes.

'And I love you more than life itself,' he replied.

EPILOGUE

A little over three years later...

EVERY CHRISTMAS FROM now on should include a family gathering at the Tom Slater Concert Hall. Sienna decided this as she watched her own children, together with her nephews and nieces by marriage, having the time of their lives. There was so much space here, so much light, and Alejandro had arranged the entertainment, making sure there was something for everyone. He'd booked children's entertainers, film shows, petting zoos, spa treatments, and now they were all playing the most ridiculous charades that had everyone in hysterics, and even more ridiculous quiz games where everyone cheated, and, of course, there would be the inevitable polo match to follow.

Alejandro had insisted on including the children of every-one who worked for him, which made everything so much warmer and more special, Sienna thought. He'd even flown in families who worked in the UK—though on this occasion his butler was not wearing white gloves, and looked a different and very happy man in blue jeans.

Smiling around, she felt the warmth of the Acosta family envelop her, as it had from the start. The Acosta men's wives, and Alejandro's sister, Sofia, had accepted Sienna without question, and with great enthusiasm. 'About time!'

Sofia had declared, giving her brother a hug. 'I've got you back at last. Thank you, Sienna.'

Lucia had been wonderful, on hand for advice with each new Acosta baby. They had become the closest of friends. Sienna made Alejandro happy, and that was all his family cared about. She'd even headed up a team at the last polo match that had thrashed the Acosta men—though whether the guys' team riding reversed in the saddle counted as cheating, she couldn't possibly say.

Sienna and Alejandro had been blessed with three children. Carlos, the oldest, was nearly three, while twins Ellie and Tiago, who were currently fast asleep by her side in their Moses baskets, would soon be crawling, creating happy chaos with their cousins. Laughing, she covered her ears in mock horror when the children started to scream with excitement as Alejandro made the announcement that it was time for presents.

A storm of wrapping paper later, silence fell as toys were assembled, and everyone was absorbed in investigating their gifts. Sienna had bought a new bridle for Alejandro, as well as a headband for his favourite horse.

'And I've got nothing for you,' he observed with a frown.

'Do you really think I need anything more than this?' she asked, looking around. 'And on top of this, staff for the facility is already in place and ready to start working with our first visitors, and foundations have been laid for our site in London. That's more than enough for me.'

'Lucky for you,' Alejandro observed, 'that there's more pleasure in giving than receiving.'

Sienna smiled at the man she loved. How many times had they proven that between them?

'As it happens, I have got something for you,' Alejandro revealed. Delving into the back pocket of his jeans, he brought out a small midnight-blue velvet box. 'And don't say you don't need this,' he scolded with a grin, 'because you're going to get it, whether you want it or not. We both know your vine ring disappeared on the day Carlos was born.'

'I was frightened he might chew on it.'

'He'll be quite safe chewing on this.'

As Alejandro flipped the lid of the ring case she gasped with amazement. 'Alejandro! What have you done?'

'Arranged for you to have the most beautiful diamond ring in the world. It used to belong to my mother.'

'I'll treasure it,' she vowed.

The blue-white sparkle of the pear-shaped diamond was mesmerising. It was easily the most beautiful ring Sienna had ever seen, but its sentimental value made it all the more precious.

'Do you like it, *mi querida*?' Alejandro asked as he hunkered down at her side.

'I love it,' she breathed as he slipped the magnificent jewel onto her finger. 'But that's not even close to how much I love you.'

'For ever,' Alejandro whispered as he drew her close for a kiss.

'And always,' she breathed.

* * * * *

RIVALS AT THE ROYAL ALTAR

JULIEANNE HOWELLS

MILLS & BOON

For Denley, Moira and Richard.

I can't begin to express how much your help
and support has meant to me.

You deserve the very best of all good things.

Love you loads. xxx

CHAPTER ONE

'NO, NO, AND *NO*!'

Her Majesty, Queen Agnesse of Ellamaa, was not amused.

It was not only that her perfectly ordered plans were being rearranged at the last minute. But worse, so much worse, her secretary had announced that her co-host for tomorrow's charity gala had been replaced. The Crown Prince of Grimentz was unable to attend and in his stead he was sending his cousin, Prince Sebastien: not just Europe's most notorious royal playboy, but also a man with whom Agnesse had a brief but unfortunate history.

'He'll make a handsome escort,' Keert suggested.

Stunning green eyes and a mouth that promised all sorts of wickedness came to mind, but Agnesse would not be swayed by his dazzling looks.

'I am not having that Lothario within ten miles of me. And have you forgotten he broke my sister's heart?'

'That was more than five years ago, ma'am, and wasn't it merely a youthful infatuation? Princess Isobel was only sixteen.'

'Exactly. She was a baby.'

Her secretary tried again. 'All you'll have to do is sit at dinner with him and make polite conversation.'

'Make conversation with that...that *reprobate*?' Her voice rose to an unregal screech. Had her mother been present,

Agnesse would have been instantly on the sharp end of a withering glare.

'Come now, ma'am. Is that not a little harsh?'

'Harsh? He has the morals of an alley cat.' Agnesse began pacing. The mere mention of Prince Sebastien von Frohburg was enough to make any woman pace. 'And he broke Isobel's heart.'

'Yes, ma'am, you said.'

'My innocent baby sister.'

Keert's eyebrows rose.

Perhaps that *was* an exaggeration. Her middle sibling had always been a little wild, the bane of her parents' lives, and now at twenty-one, had developed into something of a man-eater. But maybe the actions of Sebastien von Frohburg had started her along that path.

'Perhaps we can allow he has changed in the interim, ma'am.'

Agnesse halted by her desk and twitched angrily at the positions of her pen and diary until they sat precisely side by side again. 'Five years is nothing to a man like that,' she muttered.

And no time at all for him to forgive what she'd done in revenge. Agnesse could feel no pride for what she'd done back then. In fact, she was thoroughly ashamed. It had been her lowest moment. But for some reason the prince brought out an impulsive side of her that no one else ever had. He'd made her see red by callously brushing aside the tender feelings of a love-struck teenager, when he could have stirred himself to be kind and let her down gently instead.

Agnesse had absolutely no desire to face him again. Then she brightened. 'Couldn't Carl do it?'

Her nineteen-year-old brother had stepped in before as her escort during this period of official mourning for their late father.

'It's a joint event for Ellamaa and Grimentz, ma'am. A representative from the principality needs to attend, and Prince Sebastien would be a natural choice.'

Of course, she knew Keert was right, as the event supported a charity jointly set up by her father and the crown prince, Leo.

Despite having a twenty-year age difference between them, and their respective countries being hundreds of miles apart, after meeting at a European summit the two men had become friends. They'd discovered a shared interest in supporting youth work and established a charity which, over the past few years, had helped thousands of disadvantaged youngsters across Europe.

Agnesse doubted that Prince Sebastien was equally altruistic. He offended every value she stood for: decency, constancy, service. And except pursue his own gratification, what did he even *do* all day? He'd sometimes be seen at public occasions, lurking at the side of his cousin, or as in the case of the upcoming gala, standing in for him at social events, but really, what else was there? It was too much that Leo's absence would oblige her to associate with such a man.

'Has the crown prince said why he can't attend himself?'

'A family matter, I understand. It must be quite pressing. He wouldn't have pulled out at this late stage otherwise.'

'Perhaps he's dealing with the fallout from yet another of his cousin's scandals,' she said tartly, then sighed in exasperation. 'Are you certain we couldn't suggest Carl?'

'Ma'am, forgive me, but you know what the press would say. That you resort to your brother as escort because no other man will accompany the Ice Queen.'

Agnesse didn't care about that. She'd embraced the sobriquet and had cultivated as haughty and unapproachable a demeanour as she could. It had succeeded in deterring all but the most determined would-be suitors—to her mother's endless dismay. How would her daughter ever marry and produce an heir if she never allowed a man close?

Agnesse wanted children. Of course she did. But she wasn't

just choosing a husband for herself; she was choosing a prince for her country. She must find a man who'd be drawn to the role first and the woman second; who'd care about serving her people, not his own pleasures.

Deep down, hidden away in a corner of her heart, she yearned to experience what her parents had had. The joys of a love match. She remembered how her mother lit up around her husband, and her father's gaze restlessly seeking out his queen wherever she was in a room. Then their eyes would meet and hold, as if not another soul existed. In a world where most of her life was public property, how Agnesse longed for such precious moments of true intimacy.

But she couldn't afford to let her heart rule her head. She was Ellamaa's first ever queen by succession. Before her birth the law had been changed so the firstborn would inherit the throne regardless of sex. The Toivonens were a fecund line, blessed with sons in every generation, so even with that recent amendment, she was the first female monarch to rule. The weight of history sat doubly heavy on her shoulders and she had much to prove. The eyes of her countrymen were upon her and some of them were expecting her to fail. Not least of whom was her prime minister, a stalwart of her father's who'd nevertheless voted against the new law of succession. After her father's death he'd practically told her not to worry her pretty little head and to leave all the hard work to him and her government.

That wasn't how her beloved papa had raised her. He'd believed she could be queen as he had been king. A true figurehead for Ellamaa. She would not fail the trust he'd put in her.

He'd also believed she would find a partner willing to take on the role of consort to a queen. For love of *who* she was and not *what* she was. Someone she could love in return. In that belief she had much less faith. How could it be when none of the men she met made her *feel* anything?

Once she'd thought herself in love. She'd even said a breathless 'yes' to Eerik's marriage proposal. The twenty-two-year-old scion of a banking dynasty had been charming and attentive, and she'd thought he was *the one*. How foolish she'd been. Young, green, and foolish. She'd been nineteen then, and though she was only twenty-five now, it already felt like a lifetime ago.

She'd even given herself to him, but it had been awkward, swiftly over, and surprisingly painful. Eerik had told her that she just needed to relax and it would be better next time. But before there was a *next time*, he'd discovered the realities of his role as her husband. That he'd always walk a pace behind her, always play second fiddle to her and, while he'd be granted the honorary title of prince, he would never be king, never have any real power.

So he'd ended their relationship. Saying she was 'borderline OCD and frigid' anyway and that there were no compensations worth sticking around for. In an infamous TV interview he'd repeated that phrase publicly, claiming that the split was all her fault, that despite appearances he'd discovered she was only beautiful on the outside and, almost tearfully, went on to paint her as difficult and cold. His comments had never been contradicted. Palace policy was to remain silent on such personal matters.

For Agnesse, it had been devastating. Eerik hadn't wanted her, after all. Just a royal title and the power it might grant him. And more hurtful still was the anguish of what he'd claimed. Oh, not the OCD remark. She knew that was incorrect. She had high standards and liked order. How else did you get through a packed work schedule?

But he'd said that she was frigid. Was it true? If it was, she feared there was even less chance now of her finding love.

Her beloved papa had tried to counsel and console her, wrapping her in his arms and dismissing the young man as an opportunist and utterly beneath her. How lucky they were, he'd said, that Eerik had revealed his true colours before any official engagement had been announced. She was young. She had all the time in the world to find her mate. A good man waited out there, he reassured her, and she'd find him when the time was right.

But Agnesse had never got past the hurt, or the fear of getting hurt—and humiliated—again. She'd spurned the advances of every man since Eerik. It hadn't been hard. None had attracted her.

So be it. She wasn't Isobel. Perhaps men were never going to fascinate her in the same way.

But before Eerik there was someone, a quiet voice taunted her, *the prince...*

Him? That had meant nothing. One afternoon of silly infatuation, at the end of which he'd brutally crushed any dreams before they'd really begun.

It had been Speech Day at her school and as Head Girl, she was giving the end-of-year address. She'd waited nervously at the side of the stage. Prince Georg von Frohburg was presenting the awards and he'd brought his younger son with him. Prince Sebastien had been seated in the front row of the audience. Perhaps he'd seen her anxiety because he'd winked at her and somehow settled her nerves. When she'd finished her speech, she'd caught his eye. He'd joined in the applause, raising his hands higher in salute, as if he thought she'd done well.

At the reception afterwards, her gaze had been drawn over and over to Sebastien. There'd been something so arresting about his handsome face. And then, while she'd been gazing at him, he'd looked up and his expression had grown softer, warmer, and he'd smiled. Just for her. Agnesse had never experienced anything like it. She'd been standing in a pool of sunshine but it was the warmth of that glorious smile that had filled her with heat. Instinctively, she'd sent an unrestrained smile back at him. A moment of stunning intimacy in that crowded room and her heart had fluttered in her chest. Then his attention had been pulled back by a fellow guest, and their moment was over.

But afterwards, unobserved by either of them, she'd overheard the prince talking with his father as they left.

'You're mistaken,' he'd said. 'I have no interest in the girl. She might be a pretty face, but as that speech just proved, intellectually she's not, nor ever could be, in my league. God help Ellamaa when she's queen.'

Those smiles, that intimate look, that beguiling moment of connection? They'd been nothing but a cruel lie.

Her secretary cleared his throat, drawing her back from her bitter memories.

'Ma'am, why not look at this another way,' he said. 'Imagine how it will appear if you are escorted by Europe's most celebrated ladies' man and you make it appear as if he were dangling after you.'

'Why on earth would I want that?' she asked. Keert had served her father faithfully for twenty years. He'd served her well for the past nine months and she valued his counsel, but that suggestion was ludicrous.

'For the sweet revenge of being one of the few women to ever say no,' he pronounced with an enigmatic smile.

She studied Keert's face, which gazed back serenely. She could read nothing there. He was the consummate courtier. He might simply be using his skills to gain her agreement for something he knew was unavoidable anyway—or he might actually have a point.

Further revenge on the prince would feel rather…satisfying. Whether he was dangling after her or not, if she was as publicly disdainful as politeness would allow, the press would do the rest. They'd love the story.

The Ice Queen resists the irresistible charmer.

Yes, that had a certain ring to it and would deliver up more retribution on Isobel's behalf. And for that other, older, and even more personal incident. Which he'd probably forgotten anyway.

Agnesse never had, never would.

As the charity supported young people, her father had thought a younger Toivonen should co-host the actual gala, and Agnesse had done so for the past four years. This time it was being held in Vienna. It would be her first royal engagement outside Ellamaa since she'd become queen.

Grief knotted in her chest. Last year her beloved father had still been alive. But then came the heart attack, when one night, completely without warning, he'd collapsed in his rooms. Gone before he'd even hit the floor.

Her precious papa, who had been steadily preparing her for this role, when they both thought she'd have another twenty years at least before she would step into it.

Of all the people she'd have wanted as escort for this first gala without him, Sebastien von Frohburg was at the bottom of her list. Scrub that. He wouldn't have been on her list at all. Such was her aversion to the man.

Absurdly handsome, charming, rich—and titled, of course—the prince got any woman he wanted. He just didn't want them for long. Broken hearts and shattered dreams lay like so much debris in his wake.

And scandal was never far behind. Oh, the salacious stories about him. Agnesse supposed she should be grateful Isobel had once been too young for him, and now that she was not, that her tastes had switched from aristocrats to trashy rock stars and fast-living sportsmen. Creating her own scandals to rival the prince's. Their mother despaired.

'Ah. That's unexpected,' Keert said, frowning at a notification on his tablet. 'The Comtesse d'Onzain has just appeared on the guest list.'

Oh, that was just marvellous. Europe's biggest female flirt in the same room as its most celebrated royal playboy. Could it get any worse?

'And…um…' Keert shot his queen a swift glance. 'Both her daughters.'

'What?' Shocked into completely forgetting her manners, Agnesse wrenched the tablet from her secretary's hand. She stared in horror at the confirmation right there in black-and-white. 'All three of them. And the prince. Under one roof?'

Keert made a sympathetic face while Agnesse sank into a seat.

Just her luck that the comtesse had chosen this year for her first attendance at the gala. Where she went invariably so did her two girls, and the story was that her new co-host had once taken all three of them to bed. Satisfying each of them in turn in the space of a single debauched weekend. One might almost admire the man's stamina—if his behaviour wasn't so thoroughly reprehensible.

'Might I be required to referee a cat fight when the d'Onzains set eyes on him?' Agnesse said caustically.

'I'm sure that won't be the case. I understand their relationship is most amicable. I doubt it will come to…er…actual blows,' her secretary added.

'Thank you for that grain of comfort.' Agnesse dropped her head into her hands. 'I suppose it's too late to cry off and send my mother instead?'

Keert's silence was answer enough.

Agnesse gave herself a shake. Really, why was she worrying? The prince had probably forgotten all about their altercation. A man of his predilections would be more focused on the rich female pickings he'd find at the gala. The guest list read like a who's who of European society. Including the comtesse and her daughters. At the implications of her co-host and those three women being together, Agnesse's heart gave a worrying thud. But she breathed through it as she'd taught herself to do and the anxiety quickly subsided, with Keert none the wiser.

No, wherever the prince was right now she would probably be the last person on his mind. He was more than likely delighted to be asked, and already breaking out his best tux and practising his smoothest one-liners in anticipation of a successful night of seduction.

'Spend an evening with Agnesse Toivonen? That termagant? When hell freezes over!'

The roared answer reverberated round the office of the Crown Prince of Grimentz, and was so unlike the usual laid-back manner of Prince Sebastien von Frohburg that the other occupants of the room stilled.

'Come now, she's not that bad,' said his cousin Leo, the crown prince himself, and the one asking the impossible favour. 'Apart from that single…ah…unfortunate incident, she's been a model of propriety.'

Seb was having none of it.

'Don't you remember her insults? She branded me a louse, and so beneath her and her family as to be unfit to even wipe their shoes.'

Seb stopped abruptly, breathing in hard. Those comments had stung. For so many reasons they had stung deeply.

'That was just the media. We don't know that she said those things precisely,' Leo ventured.

'No, but we know she punched me.' Seb jabbed a finger at a small, silvery scar on his jaw. 'Gave me a right hook while she was wearing her royal signet ring. The thing was practically a knuckle duster. I'm scarred for life, yet still you expect me to socialise with her. I can't believe you've asked me. How could you ask me?'

'Violetta's pregnant.'

Instantly, the fight went out of Sebastien. It was the one name his cousin could invoke that would stop any Grimentzian in their tracks.

Violetta. Leo's wife of two years. From road sweepers to society mavens, to Leo's picky valet—who didn't like anybody and who slanted Seb a pleading look now—she was adored by everyone. Seb was no exception. He'd throw himself in the path of stampeding elephants for her.

Elfin Violetta, who'd suffered two miscarriages in the past two years and whose every desire had now distilled down to just one—giving her beloved husband an heir. Otherwise, Max, Seb's older half brother, would inherit the throne, making Seb second in line, and that was the last thing anyone wanted. Certainly not him. And, as his father had once made abundantly clear, neither would the people of Grimentz.

They won't want you, boy. They never will. And what's more, they don't need you. They have Leo. They have Max. There's nothing you have they could possibly want.

Abuse came in many forms. A father telling his only son he had no worth was only one. But that had been enough to forge Seb's view forever. The people were probably praying for the day their crown prince had children of his own. Pushing the stain of Seb further down the line of succession. He'd never been prepared to test the truth of that. His wider family had rejected him—except for Leo—and his own father had barely tolerated him. Why would the people be any different?

Seb slammed the door shut on those thoughts.

'How far along do you think she is?' he asked.

'My guess would be about three months. But she hasn't told me yet. I think she's planning to do it tonight.'

Today was the anniversary of Leo and Violetta's first botched wedding attempt when she had fled in her wedding dress. They'd been two strangers contracted to an arranged, loveless marriage when, oh the irony, they'd actually fallen in love.

'She's given the staff the night off and she's cooking dinner,' Leo said. 'Her specialty, spaghetti al pomodoro.'

Seb's brow lowered. 'You're asking me to abase myself before the world because of a menu choice?'

'She only cooks when she has something important to tell me.'

'You know that right hook will be all over the press again,' Seb said, running a hand across his jaw.

Leo grimaced. 'I know what I'm asking. I know it will be tough, and I wouldn't ask this of you under any other circumstances. But if Violetta tells me tonight, I don't want to leave her alone tomorrow. You know how she'll be.'

Yes, Seb knew exactly how she'd be. Stoic on the outside but inside she'd be falling apart. His cousin would be strong for the two of them and how he did that, Seb couldn't fathom. His blood ran cold at the thought of what could happen. Leo had an example standing before him of exactly how badly a pregnancy could end. Seb had never known his mother. She'd died giving birth to him. Which was one of the reasons why he would never lose his heart, never marry. How would he live with the fear or the guilt if things went wrong? As they could, so easily.

But he couldn't say no to Leo's request. Seb never let him down. The man had been like a brother to him, helping Seb carve out some kind of place in the world when the rest of his family couldn't have cared less. All because his father had had the temerity to divorce his first wife of impeccable lineage, and then gone on to commit the unpardonable sin of falling head over heels in love with his secretary, marrying her and producing a son. He may be a prince but to the von Frohburgs, Seb would always be the son of the help and never accepted by them. Since Leo's marriage, Seb had had more of a relationship with Max, but even that had been due to Leo's efforts.

He owed Leo—big time. So he'd do it. Spend an evening with his nemesis: Queen Agnesse of Ellamaa.

Such a pretty, fairy-sounding name for a woman who was anything but! Not that she wasn't beautiful. She was, extraordinarily so. Fine-boned, blue-eyed, with hair like spun gold. A man could lose sleep over her, and many had. Her former fiancé for one. He'd publicly choked back tears when he'd announced the end of his engagement to the then crown princess. Irreconcilable differences, he'd said.

The palace had been entirely tight-lipped on the matter. But it hadn't stopped the press extrapolating, even going so far as to dub her the Ice Queen, particularly after Eerik had given an exclusive interview to a major TV network and hinted that the princess was 'hard to please'. Whatever the truth of it, Seb considered that interview, and its revelations, was not the act of a gentleman.

He was less inclined to be sympathetic when, two months later, the crown princess had landed her fist on Seb's jaw.

Perhaps Eerik had decamped when he discovered Agnesse Toivonen had a tendency to get punchy. Though so far as anyone knew, Seb had been the only one on the receiving end of that. She'd been a model of propriety since then. And after her father's death, she'd comported herself with great dignity in the face of her country's grief and her own. The king had been an exemplary monarch and well beloved and, while it was a constitutional monarchy, Ellamaa had definitely thrived with him on the throne. His daughter had quite an act to follow.

His daughter, the renowned beauty.

Seb had no trouble attracting beautiful women to his side. Never had. He had no desire to get entangled with an innocent-sounding witch like the Queen of Ellamaa.

Even if once, on a golden afternoon, she had stood in a halo of sunshine and so bewitched him he'd thought he was gazing at an angel.

An angel who, regardless of his own title, was way out of his reach—as his father had bluntly pointed out at the time. Because, despite Seb's royal status, he was only the second son of a second son. In contrast, Agnesse was descended from royalty on both sides and from birth had been heir to the throne of an ancient kingdom.

Above him in every way.

Seb shoved his hands in his pockets and scowled at the view

from Leo's windows. Lucky for him, then, that the angel had later proved herself to be a quick-tempered devil and the illusion had shattered.

'Have you considered your problem is that you actually like the woman?' Leo said into the silence.

Seb's jaw fell open. '*Like* her? Married life has addled your brain. You may be happily loved up but that's because Violetta is adorable. As I recall, she never accused you of being beneath her, and then socked you in the jaw.'

Leo's expression was one of sympathy and indulgence. Neither of which Sebastien could stomach right then. But he'd attend this event because he owed his cousin. He'd be polite; he'd be charming. As for the rest of it, he'd be keeping his distance and interacting as little as possible with the woman.

He hoped she'd do the same. Then, unlike at their last meeting, he and the queen could get through the evening with no drama and certainly no repercussions.

CHAPTER TWO

EARLIER THAT AFTERNOON there had been an ominous thunderstorm in Vienna, but the gods had been kind and the skies had cleared. With the setting sun as its backdrop, the facade of the hotel appeared gilded by the floodlights trained on every floor. Above the former palace, once home to a Hapsburg prince, flew the Austrian triband, while to its left and right fluttered the flags of Ellamaa and Grimentz. In honour of tonight's illustrious visitors, the grand Viennese hotel had laid on a dazzling welcome.

As the senior royal at the gala, Agnesse was the last to arrive, which meant that, as she stepped from her car, Prince Sebastien was already waiting for her at the top of the entrance stairs. She was obliged to suffer his scrutiny as she ascended the red carpet amidst the flash of cameras and cheers of gathered well-wishers. She kept her attention on the hotel manager, who was formally welcoming her.

Agnesse was accustomed to the impact she had on people. It embarrassed her but she knew she was considered beautiful, and that this sometimes threw even the most experienced of staff. She took time to settle the blushing, stammering hotel manager now. For herself, it also delayed the moment when she would have to look the prince in the face again.

From the earliest days her father had tutored her on how to behave at such events. 'Smile and be gracious,' he'd said. 'It is up to you to put others at ease.' He'd been a careful and thorough teacher, and she'd studied hard. No one would have guessed at her inner turmoil as she climbed the steps towards the waiting prince. To all those observing she would appear serene, composed, the very image of royal dignity, while in reality she was singularly aware that up ahead a pair of intense green eyes watched her every move.

Though she always prepared carefully for any event, she'd taken particular care with dressing that evening. Her gown was perfect. In a soft mink colour, it had a fitted lace bodice that skimmed her collarbone and close-fitting three-quarter-length sleeves. The skirt was layer upon layer of toning chiffon that fell to her toes. She'd chosen to wear little adornment. Just a pair of diamond and pearl drop earrings—her father's last gift to her—and the gold mourning medal for him, that she and all her entourage wore, secured high up on her shoulder with a black ribbon. She resisted the urge to seek the comfort of touching her fingers to it.

She could do this.

A little mingling at a predinner reception, where she would deliver the speech she'd written days ago and practised until she was word-perfect. Then dinner. What was so hard about that?

As she reached the final step, she was grateful that her maid had insisted on creating a more elaborate hairstyle than Agnesse had intended.

'I know we're still in mourning, but this strikes the perfect note between sombre and sexy,' Dorel had said, pinning a final curl of her blond up-do. 'The prince will be struck dumb.'

'I can but hope…' Agnesse thought desperately as a pair of shiny black shoes came into view. Her gaze rose slowly upward, along the length of his legs, then to the lean hips and waist. The deep V of an immaculate dinner jacket that emphasised the breadth of his shoulders, the snowy white shirt, the deeply tanned skin of his throat above it. A man had no right to look that good in his clothes. She would not dwell on her next shocking thought. How good he might look *out* of them...

At last, she had no choice but to raise her gaze to the glory of his face.

His mouth was smiling and that mouth was something else. With full, sensuous lips that made her tongue flick out to lick her own—they'd become so dry suddenly. His rich brown hair gleamed in the lights. Cut short at the sides and only slightly longer on top and swept to one side in a quiff that begged to have female fingers run through it. She did not look too closely at the tiny scar marring the perfection of his jaw. Not that something so trivial could truly mar this stunning man. If anything, it added to his allure by making him look even more dangerous. In bow tie and tux, he was the bad-boy prince dressed to perfection and she could barely look away. The heat in his gaze telegraphed that he, too, was liking what he saw and, despite her best intentions, Agnesse was flushed and a little breathless by the time she gained the top step and stretched out a hand.

She could not fault his greeting of her.

'Good evening, Your Majesty,' he said in perfect Ellamaarsque with only the hint of an accent from his native French. She should have expected that. Amongst their many talents, the princes of Grimentz were raised to be accomplished linguists. Taking the hand she offered, he gave a very proper bow, adding the heel click the von Frohburgs always did. They had such impeccable manners, with an old-world charm to them, and despite what she knew of him, it felt so gallant. Unwanted pleasure purred along Agnesse's spine.

She murmured an appropriate response as they paused for photographs.

She couldn't help but recall the last ones they'd been in together. Well, not together precisely—because in one she'd been in the foreground, marching away, while he stood behind, clutching his cheek, gazing after her in shock. The shots taken moments before that had been much worse. A blurred flurry of motion as her right hand, and its royal signet ring, connected with his jaw. Agnesse could barely think of it without dying of shame.

If he was thinking of those same moments now, he didn't show it.

'You are looking very beautiful tonight, ma'am,' he said as he offered her his arm. Her fingers settled on his sleeve. She was acutely conscious of the shift of muscles beneath but pretended that she felt nothing, that she was unmoved by the man beside her. Agnesse had steeled herself for the embarrassment of dealing with a lingering resentment or bitterness, but she hadn't expected that seeing him again would be so physically affecting: the sharp, dizzying sizzle of awareness when his hand had touched hers, the way she instinctively breathed deeper to savour the scent of him.

He was more than she remembered. Taller, broader, more compelling. But seeing him again brought back those other emotions. How he'd treated Isobel was neither forgotten, nor forgiven. Nor that other cruel slight. His crushing comments that were seared into her memory. No, she could not be amiable to this man.

She disguised the barb of her response with a polite smile. 'I'd be grateful if you'd spare me the empty compliments. A man of your reputation must use them so often they become meaningless. I don't believe them.'

The arm beneath her fingers tensed but his own smile deepened.

'Ah, but a man of my reputation is a connoisseur of women,' he said. 'Uniquely placed to appreciate true beauty when he sees it. In which case, perhaps you should believe me.'

He was tall enough that, even though she was in five-inch heels, she had to look up at him, making her profoundly and meltingly aware of her own femininity.

And, of course, there was that stunning smile, which he'd

once turned on her to such spellbinding effect. He was every woman's fantasy. If you could overlook the promiscuity, of course. Agnesse wondered how many of the female guests here tonight had shared his bed. If the rumours were true, three at the very least.

They approached a sumptuous reception room. The light from crystal chandeliers reflected in the ornate gilded wall mirrors and across the VIP guests who'd paid extra for the privilege of meeting their royal hosts. A buzz of anticipation raced around the salon at the sight of the two of them together. Even the dimpled cherubs, cavorting on the ceilings above, seemed to pause as Agnesse made her entrance on Sebastien's arm.

The Ice Queen and the Playboy, side by side and with such a juicy history between them. The evening had suddenly taken on an extra excitement.

When she'd attended this event last year with Leo they'd broken apart at this point to work the room separately and ensure every guest met at least one of them. But as Agnesse began to pull away, Sebastien captured her hand and tucked it firmly into his elbow, forcing her to walk beside him longer.

'Let's really give them a show, hmm?' he murmured. 'Imagine how much more they'll spend at the auction.' The hand imprisoning hers at his elbow was warm and strong, and sent such a thrill through Agnesse she couldn't quite find the voice to say no.

She'd co-hosted with Leo on four occasions before. A von Frohburg prince always furnished an event with added cachet. Royalty usually did. But the cousins had that extra allure: charm, intelligence, and both were of course outrageously good-looking.

Even so, Leo had never made her heart beat faster like this.

Breaking with protocol, a guest approached them.

In a scarlet silk dress slit to the thigh and oozing French chic, the Comtesse d'Onzain sashayed up. She had twenty years on him, but it didn't stop her eyeing Sebastien like a hungry lioness sizing up a wildebeest.

She placed a proprietary hand on his chest. 'Divinely handsome as ever, Your Highness.'

Agnesse had the strangest impulse to place herself between the comtesse and her quarry. As if the man was not perfectly able to take care of himself. And more. He proved it as the comtesse's daughters arrived. They crowded round him, simpered and twittered for him, brazenly competing for his attention. Really, had they no shame?

He graced them with a smouldering smile, taking their hands in turn and making a production of lifting them to his lips to lavish each with a showy kiss.

Agnesse rolled her eyes. Had *he* no shame?

Finally, he remembered her presence and turned his attention to her.

'Madame la Comtesse, mademoiselles, permit me to introduce my date for the evening, Her Majesty, Queen Agnesse of Ellamaa.'

The sisters curtsied prettily. The comtesse bowed her head. 'Your escort is a magnificent beast, is he not, Your Majesty?' The woman practically licked her lips. 'I do hope you don't intend on monopolising his attention all evening?'

Agnesse bristled.

'Sadly, I must contradict His Highness. I'm not his date. We're co-hosts. Nothing more. And as I'm not the kind of woman to hold the attention of a...a *beast*, Comtesse,' Agnesse said, freeing her hand from Sebastien's grip, 'I'm happy to release him back into the wild at once.'

The comtesse laughed. 'Poor Sebastien. Her Majesty appears quite unimpressed. Are you losing your touch?'

Before Agnesse could walk away, he caught her hand and pressed his lips to it. Those stunning eyes fixed her with a bold seducer's gaze. 'I'd be content to return to captivity anytime, ma'am. Just say the word.'

She snatched her fingers from his and walked away, joining the first group of guests she encountered. For the next half hour she chatted and smiled, doing her duty.

And if she was acutely aware of every woman those green eyes flashed for, every female hand his soft lips kissed, well, that was no one's business but hers and after tonight she'd forget all about the strange effect Sebastien von Frohburg was having on her.

Seb let her go. Even though every instinct screamed to haul her back and clamp her to his side. The haughty, uncivil, infuriating...*beauty.*

He'd been prepared to overlook the outcome of their last meeting. He was representing Leo and Grimentz, and it behoved him to keep that in mind. But the queen had come at him all guns blazing, throwing his genuine compliment straight back in his face, later dismissing him—much to the amusement of the comtesse—and all despite his attempts to be pleasant.

For any other woman he'd turn his back and walk away. But the Queen of Ellamaa was no ordinary woman, and the truth was she'd had him on the back foot the moment she'd emerged from her car and stepped gracefully onto the red carpet.

For a moment there he'd forgotten where he was. She'd taken his breath away. Sheer perfection from the top of her head to the tips of her toes and all the woman in between. The curve of her cheek, the little pointed chin, and that mouth, *Lord*, that mouth. If ever lips had been made to be kissed...

The young woman who'd once punched him had developed into a goddess. More dazzling than he remembered.

As she'd climbed the steps, she'd been thoroughly sweet to the hotel manager, who'd been so obviously bedazzled by his stunning guest. He couldn't blame the man. Seb had been experiencing a similar reaction. And not just in the tightening of his groin.

He'd witnessed the infinitesimal falter when she'd reached him, the faint tremor of her hand as she'd placed it in his—that first touch had also sent a jolt of energy through him—and it had brought out the overprotective, chest-beating alpha male in him. It was just as well he was her official escort for the evening. At that moment he could have flattened any other man who'd dared to touch her.

All his former lovers would say he treated them with respect and care. But this? This was something new. Underneath all that icy reserve he'd sensed a vulnerability about her, and with it came the fierce certainty that it was he who must step into the role of chief protector.

How was that even logical, when she had a team of security to do just that, and when he was the one on the receiving end of the attacks? She'd loaded a poisoned barb into every one of their exchanges so far.

When she'd fully raised her eyes to his—bewitching, blue as a summer's day—for a tantalising moment they'd telegraphed that she liked what she saw, but then hardened with challenge and barely veiled hostility. Agnesse Toivonen had not forgiven his supposed transgression against her spoilt younger sister. Even after five years. Damn it, the woman knew how to hold a grudge.

But then the comtesse arrived, flirting outrageously, and he'd seen an interesting flicker of possessive anger in Agnesse. She might have walked off, dismissing him in the process, but Seb could tell she wasn't as immune to him as she pretended.

He'd give her one more chance to be even halfway civil. If not, then the gloves came off. He'd show Agnesse Toivonen that even the Ice Queen herself could melt for him.

CHAPTER THREE

THE MOMENT FOR Agnesse's speech had arrived.

She extracted the discreet bundle of cue cards from her evening bag and advanced towards the podium. Over the years she'd made so many speeches, two of them at this event before, so there really was no need for the churning in her gut. But it was there all the same, and it was getting worse. As was the tightness in her chest and the plea playing over and over in her head.

Let me be good enough tonight.

She plastered on her most serene of smiles and bought some precious time by arranging her cards on the lectern before her, willing her heartbeat to slow and her clammy palms to stop sweating.

Please, God, not here. It couldn't happen here.

There were so many eyes on her and as she looked up, she forced herself to scan them calmly, praying no one would notice her trembling. And if they did, to put it down to stage fright. Not the fear that she might be about to lose the ability to breathe, right here in front of everyone.

But the speech calmed her. The familiar routine and the words she'd learned by rote, the question here, the pause for laughter there—it lowered her heart rate, steadied her breathing. And the memories, the things she wanted to say about her father, filled her with pride. Not panic.

She spoke of his legacy, his hopes for the future of the charity, and of her intention to keep those hopes burning bright for all the youngsters who'd benefit from the money raised tonight. When she left the lectern Sebastien waited for her, his gaze burning with concern. Had he seen? Had he spotted her moments of weakness?

'You spoke movingly of your father,' he said, reaching out an arm to support her as she stepped down from the stage. 'He would have been very proud of you tonight.'

He sounded sincere but it reminded her uncomfortably of that other occasion, where he had appeared impressed. Until later, when she'd overheard him reveal what he truly thought of her.

'Shall we go into dinner?' she said, cutting across him. Not trusting his motives at all.

The fear had subsided, the faint nausea gone, so she barely leant on his arm at all and averted her gaze from the shadow of concern she saw in his. He must not see. *No one* must see. The first queen regnant of Ellamaa could not appear to be weak in front of any of them.

Be good enough, Agnesse.

'I wonder why your brother wasn't sent tonight instead,' she said to divert his attention.

'Max? This isn't his thing at all. He'd have had guests demanding a refund.'

'And you, I suppose, will be doing the opposite?' she said.

He sent her a smug grin that told her he had every confidence of that. She wanted to despise him for it but couldn't.

This gala was designed to attract those with very deep pockets, and the event team had created an appropriately lavish spectacle. The ballroom was already a rococo masterpiece, lined with wall mirrors, richly gilded stucco, and a second painted ceiling, this one depicting the story of Cupid and Psyche. But the addition of floral arrangements, statues, and dramatic lighting made the room even more splendid. The designers had taken their theme from the painted ceiling overhead. The stage was graced with a giant ice sculpture of the lovers entwined. Each table bore its own Cupid statuette primed with an arrow of glimmering gold. As Sebastien helped her to her seat, Agnesse noted their Cupid's arrow was directed straight towards her. She sent the impertinent immortal a glare as she arranged the chiffon layers of her dress neatly around her feet.

As Sebastien took his own seat the artful lighting cast him in the strangest shadows. He was darkly handsome, like a god of the Underworld. Alluring, dangerous, and forbidden. Definitely forbidden. Royal playboys were off-limits to queens attempting to stake a serious and dignified place in the world. However affecting he might be. She flexed her fingers as the back of her hand tingled from his remembered kiss.

Dinner was served and her situation became easier. The comtesse, who had been assigned to their table, sat to Sebastien's left and monopolised his attention. He seemed more than happy to oblige her, chatting easily, laughing, and getting cosy with the older woman. Not seeming to mind how often she touched her hand to his arm, or that it dropped on occasion to his thigh and lingered there.

Of course, it didn't bother Agnesse, either. Why would it? She was engaged in conversation with an elderly duke who regaled her with a monologue on his pet topic: the life cycle of the Mason bee, which was fascinating. Really, it was.

When it came time for the charity auction, which was to be compèred by her co-host, she discovered that Sebastien's skills ran not only to charming a comtesse, but also captivating an entire room of people. He had them eating out of his hand, and emptying out their pockets. Cookery courses with celebrity chefs, holidays on private islands, coaching sessions with tennis stars, all went for outrageous sums.

He flirted, he cajoled, he feigned abject disappointment when a sum achieved wasn't to his liking, and the laughing bidders found themselves parting with small fortunes. Agnesse even bid on an item herself: a photo shoot with a celebrated portrait photographer, which she would gift to Isobel. Her sister would adore it. But the royal auctioneer sent her a pirate's smile from the lectern as he talked up the lot and sent the price higher.

'I paid four times what the photo shoot was worth,' she said as he returned to her side once the auction concluded and the dancing began. She was impressed by how much he'd helped to raise but wild horses wouldn't drag that from her. He was already far too pleased with himself.

His eyes twinkled down at her. 'And the children it supports will be grateful.'

She softened. 'Of course, I don't begrudge a cent of it. I know how much the money is needed. I often accompanied my father when he visited the youth groups and I was humbled by the resilience of those children.' She waved a hand to encompass the room of wealthy partygoers. 'We live a life of such privilege. How can we begin to imagine what they've suffered?'

'I can,' he said with a dismissive snort, and then his jaw tightened as if he regretted speaking.

'But you've been raised as I have, in luxury. How can you have known a moment's want...?' Agnesse halted abruptly. She'd sounded so dismissive, so heartless, when she'd really not meant to.

'Deprivation isn't only an absence of material things. We aren't all blessed with kindly fathers, Your Majesty,' he said, tightly.

The bleakness in his eyes was in such marked contrast to the laughing man of moments before, and so unlike everything she thought she knew about the infamous pleasure seeker that she wondered, did Sebastien von Frohburg have a darker past than appearances would suggest? Had she just glimpsed the real man behind the fine manners and handsome face?

He was gazing out calmly enough as couples began filling

the dance floor, but a muscle worked in his jaw, and Agnesse had the crazy urge to reach out and caress it to stillness. She curled her hands firmly in her lap.

That strange sadness in his eyes had simply been a trick of the light, or maybe she was just being overly sentimental. The impudent little god glinted in the centre of the table. She reached out and swivelled Cupid so that he—and his ruinous arrow—faced safely in the opposite direction.

When she sat back Sebastien was watching her. All the melancholy had gone and the playboy's smile had returned. His glance went from her to the statuette and back. The smile widened. He was laughing at her.

Suddenly, her heart rate increased. Usually, she could fight off that telltale hitch in her breathing, the clatter of her heartbeat. She'd push it back, in the way she'd taught herself to do, and any moments of discomfort would start to pass. But this time it wasn't working.

On the little finger of her right hand was her signet ring. The ruby-and-gold ring had been presented to her on her eighteenth birthday, as it was with every Ellamaese heir. She spun it mechanically round and round her finger, but she caught Sebastien's sharp gaze watching the action. It was the very ring that had carved the scar on his jaw.

She covered the ring with her other hand.

She desperately searched the table in front of her.

Amongst the dregs of dinner sat her glass of white wine, another of champagne—both barely touched—a chilled bottle of sparkling water, damp with condensation, and beside it an unused goblet. She fiddled with them, taking her time until they were all neatly lined up. And her heart began to slow at last. But she needed some water and not the kind on their table.

She beckoned to their waiter. 'A still water, please. At room temperature. One ice cube. One slice of lime.'

As the waiter left to do her bidding, there was a soft snort from the man beside her.

'You have a problem with my drink order?' she said.

'That wasn't a drink order. It's something you'd take on a cleansing retreat.'

Forcing herself to do it, and appear calm and in control, she looked him up and down as if his proximity was distasteful. 'Perhaps I feel in need of cleansing.'

'Perhaps,' he said. 'However, at this moment, Your Majesty, you might be wiser to retreat.'

She sent him a glacial stare. 'A Toivonen never retreats.'

'Ma'am, neither does a von Frohburg. If it's a fight you want, which you seem to have been spoiling for all evening, you may have one. But I'll warn you. I play to win.'

Sofia, the elder Onzain sister, passed by their table, hand in hand with a partner, on the way to the dance floor. He watched them for a moment.

'Although, instead of fighting I suppose we could dance,' Sebastien mused.

'Dance with you?' Agnesse said a little unevenly, ruffled by the intense glitter in his eyes. 'Thank you, but I'd rather wrestle with a hungry bear.'

He tilted his head and studied her, green eyes alight with challenge.

'Role play? I could do that.' His voice lowered to a veritable purr. 'If that's what you want.'

Thank goodness for the dim light in here. She'd just gone pink to her ears. What a schoolgirl error to encourage such familiarities. Keert would have been disappointed in her.

'But it's just a dance,' Seb said, studying the crush of couples. 'And it will be expected of us. What do you say to getting it over with? Strip the plaster off in one swift move.'

Agnesse's chin lifted in defence. 'If it's going to be that distasteful to you, let's not.'

'No, that won't do.' In a surge of power he was on his feet. An unfurling of legs and a flexing of broad shoulders that sent a flurry of excitement through her. He stretched out a hand. 'Do me the honour, hmm?'

Interested eyes had turned their way. Cameras, too, no doubt. She wanted nothing controversial to appear in tomorrow's papers. At the very least she'd promised her mother. Reluctantly, she stood, gave him her hand, and allowed the prince to escort her to the dance floor.

Of course, he moved beautifully, expertly guiding her round the floor. It was so easy to follow his lead she even allowed herself to relax a little. Those moments of panic had passed and the challenging part of the evening was over.

'See,' he said, smiling down at her. 'This is perfectly pleasant.'

'I suppose you dance well enough.'

He inclined his head. 'Even if it feels like that compliment was grudgingly given, thank you.'

'I'm sure it's only because you've had so much opportunity to practise,' she added quickly.

There was no flippant response this time. Instead, his brow creased.

'Yes, there's been women. I like women and I'll make no apology for that.' He held her gaze, ramping up the heat in her belly. 'I might even like you. If you'd let me.'

She made a sound that she'd meant to be derisive but actually came out more of a whimper. She stared at the knot on his bow tie, helplessly wondering what he might do with a woman he liked.

'You're prickly but not that hard to like,' he said.

The scarlet gown of the comtesse danced into view. She was in the arms of a young diplomat who looked thoroughly entranced. How did women do that? Agnesse had no idea how to flirt, how to attract a man, and anyway, what would be the point when ultimately she was the Ice Queen and he would only be disappointed?

Sebastien followed the direction of her gaze.

'She's not what you think, you know. It amuses her to be seen as a femme fatale but much of the gossip is untrue. The comtesse uses her influence to raise millions for charities across Europe. She prefers not to make a big thing of it.'

Sofia passed by with her dance partner again. Agnesse felt a sharp stab of something like jealousy as Sebastien's gaze lingered briefly on the couple.

'You're saying that all the stories are false?'

He turned his attention back to her. He knew exactly which story she was referring to.

'Not entirely. But it wasn't a weekend. It was one night. And only *one* woman,' he said for emphasis. 'It meant nothing. For either of us. We were both bored and in need of entertainment.'

'You engage in the most intimate of acts out of boredom?' She could have bitten off her tongue. How prim had that sounded?

'Ma'am,' he purred, 'if you haven't derived pleasure from the intimate act, as you call it, I venture your lover hasn't been doing it right.'

Her lover was long gone and since that first and only time with him, she hadn't been doing it at all. But she wouldn't dare divulge that to this man. He'd probably see it as a challenge.

'But I did nothing to correct the story,' Sebastien continued. 'The d'Onzains are amused by their notoriety and the embellished story helped my cousin at the time. He'd just been jilted by his fiancée. It gave the press something more scandalous to salivate over.'

'Oh… I see.'

Sebastien's amused gaze settled back on her. 'Yes. I'm not the faithless creature you think I am.'

She wrestled with that surprising revelation for a moment. That he'd brought censure down on his own head to support his cousin.

'Difficult, isn't it? Admitting I'm not the complete scoundrel you thought.'

She tipped her chin upward. 'You still broke my sister's heart. She was only sixteen.'

His gaze narrowed sharply on her. 'And that fact alone should have told you I would have done nothing inappropriate. I was mindful of her youth. We'd met a month before at a friend's house. I remember we had a pleasant conversation but nothing more. Then at that wedding reception we all attended, she walked into a room, without preamble or invitation, where two adults were holding a private conversation. She behaved like an ill-mannered child and she was reprimanded as such.'

'You could have let her down gently.'

'There was no *letting down* to be done. All the interest had been on her side. I had done nothing to encourage it.'

The other dancers had all edged farther away, leaving a gap for the queen and the prince to dance unhindered. But Agnesse barely noticed.

'That's not her version of events.'

He stared down his nose at her. 'I'm not surprised she lied to you about what happened.'

'Or she isn't the one who lied.'

The hand at her waist tightened, then relaxed again.

'Look. I'm trying to be the gracious one here. Another man may try to get even for your very public slight that day.'

'Get even? I was defending Isobel. You were in the wrong. We are already even.'

'No.' He swirled her round. 'We are not.'

They danced in silence for a moment. She tried to ignore the impact of the strong, vital body close to hers and the realisation that she might have placed herself in the grip of a hungry bear, after all.

'I had no interest in your sister,' he said at last. 'Still don't. I am, however, finding myself drawn to *her* sister. Even if she is rather difficult.'

'I'm not difficult. I'm merely disinterested and I assure you, I'm immune to whatever charms you think you have.'

'Is that so?'

Had she imagined it or had he just inched her closer? 'And what charms are those, hmm? The good looks? The wit?'

'The arrogance? The conceit?' she suggested, tartly.

He chuckled. 'I know you enjoyed watching me conduct the auction. I saw every emotion that crossed your face. You can't hide it. You like me.'

'You're deluded,' she said through her teeth, but her breasts tingled as they brushed his chest. She summoned a smile for a couple dancing by and fought to contain the growing feeling of giddy excitement at being in this man's arms.

'You didn't like the comtesse putting her hands on me.'

'Whatever happened at the dinner table was between—'

The corner of his mouth tilted. 'So you were watching me then, too? But I meant before that. When she approached us at the start of the evening. I thought you were about to leap between us.' He pulled her closer and rested his cheek against her temple. She felt the warm caress of his breath as he murmured, 'You've no need to be jealous, Your Majesty.'

How was he doing this? Making her feel so defenceless and unsteady and yet so thrillingly awake at the same time.

But this was the man who'd appeared so beguiling once before and then dismissed her as being unworthy of him. Her? A woman who took her role seriously and worked hard to earn the respect of her people. He may have forgotten that but she had not. Despite what she'd discovered about him tonight, wasn't he still essentially a man who used his royal title for nothing but his own gain, who enjoyed his status but assumed none of the responsibility that went with it?

She leant away so she could look directly into his eyes. 'You're quite mistaken. I wasn't at all jealous. You might have a handsome face but I have no interest in you. How could I? The second son of a second son who pursues pleasure and little else? You are not, nor ever could be, in my league.'

She felt the anger rip through him like a wildfire, consuming the softly teasing prince. In its place it left a man whose charming expression had become a cold mask.

She hadn't meant to insult him so badly and regretted it at once. But she was struggling to cope with his charm offensive and her body's wayward reactions to the closeness of his.

She was completely unprepared for what he did next.

He shifted his grip, tipped her backwards in his arms, and before she could stop him, fastened his mouth over hers. Too shocked to respond, she let him kiss her. His lips and his tongue taking shocking liberties.

He tasted of things she could hardly name but wanted more of.

It's passion, she thought dimly. Wrapped in a masculine feast of soft lips, and an enticing body that was hard and hot. She would've been breathless if she could breathe at all.

It had never felt like this with Eerik. Not even for a moment. This need to be closer still, to mould their bodies together. She slid her hand from his shoulder to curl about his neck. She arched her hips to press closer to his, revelling in the feeling of being weightless, of being held so securely in his arms.

Then suddenly his mouth, and all that tempting softness, was gone. Her eyes fluttered open, her gaze refocused to clash with his, oddly dark and forbidding.

'Now I think we are even,' he said.

And in a move, so swift she hardly felt it happening, she was upright, back on her own two feet, and he was striding away.

Leaving her marooned amongst the cream of European society who, stripped of their elegant manners by the sight, gawked at her like fishwives at a street brawl.

CHAPTER FOUR

It was ten minutes in his limo across Vienna, then a farther five, striding across foyers and into lifts, before Seb reached the sanctuary of his hotel suite, where his simmering temper drove him straight to the bar. He dumped a generous measure of whisky into a tumbler and knocked it back, grimacing at the burn as it went down. The label identified it as a very fine thirty-year-old single malt, but Seb tasted nothing. Nothing but her seared onto his lips.

He should never have kissed her.

He tore his bow tie loose, flung his tux jacket onto the nearest sofa, then refilled the glass.

Why the hell had he kissed her?

Because she'd offended him, dismissed him in the worst possible way. Agnesse of Ellamaa had crossed a line by insulting him again. *Second son*: the moniker that had tainted his entire life. This time she'd actually dared say it to his face.

But his instinctive retaliation had seriously backfired when he'd tasted all that honeyed sweetness, when he'd felt her melt in his arms.

She was a beauty, yes, but there was more. Was it because she was firmly off-limits? Because he had no intention of getting entangled with her. That kiss was the end of it. He never let a woman trouble him in this way. Especially not a royal one. He preferred to give any kind of royalty a wide berth. He'd had his fill of its pettiness and politicking that surrounded his family. He wanted as little as possible to do with that life. He'd have renounced his own title but the von Frohburgs would love that, and he wouldn't give them the satisfaction.

And he owed Leo. The best of them by far and the only one he considered family, who'd been in his corner for as long as Seb could remember. More of a brother than Max, his actual elder brother, would ever be. Seb kept his title and his link to the von Frohburgs to support Leo.

And for his mother.

The young woman of humble birth who, despite what the von Frohburgs believed, had married a prince for love and nothing more.

He had a handful of photos of her. In all of them she was simply dressed, wearing a wedding band only. Obviously no interest in the trappings of her husband's wealth and status. She'd never even allowed them to call her *princess*, though royal observers noted she'd behaved with all the dignity of one.

Fabienne Bonfils had wanted Prince Georg the man, and not his title. But Seb would keep his, in honour and remembrance of her. And to spite his pompous relatives who hated the fact it was his by right.

Did Agnesse share their prejudice? Was that why she'd taunted him?

'We are already even,' she'd told him, lifting her chin in challenge. But the light had glowed on the lustrous pearls of her earrings, and the luminous perfection of her skin, and for that moment all he wanted was to discover if that place just beneath her jaw was as tender as it looked, and would she moan for him if he pressed his lips there?

She'd been wearing pearl earrings the very first time he'd set eyes on her. Tiny pearl studs and a delicate gold necklace, with a pendant in the shape of an 'A'. He remembered she'd tied her hair back with a blue scarf, the same colour as her eyes. Seb had been in the audience at her school prize giving.

From time to time and for appearances' sake, his father behaved as if he actually cared about his younger son, which was why Seb had been with him that day. Prince Georg presenting prizes to youngsters while enthusing over their achievements would be more credible if he had one of his own children in tow.

Seb had winked at her as she waited anxiously to give her speech. In the reception afterwards she stood talking to other guests. Bathed in a pool of sunshine that transformed her blond hair into a golden halo, he was convinced he was looking at an angel. Then she looked up, their eyes had met, and she smiled at him. In all his life he'd never seen anything more enchanting.

But his father had seen the direction of his gaze and later, as they'd descended the stairs to the exit where their car waited, he'd chastised him. 'Take your thoughts off the Toivonen girl. She's heir to a throne and not for the likes of you.'

He'd snapped back. Hiding his hurt at yet another of his father's slights by dismissing the girl. Something about her pretty face, but that intellectually she was not his equal and so of no interest.

It was almost word for word what Agnesse had flung at him tonight.

Seb slugged back more whisky.

She'd heard him that day.

The smart of his father's dismissal had made him lash out, belittling the girl without a thought to ease his own hurt, never imagining she would overhear.

His fingers went to the scar on his jaw where her ring had gouged a sliver of skin. Was that what the punch had been about? The excuse about Isobel hiding the real hurt Agnesse had felt?

Well, he'd never have to see the Queen of Ellamaa again, or suffer any more of her insults and jibes. Nor wonder how it would be to bed the woman who'd melted so thoroughly in his arms.

Ellamaa. It had the sound of a magical kingdom. Where a man might find himself enchanted by its Fairy Queen. Or, more likely, frozen to death by one of her glacial stares.

But as he'd just discovered—or perhaps known all along—Ellamaa's queen wasn't cold. Beneath all that icy reserve the woman burned hot. The sweet temptation of her response had made it hard to set her away from him back in the ballroom.

She was a warm, sensual creature. He'd seen the seeds of it that day at the prize giving. When she'd smiled at him and he'd been unable to stop himself smiling back.

But a few years after that not only had she punched him, she'd also belittled him, and today she'd repeated that he was beneath her.

She'd got off lightly. A kiss—it had just been a kiss—to prove he wasn't as repellent and beneath her as she'd claimed.

Seb shoved a hand through his hair. Even so, it had not been the act of a gentleman to try and prove that so publicly. He certainly shouldn't have abandoned her on the dance floor. He took another slug of whisky.

Why did the one woman in the world who could practically scramble his DNA have to be so difficult you needed a black belt in ducking and diving just to hold a conversation?

Voices raised in the corridor outside interrupted his musings.

His suite shared the top floor of the hotel with only one other. He'd dressed for the evening on his private jet and gone straight to the gala from the airport so there'd been no chance of bumping into its occupant in the hotel corridors.

Though of course, Seb knew exactly who it was.

Your Majesty. Please open the door.

Ma'am, you must let me back in.

Yes, Agness of Ellamaa was just across the hallway and still causing trouble by the sounds of it.

The voices were getting louder and more agitated. Seb tried

to tune it out. It was nothing to do with him. Let her team see to her.

But now the pounding of a fist and a more determined female voice. 'Ma'am? Agnesse? Open the door.'

That they'd resorted to her given name was an indication of their concern. It got him to his feet and out into the corridor.

Gathered outside the queen's door was her security team, a small, agitated woman whom he presumed was a maid, and the hotel butler assigned to the Royal Suite.

'What's going on?'

The maid rushed towards him.

'Oh, sir. The queen asked me to get Christina for her and then she locked me out. She's never done anything like this before. I don't know what's come over her.'

'Maybe she wants some peace and quiet after an evening doing her duty.' He sent them a pointed look but they didn't appear to get the irony.

But her maid's alarm was genuine and worrying. Seb felt a prick of conscience. After what he'd done, he should at least reassure himself there was nothing seriously wrong.

'What about the staff entrance?'

The butler looked uncomfortable. 'That key card isn't working. I've sent for another.'

On cue the hotel manager arrived. Apologising to Seb while simultaneously scolding the butler for the grievous sin of inconveniencing His Highness. Seb doubted it was the man's fault and said so, gaining a grateful smile for his pains.

Seb took the key card from the manager, opening the door himself and ordering everyone to wait outside, reassuring them he'd summon them if they were needed. Agnesse had kicked her staff out for a reason. Whatever was happening she didn't want them to witness it. He could identify with that. Hadn't there been times when he felt the same?

He began searching the suite, calling for her. The sitting room was empty. The door to the private terrace stood open, but the elegant space, with its magnificent views of the city and its planters of roses and cherry trees, was deserted. So, too, was the bedroom, though someone had been there because the covers were awry as if desperate hands had tried to drag them off. Then Seb heard a noise coming from the bathroom. He headed for the door. Pushed it wide.

And there she was, crumpled in a heap on the tiled floor: bundled in a white robe, hair an untidy mass of gold, and face scraped free of makeup. His glorious nemesis.

In the midst of the mother of all panic attacks.

There'd barely been time to fabricate a reason to get Dorel out of her suite, to lock her door, and stagger back to the bed, before the nausea and dizziness overtook her. She'd somehow got to the bathroom, wanting to splash cold water on her face. But once there her legs had buckled beneath her and she'd slumped to the floor.

As the room spun and the pain in her chest got worse, she heard the hammering on her door, her team yelling her name. She regretted alarming them, but she couldn't let anyone see her like this. However bad it got. They mustn't know she had these moments. No one must know.

But now a new voice called to her, calmer and closer, from inside the suite itself. She recognised it instantly.

Not him. Anyone but him to see her this way.

But even as that thought arrived, another came quickly on its heels.

You'll be safe with him. You don't have to be alone this time.

Inexplicable though it was, after he'd humiliated her so publicly, when the prince's tall figure appeared in the doorway, she reached for him.

'Seb…astien.'

In a few long strides he was there, dropping to his haunches before her, taking both her hands in his. Searching her face, his expression all concern.

'Heart...pounding. Scared,' she told him on a series of gasping breaths.

'Agnesse,' he said, gently. 'I know this is frightening but what you're experiencing is a panic attack. You'll get through it, I promise you, and I'll be here to help you until you do.'

He was so wrong. It wasn't an attack. This was worse than anything she'd experienced before. She'd had episodes like these where her heart had raced, her breath coming in short, choppy bursts, but those times she'd managed to control them. This time she couldn't because surely she was dying. Her heart was beating hard enough to burst out of her chest.

'Look at me.' The command was gentle but a command all the same. He waited until her eyes fixed on his. 'We're going to breathe together. Breathe in, Agnesse.'

He was so calm and steady. How could he be when she was on her bathroom floor? *Dying.*

'Breathe,' he repeated, squeezing her hands.

She tried. Nothing happened. She couldn't do it. She was never going to breathe properly again.

'It's all right. I know you're frightened but it will be okay if you try and follow what I do.' He inhaled through his nose and blew out a long, slow breath from his mouth.

She copied him. Sort of. The iron fist clamped about her lungs loosened enough for her to drag in some air.

'Good girl. Now out.'

She pushed the air out, still feeling like she might suffocate. But Sebastien continued breathing in and out slowly himself, counting for her. 'In two three. Now out two three.' She tried to copy him while clutching his hands. They felt so solid, like her lifeline.

But she was doing it. Her shallow, gasping breaths were getting deeper.

'Now, tell me five things you can see,' he said.

What? She had to breathe first. Surely, that was her priority.

'How...how—'

'I've seen this before,' he said, answering the question she couldn't frame. 'At a mental health charity I work with. Now, five things, Agnesse.'

She struggled to process that. Not supported. Worked *with*. The playboy helping out at a charity? That astonishing thought shocked her enough that she answered his question.

'You,' she said.

His mouth quirked. 'That's one. What else?'

The room was still spinning but she did her best to look around.

'A gold tap.'

'Good. And?'

'Two—two gold taps?'

He smiled in earnest now. 'Nice try. But I'm still waiting for a third thing.'

'So—so picky,' she said, shivering now. 'Okay. M—mirror. Marble b—bath.' Her heart was slowing at last. 'And t—towel,' she said.

'Good girl. Now four things you can hear.'

Who put him in charge? 'Someone b—being a p—pain?'

He chuckled. 'You'll thank me later. What next?'

'My—my teeth chattering.'

'Yeah, what a racket. I can hardly hear myself think.' He reached forward to gently push her hair back from her face. 'Number three?'

'Air con.'

She'd said that without a stumble.

The wall behind her separated this suite from the corridor outside, where she could hear Dorel babbling and Christina doing her best to calm her.

'And my maid, having a fit.'

'I don't blame her. You've given us a fright.'

'Sorry.'

She breathed out. Slower, easier. That terrifying tightness

in her chest was easing. His beautiful face became serious. And kind.

'You lost your papa and became queen in the same moment. You're grieving and grappling with your new role all at the same time. I'm not surprised you're having moments like these.'

She gazed up at him, forgetting to be guarded, drinking him in. This wasn't the man she'd expected after the evening's exchanges.

'Do you think you can stand?' he asked.

Her legs were jelly. A wave of exhaustion was sapping all her strength. Standing wouldn't be happening anytime soon.

'Give me a moment. I'll be okay soon. You can go now if you like.'

He looked appalled at that suggestion. 'Not likely. I'm staying until I know you're okay. Would you like me to call a doctor?'

'No!'

He raised a brow.

'I mean, no thank you, because what could a doctor do? I'll be fine shortly and then I have work to get on with.'

'You've just spent several hours working at that gala. It's time to rest.'

'But I still have a report to read and emails to answer tonight.'

He rolled his eyes at her. 'How is that self-care, hmm? Don't you know anything about coping with panic attacks?'

Actually, no, because she'd never had one this bad before.

'I'll be fine. Honestly.' She tried to reassure him.

'Stubborn woman,' he said, suddenly scooping her up. 'You're not working again tonight if I have anything to do with it.' He carried her from the bathroom and even if she'd had the strength to protest, right then she didn't want to because in his strong arms, she felt safer and less alone than she had in months.

* * *

It felt so good to hold her, but hell, he shouldn't be revelling in it. She'd just suffered a panic attack. Lighten the mood, he thought. *Now.*

'God, you're a weight.'

The woman in his arms mumbled something.

'Excuse me?'

'I said the correct address would be, "You're a weight, Your Majesty."'

He made a derisive snort. 'Seems to me it's all the royal stuff that's got you into this state, so let's dispense with titles, shall we? Tonight I'm just Seb.'

'Okay… Seb,' she murmured, and sweet pleasure flared in his chest at the sound of his name on her lips. He set her on her feet beside the bed, careful to keep one hand on her arm in case she swayed. With the other he gave a little tug on the collar of her bathrobe.

'On or off?'

There, that was suitably avuncular. Not a hint of anything suggestive to it. Which was essential. Because everything else about this situation was screaming danger. He left her pulling at the belt of her robe while he focused on setting the bed to rights.

He could do this. He could help her and then walk away. There'd be no repeat of what happened on the dance floor and he'd give no hint, by even so much as a sideways glance, of what she was doing to his self-control.

Then he saw what she was wearing beneath her robe. Not a silky wisp of a chemise, which he'd expected—and braced himself for. Nor something helpfully chaste, falling from neck to ankle in virginal white cotton.

No, the nightwear preferences for the Queen of Ellamaa went in an entirely different direction.

The all-encompassing bathrobe had fallen away to reveal a fine linen cami with shoestring straps and ruffled hem, plus

shorts edged with tiny matching frills, the whole outfit strewn
with daisy motifs. The ensemble was not only rather adorable
but also showing way too much leg for his comfort. The shorts
had even ridden up on one side to offer a glimpse of shapely
buttock. Seb dropped his gaze and redoubled his efforts at
straightening the crisp cotton sheets and silken eiderdown.

When he'd finished Agnesse slumped to the bed, oblivious to the effect she was having on him. 'I wish I was home,'
she said.

So did he. Hundreds of miles away in gloomy Grimentz
Castle. Far removed from this sumptuous hotel bedroom, with
its plump pillows, soft lighting, and half-naked beauty.

Over the sudden hoarseness in his throat he said, 'Ellamaa?'

'Not just Ellamaa. In the Summer Palace. It's ten miles outside the city but it could be a hundred. It's so peaceful. It's the
one place I can really relax.'

She looked up at him again, with big, haunted eyes and he
knew he should turn on his heel and get the hell out of there,
before he did something reckless.

'I realise I've been difficult this evening and it's a lot to
ask, but...would you hold me again?'

Something exactly like that for instance.

Bad, *bad* idea.

The lustful beast in him clamoured to do it, to get ac-
quainted with all the luscious curves and hollows on show.
But in the mental tussle that followed—take shameless advantage of an emotionally vulnerable woman or do the right
thing—the gentleman prince won out.

Just.

'That wouldn't be appropriate,' he said.

'Please. Only for a moment.' Her luminous gaze fixed hopefully on him.

'Why don't I fetch your maid?' he suggested.

'Dorel will fuss and worry and ask lots of questions and I
can't face that right now. Surely, you know how it is? Don't

you have moments when you wished they would just leave you alone?'

Damn it.

He ran a hand through his hair, knowing she had him because, yes, he'd had times like that. Days when he wanted to hide from everyone. But always a servant stood nearby or security hovered on the other side of a door.

So he lifted the bed covers and helped her climb in, and while she snuggled down he heeled off his shoes, placed his watch on the nightstand then lay down beside her. Instantly, she flowed into his arms, tucking her head beneath his chin. Like she belonged there.

Her perfume enveloped him. An elegant classic that was familiar, but which he'd never found quite so appealing before. Seb cleared his throat.

'How many times have you experienced an attack?' That was good. Get on to something practical, something that would distract him from the heady scent, the supple limbs, and enticing curves of the woman in his arms.

'Five. Always at night. But this has been the worst.' Her fingers toyed with the edge of his collar. 'I hate how helpless I feel. Being so out of control.'

He remembered the glasses lined up at the banquet. 'And you like to be in control of everything?'

'Don't you?'

His life had been troubled much less by the protocols that governed hers. He'd taken a grim satisfaction in flouting the ones that had. Less so now his cousin was monarch, but he didn't relish control. It smacked too much of his father's regimented world.

'I prefer spontaneity,' he said. 'It's good for the soul to let things just happen every now and then.'

'I can't indulge in that. I have too much work to do.' She adjusted her position, and her thighs brushed against his.

'But surely even a queen is allowed days off,' he said through suddenly gritted teeth.

'I can't afford to. Not everyone agreed with the changes to the succession and I know some of them are waiting for me to fail. I can't give them any excuse to doubt me. Papa started the monarchy on a new path but we discussed the ways we can help our people even more. I have to make those things happen.'

Seb heard the determination in that statement. But also the fear that not all her countrymen supported her and shared her vision. What allies did this young queen have?

He tightened his embrace.

'How have you managed your attacks in the past?'

'I haven't,' she said with a bitter laugh. 'I just hid in my rooms until they were over. I've never told anyone about them.'

'Not even your doctor?'

Her hair tickled his chin as she shook her head.

Even though tonight she'd been confrontational and he bore a scar as a perpetual reminder of this woman's temper, the thought of her dealing with her attacks all alone crushed something inside him.

'Tonight you don't have to get through it alone. You have me to help,' he said, giving her back a reassuring rub, and for his pains discovering the delicate ridge of her spine.

She made a soft sound, like a sigh of relief. 'When I was a girl, if I was upset or worried, Papa would distract me by telling a story. It always made me feel better.' She nestled closer. 'Perhaps you could do that?'

Seriously? This was a first. In bed with a barely dressed woman and all the entertainment she wanted from him was stories?

'Er...that's not my forte.'

She tilted her head to look up at him. 'You told all sorts of tales when you ran the auction tonight.'

'Hardly the same thing.'

'Please.' She pressed a palm over his sternum in supplication.

Why, *why* hadn't he stayed in his own rooms? Left her team to sort this out.

She was silent. Waiting…

Okay, he'd got himself into this and if, to extricate himself again, he had to be Seb the storyteller, so be it.

'Once upon a time there was a beautiful queen,' he began, 'who was brave and strong but thought she had to slay every dragon single-handed.'

Agnesse's soft huff of breath feathered through his shirt, warming flesh and bone. Right over his heart.

Seb swallowed hard, then said, 'But when it got too bad she put on her favourite nightwear, the one strewn with magical daisies, and remembered all the faith her beloved papa had in her.'

Her face was hidden, but he knew for a certainty she'd just smiled at that.

'Daisies were his favourite flowers,' she said.

'Because he knew they contained magic. Magic that would help a clever princess become a great queen.'

Her fingers made a little fist in his shirt front. 'I don't feel like a great queen. I feel like I'm never quite good enough. I badly want to make Papa proud. But it's been hard. I miss him so much, Seb.'

His name again. And said in such a small, faraway voice. Compassion for this grieving woman made him kiss the top of her head, then turn his cheek against her hair. 'Trust me, he would be very proud of you.'

Her fingers crept higher, slipping inside his shirt to caress the hollow at the base of his throat.

'What did you mean earlier, about not everyone being blessed by kindly fathers?' she asked quietly.

He'd regretted revealing that much about himself and he'd hated the flash of pity he'd seen in her expression when he had.

When he didn't answer she lifted her head to look him in the eye. 'Seb, was your father unkind?'

And damn it, there was the pity again. But something else, too. A compassion that warmed him—and, surprisingly, loosened his tongue.

'Mostly he was indifferent. But occasionally, yes, he was unkind.'

An understatement.

'Why was he unkind?' Her soft voice was full of disbelief.

Why indeed? The question Seb had asked himself for much of his thirty-two years. He'd stopped when he'd decided the only man who could truly answer it was already gone. Or perhaps because he knew the answer anyway: it was because Seb had survived.

'On my fourth birthday my father announced to me that he wished I'd never been born.'

Agnesse gasped and slid an arm around his waist. 'I'm so sorry. Do you want to talk about it?'

Seb's earliest memory was from that night. When his father had burst into his room. Roaring drunk and savage with it.

I lost her because of you, you little monster, he'd spat, spraying spittle everywhere. *You killed her. It's your fault. I wish you had died instead.*

Then two footmen had rushed in with Leo's father, who'd yelled at his brother to pull himself together and slapped him hard across the face. Prince Georg had broken down, sobbing uncontrollably as they dragged him from the room. A nanny was sent to settle Seb again, but once she had gone, he'd crept from his bed and slept under it all night and for a whole month after, in case his father came back.

He'd never told anyone, not even Leo, about that night. No one else ever spoke of it. Certainly, his father had never apologised, never took back what he'd said to his young son. While Seb had tried to bury that memory, the agony of it had never truly gone away. His only surviving parent hadn't wanted him.

His father had been dead for seven years but all that bitter, blighting hurt still resurfaced now.

Agnesse had turned her cheek to his chest and pressed her body against the length of his. He could easily lose himself in the comfort of that. So easily. But he couldn't allow that to happen.

'That's a story for another day,' he said, shifting his weight, releasing her from his arms instead. 'And now you're feeling better perhaps it would be best if I go. Your team will be worrying.'

Better to go, yes, but not what his body demanded when she looked at him with soft, unguarded eyes, or trailed burning fingertips over his skin. Not when he felt the press of her breasts against him and the tantalising heat of her body next to his.

'They'll know you'd have called them if they were needed. Stay,' she said, lifting a hand to his jaw. 'Just a bit longer. Please.'

A fingertip found his scar. 'I'm sorry about this,' she said, stroking it gently, then shocked him by pressing her lips to it. She leant back and looked up at him with a bashful smile.

'There, I've kissed it better.'

It was the briefest of touches, but it sent his heart clattering around in his chest.

Now her gaze darkened and dropped to his mouth. 'Will you kiss me again? Like you did on the dance floor.'

Oh, God, yes.

'No. That would be a very bad idea.'

'You did it before.'

'And I shouldn't have.'

'But you wanted to get even.'

He released a strand of hair caught in her eyelashes. 'In the moment, yes. But now I apologise. That was not the act of a gentleman.'

'What if I want you to this time?'

'No,' he said firmly, as much for his benefit as hers. They were not going there.

'It's one kiss. One little kiss. How could that hurt?'

Lord, she knew *nothing*.

Her face fell. 'Is it because I'm not good enough? The famous playboy is in bed with me and he won't even kiss me. Do I lack something all your other women had?' Her eyes sparked with anger. 'You took Sofia d'Onzain to bed just because you were bored. Yet, you won't kiss me at all. She must be so much more attractive than I am,' she snapped, flinging herself from the bed and stomping to the bathroom.

Seb collapsed backwards onto the covers and stared at the ceiling. He *definitely* should have stayed in his own suite. First, she hated his guts; now she wanted kisses.

Give him strength.

He exhaled heavily, climbed from the bed, and crossed to the closed door of the bathroom.

'It's not that I don't want to,' he said, raising his voice to be heard through the heavy wood and the sound of a tap running.

The water stopped. 'Then why won't you kiss me? You were happy enough to do it when there was an audience.' The door flew open. 'Is *that* the problem? You need someone to see. Shall I call in my maid? Our security? Give them a show.'

'Agnesse,' he warned.

'Oh, don't bother.' She shoved past him and headed back to bed. 'Don't worry, your virtue is safe with me. I'm the Ice Queen, remember. No man in his right mind would want to touch me.'

He heard the hurt; how could he not? He'd have to be made of ice himself to have missed it, and despite everything his chest clenched. He padded back to the bed, sank down beside her. She'd curled up under the covers, with her back to him. A small, blonde-haired ball of misery.

'You're an attractive woman. Who wouldn't want to kiss

you? But surely, you can see it would be crazy for us to give in to the impulse. Especially in here. Alone.'

'Afraid you won't be able to control yourself?' The snide comeback was muffled by her pillow.

'Yes, actually. That's precisely what scares me.'

She turned her head to peek up at him. 'So you do find me attractive.'

'Yes. But I already told you that. Now it looks like you're fishing for compliments. And that's *not* an attractive quality.'

But Agnesse was grinning, then looking coy, and now, Heaven help him, she'd shuffled closer. Her hands were on his chest and she gazed up at him through her lashes. 'So kiss me. Just once. To show me you mean it.'

Her hand slid up to his neck and pulled his face down towards her. 'Look, I'll even make it easier for you.' She closed her eyes and puckered up.

The last time he'd had sex with a woman she'd been wearing expensive, barely there black lace underwear. She'd draped herself over the bed in a practised pose.

Yet, this woman, dressed in daisy-strewn shorts with her eyes squeezed shut, sent lust screaming through him.

'I really am trying to be the gentleman here,' he said, his voice gruff. Maybe he was attempting to convince himself even more than her.

Her fingers slid upward, to curl around his neck and caress the hair at the back of his head. A ripple of awareness tingled over his scalp.

'I don't want the gentleman. I want the playboy.' There was a thread of vulnerability in her voice now. Like a plea, not to be rejected again. Seb remembered that bastard of a fiancé, the things he'd implied about her. Cold. Unresponsive. That wasn't the woman he'd kissed on the dance floor or who gazed up at him now.

Okay.

One kiss.

Surely, he could handle that?

He wanted those shadows gone from her beautiful blue eyes. He wanted that hurt gone from her lovely face altogether. He let her bring their faces closer. Their mouths to meet. There it was again, the jolt of energy that shook him. Need and desire surged to life. But he'd control it.

It would just be a kiss.

Seb slid his hands into her hair, fingers gently cupping her skull so he could hold her closer and increase the pressure of their mouths. She tasted of everything a man could want, like sunshine and happiness and wild, untrammelled passion. He followed eagerly when she rolled onto her back and pulled him down on top of her.

A few moments more, then he'd stop.

Her hands slid down his back, her fingers tugging his shirt loose from his trousers, and then there was the hot glide of them over his naked back.

Seb groaned. Shifted his position so he was stretched out over her. But he couldn't touch anything. There were bed-clothes and an adorable daisy-covered sleep set in his way. And, boy, did he want to touch.

With an open mouth she kissed him again, sliding her tongue to tangle with his. There was more enthusiasm than skill, but the impact rocketed through him all the same. He was getting lost, losing his grip, losing control. Phrases he'd never used in connection with a woman. He always remained emotionally detached. Always. It was a matter of self-preservation.

Could he do it? Make love to Agnesse and not get involved? The woman who'd haunted his dreams since the moment he set eyes on her. Who'd been the fantasy creature he'd measured every lover against since that day. Wanting her memory to be eclipsed by another and yet never finding a woman who had.

And the fantasy was nothing compared to the living, breathing woman writhing beneath him, tugging urgently at his clothes. Her hands were trying to push his trousers down his hips; when they couldn't they dipped beneath the waistband of his trousers, caressing the small of his back, then lower to the rise of his buttocks. He groaned and ground his hips against her.

He stopped fighting it. He wasn't strong enough, after all. He rose up, dragged his shirt over his shoulders, and flung it on the floor, tore the sheets and duvet out of his way. Then he was back on her, his hands beneath the hem of that tantalising, whisper-thin cami, pushing it higher, exposing her breasts to his hungry gaze—and mouth. When he laved them with his tongue, she cried out, shoving her hands into his hair to keep his head where it was. When he took one rosy, puckered nipple between his teeth her hips arched up off the bed.

'Seb,' she panted. 'Oh, Seb.'

He'd never heard anything more profoundly arousing than that soft plea. For a plea it was. To take her higher, to show her more. And he would, all in good time. But she was wriggling, frantically trying to get out of her shorts, and they'd snagged halfway down her hips. His shirt was off. Her nightwear all but gone. His erection strained painfully against his fly.

'Slow down,' he groaned, as much to himself as to her. This was going way too fast. And not fast enough. He wanted to be inside her with a fervour he'd never known. Her body was perfection, as if some celestial creature had read his mind and created a woman just for him. The feel of her skin, the way her breasts filled his palms, the flare of her hips, voluptuous and fertile.

Fertile?

That pulled him up short.

'Wait,' he said. 'Are you protected?'

She gazed up at him, uncomprehending. Devouring him with those stunning blue eyes, but saying nothing.

He took that as a no.

He had protection in his own suite but going back for it was out of the question. The beast inside him howled in frustration, but this was stopping now. However much he wanted her he would never, *ever* risk getting a woman pregnant.

Although…

He mightn't be prepared, but this grand hotel surely would be.

In the bathroom his faith was rewarded. Amidst the high-end toiletries and designer perfumes, was a discreet but generous stash of condoms.

Seb grabbed a handful in his size, sent up a prayer of thanks to the gods of housekeeping and headed back to the bedroom.

Several condom packets landed on the nightstand. Agnesse was a little daunted by the number. How many times did he expect to do this? Seb stripped off the rest of his clothes then knelt between her splayed thighs, ripping open a packet with his teeth and rolling the condom over his erection.

She watched; how could she not? A naked Seb was a sight to behold.

He lowered himself down, supported on one elbow. But in those moments, when he'd left her to search the bathroom, reality had intruded and she'd become acutely aware that in her urgency to get naked with him, and finally banish her lingering fear that she was frigid, she'd been inexpertly dragging off her own clothes. How gauche. She hid her dismay in the pillow.

A hand slid to the nape of her neck. 'Look at me, Agnesse,' he said, gently. And she did, though not where he meant. She sneaked a glance down to the jut of his erection—and gulped.

It was thick and long. How was that ever going to fit?

'*Chérie*, you've done this before, *oui*?'

That lapse into French, with its tender endearment, stole around her heart like the caress of warm fingers.

She gazed up into eyes turned black with desire. A little of her failing confidence flowed back.

'Not for a while and even then, it was only once.' She was embarrassed at how little experience she'd had compared to

Seb. Would she be disappointing, put her limbs in the wrong place, not know where to touch, not please him at all? Would it be just another bout of sex to him?

'If you want to stop, *chérie*, we stop. We only go as far as you want.'

But the thing was she didn't want to stop. She wanted him to touch her, to kiss her breasts again, and feel sweet pleasure arrow straight to that place between her thighs. And she wanted to touch him, to run her tongue along the vein that bulged in sharp relief on his biceps, to put her mouth to that ridge of muscle low on his abdomen. Perhaps even lower, if she had the courage.

She reached up to cup his jaw, and her confidence soared when he closed his eyes and turned his head to press his lips into her palm. Maybe he did that with his other women, but she didn't care. Tonight he was with her.

'No, I don't want to stop.'

'As long as you are sure?'

She nodded.

But as he eased into her she gasped; it was too tight, too much. She struggled against him. But then his mouth was at her cheek, breathing soft words of encouragement. A litany of delight, matched by the caress of hands as one slid along her inner thigh, hooked beneath her knee and opened her wider for him. When he pushed in next time it was easier.

And it felt good.

He pulled back, and she felt him brace and this time sink deeper.

She felt so full of him, almost overwhelmed by the sensation. But she wanted this. She wanted to get lost in him and leave nothing of the old Agnesse behind. Tonight she would finally say goodbye to the Ice Queen.

She wanted something else, too; she wanted to see him come undone. This man, who'd been a lover to so many other women. She wanted a piece of him that was just hers and would only ever be hers. A sliver of emotion, of his *heart*; something of his that she would hold forever, even after this night together had become a distant memory.

Her first and only time had been with Eerik, and it had been painful. But that was so long ago, did it even count anymore? Nothing she'd felt then could compare with the glide of Seb's body inside hers.

Something within her that had been closed off and wound tight was unfurling. Because of him.

This.

This felt like her first time.

She forgot he'd ever been her enemy. As his hands caressed her, cupped her breasts, sent her pleasure soaring, she wondered if that man had ever really existed. His breathing was shallower, harsher; sweat glistened over his body. He was moving faster, thrusting harder. But she was with him, matching every groan, every sigh, every devouring kiss.

Until his hand slipped between them and his thumb slid right to where she was wet and hot.

Her breath stuttered in her throat. He rolled his hips and thumb with the same relentless rhythm, and now she was gasping and writhing and crying out. Incoherent, abandoned.

Triumphant.

Agnesse, the Ice Queen of Ellamaa, buried her face in her lover's neck and gave herself up to glorious, transcendental passion at last.

CHAPTER FIVE

THE GLIDE OF a palm along her flank roused Agnesse from her sleep. She cracked open an eye.

Oh now, there was a sight to wake up to. Propped up on one arm and gazing down on her was a tousled sex god, sporting a gorgeous lopsided smile.

'You're looking very pleased with yourself,' she said.

'I've just made love with a warm, giving beauty.' He took her mouth in a soft kiss. 'Why wouldn't I be pleased?'

She trailed her fingers along his jaw, fascinated by the scratch of early-morning stubble. 'Made love?' she repeated, dreamily.

The shutters came down at once.

'It's a figure of speech, Agnesse. Call it plain sex if you want. A coarser term would fit, too.' He captured those caressing fingers and pressed a perfunctory kiss to them. 'But I think that would jar in this beautiful room.'

Not love, then, or anything close to it, and he was keen she knew it. But there was nothing plain or coarse about what they'd done together. It was a revelation more like. Her body had responded in ways she'd never imagined it could. Already it was hungry for more. A throb of need beat low in her pelvis.

But he was untangling their limbs, throwing aside the sheets. 'It would be better if I weren't seen leaving your suite, and there'd be much less chance of that if I go now.'

She forced herself not to cling. Not to ask if they could meet up again.

What for, Agnesse? More casual sex? That was all there was on offer and however tempting that might be, what would be the point? Seb was not the man to give her what she really needed. A reliable prince consort for her country. A steadfast man to support her.

However, there was no reason to deny herself the pleasure of ogling as a stark-naked Seb walked about the room, gathering up his clothes. She rolled onto her stomach, propped her chin on her hands, and watched him. The spectacle of him taking *off* his clothes would be better, but this came a close second. She'd had no idea it could be so engrossing. He was tanned all over except for the paler skin of his buttocks. They disappeared from view as he stepped into tight black jersey boxers. But the fabric clung lovingly to every taut muscle so her gaze lingered there, until they, too, were covered by beautifully tailored trousers. Agnesse bit her lip as the zipper went up, recalling the pleasure she'd received when that zipper had come down. She mourned the loss of his bare torso but there was something enthralling about the flex of muscle and sinew as a man shrugged into his shirt.

He came back to her, smiling slightly at her rapt attention. He collected his watch from the nightstand.

'Thank you. Last night turned out much better than I'd anticipated.'

Her brows shot up. 'If rescuing me from my bathroom floor was better than you imagined, you must have had really low expectations.'

His expression tightened with concern then warmed again as it dropped to her breasts, plumped up between her and the mattress. 'But how much more delightful did our evening become after that?'

She fluttered her eyelashes at him and he chuckled as he bent to drop a parting kiss to her brow.

She was okay with him leaving like this. Really, she was.

She would revel in the discovery that Agnesse, the frigid queen, was not so cold, after all, and not let Seb's departure spoil the moment.

Only once he'd gone she felt the keenest disappointment, as if some vital element of her peace of mind had just walked out the door with him.

The stroll back into his suite was short, uneventful, and more importantly, unobserved. Other than by the respective security teams who were paid well for their discretion. Walking away and leaving Agnesse, all warm and willing, in bed had been the harder act to accomplish. Her blond hair tumbling about her shoulders, the plushness of her breasts, and her absolute focus as she watched him dress, nearly had him stripping off again and climbing back into bed beside her. He didn't do it because what if he'd slept again afterwards?

Slept? That had been a first. He'd never actually *slept* with a woman. It could lead to them getting the wrong idea. So he'd always left.

Until he hadn't.

Agnesse Toivonen was no Ice Queen but a woman of warmth and passion and curves—Lord, *those curves*. She was vulnerable, too, though she tried to hide it, and even as he told himself there would be nothing further between them, something warm and tender settled deep inside him; a need to protect her.

That was impossible, of course. When did Seb get involved with a woman who needed anything but sex from him? He *never* promised more and steered clear of any woman whom he thought might have longer-term expectations.

Still, last night had turned out a thousand times better than he'd imagined. He was still musing on that when his phone rang. Seb's brow creased when he saw the caller.

'Sofia?'

'Sebastien, thank God. Please tell me you're still in Vienna. I'm in a scrape and I need your help.'

What was he now, Chief Rescuer of Damsels?

'I've been seeing someone, and I don't know how it happened, but he's started talking love and marriage and—' her voice dropped to a horrified whisper '—*babies.*'

Seb almost laughed. A woman less inclined to settle down than Sofia d'Onzain was hard to imagine. A darker thought occurred. She was the same as he was. Just as determined to stay single and childless.

'He's got in touch to say he's coming over. With something important to say. I think he's going to propose. He's awfully sweet and I don't want to hurt him, but he's not getting the message. Could you come down to my room? Be here when he arrives. And answer the door to him, half-naked or something. Surely, then he'd realise I'm not right for him.'

'You're a grown woman. Just tell him marriage isn't what you want.'

'Don't you think I've tried that? He's determined he can change my mind. *Please*, Sebastien.' He could practically hear her eyelashes batting.

'Okay, if only to save some poor devil from losing his head over the least marriage-minded woman on the continent.'

There were squeals of delight and a babble of effusive thanks, so he raised his voice to make sure she heard his one condition.

'But my shirt stays on, Sofia.'

Agnesse was due to leave the hotel at ten. But by eight she was already showered, dressed, and seated at the desk in her suite, giving her two precious hours to catch up on the work she'd failed to do last night. Her late-evening plans had been thoroughly derailed. A panic attack followed by a night of mind-blowing passion with her former arch-enemy had not been on her agenda.

She'd apologised to Dorel and Christina for kicking them out. She told them she'd been feeling overwhelmed by the events at the gala and needed some time to herself. Neither woman made mention of the guest who *was* allowed into the suite and who'd remained there until 5 a.m.

A tray with a full cafetière and a pretty china cup and saucer sat on her desk. Agnesse rarely ate breakfast. She preferred starting her day with coffee. And the aroma wafting towards her was especially inviting this morning. She took a sip and sighed in contentment.

'Dorel, can we find out which coffee this is, please?'

Her maid, busy with preparations for their departure, paused.

'It's the one we always request,' she said, looking puzzled. 'I checked with the butler.'

Agnesse sipped again, savouring the deep, dark flavours that rolled across her tongue. 'Perhaps it's something about the roast they've used.' It really was superb. 'Will you ask them for a bag or two to take with us?'

Dorel raised a brow but picked up the house phone to relay the queen's request.

In the middle of Agnesse's desk sat her laptop. A manila folder containing the report she failed to read last night was by her left elbow. And to the right, her pen and notebook. Her brow creased. Its elastic closure was twisted. She quickly set it to rights.

There, perfect. Now she could start work.

Yet still, that manila folder lay untouched.

Out on the roof terrace the trees swayed and their leaves rustled faintly in the breeze. Agnesse listened to the pleasant sound as her fingers dawdled across the smooth, polished marquetry of the desk and recalled, with a shivering delight, the astonishing feel of silken skin over rock-hard muscle. With a dreamy sigh, she propped her chin on her hand and studied the floral display on a nearby side table. A bowl of roses in such gorgeous shades of blush and dusky pinks that she couldn't help but smile at them. She'd stayed here on several occasions, but the hotel really had pulled out all the stops for this visit. It had never been quite so enticing before. She was genuinely sorry she was having to leave soon.

'Are we working this morning or daydreaming?' Dorel said with a wry look. 'It's all the same to me but don't expect my sympathy when you get grumpy later about everything left on your to-do list.'

'I do not get grumpy,' Agnesse said, sitting upright then wincing as she felt the sharp pull on tender flesh. The stash of condoms at her bedside had shrunk by three by the time Seb had left her. The man had some stamina. But then, so did she. She'd matched him, pace for pace.

And how she marvelled at that.

Eerik had said she was frigid. She knew now she wasn't. At least not with Seb. The things he made her feel with his hand and his mouth, and his...

She pushed the manila folder away from her. It was pointless. No stuffy old report was going to hold her attention after last night.

'I'll read the morning papers instead,' she announced.

Agnesse usually read a curated selection of stories online, and her maid looked surprised by this break in routine.

'Don't you know that spontaneity is good for the soul, Dorel?'

'Judging by how gingerly you sat in that chair,' Dorel muttered, 'I don't think it was your soul enjoying spontaneity last night.' She collected the newspapers from the sideboard then abruptly dumped several back down again.

'What's wrong with those?' Agnesse said, alerted by the maid's suspiciously innocent expression.

Dorel waved a hand. 'They're far too trashy. They won't be of any interest.'

But Agnesse knew her maid too well to be mollified by that.

She pushed to her feet and crossed to the sideboard, gasping in horror when she saw versions of the same story splashed across every front page of the abandoned papers.

Her dreamy recollections of last night evaporated instantly.

They all bore the same photo, which was almost a mirror image of that infamous one. Only this time it was Agnesse staring, frozen in shock, as Seb walked away.

Her hairdo askew, the back of her hand to her burning cheek, her precise emotions at that moment were writ large across her face. Years of careful image management, her father's patient tutoring, had been blown to pieces by fifteen seconds of that playboy's mouth on hers.

Love Struck, read the headlines. *Smooching with the enemy.*

Agnesse threw the newspapers back in the sideboard. Oh, that man! Why did their every encounter have to end in lurid headlines?

Because he turned her into a crazed version of herself. Her mind rebelled at everything he represented while her body couldn't get enough of him.

Events late last night had rather eclipsed the earlier parts of the evening, but looking at that photo brought Seb's behaviour on the dance floor back into searing relief.

Now I think we are even.

He'd rescued her from her panic attack so she could forgive him that kiss—but not the smug expression as he walked away from her. The look of triumph on his face was galling. In their previous altercation, when she'd been the one walking away, at least she'd had the decency to look filled with righteous anger.

At the time, her mother had been furious, of course. But her father, in his usual calm way, had simply asked why she'd done it. When she'd explained he said he could understand why a protective older sister had behaved the way she had, but perhaps she should reflect on it. He couldn't condone violence and he'd asked her to consider the full story, which he was certain Agnesse probably didn't have. Did she really believe the prince would have ever encouraged Isobel? Was his supposed interest not all in her head? *We know,* he'd said with a rueful glance, *what Isobel can be like.*

And after hearing Seb's version of events, Agnesse knew her papa was right.

But he hadn't known about the other thing, about *the smile…* and those cruel, dismissive things she'd heard the prince say about her afterwards. That, as much as Isobel's tears, had made her act the way she had. That and something about Seb himself. Something about the effect he had on her. As if he reached beneath all her careful composure and found the living, breathing woman, not the painstakingly constructed royal image.

Part of her wanted so badly to be found. It was why she'd seduced him.

She'd seduced *him.* She went hot at the thought.

Last night she'd not been Agnesse, the Ice Queen. She'd been another woman entirely. One able to give and receive pleasure. That it happened in the arms of Sebastien von Frohburg was astonishing but also not. The spark had been there from the first time she'd set eyes on him. A spark she'd never felt for another man.

Of course, there was no future in it. Despite what she'd learned about him last night, he was still the unapologetic ladies' man, and hell-bent on pleasure. He could never be the man she needed as her mate through life. If she chose him, she would be choosing most unwisely for Ellamaa. Better to scotch any rumours now before they took hold. The small pang of regret she could live with. But not the disaster of making someone like him prince consort of her people.

The beguiling room and its pleasures had suddenly palled. Even if it meant sitting in her jet on the tarmac for several hours to await their flight slot, she wanted to leave Vienna now.

Christina counselled against using the hotel's main entrance. 'The press are there in numbers, ma'am.'

But Agnesse wasn't going to hide. So Seb had kissed her.

So what? If she pretended it was nothing, the press would get bored and move on. The best way to do that was to front it out. Take the positives—that she wasn't made of ice after all—and get on with her life.

The questions came at her as soon as she exited the hotel.

Were she and the prince an item now?

'No.'

Was he a good dancer? Was that a real kiss?

'Yes and no,' she said with her very best regal smile.

Did she know he'd spent the night with Sofia d'Onzain?

She couldn't help it. The smile slipped and her moment's pause was enough for the journalist to pounce.

'Mademoiselle d'Onzain's boyfriend caught them together in her hotel room early this morning. Sofia was barely dressed, apparently.'

The world dipped and swayed. Seb had gone from her bed straight to that of another woman's? How could he? She thought he'd found pleasure in her arms. Was she so disappointing, then? The tightening of her chest almost took her breath.

But she was a Toivonen. They never retreated, nor did they leave the battlefield before delivering the killer blow.

'Where His Highness chooses to spend his time has nothing to do with me,' she said through the lancing pain.

'So you weren't hoping for a relationship with him, then?'

The words spilled out from a place of deep hurt before she could stop them.

'A relationship with Prince Sebastien?' She conjured a tinkle of incredulous laughter for good measure. 'He makes a great show of kissing one woman then takes another to bed in a matter of hours. I'd be scraping the bottom of the dirtiest kind of barrel to have any kind of involvement with the biggest man-whore in Europe. Don't you think?'

She turned her face from the cameras and the rabid interest

of the journalists and climbed into the safety of her waiting car before they could see the truth etched across her features.

That somehow she'd permitted Sebastien von Frohburg to upend her life yet again.

The days and weeks that followed were impossibly busy. No chance at all for Agnesse to meet Seb in person and apologise, because if she knew nothing else, she knew that she had to make a heartfelt apology to him.

Even after she'd been rude to him all night and with little provocation from him, he'd come to her aid. Then *she'd* begged him for sex. Not the other way around.

Oh, the sex. The memories of it consumed her. She knew, with every sensible bone in her body, it could never happen again, but that didn't stop her replaying it over and over in her mind. Mostly when she was alone. So that meant at night. When there was absolutely nothing to distract from her need for him. From the longing for his big, hard body in the bed beside her. Some nights it was so bad she could have wept with frustration.

And with shame.

She'd called him a terrible name. In public. So what if he had gone to another woman's bed after hers? He'd made no promises. He wasn't even acting out of type. And he hadn't said a solitary word to the press in retaliation. In one comment on that fateful morning, he'd told a journalist that she'd been a charming companion all evening. The punch? That was long forgotten. And that kiss? He'd overstepped the mark, but she was a beauty, and who wouldn't want to kiss her?

But then they'd repeated the man-whore remark and that she'd said he was beneath her. After that, his replies had all been *no comment*, until he'd disappeared from the public eye altogether.

Agnesse knew she'd wronged him and that this time she had to make amends by apologising.

She could have phoned him. But the moments when she was free never seemed appropriate. Too early in the day. Too late. Who called to make a grovelling apology in a few minutes shoehorned between meetings or in the car heading towards an evening engagement? Her wrongdoing required more of an occasion than that.

A handwritten letter, even an email, appropriately contrite, may have sufficed, and she'd tried, really she had, but every effort had been abandoned before it was ever sent. Nothing short of seeing him in person would do, so he would see the genuine remorse in her eyes. But she knew she was making excuses and as each day passed, she was only making things worse. Then he'd even disappeared completely from public. Which finally drove her to act.

At last, she summoned her courage and rang...

Leo.

'Hello, Agnesse.'

'Hi...um...how's...how's Violetta?'

'Violetta?' She heard the bemusement, like he knew she'd meant to say another name and bottled it. 'She's good,' he said. 'She's pregnant.'

Agnesse sensed the pride, the joy, and the love all bundled up in that simple statement.

'I'm so happy for you both,' she said, and meant it. Anyone seeing those two together could not mistake the love they shared. It shone from them. And at last, they were going to be parents. She couldn't be happier for them and was only a little ashamed of the stab of envy and longing at their news. A man to love her, a family of her own, it was what she dreamed of for herself one day. If being the Ice Queen didn't get in the way of that hope. But that wasn't why she'd phoned. She stiffened her spine.

'Leo, I need to see Sebastien. But he's apparently disappeared from the face of the earth.'

'Can you blame him?' There was censure there now, which

Agnesse knew she deserved. 'He didn't take those last remarks of yours well. He's not speaking to anyone much.'

'And I'm genuinely sorry for it, Leo. But I need to see him so I can apologise. Properly.'

There was a pause. A prince considering if this queen deserved his help. A fond cousin deciding if he should reveal the whereabouts of his wronged relative.

Eventually, he said, 'Okay. If you really want to see him, I can tell you he's in London. Hiding out at a friend's house. But I'll warn you he's not good company. Snaps your head off at the slightest thing. He may well just fling your apology back in your face.'

Maybe so, but she'd heard a magic word.

London.

She was in Paris. Only an hour or so away, and with a day free of commitments. She could easily be there and back in a few hours with apology delivered, her conscience salved, and hopefully both of them able to move on.

There might never be a better opportunity. She couldn't put it off any longer. She thanked Leo and hung up the phone, then called for her maid and head of security.

'Dorel, you're getting your dream morning. A chance to shop in Paris to your heart's content. But, Christina, we're going to London for the morning.'

CHAPTER SIX

MAN-WHORE.

He'd been called worse and shrugged it off. But Agnesse had believed the worst of him and that had proved harder to dismiss. Why the hell couldn't he move on? It was a month, a whole month, and still he couldn't shake the feeling of regret, the sense that he'd let something of incalculable value slip through his fingers.

Nor the want. He definitely couldn't get that out of his system, and the most unsettling aspect? It wasn't entirely physical. He'd never wanted a woman before for anything other than the obvious. He didn't *need* a woman in his life. So what the hell was wrong with him?

Agnesse represented everything he was determined to avoid—being trapped within the unforgiving hierarchy of a royal family.

He'd thought to divert the strange energies coursing through him by focusing on work. With a laptop and an internet connection he could do that anywhere. Something he'd started as a way to make him financially independent of his father, and the von Frohburg coffers, had grown into so much more.

He'd begun investing at sixteen: start-ups by young people in Grimentz, coffee houses, jewellery designers, fledgling market gardens. Each offered a few thousand euros at most, saved from his allowance. But mostly they worked out and he'd discovered he had an eye for it. He'd branched out, investing more. Bigger, bolder projects: green energy, waste management, as far removed from the realms of a playboy prince as you could get. All done anonymously, so, except for Leo, no one knew. It suited Seb. Let the world judge as it wanted. Let his pompous, elitist relatives continue to see him as feckless and dissolute, beneath them. Because all the while he was amassing a fortune that surpassed any of theirs, that he could wield as he saw fit.

And he was wielding it for good.

After the debacle with Agnesse, he'd tried to bury himself in his work. But Grimentz was a fishbowl and short of locking himself in his rooms, there was no peace to be had from the press.

He'd stayed with a series of friends around Europe, but each time the paparazzi tracked him down. The media wouldn't leave it alone. They were determined there was something between the former enemies.

Yeah, even more enmity.

But Seb maintained a stubborn silence on the matter. Even to Leo, though he knew his cousin had probably guessed. Maybe he'd been right all along. Seb did *like* Agnesse of Ellamaa and maybe that was why it hurt. Not the man-whore insult. With his reputation he couldn't blame her for that. But after their night together, after what they'd done, how they'd talked, that she should still believe without question that he'd gone to another woman's bed? That she'd automatically thought the worst of him? It was that he couldn't bear.

A friend in London was having his Belgravia town house renovated. A planning issue had called a temporary halt to the work, and the property would be sitting empty for at least a week. It was a measure of his state of mind that Seb considered a bare-bones house to be the ideal bolthole. A bed, a bathroom, a fledgling gym in the basement. An annexe out the back for his security team. None of it in the least bit finished yet, but spartan living would suit him.

So he'd thought.

But he hadn't been able to settle. By day, hood up, head down, he'd run incognito through Hyde Park, or hit the basement gym and worked out until he could hardly stand. But the nights were another matter. He'd prowled about the empty house. Restless, confined. On the third night of that torment, he'd gone out.

The bar he'd chosen was cheap and nasty. Perfect for anonymity. Who'd expect a prince to be slumming it in there? Just the place to get blind drunk where no one would notice or care. Except for his security, who'd tried to dissuade him, and when they couldn't, found a table in the shadows and hunkered down to wait it out.

He ignored them, because he was determined to sit there and order whisky until a blonde angel, with a devil's temper and a vicious line in insults, became nothing but a blurred memory.

So it was pure bad luck that the TV in the corner was on a news channel, airing a report about Ellamaa's glamorous young queen and her visit to Paris, the city of lovers, and the lowlife propped at the end of the bar just had to comment.

'City of lovers? She's alone there, though, isn't she? She's a ball-breaker. No wonder she got dumped.'

Seb, nursing drink number seven—or was it eight?—had thrown it back and ordered a refill.

'Needs bringing down a peg, that one. Thinks she's too good for us. Rejecting every man. Look at that poor devil of an ex-fiancé. He practically spelled it out. She's no good in bed.'

The refill went down in one. The empty glass landed with a clatter on the bar.

But the worthless creature hadn't finished. 'Sleeping with Agnesse Toivonen would be like bedding a hunk of frozen meat.'

At that, Seb had got to his feet. He might have staggered as he stood but nevertheless, he'd remembered he'd moved forward, advancing on the owner of that voice. Every instinct in him rebelling against those…those *lies*.

Agnesse of Ellamaa was warm and responsive and brave and vulnerable. And that vile piece of humanity had dared to even breathe her name.

He'd told him to shut his worthless mouth. Seb had received a punch for his pains and another stream of insults aimed at both him and Agnesse.

After that, the swirling, savage red mist had come down.

Seb couldn't recall many of the details, but in the altercation that followed he knew his security team had gone above and beyond their duty. While he, in contrast and to his everlasting shame, had scraped the very bottom of the filthy, slimy barrel that Agnesse had accused him of inhabiting.

The four-storey town house was swathed in scaffolding. A rubble-filled skip sat concealed behind a neat box hedge. The windows were bare of curtains and the rooms empty of furniture, though paint-strewn buckets and ladders were piled in the centre of the room, visible from the front steps.

Behind Agnesse a line of parked cars ran the full length of the street but otherwise, it was deserted. No one around at all, except for Christina and her team, occupying two vehicles at a discreet distance and ordered by their queen to keep a low profile.

Taking a deep breath, Agnesse rang the doorbell.

She wore skinny jeans and a baseball cap, tugged down to hide her face. She carried a big, flat pizza box emblazoned with the logo of the chain it came from. The same logo was splashed across the back of her hoodie. For all anyone knew, workmen in the house had ordered takeaway.

It may be a fancy part of London, but the house was still essentially a family home and small enough that Sebastien might answer the door himself. But despite ringing twice, no angry sex god appeared. Maybe he was somewhere in the bowels of the house and couldn't hear the door. But Leo had said he was definitely here and she'd come here especially, taking the risk of being spotted. She was prising him out of his hidey-hole whatever.

Agnesse jammed her finger against the bell and kept it there. But when almost a minute later there was still no answer, she admitted defeat and swung away. She'd taken three steps down, when the door flew open.

She opened her mouth to speak but the words died in her throat. This house did have a sex god within and it looked like she'd just got him out of bed.

Sleep-mussed hair. Acres of bare chest. Dressed in nothing but button-up jeans with the top one still undone as if he'd just tugged them on. On this lower step she was at eye level with his hips. A narrow line of chest hairs trailed downward to disappear beneath the waistband into the pieces of his anatomy causing the impressive bulge beneath the button fly. Inconveniently, her own nether regions spasmed in recognition.

'You know it's polite to say hello before you start ogling a man.'

Her gaze swept upward to encounter an expression, chilly as a winter's morning. Then she noticed his jaw sported a bruise. The knuckles wrapped round the door were grazed. There were even angry marks on his arms and torso.

Instinctively, she took a step back up towards him. 'You're hurt.'

He shrugged. 'You should see the other guys.'

Guys? There was more than one. He could have been badly injured; he could have ended up in hospital. Her heart twisted; she could have lost him.

Stupid. He wasn't hers to lose, and judging by his expression he'd prefer her to get lost herself right now.

But then—the relief—he stood aside for her to enter the house. He closed the door behind her and led the way down a long passageway. Past walls of bare plaster and wires, poking out where lamps would be fitted. Into the kitchen space at the back of the house. At its centre was a vast marble-topped island unit. The rest of the space was littered with cupboards and appliances awaiting installation, all still wrapped in their protective coverings.

Here, Agnesse discovered she hadn't got Seb out of bed at all. She'd interrupted his breakfast. On the marble counter was a plate of half-eaten toast, a cafetière of coffee, and a pink mug with its handle missing and bearing the logo Gin o'clock. Where had he found that? Dug it from that skip out front? Such a frivolous thing in his big hand was so incongruous she almost laughed, but she knew if she started she wouldn't be able to stop, and nervous, hysterical giggling would not impress this man.

As she set the pizza box on the counter, he took a swig from the mug. 'What do you want?'

You, she nearly said—battered and bruised, unwelcoming as he was, and now drinking out of that crazy mug. Had she ever seen anything more adorably sexy? How inconvenient that the only man to ever make her heart beat faster could not have been less suitable as husband material, and clearly was not happy to see her.

The knuckles wrapped around the mug looked painful.

'What happened to your hand?' she said, fighting the mad desire to press her lips to them and soothe the hurt.

'A small disagreement,' he said.

'A disagreement that got you hurt? What was it about?'

His gaze clashed briefly with hers. 'It doesn't matter.'

'But you were in a fight?'

A curt nod.

'Where on earth was your security team?'

He sent her a long, level look and remained silent.

He couldn't possibly mean… Her jaw fell open. 'It *was* your security team. I hope they've been fired.'

'Certainly not. They received a substantial bonus and an abject apology from me. I picked a fight with a…' He bared his teeth in a grimace. 'With a worthless lowlife. The team had to step in. Apparently, I took violent exception at their attempts to restrain me.'

'Apparently? You don't remember.' Her eyes narrowed on him. 'You were drunk.'

He stared over her head at the shell of a kitchen with all its swanky appliances still concealed in their packaging. 'I was in need of a crutch. Alcohol fit the bill last night.'

Why did he need that last night? Why did he need a crutch at all? A horrible notion nagged at her. 'Was the fight because of me?' she asked.

His gaze locked on hers and held but he didn't say anything.

And that was answer enough because then she knew. He'd been defending her reputation. Not his. The sting of shame burned like acid in her stomach.

It was well past time for that apology but faced with his hostility and this new, humiliating revelation, her courage failed her. She twisted her hands in the hoodie front. It smelled of the previous owner's perfume, sickly and too sweet. Agnesse's stomach gave a heave.

He watched the movement then tipped his chin at her. 'Where did you get that?'

'From the same place I got the pizza.' She smoothed the front out again. The nausea had passed.

His brow knotted. 'You bought it?'

She chewed on her lip. 'I actually got one of the team to buy it.'

His mug landed back on the counter with such a clatter she marvelled that it remained in one piece. 'How, *buy*?' he said.

'We ordered pizza and when it arrived Christina offered the delivery driver a fifty pound tip for the pizza and the uniform.'

When he stared at her open-mouthed, she added, 'I thought she'd be less intimidating to the girl who delivered it than one of the men on my team. To be fair, Christina was quite reluctant to do it at all.'

'I bet she was. She's one of *the* most recognisable close-protection operatives on the planet, who everyone knows works for you. Whatever you paid that delivery driver it won't be enough. She'll have gone straight to the press. The story will be everywhere by lunchtime. They've probably already got pictures of you dressed like that standing on the doorstep.'

'How could they? I looked like someone delivering pizza. That was the point and no one even knows I'm in London.'

'You can't be that naive. They'll know. They always know where we are.'

'They didn't know *you* were here.'

'They will now,' he said with a glower.

Her chin went up. 'Look, I came all this way and went to all this trouble to apologise for what I said about you to the press.'

'You could have phoned to do that.'

'And would you have taken my call?'

His mouth tightened. Well, that was a no. But she *had* come to apologise and even if he wasn't in a receptive mood, she might as well get on with it.

'I'm sorry. I was in the wrong, but you could be a bit more gracious about it. And you did go straight to the bed of another woman after mine. I wouldn't have minded but you made up some story about not wanting to be seen leaving. That was a lie. You had another date that night.'

'Not true, but you believed it without question.'

'You were *seen*,' she accused him. It had hurt then, and damn but this was hurting her all over again.

'Said who?'

'The press.' She wanted to punch him again. So smug. So calmly standing there when he'd had a second assignation that night. How had she believed that being with her would be somehow different? Once a playboy, always a playboy.

'And they always tell the truth, do they?'

'You were seen in the rooms of Sofia d'Onzain and she was wearing little more than a satisfied-by-Sebastien smile. Isn't that a signature look for your conquests?' she said, nastily, trying to contain all the hurt that was threatening to overwhelm her. Why was she allowing this man to have such power over her?

Emerald splinters flashed in his eyes. 'How is it you claim you're here to apologise and yet once again you're throwing insults at me?'

'You're right. I should never have come. Who you sleep with is none of my business.'

'Then why does it bother you so much?'

'It doesn't.' Though a silly knot of tears was forming in her throat.

He took a step closer. 'And yet, I think if I say one more hurtful thing you'll cry.'

'Nonsense.' She dipped her head, hiding her face beneath the brim of her cap.

He was right in front of her now. 'I did not sleep with Sofia,' he said, lifting her chin with a forefinger so she had to meet his gaze and see the truth there. 'She asked me to make it look as if I had to deter an overeager suitor of hers.'

'Is that supposed to make you sound good? Hurting someone else doesn't exonerate you.'

He was carefully disentangling her ponytail from her cap. The brush of his fingers sent shivers down her spine.

'Trust me. I thought I was doing the man a kindness.' Seb placed the cap on the counter beside her. 'He was the sort Sofia would normally make mincemeat of. The irony is she's the one besotted now.' He shook his head in disbelief. 'They've even got engaged.'

'Not everyone is as commitment averse as you.'

'I'm not averse to others getting hitched,' he said. 'It's just not for me. I thought it wasn't for Sofia, either. Let's just say the examples we've both witnessed haven't given either of us much confidence in the institution of marriage.'

He sounded oddly wistful, regretful even, and a new and surprisingly painful thought occurred to her.

'Do you love her?'

'Sofia?' He barked in laughter. *'Mon dieu, non.'*

Agnesse nearly slumped in relief. And finally understood then that she'd been fooling herself. The need to apologise in person, while real, had also been a convenient excuse.

She'd been desperate to see him again.

That was what all those sleepless nights had been about. Seb had got under her skin.

'I like Sofia. I sincerely wish her every happiness with her fiancé, and I've no regrets about our times together.'

Agnesse couldn't help it. The words were out before she could question the wisdom of them.

'Do you regret our night together?'

The corner of his mouth titled. 'After all those terrible things you said about me, you mean?' He grazed the back of a knuckle along her cheek. 'No,' he said. 'Not even for a moment.'

He'd meant that gesture as something gentle and soothing, she was sure, but it didn't soothe. It ignited the torch she held for him and sent it roaring into a full-on furnace. The flame he'd first set burning that night in Vienna. No, it went further back than that. He'd set something alight in her all those years ago with that smile of his. As no one else ever had.

Or perhaps ever *could*? And this might be her last time with him. Her last chance to feel again what he made her feel that night.

There was no other way to describe what she did next; she *launched* herself at him. Her mouth, her hands, her ice-maiden's *heart*; she plastered everything she had to him. He staggered a little, caught off balance, until his backside hit the marble counter and he braced against it, using it to keep them both upright.

She didn't notice. She just kissed him, open-mouthed and ravenous. Until he hissed in pain.

She pulled back, 'I'm so sorry.'

'No, it's okay, it's just…' He gestured to the bruise. Gentle hands cupped her face, pulling her back towards him. 'Kiss me again.'

She pressed her lips tenderly to the bruise at the corner of his mouth. 'There, is that better?' She took his hands from her face and pressed soft kisses to his grazed knuckles.

She held his gaze and watched it darken. Felt the sudden shift in his body, the surge of energy, of a new and thrilling tension.

He untangled their fingers so he could snake a hand to her waist, then lower to her behind, so he could press their bodies closer. She heeled off her shoes and they flew to land with a bang against one of the boxes.

Breaking the contact to strip off their clothes was a torment in itself. Who knew where her jeans and panties ended up. They were gone from her and that was all that mattered.

He stripped off the jeans, kicking them away. He lifted her easily onto the counter. The marble was shockingly cold against her naked skin, but then he was there, hot and hard and right where the persistent ache had been since that night in Vienna. She groaned as her head fell back. How much she'd yearned to feel this again.

But...

'Wait,' he said, dragging his mouth from hers. She didn't want to. She spread her legs wider, crushed herself even more intimately into him. But his hands on her hips held her back. *'Wait,'* he repeated.

She was panting and naked in a stranger's kitchen and she didn't care. She wanted him.

'Chérie, we need protection.'

Of course. She hadn't even thought about it.

'I'll be right back.'

She heard him pounding up the stairs and into a room overhead. It was dispiriting to discover he was prepared, even here, in case a willing female happened along. Did it matter to him that it was her? Could it just have easily been another woman

as far as he was concerned? With his history would he really
have been celibate this last month?

Then he was back and sheathed and ready, just for her, and
she no longer cared about his other women because at that
moment he was hers alone.

She was as shameless as the Comtesse d'Onzain and yes,
both her daughters. She crooked a finger at him and spread
her thighs wider in invitation. Because the comtesse was right;
standing there in his naked perfection and fully aroused, Sebastien von Frohburg really was a magnificent beast.

With a growl he strode over to her, possessing her mouth,
grasping her hips, and sinking to the hilt in one sublime move.
Agnesse moaned in relief. This was what she'd dreamed of
every night since Vienna. The hot, hard, remorseless power
of him surging into her, her legs clamped about his waist, his
hands fisted in her hair. Nothing but his body and hers locked
together.

It was fast and furious. Neither of them in control. Just
a frenzied coupling in an empty building site of a house. It
could have been sordid. But it wasn't. It was exactly what
she'd craved. Seb moved her, made her feel things she never
had before. But then the doubts crept in. Did he feel the same?

He rested his forehead against hers, chest heaving, catching his breath.

'That was—'

'Good,' she interjected. Fearful she was about to hear 'am-
ateurish' or 'regrettable.' Any of the epithets she was imagining for herself now the glow of release was waning. She'd
thrown herself at him twice now. Had any of his other lovers
ever been so gauche?

'I was going to say *surprising* but it was good, better than
good.'

Surprising how? That he wanted her at all?

He lifted her down and once she moved away to gather her
clothes, he retrieved his jeans from where they'd landed, cur-

rently adorning a shiny steel fridge. Her own jeans were in a heap on the floor. Her panties two feet away. She grabbed them and tugged them on.

He was dressed before her. Well, back in those jeans at least. The midday sun bounced through the window and glinted in his hair, off his golden skin. Her breath caught.

'We may as well have some of this,' he said, lifting the lid of the pizza box and retrieving a slice. The smell wafted towards her and that nausea came back with such a vengeance she had to fling a hand to her mouth.

They'd passed a cloakroom on the way to the kitchen and she fled there now. Only just reaching it in time. This was the third or fourth time this week. She'd eaten seafood in a restaurant a few evenings ago. Maybe something had been off.

When she returned to the kitchen Seb's slice of pizza was lying on the counter untouched. 'Are you okay?' He sounded rather more concerned than a bit of mild nausea warranted.

'It's happened a few times over the last week. I think I ate something I shouldn't have.'

'A few times. Could you have picked up a bug?'

'I'm not sure. I've felt a bit off for...' She thought about it. 'Actually about a week. At least.'

'More than a week, then?'

'Yes, now you mention it. Hmm?' She mused aloud. 'So that would have been before the restaurant.'

Seb had gone deathly pale. She frowned at him. 'What?'

'Agnesse,' he said, 'could you be pregnant?'

'Of course not. We used protection. You were most careful.'

'Then when was your last period?'

'Two weeks ago.' Though it had been much lighter than usual, and she'd stopped wearing her favourite perfume because suddenly the smell had become so cloying and then her breasts were rather tender and...and...

The room spun; she felt the blackness coming on. Then nothing but a stream of curses in French and a pair of strong arms grabbing her, lowering her down onto the only chair and pushing her head between her knees.

She couldn't be pregnant. She had things to do. Things to prove. Ellamaa's first ever queen regnant was going to show those doubters how wrong they were.

Was she going to fall at the first hurdle? Who ever heard of a single-parent queen? Oh, God. The wave of nausea and faintness came again.

Seb was by her side again, pushing a glass of water into her hands. She took it and gulped some down.

He'd recovered quicker than she had. He was on the phone, rattling off instructions in French. She heard *pharmacist* and *pregnancy test*.

She focused on getting the room to stop spinning and the basics of staying upright and conscious. One hand clutched the counter; the other was wrapped around her seat.

This couldn't be happening. They'd been careful. But even as she thought that, she knew…she just *knew*.

Since that night something had been slightly off. She couldn't have described exactly how but she'd felt different. She thought it was unrequited lust. Because she'd craved some little piece of Seb that no one else could claim, that she could tuck away in her heart.

He'd left a piece of him lodged inside her all right. Just not in her heart.

The room spun again.

Seb was by her side, placing a damp towel to her forehead, talking to her, telling her it would be all right. How was this going to be all right?

Five minutes later there was a knock on the rear door, and when Seb came back from answering it, he clutched a white paper bag. He pushed his plate and mug aside and unpacked its contents onto the countertop. No less than three identical small boxes. He opened one, scanning the instructions.

'Take this. You'll need to… Well, I guess you might already know what to do.'

'I've not used one before if that's what you mean. But I'll work it out.'

'Do you need help to the bathroom?'

She sent him a glare. She wasn't an invalid. She was a queen and she needed to start behaving like one. Shoulders back, straight spine and if her steps wove in a less than straight line, well, at least she was walking unaided.

The news was the worst.

Agnesse sat on the closed toilet seat in that gloomy room, amidst the part-tiled walls, the window grimy with masonry dust, and wondered if a future monarch had ever announced their presence to the world in such an inauspicious space.

She splashed cold water on her face, tidied her hair then returned to the kitchen, clutching the little white stick with its tiny pink line.

Pregnant.

But behind it all was the thrill. They'd started their own little blip of life. A tiny thing, but hers to love. She was going to be a mother and even the ruinous circumstances couldn't fully extinguish a glimmer of happiness.

The father, in contrast, was grim faced. Not a speck of joy there. Quite the opposite. His look was one of cold resignation overlain with a helping of sheer terror.

'What do we do now?' she asked.

'Considering who we are and who the child will be, I'd thought that was blindingly obvious.' He straightened then gave a small bow. 'Your Majesty, consider this an official proposal. We are getting married.'

CHAPTER SEVEN

HIS PROPOSAL SENT Agnesse staggering towards a seat again. This time she stuck her head between her knees herself. It wasn't the most flattering reaction to the offer of his hand, but Seb supposed he couldn't blame her. He wasn't overjoyed at the prospect himself.

From beneath the tumble of her hair came a plea. 'Can you give me a moment?'

Perhaps he could use one himself. She was okay on that seat. There was really nowhere to fall if she did pass out. Seb quit the room and in the hallway turned to the stairs, taking them three at a time on a burst of restless energy.

Marriage? He nearly stumbled on the last step. But there was no use in regretting his decisions. There was no alternative. He would get on with it and do whatever was required. He pulled out his phone as he strode into the salon at the front of the house.

On the other side of the street was a park. Beyond the bars of scaffolding caging the front of the house, Seb could see birds flitting busily from tree to tree. Overhead, cotton-soft clouds floated across a sky of clear blue.

He waited for his call to be picked up.

'I'm getting married,' he said as soon as Leo answered. No point in any preamble. Action was needed now. It might help tamp down the terror he was feeling.

'The Ellamaa Queen, I presume? Congratulations.'

Why did Leo not sound surprised?

'She's pregnant.'

'Ah, I see. Well, a family of your own could be the making of you,' Leo said with absolutely no censure. Actually, he sounded annoyingly upbeat.

'I didn't call for a heart to heart. I called to inform my monarch of my intentions and ask him to be best man.'

'Of course. I'd be honoured. I assume my services will be required sooner rather than later.'

'In the next few days…' Seb inhaled sharply. He'd always told himself he'd never marry. Never risk an emotional commitment to a woman. He'd never wanted to live with the endless fear of things going wrong… How quickly a life could change irrevocably. Well, far better to be in the driving seat when it did. 'As soon as I can arrange everything. Although we won't be announcing the pregnancy yet.'

'Very wise. Make it sound like a love match and not a marriage of necessity.' There was a short silence from the other man, then, 'I hate to ask but it probably needs to be said. You're sure it's yours?'

Seb's quiet 'yes' concealed the blazing need to hit something in lieu of his cousin for suggesting otherwise. Of course the child was his. It never crossed his mind that it wouldn't be. Agnesse was practically a virgin that night. That pitiful excuse of a man who'd called himself her fiancé didn't count, and there had been no other lover since their night together. He'd bet his life on it. He also didn't like the snarling, jealous beast that reared his head at the thought of another man with his hands on her.

'Those photos will be back, of course.' Hell, would they ever. The punch, that kiss in Vienna… Seb could see the prurient headlines now. 'But we'll spin it to our advantage. A classic enemies-to-lovers story.'

'I never knew you could be so romantic.'

'I'm not.' That misapprehension was definitely getting corrected. 'I'm being pragmatic.'

'How's Agnesse with all this?' Leo asked.

Seb thought of her gripping that chair as if her survival depended on it, while her future coalesced around her without input from her.

'She's nearly fainted twice in the last ten minutes, if that's any indication.'

'It's a lot to take in. Marrying the man you're supposed to despise. And dare I ask… How are you?'

There was a squeal from somewhere near Leo and Violetta's excited voice called out, 'He's getting married? Give me that phone.'

'I apologise but apparently my wife would like to speak to you.'

'No, don't, I—'

'Seb? Is it Agnesse Toivonen? *Please* tell me it's her. You two would be perfect together.' She knew that based on what? A punch and a few insults? 'We all saw that kiss. It was hot. You've won her over at last. I knew she'd eventually see what a catch you are.'

'Something like that. Hello, Violetta.' Her boundless optimism usually made him smile. Today, not so much.

'Oops. Judging by my darling husband's face I've just interrupted some serious manly stuff. Bye, Seb. Please bring Agnesse to meet us all soon.'

Leo retrieved his phone again. 'As I was saying… How are you?'

Seb considered that question. Not running for the hills as he might have thought. Amongst the ever-present fear was a sliver of excitement. A father. Him?

He'd not learned much from his own that he could use, except how *not* to parent a child. The man had barely figured in his life at all. When he deigned to grace Seb with his presence, it was only to remind his son of his lowly place in the von Frohburg family hierarchy, and what a curse his arriving at all had been. From his example Seb also knew that giving your heart bore a terrible risk. Leo had been lucky, but Seb was never going there. Yet, neither would he shirk his duty. He'd never condemn another child to the curse of an indifferent father. For better or worse he'd be there for it. For Agnesse, too.

If mother and child even survived...

His gut roiled. What if by getting her pregnant he'd already condemned Agnesse to the same fate as his mother? He crushed that thought before it could take hold.

'Dealing with it,' he said at last.

'Good man. What else do you need?' Leo asked.

'The use of the Mayfair house tonight?'

'It's yours. I'll make the arrangements at this end.' Leo chuckled. 'So Prince Consort of Ellamaa, eh?'

'No. I won't be taking any new titles.' Husband to Agnesse. Father to her child. That would be the extent of it.

'You might like it.'

'No.' He already didn't like the lurking fear of how this might end for Agnesse. He wasn't about to risk any further emotional damage by taking on a royal role that no one wanted him in. Seb the playboy had been a deliberate choice designed to deflect the offers of any unwanted promotions.

'You'd be *good* at it.' Leo wasn't leaving this alone. He'd make him.

'My father crushed any faith in a royal life out of me. And forgive me, but so did your family.'

'Whether you like it or not, they're your family, too.'

'Don't let them hear you say that. They've spent a lifetime doing their best to pretend I'm not.'

'They may change their minds now you're about to marry into the Toivonens, and the queen, no less.'

'They can all go to hell,' Seb snarled and cut the connection.

At last, the room stopped spinning. Agnesse cautiously lifted her head, but maintained her grip on the chair just in case. She opened her eyes to find she was alone. Seb had given her the space she'd requested. Just as well. It was hard to have any sensible thoughts with his naked torso to stare at. How was it, in the midst of this crisis, her body still craved his? Perhaps it was pregnancy hormones.

Pregnant.

That simple fact had changed everything. The cold, stark reality sank in. Seb was right. There was just one solution for someone like her. Remaining unmarried was unthinkable. Her only option was to marry the father of her baby.

Gone was the chance at love like her parents had shared. That had always been a distant hope. Her duty had to come first, but still there had been a possibility. Not anymore. Seb did not love her, nor was he the kind of man to develop those feelings in time. He'd been pretty clear about that. She supposed she should be grateful he believed in duty, at least.

Time to find him and accept his proposal.

His voice came from the floor above. She followed the sound and found him at the front of the house. In a room that would one day be a glamorous lounge with a pretty view of the park on the other side of the street.

Now the only thing lending the bare room any glamour was the stunning, shirtless man standing at the window. His back to hers, arms folded across his chest, legs planted wide, he looked like a warrior ready to take on the world.

He'll keep us both safe, she thought. *Me, and this little one.* Her hand went to her belly.

Seb's head swung towards her, his gaze dropping swiftly to where her hand rested.

'Are you all right? I wasn't too rough before?'

Oh, all that concern in his stormy green eyes. It warmed her to her very soul. She nodded. 'Who were you speaking to?'

'Leo. I was asking if he'd be my best man.' Uncertainty clouded his expression. 'If I require one?'

Agnesse swallowed hard. What other choice did she have? 'Yes, I'll do it.'

His look of relief was so profoundly different to the tension of moments before. When he stretched out his hand to her, she went to him at once, her feet carrying her towards him of their own accord. Her body simply couldn't resist him. And the warmth of his hand as it engulfed hers was so comforting that she didn't hesitate when he drew her closer into his embrace and kissed her. A slow, sweet, drugging kiss that mightn't be about love but still had a tantalising air of romance about it.

When he lifted his head at last, she opened her eyes to gaze up at him. But he was looking elsewhere, to the street below and with a determined and decidedly unromantic expression on his handsome face. She glanced in the same direction and saw movement. There was a lone figure on the far side of the street. With his camera lens pointed directly at them, a photographer stood snapping shot after shot.

Seb tightened his grip on her, took her jaw firmly in hand so she couldn't move as he looked down on her.

'So our story begins. We fell in love. We tried to fight it but it's too strong for either of us. We met in secret but alas, we've finally been discovered.'

Love? Wrapped in his arms like this, the absolute focus of those burning green eyes, she feared that it would be all too easy to fall deeply for him. But would those feelings ever be reciprocated? She freed her chin and turned her cheek to his chest, feeling shaky again. This would be a marriage of convenience only. Of lust, yes, but not love, and she would do well to remember it.

'How will anyone believe that?' she said.

'Easily, if we feed them the right images. And when the baby comes and they realise you were already pregnant when we married, it will still be seen as a love match and that the child is...' His voice caught. 'That this child is wanted and loved.'

Beneath her cheek his heart beat a furious tattoo and she knew in that, at least, he meant every word. Then he slid a hand into her hair and tilted her head back, angling her face up towards him.

'Now, kiss me again and look like you mean it.'

His mouth came down on hers in an all-consuming kiss so profound that Agnesse didn't have to pretend. She couldn't help it. She was lost in him.

Thirty minutes later they were gathered in the hallway. One of Seb's team, with a bruised jaw to match his employer's, stood poised to open the front door. Behind them were the remainder of the team, carrying various pieces of luggage, and between them sporting a selection of split lips and black eyes. They'd clearly shown commendable restraint in saving their royal charge from himself last night.

Outside, Christina waited with Agnesse's protection detail, keeping the press back from the front steps. That single photographer had been joined by two dozen more journalists.

Agnesse had replaced the pizza uniform with the navy blazer she'd been wearing that morning when she'd left Paris. But she almost wished she were wearing one of Seb's sweats. It would have swamped her, but she wouldn't have cared. She'd have happily hidden away inside it completely and never come out again.

Seb was devastatingly handsome in a sharp charcoal suit and white shirt, open at the neck. She could barely drag her eyes from him.

'Ready?' he asked her.

For what awaited them on the other side of that door? The scandal, the scrutiny, the disapproval of her prime minister. Her sister's surprise. Her mother's disappointment. And marriage to this man?

Hardly.

But his arm was a protective shield about her; his body her safe haven as he tucked her in under his shoulder and their joint teams cleared a path through the jostling cameras and baying journalists.

'You're loved up now but what about that punch?' one of them shouted.

'All forgotten,' Seb answered, flashing a brilliant smile for the cameras.

'By the look of that bruise she's been at it again.' A ripple of humiliating laughter ran through the pack around them.

Agnesse turned her face into the wall of his chest, grateful for her big paparazzi-proof sunglasses. She knew her eyes would have instantly given her away. Unlike him, she could not have put on a show. Everyone would have seen the bald shock and they'd have surely guessed the calamitous truth.

Pregnant.

By this man. Who was insisting they marry.

Would her people believe she'd fallen at the first hurdle? Thinking she was imposing the most unsuitable of prince consorts on her country, a man whose only real achievement, they'd think, was seducing half the women of Europe.

'It's an odd location for a romantic tryst. Why were you here?'

'Privacy,' Seb told them over her head. 'We thought we'd escaped notice, but you found us anyway.'

'That pizza stunt was a dead giveaway. Were you hoping to be discovered so you could force him, Agnesse? You want the man-whore after all?'

She missed her footing on the kerb, but Seb was there, supporting her, helping her into the backseat of the car, then following her in. The door slammed shut against that mob outside. She sat there, numb, unable to move, and he leant over to fasten her seat belt. Now they'd left the sanctuary of the house, this had all become so real.

'Agnesse,' he said, gently taking her chin in his hand. 'Breathe.'

For all its softness, that command could not be disobeyed.

Her body responded. Air whooshed through her teeth; her lungs expanded.

He was the captain of her stricken life and he'd just saved her from foundering on the rocks. But how, *how* could she go through with this?

'I don't think I can marry you, after all,' she said, weakly.

'It makes no difference. I'm the father of your baby and I'm staying at both your sides.'

Her body thrilled to that even though her mind and heart rebelled.

He doesn't love you. He'll never love you.

'What if it's not yours?' she said, breathless and panicky, and suddenly desperate to find a way out.

He turned angry green eyes on her. 'Are you telling me you've been with someone else in the last month? You'd play that old trick, would you? Foisting another man's child on the poor sap who'd marry you because he believes in duty?'

'No, of course not.' She sank down in her seat. Ashamed of herself. He hadn't questioned that the child was his. Believing in her straightaway. Which was more than she'd done for him in Vienna. Was Sebastien von Frohburg, the louche playboy, actually an altogether different kind of beast? An honourable man?

It was a short drive to the von Frohburgs' London residence. Agnesse's base was in Paris and she had no home here. Otherwise, she would have insisted that was where they went. Though it might have fallen on deaf ears.

'You should rest when we get to the house. Give me a few hours to arrange everything.'

'Everything?'

'The wedding.'

'Wedding?' This was moving too fast. She swayed forward in her seat, but he flung out an arm to stop her toppling.

'The sooner I get you home, the better.'

'Home?' she repeated.

Oh, for Heaven's sake. Had pregnancy turned her into a parrot now?

'Ellamaa. The Summer Palace, to be precise. What could be more appropriate than taking your new fiancé home to meet your family?' His hand hovered just in front of her, a precaution in case she swayed again. 'You said it's the one place you can truly rest. A pregnant woman needs to take care of herself.'

'But I will still have things to do,' she argued. 'I'm the queen.'

Yes, she was. And it was time for her to start behaving as one. She couldn't let him take over this way.

'You're pregnant with my child,' he said. 'That supersedes everything else.'

The hell it did. She stiffened her spine. 'I won't agree to this.' But she was protesting to an empty space. They'd arrived under the portico of Leo and Violetta's London home. Seb was already out of the car and was crossing to her side.

'I can manage,' she said crossly, refusing the hand waiting to help her out.

'I'd be more convinced of that if you didn't look like you were about to faint at every comment I make.' He followed that up by clamping her to his side as they walked into this new address.

If Seb's temporary bolthole had been a luxurious London home in the making, the official London residence of His Serene Highness, the Crown Prince of Grimentz, was a fully-fledged, statement-piece palace, with marble staircases, crystal chandeliers, and priceless artwork everywhere she looked. She spied at least one Tintoretto hanging in a reception room and a pretty little Vermeer landscape peeked out from a corner of the hallway.

This wasn't a family home, at least not the ground floor. It was designed to demonstrate the wealth and status of its owners. Was this what Seb had grown up with? How different would he find the Summer Palace? There were treasures there, and in her family's other homes across Europe, but mostly the emphasis was on luxurious comfort and ease.

The butler and housekeeper greeted them warmly. It was obvious there was genuine affection for Seb. They *liked* him. They fussed over him, anxious about his cuts and bruises. He brushed that off and he greeted them like old friends.

Then at word from Seb, the housekeeper was whisking Agnesse away to a guest suite and he was disappearing into one of the salons, his phone clamped to his ear and barking out commands in French.

The rooms she was shown to were as grand as the rest of the house, though they were divinely comfortable. Agnesse sank down into a silk-upholstered couch. Grateful to sit. Despite what she'd told Seb, she was still feeling wobbly.

But it was time she made a call of her own. Her mother should be informed, and Agnesse sorely needed to hear her voice right then.

Mathilde Thiset-Toivonen could be tough on her children, but then she wasn't just a mother; she was a queen, too, with all the demands that entailed. Agnesse knew it was her way of helping her children navigate the inescapably public lives they'd been born into. When they erred, they might be subjected to a thorough dressing down but in the end she was always there for them, no matter what they'd done. Just as she'd supported her husband throughout his reign. His 'rock' he'd called her. Agnesse wanted to find a similar partner in life. Would Seb be that for her? She certainly couldn't fault his reaction to her pregnancy so far. Maybe her mother would be impressed with that. She might even like Seb. If she gave him a chance.

The phone was answered on the second ring.

'Agnesse, what's this I hear about you being in London with that dreadful womaniser?'

So much for Mathilde liking her future son-in-law.

'I came here to apologise for the terrible things I'd said about him in Vienna.'

'I'm sure you didn't say anything he hasn't heard before, and whilst you might have been a little uncouth, you essentially spoke the truth.'

But she hadn't. She'd been mistaken, about his night with Sofia and perhaps more than that. Hadn't he proposed to her in a heartbeat? Was that the behaviour you'd expect of an irredeemable playboy?

Agnesse steeled herself for the next part. 'He's asked me to marry him and I've… I've said yes.'

'Marry that man?' her mother stuttered. 'Why on earth—'

'Mama, I'm pregnant.'

The silence was mercifully short, and her mother's observation when it came had no judgement in it.

'In that case, my darling,' she said on a sigh, 'you'd better come home as soon as you can.'

CHAPTER EIGHT

HER FUTURE HUSBAND sat still and silent beside her. His gaze was fixed on the view unfolding beyond the car window; his first glimpse of the grounds of the Summer Palace.

And his new home.

He'd have a harder time taking charge of everything here than he had in London. Whisking her to the von Frohburgs' London residence. Organising her staff, who'd fallen in with his plans far too readily. He'd made sure she ate something, told her to rest, even charming Dorel, whom he'd had flown from Paris, into obeying his commands.

'Traitor,' she'd muttered as her maid had hurried to do his bidding. Dorel had shrugged and done it anyway.

They'd left Mayfair in the early hours. Seb arguing that they should travel through the night to be with her mother by morning, and before the story broke properly in that day's news schedules.

He'd hustled her onto the plane—*her* plane—and ushered her straight to the bedroom, where he'd insisted she got into bed. Then promptly left her. She'd been too wrung out to argue, falling asleep the moment her head hit the pillow.

What Seb had done on the three-hour flight was anyone's guess. When he'd woken her twenty minutes before landing, he'd looked as fresh faced and in control as when she'd closed her eyes.

Agnesse desperately wanted to know what he was thinking now as his new home appeared before them. One not really of his choice. He was only marrying her out of his sense of duty. How different might this homecoming have been for them both had there been any love involved?

The physical attraction was there. She'd happily ravish him on the plump leather seats of this stately limo. Despite the driver and security sitting up ahead. She sighed in frustration and instantly Seb's head swung towards her.

'Is everything all right?' There was an anxious glance, an all too fleeting brush of his hand, but there wasn't a flicker of heat in it. If there was, he'd tamped it down so well it was completely hidden. The ache of lust and longing had become all hers, apparently.

The familiar landscape slipped by. The parkland with its ancient trees, the deer grazing at the edge of the lake. Her home itself was partly obscured by a haze that often rose from the lake in the summer months. It would clear in an hour or two but until then, only the upper stories were visible, floating, as if by magic, above the tendrils of mist. The palace's pale lemon walls and white-tiled sloping roof were dazzling in the early-morning sun.

'Ellamaa,' Seb said, softly. 'The land of fairies.'

Agnesse knew her principal home was nothing like the one he grew up in—a hulking fortress built primarily to keep its owners safe and intimidate its enemies.

Not this elegant palace. Yes, created to impress visitors but still more, made for the pleasure and comfort of its occupants, with its formal gardens and sprawling parklands, its sumptuous staterooms and forty bedrooms. The von Frohburgs of Grimentz might be fabulously wealthy, but for comfort and sheer beauty the principal residence of the Queen of Ellamaa knocked their forbidding fortress into a cocked hat.

She'd always loved this approach to her family's home. On mornings like this it could take her breath away.

Their car turned into the drive that would take them to the

private entrance used by the family. It took them past the east wing, past the grounds remodelled by her father where he'd had the parklands restored to a wildflower meadow. Protected by a deer wall to keep them safe from the grazing livestock, a sea of poppies and daisies ran uninterrupted to the tree line. Her father would have loved it.

They passed the end of the wing where the chapel was situated. Tomorrow, if Seb had his way, the archbishop would conduct their marriage in its hallowed space, with Leo and her mother standing witness.

Leo was arriving tomorrow. Along with Sebastien's hastily packed possessions.

'Wouldn't you have wanted to oversee that yourself?' she'd asked him as they'd climbed onboard the jet in London.

'It's fine,' he'd said with a shrug. 'I don't have much.'

And her heart had squeezed. Who *was* this playboy prince with apparently so little to his name?

Keert was waiting for them at the family entrance. Agnesse made the introductions. Her secretary bowed low then looked startled when one hand landed on his shoulder and another grasped his in a firm shake.

'The secretary famous for seamless organisation. Your reputation precedes you,' Seb said with a broad smile. 'You're the envy of royal households across Europe.'

Completely disarmed, Keert stammered his thanks.

The next introduction was more frosty.

The dowager queen awaited them in her private sitting room. Seated on an elegant chaise, she rose in all her state as they entered. There was a warm embrace for her daughter. The interloper received a haughty glare and the barest fingertip stretched out for him to take. 'You must be Sebastien.'

'Your Majesty,' he said, bowing over her hand and adding that heel click that Agnesse found so...so *distracting*.

'Forgive me, ma'am,' he said, slewing a glance to a painting hanging to one side of the fireplace. 'But is that a Raphael?'

Her mother's gaze flickered to the portrait of a golden-haired Madonna. 'It is. My late husband gave it to me on our last anniversary.'

Seb studied the canvas in open admiration. 'It's a very fine piece. He had excellent taste, ma'am.'

'Yes, he did.' Mathilde's gaze softened as she studied the painting, then she turned away and drew Agnesse down to take a seat on the sofa beside her. She did not invite Seb to sit.

'I've arranged for you to see the family physician. He'll be here later this morning,' her mother said, ignoring Seb still standing politely.

'Can't it wait a day or two?' Agnesse asked, not wanting to be prodded and poked. 'I've taken a pregnancy test. I think it's clear.'

'I know, my darling—' her hand went to her daughter's cheek '—but you're planning such a big step. Let's be absolutely certain about everything.'

'Your mother is right, Agnesse. It's wise to be seen by your own doctors as early as possible. So they can monitor how you and the baby are doing.'

At Seb's words, her mother's lip curled, as if she was fending off an unpleasant smell. 'Quite,' she said.

At last, Mathilde waved a hand, indicating that Seb should sit. Agnesse watched transfixed as he undid the button on his jacket and sank gracefully into the sofa opposite. But she couldn't mistake the expression. Her fiancé was being polite but beneath the elegant manners, she sensed the steel and determination. Her mother might have met her match.

'I've had a request from Grimentz Castle for a visit by the crown prince tomorrow. I have, of course, said yes on your behalf, Agnesse. But really, does the marriage have to be quite so hasty?' She took her daughter's hand and stroked it.

'Ma'am,' Seb cut in. 'There seems to be little point in delaying. A small, quiet wedding would not be inappropriate during the period of official mourning, and the sooner Agnesse and I are married, the better it will appear once the pregnancy is announced.'

'And is that the life you want, young man? Forever standing two paces behind my daughter? Because, make no mistake, that will be the reality of your position. Even if you are the prince consort, there will be no transfer of power to you.' She sounded so angry but what else did her mother think could happen? Was she hoping Seb would change his mind? Because that would be disastrous. Agnesse couldn't raise their child alone. She and Seb were tied together even if protocol demanded he stand a hundred paces behind her.

'I assure you, power is the last thing I want. In fact, I won't even be taking the title.'

Her mother swivelled towards him in surprise. 'But it would be expected of you.'

'I'm sorry, I should have apprised Agnesse of this sooner, but I have no desire for a formal royal life. I will of course support my wife in any way I can, but as husband only, not as consort.'

'In our world there in no difference,' her mother said, angrily. She turned back to Agnesse. 'And if you think there is, you can both explain that to the prime minister. He's requested an audience with you. Keert has made the space in your diary after lunch.'

Seb's declaration was a bombshell. She was already marrying a man with a problematic reputation, and now he'd revealed he had no intention of supporting her by taking a formal role. How was Agnesse expected to explain that to her prime minster? A stuffy traditionalist who already believed she wasn't up to the job of being queen.

'Does he know about the baby?' Agnesse asked. God forbid she'd have to discuss that with him, too. She was already imagining his disapproval and attempts to retain some control over her once he knew she was about to take a husband.

How would he react if he knew there was a child conceived out of wedlock, too?

'Of course not. There is no need for anyone to know yet. It's too early. You're barely a month gone. When the time comes you could say it's a honeymoon baby.'

Agnesse dismissed that idea. 'People can do maths, Mama. Besides, I don't have time for a honeymoon.' She ran a mental tally of the work she'd already delayed over the past two days. She couldn't afford to fall any further behind.

Her mother shot a disapproving glance in Seb's direction, as if she wasn't surprised her daughter didn't want to spend any time with him.

'Until things are settled, for the prince tonight I thought the Rose guest suite.'

Agnesse silently added 'would do' because surely that was what her mother had meant.

'It can be changed of course if it doesn't suit. But it seemed sensible as you may choose not to stay at all.'

Seb stood, fastened the button on his jacket, and advanced towards their sofa. 'You could house me in the stables if you want, ma'am,' he said with a martial gleam in his eyes. 'But I assure you, I'm staying.'

He took Agnesse's hand, lifted it to his lips. The touch sent a shimmer of need over her skin.

'I will leave you to talk with your mother, Agnesse. I'll find a servant to direct me to my rooms. Your Majesties,' he said, and with a formal bow and click of his heels he quit the room.

Her mother's eyes narrowed on the doorway through which Seb had departed.

'I can see how you might have been seduced by him. But if he thinks all will be forgiven with fine manners and a few pretty compliments about your father, he is very much mistaken.'

After lunch, during which she ate almost nothing—and despite Seb's best efforts to pile tempting morsels on her plate—

Agnesse settled in the Prince Josef salon to await the arrival of her prime minster.

They met regularly, but today she'd dressed especially carefully. A fitted, knee-length dress in sombre grey, pearl earrings, her father's mourning medal, and grey leather pumps with five-inch heels. Royal power dressing at its best.

She wished Seb could have joined her from the start, but he'd declined.

'You can do this,' he said with a kiss to her cheek. 'And I'll be there as soon as you need me.' And off he went to wait in the adjoining salon.

From the corridor she heard Keert greeting her guest.

Andris Nilsson had served as head of government for the past decade. She'd been fourteen when he'd arrived at the palace for his first audience with the king. Despite all the intervening years, he couldn't see that she was a grown woman. He was frequently patronising, and since her accession had tried to control her, doing what he could to constrain the changes she wanted to make in her role.

The door opened. After making his usual bow, which was never quite as deep as the one he would have made to her father, the prime minister strolled towards her. 'Your Majesty, how lovely you look today. Quite the young lady.'

I'm twenty-five, she wanted to snap, but held her tongue.

'Prime Minister,' she said, rising to shake his hand.

He took hers in both of his and held on. 'Now, what is this I hear about some hastily concocted marriage plans, hmm? I'll convene the cabinet and we'll discuss it next week.'

'By all means, but you were informed as a courtesy only.' She reclaimed her hand and returned to her seat, waving him to a seat facing her own. 'I'm not asking your permission. I don't need it.'

'Ma'am, you're young and, forgive me, rather inexperienced.' He was still standing so she was obliged to look up at him. Giving him an advantage. No doubt as he intended.

'I must advise caution. His Highness, Prince Sebastien, is a foreign national, after all.'

'Yes, from Grimentz. With whom we share a deep and abiding friendship. My father and the crown prince were great friends.'

'With all due respect, you're not marrying the crown prince.'

'I should hope not. His wife would have something to say about it.'

Her country's senior official did not smile at that. In fact, his expression hardened. 'Your father would have counselled you against this union.'

'No, he would not. He would have trusted my judgement. And I'm not ignorant of the protocols. I would only need your permission if I were marrying an individual from a hostile state or whose position may be thought to outrank mine.'

At last, he sat. 'Ma'am, I think you know what I'm really trying to say here.' He sent her an oily smile that set her teeth on edge. 'Prince Sebastien's reputation is a cause for concern. I do wish you'd allow yourself to be advised by those older and wiser.'

'And I wish you would recognise that I'm perfectly capable of making this decision myself. The prince is not the man you think he is. He has qualities and depths beyond those the world chooses to see.'

He snorted. 'Oh, he has hidden depths all right. I had hoped to spare you this, but as you appear determined to run headlong into this mistake, I must tell you some shocking images have recently come to light.'

He drew a series of photographs from a file he carried. Blown-up, grainy images of a grubby back alley, where Seb wrestled with three men, who were restraining him while he bared his teeth at someone out of shot. A second showed her fiancé throwing a drunken punch. Another caught him flailing while he was forcibly bundled into the back of a car.

'These were taken only the other night. Your fiancé was involved in a street fight. A common brawl, ma'am. And one that he started because he was intoxicated, I'm told. I am deeply shocked by these behaviours. How can you possibly believe this man suitable to be prince consort of Ellamaa?'

'I know of this incident, Mr Nilsson. The prince has explained the circumstances to me. And my intentions have not changed.'

His brows lowered and he leant forward in his seat, like a bull about to charge.

'You would still take him as husband, after learning about this and what else besides? A drunk, a known womaniser to boot? One might, respectfully of course, wonder have you taken leave of your senses, young woman?'

'No, but I think you may have taken leave of your manners, Mister Nilsson,' Agnesse said, never taking her gaze from his. 'May I remind you that I am your queen.'

The prime minister flushed red. 'Forgive me, ma'am.'

Agnesse continued, 'While I do not condone his behaviour, I cannot condemn the intention behind it. The prince had already informed me about this incident. He was defending my reputation and was prepared to suffer harm to do so, even after all he'd received from me was shameful insults. Could you say the same, Prime Minister?'

She was done with diminishing Sebastien von Frohburg.

'So you are determined to marry this…this brawling prince?' The prime minister nodded towards the photographs.

'I have found the man I…love.' She could say that because it was important. 'One I believe will support me in my role. Naturally, I have taken the advice of my mother.' Who probably shared the prime minister's misgivings though Agnesse wasn't going to tell him that, and she knew with a certainty, neither would the dowager queen. 'But in the end, the decision about whom I would marry was only ever going to be mine.'

'You would elevate such a creature to the lofty position of consort?'

A creature? Seb was a *man* of principle and kindness and duty. Agnesse lifted her chin and held her ground. Seb deserved all the protection she could give.

'Actually, my future husband will not be taking the role of consort. He has no interest in the trappings of status and power. Instead, he has stated his desire to continue to live a private life.'

The prime minister's jaw tightened in disbelief. 'Then what, may I ask, is he going to do with his time?' His voice was rising to a disrespectful volume. 'Run around whoring again?'

'I'll be doing whatever Her Majesty asks of me.' Seb's cool voice came from behind her. Even without that, Agnesse would have known he'd just entered the room. The look of astonished fury on the minister's face was priceless.

'I understood our conversations were private, ma'am,' he growled. 'At least they were in the old king's day.'

Seb's hand arrived on her shoulder. Agnesse felt the subtle squeeze of support and allowed her fingers to float up and settle over his, more grateful than she could say for his solid presence.

'Tell me,' Seb said, 'did you attempt to bully and brow beat the old king, too? Because from where I was sitting, I heard little respect for your monarch.'

The man huffed and blustered but didn't answer.

Agnesse rose to her feet, signalling the meeting was at an end.

'By all means, Prime Minister, if you think it will be in El-lamaa's best interest, release those pictures,' she said. 'But you should know that it won't change my decision.'

It couldn't. She carried Seb's baby. But it surprised her to discover that regardless of that, she'd still mean it. Her fiancé was a good man.

He glared at Seb, his mouth twisting when he spotted the bruise to his jaw.

'Very well, ma'am. You have made your intentions clear. I can only hope you won't come to regret it.'

With a fleeting bow for her and nothing at all for Seb, the prime minister spun on his heel and stalked out.

'Perhaps we shouldn't have done that,' Seb said when the door closed and they were alone again.

'Yes, we should. Odious man. Because I'm young and female he thinks he can push me around. That's not how my father raised me. It's time the prime minister got used to that idea.'

She felt good. That was the first time she'd properly stood up to him.

'Thank you for defending me,' he said, 'but I'm sorry about those photographs.'

'I'm not. It's made him show his true colours at last. He doesn't respect me. It's useful that I finally know that for certain. But he won't release them. It would be seen as an attack on the monarchy. He's already losing popularity and that might weaken his position further.'

'It's pretty certain someone else will, though, and it's going to cause a world of trouble for you.'

'I don't care. I know that's not who you are. And you should let others see the real you sometimes.'

He spread his hands wide. 'But I do,' he said with that lazy smile of his.

She narrowed her gaze. She wasn't fooled. She knew he'd just retreated behind the persona of the playboy prince. She could see the difference now.

The family was to gather for dinner. Her mother suggested it was the perfect opportunity for Isobel and Carl to meet their new brother-in-law before the wedding.

'As you both seemed determined you are going through with this,' she said to Agnesse as they waited in her sitting room for her other children and Seb to arrive. 'I heard that the prime minister was practically puce when he left you both this afternoon. I wish I'd been there to see you stand up to him at last. Though Sebastien also played a part, I hear.'

God bless Keert for sharing that. Her mother needed help seeing past Seb's former reputation.

'I was supposed to be dining with friends in the city tonight.' Isobel burst through the door, in skin-tight jeans and a protest T-shirt. 'But after all those photos of you and a naked Sebastien von Frohburg practically broke the internet, I had to stay at home and discover all the juicy details.'

'*Naked?*' Mathilde said in alarm as Isobel crossed the floor to gather her sister in a hug.

'He was missing his shirt, that's all,' Agnesse quickly reassured her.

'Didn't look like that in the clinches I saw.' Isobel bent to kiss her mother on both cheeks. 'And I thought I was the scandalous one in this family.' She plonked down beside her sister. 'So where is he?'

'On his way. Be nice, Issy, won't you?'

'You know me. I'll be charming,' she said, all innocence.

'Like the last time, you mean? When you convinced me he'd broken your heart?'

She had the grace to look at least a little contrite.

'I'm sorry, Ness. I wasn't being truthful,' she said with a rueful smile. 'He'd actually been sweet to me when, you know, I'd probably been a bratty teenager.'

'But I punched him, Issy.'

'I know. Go you.'

Agnesse threw up her hands. 'No, it's not *go me*. I'm so ashamed. It was a terrible thing to have done.'

'But it's all worked out okay because you're getting married.' Isobel flashed her an angelic smile. 'So tell us. How long have you been secretly seeing him?'

'I haven't. That time in Vienna was our first meeting in years.'

'He got you pregnant after one night?' Isobel whistled. 'He should have *stud* tattooed on his forehead?'

'He should have a health warning tattooed somewhere,' Agnesse muttered. 'But I wasn't thinking of his head.'

Her sister's eye widened in interest.

'Big, is he? Like being impaled on an elephant trunk?'

'Isobel,' their mother scolded. 'A little decorum, please.'

'Come on, Mother. We're all grown women in here. Surely, you know what I'm talking about?'

After a moment a wash of colour stained Mathilde's cheek and a smile played at the corner of her mouth. 'Well, your father was rather...well made.'

Isobel snorted. Agnesse blushed. Then mother and daughters dissolved into laughter. Exactly at the moment Seb walked in.

'Oh, look,' Isobel said with a wicked glance at her sister. 'It's the head of the herd.'

That comment and Seb's adorable, frowning confusion had Agnesse laughing so hard she had to stuff a handkerchief in her mouth. It was nerves or stress or baby hormones. Maybe all three. She wasn't normally so unrestrained. She peeked up at Seb. Or perhaps it was something about her soon-to-be husband. He was dressed in a navy suit and matching shirt and looked good enough to eat. Agnesse's mouth went dry.

Isobel saved her by getting to her feet to greet her future brother-in-law.

'Sorry for being a nightmare and causing all that trouble. No hard feelings, and welcome to the family,' she said, lifting up on on tiptoe to peck Seb's cheek. 'And be good to my sister, or else.'

As apologies went, Seb supposed it covered the essential points, but Isobel Toivonen appeared to be as much a force of nature as ever.

Whilst she didn't have the delicate, arresting beauty of her elder sister, she was a handsome young woman with a vivacity about her that drew the eye. Seb could understand how she could break hearts and cause all the turmoil that dismayed her mother and filled the gossip columns. And he would forgive her much of that when he saw how devoted she appeared to be to her sister. They'd had their heads together, giggling over some joke, as he walked in. He got the impression he was the butt of it; not that he cared if it brought him the sweet pleasure of hearing Agnesse's unrestrained laughter.

But then she stared up at him with hungry eyes and the rest of the room faded away. She'd defended him earlier. Standing up to her country's chief government official. Apart from Leo, who'd ever done anything like that for him? Seb had been moved.

Then she'd urged him—*let others see the real you.*

Not likely. Never had, never would. Except in that moment he'd had the alarming impression that she was beginning to see precisely that. Curiously, he still wasn't quite sure how he felt about it.

The youngest of the siblings stuck his head round the door. Carl, who in most other royal families of Europe would have been king now instead of his elder sister holding the title of queen.

He kissed his mother, hugged both his sisters, but appeared completely star-struck as Seb put out his hand.

His handshake was firm but his greeting was mumbled and after that, he fell silent, leaving the conversation to his older sisters. Which meant mostly Isobel. She peppered Seb with questions about Grimentz. About Leo. About his views on world events.

'Isobel, for Heaven's sake,' Agnesse scolded. 'Let the man draw breath, will you?'

All the while Carl had watched and listened and used the sudden silence to finally find his voice, asking the one thing that at least sixty percent of those present would have preferred he had not.

'So are the stories about your conquests true?'

Seb wasn't responding to a question like that. Not with his future wife and mother-in-law present. He'd hoped his raised brow might have prompted the young man to change the subject. Unfortunately, Carl took it for affirmation and slapped his thigh in glee.

'I knew it. Oh, you absolute player.'

Mathilde inhaled sharply while Agnesse dropped her head into her hands on a groan.

'Whatever happened in the past,' Seb said, 'a wise man knows when to move on. We learn, we find new loyalties, new alliances. And the past stays firmly where it belongs.'

That right there was a lesson in diplomacy if the impertinent boy was able to see it. The blush and hurried apology suggested that he had. Perhaps the young man had potential, after all.

'Thank you, Sebastien. That was most informative,' Mathilde said, rising abruptly to her feet. 'And on that note, let's go in to dinner, shall we?'

CHAPTER NINE

IF THE DOWAGER QUEEN had meant to insult him with her choice of guest rooms, her intention had missed the mark. Seb found them to be perfectly comfortable and had quickly discovered that the feminine-sounding Rose suite was in fact named for its garden view and not for its decor, which was a restful mix of blue and ivory.

Perhaps the intended insult resided in the distance between his quarters and that of his fiancée's. Any clandestine visit would have required directions from a passing footman, and even then would have taken some time to accomplish. The Rose suite appeared to be as far from the family wing as possible.

Not that he'd had any intention of seeing his bride last night. While she was pregnant he was going to be extremely careful when, or even *if*, he touched her again. Yes, he knew the science; his rational brain knew the risk would be minimal if he made love to her. But knowing and actually *believing* it would be okay were two different things in his world—a world where his mother had lost her life and his father had then lost the ability to care for anything.

Last night's dinner and Seb's introduction to his new family had been surprising. He'd expected strained conversation and inevitable silences. But the family had been relaxed from the start.

He'd made it his particular business to draw the mother out.

She rebuffed most of his attempts with a stilted politeness. She would be harder to win over than her children. But what she didn't understand was Seb had been raised with that level of indifference and even outright hostility. It didn't touch him.

What did concern him was the impact it was having on Agnesse.

Her sister and brother chatted and sparred in dizzying changes of direction until Mathilde reined them in, scolding both her younger children. For Isobel and Carl it seemed to have no impact; they carried on as before. For his future wife, even though they were not directed at her, he saw the admonishments landed a small blow each time. On the surface she appeared serene, but Seb sensed that beneath that calm surface each rebuke or correction increased her unease.

He didn't doubt Mathilde loved her daughter, but Agnesse was young and had not long ago become queen. Was her mother inadvertently putting undue pressure on her? If his future wife needed protecting from her mother, too, so be it. He'd not hesitate to step in if necessary.

He woke early and took the opportunity to walk part of the terrace below his suite. As with his arrival yesterday a soft mist lay about the grounds, but the palace itself was visible to him.

It spoke of generations of power and wealth enough to create comfort and grandeur all at the same time. In many ways it would be an easy place to call home. Who would not be soothed by its grace and beauty?

It was a long way from the hulking fortress he'd been raised in. So much softer, gentler.

However, judging by his future mother-in-law's behaviour yesterday, would he be any more welcome here than he had been by his own so-called family?

It made no difference. He'd have to get on with it. He may not have wanted a royal life and, if his family's beliefs had been any indication, it didn't particularly want him. Apart from Leo, who'd ever thought him capable of a role in the public eye?

Didn't mean he didn't know how to behave in one. He would carve a path somehow.

He'd worked privately with his chosen charities before. Supporting them with his time in person. Privately raising funds. He could do similar here.

He'd also stood in for Leo at social functions. Though never official ones.

He'd gone through women so he never had to test the limits of their affections. What if they were like his family underneath? Mercenary, obsessed with his status and not caring about the human being behind it.

And he adopted the persona of the playboy so he would never have to test the limits of the people's affections, either. Never try to win their respect and never be disappointed.

He turned away from the peace of the early morning, striding back in the direction of his rooms. His best man was due to arrive within the hour. Two hours after that they'd both be waiting in the chapel for the arrival of the bride. His days of sitting on the fence were over. He had to make a choice now.

The palace PR team had already written the press release that would announce the marriage of the queen. No mention was to be made of the pregnancy; only the immediate family knew about that. Instead, the union was to look like the result of an irresistible love match. The period of official mourning precluding any undue celebrations, they had the perfect excuse for a quick and low-key wedding.

A single photographer and journalist had been summoned to document the wedding celebrations, such as they were. All Agnesse would have to do was look happy and pretend that she'd married for love. She could gaze at Seb as if she wanted him. That was easy. Because, Heaven help her, she did. She wanted the comfort of his touch, a sign that they might have the chance at being a proper family. She wasn't ready to give up on that dream just yet.

Last night, as they were about to go to their separate rooms, she'd blurted that he could stay with her.

He'd declined.

'I think we should respect tradition and not see each other until we meet in the chapel. And an early night might be beneficial.' He glanced down to her still-flat belly. 'It's not just you to consider now.' Then the corner of his mouth had lifted in an ironic smile. 'As for me, the delights of the Rose suite await.'

She'd longed for the reassurance of his touch, but he'd not so much as taken her hand, just bowed, clicked his heels, and left her, calmly walking away while she was a churning mess of unrequited longing.

Her mother and Dorel had arranged a selection of suits and dresses for Agnesse to try. She'd opted for an elegant ivory silk two-piece. It's fitted jacket hugged her still-slim waist; a peplum fell to her hip. The straight skirt finished just below her knees, demure, but elegant and showing off a hint of tanned leg. But peeking out along the jacket lapel and skirt hem was a trim of ivory Guipure lace. A nod to her bridal state without being too ostentatious. Her hair was caught up in an elegant side chignon. Topped by a veiled ivory pillbox hat.

Her mother fussed at it.

'I'd so looked forward to your wedding one day. But that man, *that man*, has robbed us of it all.'

'He didn't get me pregnant on his own. I was there, too,' Agnesse said. She wouldn't tell her that Seb had been the one to call a halt until they had protection and she'd admit to no one that they'd have not been in this position at all if she hadn't seduced him. 'He's not to blame.'

'Of course he is. He can't help himself. He sees a beautiful woman and he has to have her. However beyond his status she may be.'

'He's a prince of Grimentz, Mama.'

'Only just. And who was his mother? The secretary. A nobody. Snaring herself an unwary royal. Like mother, like son.'

'Mama!' Agnesse scolded. Her mother wasn't normally a snob.

She looked shamefaced. 'I'm sorry. He's just not what I'd

hoped your husband would be like. I'd so hoped you'd love each other.'

Agnesse swallowed the pain of that truth as best she could. Even though she knew from the start he could not offer her love, it still hurt that her mother could see it. He didn't love her.

She tried not to focus on that, turning instead to slip on the shoes Dorel had found. A pair of gorgeous, sky-high stilettos in ivory silk with a line of Swarovski crystals running up the heels and onto the shoe itself. Agnesse adored them and here was a little bling to match the diamond-and-sapphire ring Seb had presented to her at dinner last night. When she'd looked up at him in surprise, he'd done that little shrug again.

'I may not have many possessions but that's by choice. I didn't say I wasn't rich. I am. Rich enough to buy you as many baubles as your heart desires.'

She didn't want any more because this one was already quite perfect. Despite everything, her silly heart had skipped in delight. The sapphire matched her eyes; the surrounding tapered baguette diamonds gave the ring the look of a daisy.

Agnesse trembled. Soon, he'd add a matching gold band to her finger.

The only other adornment she wore were her pearl studs and her gold mourning medal. As would Seb. He was joining the Toivonens and would be required to mourn a man he'd never met. For today only she and her family would swap the black ribbon for one of pale grey.

She felt that her father would have approved of her new husband. Her mother couldn't see beyond his scandalous past. But her father would have seen the man behind the apparent indolence, to the intelligence and compassion that she was beginning to see in him. Perhaps that would be enough for their life together. Mutual respect.

She picked up her posy of daisies and meadowsweet. At her request, the wildflowers had been gathered from the meadows surrounding her father's mausoleum. A bee drawn by the promise of nectar flew in through the open window and settled on a daisy.

It was a much-needed symbol of good fortune on a day that should have been full of celebration. She took her mother's arm, and the dowager queen smiled at her when she knew both of them wished her papa was there to walk her down the aisle.

She gave her mother a hug and headed for the door.

Generations of Toivonens had worshipped in this chapel. Been baptised, wed, or dispatched on their final journey to ever-lasting rest. They were high-born, every one of them, and yet, despite the vaulted ceilings, the elaborate carving of the dark wood pews and chandeliers overhead, the interior of this hallowed space felt humble. As the monarch who'd built it had intended. He'd been a devout man and wanted the simple whitewashed walls to be a sharp contrast to the gilded stucco of the palace staterooms. An earthly reminder of the peace awaiting him in Heaven.

Waiting at the altar now, Seb would have preferred some-thing grander and more anonymous. This intimate family space was making him want to run like hell away from it all. Did the archbishop pick up on his turmoil? He chose that mo-ment to give him a reassuring nod.

Seb stared resolutely ahead.

But the daisy boutonnières that he and Leo had been given to wear glowed in his peripheral vision. The scent of them, and the riot of roses and hedgerow greenery adorning the altar, mingled in the air. A fresh, vivid scent that Seb suspected he'd remember forever.

Behind him, at the rear of the chapel, Isobel and Carl whis-pered together like excited teenagers. But otherwise, the pews were empty. This was to be a perfunctory affair. No extended family, no other guests. It added uncomfortably to the feeling of intimacy. This time it was Leo who picked up on the fresh jan-gle of nerves and clapped a reassuring hand to Seb's shoulder.

Seb tugged at his collar. Not that it was needed. He was impeccably dressed in a charcoal suit and ice-blue tie. His best man similarly attired.

The chapel could be reached from inside the palace, but that entrance remained closed. Instead, his bride had elected to walk to her wedding through the morning sunshine. And behind Seb, at the rear of the chapel, the great oak doors stood open with a view to the late king's summer meadows beyond.

The archbishop cleared his throat and Seb finally turned to look back down the nave. He heard Leo's sharp intake of breath.

Seb wasn't sure he'd be able to breathe at all.

Silhouetted in the great stone arch of the doorway stood his bride. She waited until Isobel and Carl fell in behind her, then on her mother's arm, the Queen of Ellamaa advanced towards him.

Outside the chapel there was an elm tree; a breeze set its leaves fluttering and the light pouring through the stained-glass windows became a dancing kaleidoscope of green and gold. As Agnesse moved through it her beauty was almost unearthly, like she belonged more to the next world than this.

And yet, she carried his child.

Seb's mouth went dry. How could he protect such an ethereal creature when he was just a man, with feet of clay? The terror threatened to claw through his chest.

Would she be safe? Please God, let her be safe.

Her ivory suit revealed only a hint of neckline and the lower part of her tanned legs. But that modesty was deceptive. The suit hugged her figure, emphasising her lush curves, her breasts, the flare of her hips. It heated Seb's blood.

His heart pounded as she arrived beside him and Mathilde symbolically presented her daughter's hand to the groom. He closed his own around it, like a priceless gift he must treasure. But her veil hid her eyes from him. He desperately wanted to push it aside so he could see her expression, to be reassured that she was real.

Of course she was real: her fingers trembled.

Or was the tremor in his?

He hadn't expected this, to be so moved by his bride. He closed his heart to it. It would serve no purpose. She needed him to be strong for her and their unborn child, not behave like a lust-struck fool. Because surely that was all it was—lust.

He wouldn't allow it to be anything else.

They turned as one to face the altar.

Beside her stood the Dowager Queen of Ellamaa. Beside him, the Crown Prince of Grimentz, both there to bear incontrovertible and unassailable royal witness; there would be no denying the validity of this marriage.

It might have been rapturously romantic had the groom not worn such a grim, dark expression and the woman beside him not been choking on her replies as if she could barely get them out.

But their eyes met, briefly, and hers flashed with a yearning that caught him off guard and somehow seared him to his soul.

Then it was done, rings exchanged and the register signed. Seb tucked her hand into his elbow and led his bride back down the nave towards the sunshine.

The photographs were to be a cursory affair. Like the service. There to simply get the job done. They would be disseminated through the press this afternoon. One interview had been organised for after the wedding breakfast so the couple could announce their nuptials to the world.

Watching his bride's pale face, the way she clung to his arm, convinced Seb that he would be taking the lead in that interview and he would insist they keep it short. They wouldn't be announcing Agnesse's pregnancy anytime soon; another two months at least. After the first scan. But she was a monarch of only nine months standing and still on a steep learning curve. He could legitimately step in protectively at this stage. She might have nearly fainted when she'd discovered she was pregnant, but there'd been no more panic attacks that he knew of. The arrogant alpha in him preened. Was his presence protecting her from those, too?

He could be the one to spout some nonsense about them falling in love; he could make it sound convincing, make it *look* convincing for the photos.

That his wife, and, since he'd officially joined the Toivonen family, also his queen, could deliver the same impression, he was not so certain.

Wife.

Pregnant wife.

Could his lifelong fears, his nightmares, have become any more real? A spouse and an unborn child to protect from all that could go wrong for them.

Then Seb saw what awaited them outside.

The palace staff had gathered, forming an impromptu honour guard along the route he and Agnesse were to take back into the palace. He'd been the focus of the public gaze before; of course he had. Countless times. He was used to it. But not like this.

Whether he took the title of consort or not, here, in the small, intimate world of the Summer Palace, he was their prince. Husband to their queen and, not that they knew it yet, father to their unborn heir. He had no playbook for this. In Grimentz the people knew him for what he pretended to be, the pleasure seeker. They had no expectations of him beyond that. But here they were looking at him with genuine regard. What happened when they discovered he wasn't worthy of it?

He nearly tripped down the final step from the church to the flagstones beyond.

So it was Agnesse who summoned the smiles, stopping to chat with a footman, or the cook and her sous-chefs. Sharing a joke with a gardener. Graciously accepting all their good wishes while he walked stiffly beside her, wearing who knew what kind of expression on his face.

Behind him he heard Mathilde and Leo similarly working their way along the line. Even Isobel and Carl were doing their duty.

A young housemaid curtsied to him.

'Congratulations, sir, and welcome to Ellamaa.'

Seb might have muttered an acknowledgment. He doubted it had been that polite. Agnesse made a quip about them both being nervous, which raised a chuckle, saved the day, and they moved on.

He was experiencing emotions he didn't know how to deal with. Things he hadn't expected to feel. About Agnesse, about their baby. About the people of Ellamaa. A desire to be everything they needed him to be. His father would have laughed in his face at that.

Let others see the real you, Agnesse had said.

Impossible.

'Come on, brother, hurry up. We're starving.' Isobel and Carl sped past him, leaping up the steps and through the French windows into the palace, disappearing from view. Precisely what he wished he could do right now.

But perhaps he could. If he pushed this emotionally stunted creature aside and turned to the old, familiar Seb.

The staff began to disperse, returning to their duties. The photographer was ready, snapping informal shots as he waited for the royal newlyweds.

Seb took Agnesse's hand and with a practised smile, raised it to his lips.

'You are more lovely than I can say, *ma chérie.*'

And if her beautiful face suddenly clouded over, well, he wouldn't let that bother him. She thought she saw right through his mask to the real Seb. Maybe she did. But he needed that mask right now. He'd promised her the protection of a husband and father for their child, nothing more. Certainly nothing deeper…

So that mask was staying firmly in place.

He posed for the photographs. Gazed feelingly into his bride's eyes. Kissed her and felt her lips trembling as they clung to his, but once that image had been captured, he pulled away. Convincing himself that he felt nothing. It was just the emotion of the day.

Then he smiled as he stood amongst his new family. He chatted pleasantly with the archbishop and politely with his mother-in-law. Sampled the delicacies laid out for the wedding breakfast, sipped champagne and fielded the teasing of his new brother-in-law and sister-in-law. Everything, in fact, that could possibly be expected of a bridegroom.

Except for the minimal attentions he paid to his bride. All the time, from the corner of his eye, he could see Agnesse watching him, her blue eyes bruised with hurt and confusion.

An hour later it was time for Leo to leave.

'Walk me to my car?' his cousin asked.

They strolled together through the gardens, heading to the forecourt where a limo waited.

'I thought the marriage service was rather beautiful,' Leo said. 'Very moving in its simplicity.'

Seb said nothing.

'And that was a genuinely touching gesture by the staff.' He paused to acknowledge the greeting of a passing gardener. 'But then the Ellamaese have always had great affection for their royal family.'

Seb made a noncommittal grunt.

Leo halted by a rose bush that was covered in lush scarlet blooms. He bent to sniff one. 'Lovely. The grounds here are exceptionally pleasant.' He glanced back over his shoulder. 'As is the palace. There are definitely worse places you could call home.'

Right now Seb couldn't think of many. Moving services, touching gestures, great *affection*. All of that scared the hell out of him and yet, here he was, helplessly trapped in the middle of it.

'Your mother-in-law might be a harder nut to crack but I've no doubt you'll charm her in the end.' Leo smiled. 'She'll eventually realise what a catch her daughter has made.'

Seb's feet scraped angrily across the crushed gravel path as he swivelled to glare at his cousin. 'Okay, spit it out. Whatever it is you're trying to say with all this nonsense give it to me straight.'

Leo studied him, his head tipped to one side.

'Just that I think you've chosen well. It could be a good life for you. If you're open to it.'

'I'll do what I did in Grimentz. What I've always done—my duty. But there can be nothing more. And you of all people should know exactly *why* that is.' Neither of them had fared well under the parenting of their respective fathers.

'I'm just saying maybe it's time to try a different way?' His solicitous tone set Seb's teeth on edge.

'No.'

'Agnesse has feelings for you. You know that, right?' Leo said.

Seb's chest tightened. His moments of weakness in the chapel came back at him. Feelings he hadn't known he could feel. If she did, it made no difference. He was only here to keep her and their child safe. He hardened the heart he didn't even know he had.

'If that's true I'm sorry for it. You know me. I can't return any of it.'

A mother he'd never had the chance to love, and a father who'd withheld all affection. How could their son know how to give anything of himself?

Leo searched his face, a scrutiny that Seb bore calmly. If his cousin was looking for anything there to refute that claim, he'd find nothing. Except that maybe he thought he had because Leo's eyes narrowed on him. 'Trust me. I really wouldn't be so sure of that.'

Seb was.

As Leo drove away, Seb knew he'd never been surer of anything in his life. He had to be.

If his experiences that morning had been anything to go by, his very survival here depended on it.

CHAPTER TEN

'I'LL BE HONEST, MA'AM. The prince has rather surprised me.'

The archbishop was on his second glass of champagne. Agnesse was still pretending to sip her first. Avoiding it would have been a dead giveaway and she was certain he already had his suspicions after the request for a special licence and the haste of their wedding.

'I really wasn't expecting such a serious-minded young man,' he continued. 'He asked me about the state of our mental health charities. He gave me quite a grilling.' The archbishop chuckled. 'Good job I was up on the facts. He seemed so interested I've agreed to make an introduction or two for him.'

Agnesse's heart swelled. Seb, her *husband*—that was going to take some getting used to—was a good man and she could only be glad that others were recognising that.

Sadly, the dowager queen wasn't currently one of them. 'I'm glad he's intending to do something useful with all his free time,' she said, tartly. 'Did he tell you he's refusing the position of official consort?'

The archbishop nodded. 'He mentioned he intends to live as a private citizen.'

Her mother sniffed. 'Perhaps he should have thought of that before he...he...'

Agnesse silently filled in the blanks: *impregnated my daughter*?

'Before he proposed to Agnesse,' her mother said with a

sneer in his direction as her despised son-in-law returned to the salon.

Agnesse felt a warning constriction in her chest. She didn't want to be caught between loyalty to her mother and loyalty to her husband, but if her marriage was to have any chance at all, she would have to choose sides, and she would have to choose Seb's.

The nausea that had fortunately held off that morning arrived now. Whether it was from panic or pregnancy hormones she couldn't tell. Nor did she care. She felt utterly miserable and needed this day to end.

As he moved towards her, she sensed that Seb had spotted her distress at once. Even though there'd been that sudden emotional withdrawal as they'd left the chapel, there was a concern in his gaze now.

'Your Majesties, Your Grace.' He took Agnesse's hand. 'My bride is looking tired. If you would excuse us, I think she should rest.'

The archbishop blustered, 'Why, of course, yes, you're a young couple and it's a wedding.' As if in the simplicity of the celebrations he'd quite forgotten the purpose of his presence here today. Agnesse wished she could, too. Suddenly, the thought of being alone with this coolly detached Seb was unnerving.

The archbishop made his farewells but as Seb led his wife away, her mother joined them. 'I need a moment of your time, Sebastien,' she said, falling in step beside them.

'Of course,' he said with a curt nod. They walked together in an uncomfortable silence. Agnesse caught in the middle of the hostility emanating from her mother and a brooding irritation from Seb.

'I wanted to give you this,' her mother said, presenting Seb with an envelope as soon as they crossed the threshold of Agnesse's suite. However much she wished it, Agnesse knew that was no wedding gift her mother had just handed over.

'As you are choosing not to take on any official role...'
Could her mother have sounded any more disapproving? 'I
feel it's important we lay down some ground rules for you,
Sebastien.'

Agnesse winced. What ground rules? The moment they'd
left the chapel it had felt as if the real Seb had withdrawn behind an invisible barrier. She didn't need any additional *rules*
getting in the way, too.

'I've had a list drawn up of palace protocols and how you'll
be expected to behave,' the dowager queen explained. 'I've no
idea about the informalities allowed in Grimentz but here you
will, of course, only ever address my daughter as ma'am or
Your Majesty whenever you are in company together.'

Agnesse sank onto a seat. She couldn't bear it. Perhaps
stuffy protocol decreed it, but that wasn't what she wanted.
She and Seb were equals.

'Thank you, Your Majesty.' Seb pocketed the envelope without even glancing at it, then crossed to the door and held it
open for her mother. 'But have no fear that I'll disgrace the
palace. I assure you, I've been most thoroughly tutored in the
niceties of royal hierarchies and court behaviours.'

Agnesse heard the lifetime of bitterness heaped into that
statement and remembered Seb's comments about unkind fathers. Was that a glimpse into what he'd meant? Had his tutoring been harsh?

'And now if you'll excuse us. My wife and I would like
some time alone together.'

Her mother's mouth fell open at being so summarily dismissed. For a moment Agnesse thought she might refuse to
leave, but perhaps something in the unblinking gaze of her
new son-in-law persuaded her that this was a battle she'd lose.

As she stepped over the threshold Seb added, 'From now
on I would ask that you respect our privacy and only enter our
suite when invited.'

'But Agnesse is my daughter.'

Despite her distress Agnesse stifled a wry smile. *Careful, Mother, that was dangerously close to shrill.*

'But now she's married. Her circumstances have changed and so must your expectations. Good day, Your Majesty.'

As he closed the door on her mother's palpable shock, Agnesse slumped in relief. Seb had stood in her corner. He'd seen her visibly crumbling before her mother's overbearing behaviour and he'd stepped in. Her mother meant well; she knew it. Like all of them, she was struggling to make sense of the world without her beloved husband in it and sometimes she misjudged, like just now.

On the sideboard sat a drinks tray. Seb went to it, filled a glass, and brought it to her.

'Still water. One cube of ice, one slice of lime.'

She looked up at him in surprise. 'I pay attention,' he said. 'I did think of adding an extra ice cube and a lemon slice but perhaps one act of rebellion is enough for you today.' He wasn't smiling exactly but there was a warmth in his eyes that seeped into her heart and took away some of the chill, nevertheless.

Agnesse took the water from him, wrapping her fingers around the cool glass. The nausea was receding. 'I know my mother loves me and only wants what's best for me.'

'But right now she can't see past the scandalous man you've installed in the palace. It was never what she intended for you. Give her time. She'll adjust.'

How was he being so reasonable after her mother's insulting behaviour? Was this yet another surprising facet to Seb?

'She never used to be like this. Since I became queen, she's been so exacting and critical. I know she's grieving and is determined for me to succeed. For me and for Papa's memory.'

'Have you told her about the panic attacks?'

Agnesse shook her head.

'Then perhaps you should. Imagine all the support she must have given to your father over the years. All the knowledge she has. She could help you.'

She couldn't bear the thought of admitting she was having problems to anyone else. It would make it real. Her father had always had so much belief in her. She couldn't let him down.

'I'm sure they'll go away soon, and I don't want to worry her. It's my job to be strong for *her*. I'm queen now.'

He took her chin and tipped her face upward. 'And when did the queen last eat, hmm? You touched nothing of the wedding breakfast.' The warmth of his hand was so welcome she would have leant into it, but he'd already withdrawn it. As if he didn't want the contact any longer than necessary.

'Last night. I couldn't face a thing this morning.'

'The sickness again?' he asked gently.

This care for her was so irresistible. In the absence of anything else more intimate she'd grasp it. She smiled at him. 'Just nerves, I think.'

'In that case you must eat.' He called for Dorel and ordered a tray be sent up for the queen.

'Anything in particular, sir?'

'Whatever you think may tempt her.'

Agnesse's gaze flickered over her husband: to the broad shoulders and long legs; to the strong jaw with its faint bruise, which Dorel, the magician that she was, had disguised with concealer for the wedding photographs; and to his wickedly sensuous mouth that haunted her dreams.

She didn't want food. She wanted him, crushing her in his arms. Pressing her to the nearest available flat surface. Spreading her thighs—

'You look a little flushed.' Frowning, he placed the back of his hand to her forehead. 'Would you like to lie down?'

Yes, with you on top of me and both of us stripped naked.

As this didn't seem to be an option, she went to the bathroom to splash cool water on her face.

A collection of male toiletries had appeared on the vanity unit. Amongst them a razor, a shaving brush, and wooden bowl containing a puck of shaving soap. She picked it up and the scent of sandalwood wafted towards her.

She brought it closer to her nose and breathed in. A needy inhalation that delivered as much of that scent as possible. She couldn't get enough of that smell. It was practically the essence of Seb.

While her own favourite perfume now turned her stomach, the smell of her baby's father had apparently become irresistible.

But what were his things doing in here? She'd had the palace team prepare the suite of rooms along the hallway, connected to hers by a door in their respective dressing rooms. She hadn't for a moment thought he'd want to *share* her rooms. She wasn't sure how she felt about it, if she was ready for that level of familiarity when the man didn't even seem to want to touch her.

She stalked back into the lounge, where he'd seated himself on her sofa and was scanning her mother's cursed list.

'What's this?'

He studied the little wooden bowl she held up. 'Shaving soap,' he said. 'My favourite brand. You might want to take note for Christmas and birthdays.'

'No, what's it doing in my bathroom—?'

'*Our* bathroom,' he said.

She remembered now, when he'd expelled her mother, he'd said *our* suite and she'd been too distracted to notice.

'You're planning to be in my rooms, not your own down the hall?'

'My duty is here so where else would I be?' For a moment he wore that same hunted expression he'd had when they'd left the chapel and saw the palace staff lined up to congratulate them. As if the responsibility terrified him.

She'd have challenged him on that, too, but the tray of food arrived. And he made her sit and hovered over her until she'd tried a little of everything and was satisfied she'd eaten enough. And then he asked if she wanted to lie down and rest now.

Like she was an invalid. Not a bride.

She could have suggested he lie down with her, but this coolly detached man felt distant and unapproachable. She'd rather spare herself the embarrassment of being rebuffed.

'I'm not tired. Perhaps we could use this time to get to know one another better.'

'Yes, of course,' he said, looking hunted again. For a moment it felt like she'd trapped a part-tame bear and the wildness in him was desperate for a way out.

'The archbishop said you'd asked about the mental health charities in Ellamaa?'

Seb's jaw tightened and he gave the briefest of nods.

'That night in Vienna you mentioned you work with one,' she said.

'I did. It's an important cause to support.'

'Do you do a lot of that? Supporting good causes?'

This time she thought he wasn't going to answer at all. He looked so closed off. But then he sank into the sofa beside her. 'I donate a considerable sum to good causes every year.'

Well, that was unexpected. 'Considerable?'

'Hundreds of millions.'

Her jaw fell open. 'Of your own income?'

He helped himself to a plump strawberry from the bowl of berries on her tray. 'Not exactly. I raise the money by investing and then donate the bulk of the profits to the charities I like to support.'

'You mean you have people manage your investments for you?'

He snorted as if she'd insulted him. 'I have a small team for admin purposes, but I've always done the bulk of research myself. It's my job, Agnesse. It's what I—' he sketched out inverted commas with his fingers '—do with my time.'

Her mother would be astonished by that, and rightly so. Agnesse was rather impressed herself.

'And how long have you been investing?'

He collected another strawberry. As his lips closed around it, Agnesse shivered in remembered delight of when he closed that mouth around the tips of her breasts.

'I started when I was sixteen.'

'*Sixteen?* You were just a boy.'

'But old enough to know I needed to find something to do with my life.'

Agnesse sensed he wasn't being entirely truthful. That the sixteen-year-old Seb had more compelling reasons for his financial planning. Why would a boy born into wealth and royalty need an escape? Unkind father, perhaps?

'You wanted to be financially independent of you family.'

His green eyes flashed. 'Yes,' he said emphatically. Well, that was an honest reaction at least. 'And I'd have gone as far away as I could. But I couldn't leave Leo. He's always been like a brother to me. I owe him.'

'So you stayed out of duty.'

'Of course, out of duty.'

Not love, then. The same reason he'd married her. Her heart deflated a little.

'Are the von Frohburgs really so terrible?'

'Not Leo and Max. But the rest of them are, and they hate me because my mother wasn't one of them.'

'Will you tell me about her?'

'I never knew her. She died giving birth to me.'

Agnesse wanted to reach out and take his hand but didn't think he'd want that sort of intimacy.

'But I have a photograph.' He dug his phone from his pocket and leant forward, elbows propped on his thighs, as he scrolled through images.

He handed her the phone.

'When my father died, they found two photographs tucked away amongst his possessions. This is one of them.'

A young woman, heavily pregnant, sat at a piano. She smiled up at the camera. Had it been taken by Seb's father? The image had a touching intimacy to it. And tragedy, too. Short weeks after it had been taken, she would be dead.

'Fabienne Bonfils. My mother,' he said.

'She was beautiful. She looks happy, too. And young.'

'She was younger than you are now when she died,' he said with a pained glance to Agnesse. This might account for the look of sheer terror she'd seen in his face today. Perhaps she could understand that. He might be worried history would repeat itself.

'You said there were two photographs.'

A host of emotions went to war in his green eyes. Whatever triumphed, it secured his decision to show her the next image. Fabienne again, but this time joined by a man.

'It's your parents.'

Of course it was. Who else could it be? The man beside her bore such a striking resemblance to them both. His father's chin and nose, his mother's eyes.

Fabienne sat smiling in the arms of Prince Georg, whose gaze was filled with love. His hand spread protectively over her rounded belly. Seb studied the image with her in silence until she looked up at him.

'It's a lovely picture but you didn't really want to show me, did you?' Agnesse said.

He ran a hand across his face. 'I have a complicated relationship with that photograph,' he said at last. 'My father's first wife came from one of the best European families. She brought wealth and good connections. The von Frohburgs have always been obsessed about protecting the bloodlines,' he said, bitterly. 'Fabienne was his secretary. She brought nothing but a pretty face, and if that photo is anything to go by, a genuine love for my father. It must have been a revelation for him. His first marriage was arranged. And not happy. My half brother remembers them fighting. By the time this photo was taken they'd been divorced for two years. It had been an ugly and bruising process. My father was not supported by the family. And then this pretty young thing arrives in the midst of that cold, loveless life and you can see it lit him up inside.'

Agnesse *could* see it. The wonder and joy in Prince Georg's eyes.

'They do so look happy together,' Agnesse said.

'The von Frohburgs hated my mother from the start. So after their wedding they moved to France. But when my mother died, he seemed like he lost all hope and went back to Grimentz, and I was raised there with Leo and Max.'

'Did your father ever speak of her to you?'

He gave a bark of bitter laughter. 'My father rarely spoke to me, full stop. I never got the chance to know anything about her from him. What little I know I've had to piece together myself. She had no family so there weren't even any grandparents or siblings I could talk to about her. She's like a ghost.' There was such loss in that statement, instinctively Agnesse reached out and placed her hand on his arm. He didn't shake it off and instead, sent her a tight smile.

Her own mother could be trying but she was there; Agnesse had at least known her and knew she was loved. By both her parents. She began to get some understanding of what Seb had lost, what he had never had. The secure bond of a family. How much harder for him to see that picture of the three of them, his father embracing his young wife, his hand spread protectively over her full belly, over his unborn son. Before that family was cruelly ripped apart.

'I don't think he could ever forgive me. The rest of the extended family certainly couldn't. Materially, I wanted for nothing, but it was like he couldn't bear to look at me. I think all the life went out of him when he lost my mother. And I was no compensation. He saw me as the opposite. The reason he'd lost the only thing he'd ever truly loved.'

Then he shook himself. 'But that's enough sadness on our wedding day. Would you like to hear about the projects I've invested in?'

Seb had never shared that much about his life with anyone. He'd always thought the bitter emotional scars his father and family had inflicted on him were better left unexplored. But sharing those details with Agnesse, seeing her smile down at his mother's image, had brought him an odd kind of solace.

It made him realise, too, that he should share more details of himself. At the very least, his new wife should know she hadn't married a wastrel, that he was a man of substance and more than just his playboy image. He owed her that, surely?

So they talked, and she'd begun to relax. And the day ahead progressed and turned to evening.

He'd discarded his jacket and tie. Her jacket was gone, too, revealing a silk camisole that clung to her breasts and was leaving little to his imagination. Not that he needed to use it. The utter perfection of her breasts had been imprinted in his mind since Vienna. Fuelling much erotic torment since that night.

She'd slipped off the sky-high, crystal heels he'd found so alluring—he knew he'd be having fantasies about her dressed in nothing but those.

She'd tucked her legs beneath her and scooted closer until she was leaning against him so she could point at the images he was bringing up on his phone.

'What's this one?'

'An artisan baker. It was one of my earliest investments. They still make the best sourdough you'll ever taste.'

He'd shown her other pictures. Other companies and initiatives he'd invested in. The latest project he'd supported was on a significantly bigger scale. A company developing hydrogen fuel technologies to heat homes and businesses with cleaner energy.

She'd sat back in laughing astonishment. 'The gossip columnists really have no idea, have they? You are nothing like the man they say.'

'Some of it's true,' he said with a glint in his eye, and she dimpled at him and his breath had caught. He could so easily have reached for her then, starting something that would have ended with them in bed together for a real wedding night.

But his mother's face haunted him. Younger even than Agnesse was now. Pregnant and so full of hope. Her death had blighted three lives. Not just his parents' but his own. He was cursed by the endless terror of losing someone he cared about.

He closed his mind to it. Tonight was not the time to think about it.

At some point she had fallen asleep propped on his shoulder. One minute they'd been talking and the next she couldn't keep her eyes open.

His beautiful bride who had secrets of her own.

He hoped she'd tell her mother about her panic attacks because he had no doubt that Mathilde would help. She was as devoted and protective as a pit bull. He and she weren't going to be friends anytime soon, but Seb couldn't fault her loyalty to her daughter. But he didn't care about her list of protocols. Nothing on it he hadn't had rammed down his throat when he was a boy. He didn't scare easily.

With the warmth of Agnesse at his shoulder and the steady rhythm of her soft breathing, he brought up his mother's photo again.

She looks so happy, Agnesse had said. He'd always thought that, too. Despite what happened next to her, it had given him great comfort to think she'd once been happy and well loved.

Seb scrolled through to that next photograph with his father gazing adoringly at his young wife.

The von Frohburgs never forgave his father, and by association, him, for marrying outside his social class. There'd been mutterings about Seb's legitimacy but fortunately he was the image of Prince Georg, except for the eyes. They were all his mother. Soft and beguiling, or so countless women had told him. Perhaps that was the reason his father had rejected his younger son. It was that or each day see the living, breathing reminder of all that he'd lost the day his wife had died.

A true von Frohburg had eyes of blue, chilly and aloof. His warm green eyes were another reason for them to snub him.

Agnesse made an adorable snuffling noise and settled again.

The thought of anything happening to her curled icy fingers in Seb's chest. This woman who at one moment could address a packed room with aplomb, and the next was fighting for breath on the floor of her bathroom.

Physical intimacy, taking a woman to bed, was easy. It was this emotional intimacy that he didn't know how to handle. He'd sought the connections he'd missed out on elsewhere in the only way he could. With endless women. But he gave his heart to no one, truly *shared* himself with no one.

Maybe it was just that she was easy to talk to. Maybe it was something to do with those blue eyes that seemed to see past the playboy prince to Seb, the real man behind it, but he'd *wanted* to share with Agnesse. And wasn't that a revelation?

But it was getting late, and she really should be in bed. A pregnant woman needed her rest.

She was so dead to the world she barely stirred when he gently lifted her in his arms and carried her to the bedroom. His bedroom, too, for the foreseeable future. She mumbled something at him when he slipped her out of the ivory skirt. She'd taken all the pins from her hair long ago and it lay in soft gold waves across her pillow. He stopped himself from running his fingers through it. He also left the camisole and panties on.

He'd vowed to himself he wouldn't touch her, and undressing her completely would have been a trial too far.

He pulled the sheet over her and she turned to her side and was deeply asleep again in moments.

Feeling like he'd had a lucky escape, Seb headed for his dressing room to ready himself for sleep.

Seb woke slowly and with an unexpected feeling of well-being. Like he'd slept the deep, untroubled sleep of the righteous. First surprise.

The second was that Agnesse was in his arms. Or rather, they were wrapped around one another, limbs entwined as if they'd found each other in the night and couldn't let go.

And right now he didn't mind.

She was soft and warm. He drifted back to sleep.

When he woke again he was alone, and from the bathroom came the sound of Agnesse retching.

'Go away,' she said, miserably, her voice echoing in the porcelain as he appeared in the doorway. Instead, he went to her, gathered up her hair and gently rubbed her spine as another bout of nausea hit.

At last, she slumped backwards and propped herself against the wall.

'All done?' he asked.

'For now, I think.'

He dampened a flannel and handed it to her.

'Is this going to be a thing for us?' she asked. 'You rescuing me from the bathroom floor?'

'It's what I signed up for yesterday. For better or worse, remember?'

'You probably weren't expecting it to be *worse* so soon in the marriage. Some honeymoon this is going to be.' She swiped the flannel back and forth over her mouth. She'd hastily pulled on a wrap; it was knotted haphazardly. Her hair in disarray. And yet, had she ever looked lovelier to him?

He told her so.

She snorted and stared at him like he'd become a simpleton.

He took the flannel from her and helped her to her feet. 'Anyway, I thought we weren't having a honeymoon,' he said.

'Just as well if I'm going to vomit all through it.'

Suddenly, yesterday's terror uncoiled and slithered through his gut. 'This is normal, isn't it? Perhaps we should speak to the doctor later, to be certain?'

'Relax. It's horrible but perfectly normal. I'll be better after a shower and a coffee. Give me fifteen minutes to do some repair work because, despite what you think, I don't feel lovely. That was a sweet thing to say, by the way,' she said, shooing him out of the bathroom. 'Sweet, but deranged.'

But when Agnesse emerged from the shower it wasn't to her usual cafetière of coffee. It was to a table for two set by a sunny window. Seb occupied one of the seats. In front of the other, a place had been set with breakfast things.

No coffee, she noted. But a teapot and toast rack with two dainty triangles of white bread with the crusts neatly removed.

'I didn't order this.'

'No, I did,' he said pleasantly. 'I understand eating breakfast can often help with the queasiness.'

'But I just want coffee. I never eat breakfast.'

'As you're pregnant, how about you start now?'

Dressed in nothing but navy silk pyjama bottoms, the sun beating down on his sculpted torso, he looked practically edible. *How about I eat* you *for breakfast?* she thought.

Last night they'd talked and she started to understand her husband a little more. His courage and determination to forge a new life for himself and help others along the way was impressive and deeply moving.

She could have talked to him all night.

But embarrassingly, she'd fallen asleep. Just like that. Perhaps that was the baby hormones, too. She felt another bout of nausea coming on.

She didn't even remember getting into bed last night. Certainly not taking off her skirt. She'd woken in her underwear, sprawled over Seb's chest, her leg thrown over his thighs. As she carefully lifted herself off him, she was relieved he hadn't woken. She'd have had to apologise to him for being plastered all over him when he'd made it clear he didn't want that from her.

Last night he hadn't made any kind of move on her. He'd slept in her bed all night and hadn't touched her.

Duty, that was why he was here. Nothing more. Just like he'd done for Leo. She'd do well to remember that.

Now he gestured to the seat beside him. 'Agnesse, you need to eat something. Please.'

He'd delivered that plea with a flash of his green eyes, and she found her feet obeying him. She sank into the empty seat. If this had been a real honeymoon she'd have perched herself in his lap and teasingly fed that toast to him instead.

On a sigh of frustration, she picked up the first slice of toast and nibbled carefully. Surprisingly, her stomach didn't rebel. She tried another bite.

Seb poured the tisane into a cup and made a point of edging that towards her, too.

'It's ginger tea. Midwives swear by it for morning sickness.'

'Aren't we the expert this morning?' She took a sip while he watched her with an expression she couldn't decipher.

'Happy now?' she said.

He blinked and that moment passed. His mouth curved into a lazy smile. 'I will be when you've finished that cup and both slices of toast.'

'Both?'

'It's hardly a banquet, Agnesse, and let's try it to see if it works, shall we?'

'I've married a tyrant,' she muttered. 'That's got to be sufficient grounds for an annulment. I might call my lawyers.'

'Please do,' he said, quite unperturbed by her bad temper. 'Just as soon as you've finished your breakfast. And if you are going to be such a ray of sunshine every morning, I might call my own.'

'Please do,' she said, shoving the second piece of toast into her mouth and chewing with a baleful glare in his direction.

But she was actually feeling better, thinking maybe the ginger tea and toast could work and feeling secretly touched by his efforts on her behalf.

And even more surprising after last night she felt the mask Seb had hidden behind yesterday had slipped, and she was getting a glimpse of the real man.

CHAPTER ELEVEN

THE DAYS PASSED and settled into a routine with a frustrating glimpse of an intimacy, of a loving relationship with her husband, that Agnesse could never quite grasp.

There was the tender care of her but also those moments when he allowed her to see the real Seb. Vulnerable, hurt, compassionate.

Oh, she wanted so much to see more of him. That man drew her in.

He would always take breakfast with her. Probably to satisfy himself that she had eaten. He was usually there for dinner with the family, too. But apart from a chaste kiss good-night, he barely touched her. She was burning up with frustration and hurt. Did he really not desire her?

If she couldn't have the emotional life with him that she craved, then she would get on with being the best queen she could be. It was the life she'd been born to live, after all. She would embrace it. She would *own* it. And she was damn well going to be good at it. Whatever the pressure. However long the to-do list that remained at the end of each day.

She met with ministers, opened hospitals, unveiled plaques, attended military parades. For none of these did Seb join her. Only on the less formal occasions, the visits to charities and organisations she supported. Then he was there, showing an interest and a surprising knowledge of the work being done at each, delighting everyone.

Her husband knew he could charm people. What he didn't understand was it happened when he wasn't even trying. It was him. There was something innately dazzling about him and people wanted to bask in it.

There were the appealing manners, the lazy smile, and for her alone, the quick but heated glances that never failed to send warmth to her belly. But there was more. There was, if you looked closely enough, a subtle vulnerability. Something guarded and fragile and perhaps not altogether under his control. Sometimes, when he thought he was unobserved, he would fold inwards and then it was like an injured bear had invaded her home and prowled its boundaries looking for an escape.

Mostly, he moved through the palace as if it hardly mattered who it belonged to. He had no need for it. But then even the walls seemed to sway closer as he passed, as if they yearned to hold him close for a moment. The palace might be Ellamaese, but now this foreign von Frohburg male had bewitched them all.

Her team was eager to please him. There were smiles, and greetings, and plans, and papers pressed into his hands for his consideration; completed tasks pointed out for his approval. She was happy that her people loved him. But whilst he was charm itself, not one of them really gained his absolute attention. Oh, none of them realised it. He managed to convey his complete focus on whomever had accosted him at that moment. But she knew that whenever she was close by his attention was on her.

Occasionally, she tested her theory. Lifting a languid hand to her brow and sighing faintly. And though he was apparently deep in conversation on the other side of the room, in the next instant he'd be beside her, his fingers lightly touching her shoulder. His green eyes full of concern.

It was irresistible, this attention. This care of her.

She felt herself falling more and more under its spell. Needing it, craving it. Like the palace staff looking for ways to draw him to her side and win a solicitous look, or better yet a smile.

Oh…the variety of smiles. The boyish one. The one filled with sexual promise that sent shivers of anticipation along her spine. And that beautiful but practised, distant one, where he went somewhere she was desperate to follow.

Emboldened one morning, she took his face between her palms and asked him outright what made him hide behind that mask. He'd closed off instantly, kissing her lightly and telling her she was imagining things. Why on earth did she think he needed a mask?

You tell me, she wanted to say, but wasn't brave enough because what if she discovered the dark truth that might lay in wait for her? That she wasn't actually that important to him and that was what he was hiding.

And then he might actually break her heart. What use would a broken woman be as queen, when what was needed was calmness, clarity, service? Where would be her strength? It would be in pieces, a tattered pile of unrequited need at the feet of this man.

All she had left by way of defence was work.

Agnesse grabbed it with both hands.

Her meeting in the city had gone well. She'd just secured extra funding for one of the youth organisations her father's charity supported. Now they could build a brand-new residential centre on an earmarked woodland site. Thousands of youngsters growing up in deprived areas would soon have the opportunity to experience all the benefits the countryside had to offer.

And the person she most wanted to tell was Seb. Last night she'd practised her speech on him, then he'd helped her revise it, and she knew it had been better because of it.

As she walked back to their suite music floated towards her down the corridor. Someone was playing her father's piano. No one had touched it since he'd passed away. Was it time for its regular tuning? There'd been no mention in her diary and Keert would have warned the family. It would be hard to hear the instrument that her papa had loved, and that had fallen silent with his death, being played again. She didn't recognise the piece, and the regular tuner rarely played more than chords anyway. The door to the music room was ajar. She peeked around it.

It was her husband seated at the piano, his fingers flying back and forth over the keyboard. So he was an accomplished pianist, too? As if she needed another reason to adore him.

She must have made a noise because his head swung towards her. The music stopped instantly.

'Hello.' He smiled and her heart swooped in recognition.

'Hello,' she answered, walking in.

'How was the meeting?'

'I got the funding.'

'Good girl,' he said with another lift of his lips. 'I knew you could do it.' Oh, she could bask in his praise all day. She dropped her bag and jacket on a chair.

'What were you playing just now? It was pretty but I didn't recognise it.' She drew closer and bent to kiss him. He may not be taking her to bed but he never refused her kisses so she gave them freely.

She noted the piano was bare of sheet music. He must have known that piece by heart.

'I think it was something my mother used to play.' He picked out a few notes with one hand. 'The music was found along with the photographs my father kept. I'd never heard it before but when I began to play, it was so familiar. I wondered if I remembered it from when...'

'Your mother playing it while she was pregnant with you,' Agnesse said, gently finishing the thought that he could not.

'Yes.'

She heard all the longing in that brief reply. A yearning to find some piece of his mother, a connection to her when all chance of that had died with her. Her heart ached for him.

She sat beside him, placing her hand over her stomach. 'Perhaps our little blip might like to hear it, too. Would you play it again for us?'

Seb lifted her hand, pressed a kiss in her palm, then turned it over and placed it gently back over her abdomen. Heaven help her, but the man had all kinds of ways to melt a girl's heart.

He began to play. It was a bright, sweet, hopeful piece and he played it beautifully. Agnesse leant against his shoulder, mesmerised by his skilled fingers, and moved by the sadness of the story behind them.

When he finished she took his face in her hands and kissed him.

'That was lovely. You play well.'

'Leo, Max, and I all had lessons as boys. I was the only one who took to it. Once I saw that picture of my mother, I figured out why.'

He looked so lost for a moment that she kissed him again, but this time she sensed a shift in him. An urgency that had been missing since they arrived here. Soon, it was he dictating the pace, his hands in her hair, holding her face to his. The brush of his lips becoming harder, more demanding.

She made a sound at the back of her throat. A call to passion. She'd wanted this from him so badly, and she prayed that he would not pull back from it as he generally did.

He answered that call, dragging his mouth from hers so he could feast on the sensitive skin of her neck. It wasn't enough for him. He popped a button on her blouse to get at more of her, then another and another until it was all but off. His panting breaths gusted hot into her hair as he reached behind her to drag it free.

Then they were on their feet, stumbling, banging blindly

into the stole, bouncing off the side of the piano, until he braced against it to support them both.

She took advantage of their respective positions, unbuttoned his shirt, and ran her greedy hands across his chest. He groaned into her mouth helplessly. Oh, she liked that. She liked his weakness for her. She'd exploit it. It made her bold.

She stepped back from him, and never breaking eye contact, sank to her knees before him. With her hands she freed him. But it wasn't her hands she intended to pleasure him with.

The feel of him in her mouth was sublime.

She stretched her lips wide to accommodate the girth of him. She teased the tip, the plump silken skin so soft beneath her tongue. Seb let out a fractured breath. An explosion of air, as if he'd been trying to stay in control and suddenly lost it.

She experimented with how deep she could take him. What the long, slow rasp of her tongue did to him as she sucked. A groan was wrenched from him this time. She smiled around him.

She reached up a hand and pressed a palm flat to his abdomen and she felt the tightening, the judder of powerful muscles as he fought to control himself. And she fought right back.

She took him deeper and watched his head drop back helplessly. His fingers clawed at the piano edge, his knuckles white. His gasps and moans filled the air. As sweet a music to her ears as the piece he'd played for her before. Perhaps sweeter, because she was the one wrenching those helpless sighs from him.

Her. The former Ice Queen. She felt thoroughly, gloriously, wanton now.

'Agnesse,' he said, brokenly, 'stop. I can't… I won't be able…'

Oh, you can and you will, she thought. And she wrapped her fingers around him, working at him, not letting up for a moment until he was beyond speech altogether. On a long, shuddering gasp he threw back his head and spilled into her mouth.

'Agnesse,' he breathed when he finally had the power to speak again. She loved how undone he was. How it made her feel so powerful. But now she had a problem.

Being a wanton was all very well—until you had to stand back up with your dignity still in place. Her skirt was tight. Her heels were high. There was no way she was getting to her feet without his help.

On a giggle she reached out to him so he could haul her to her feet. It was done but suddenly, she was beset with uncertainty. Was that any good for him? He seemed to enjoy it but that didn't mean she'd done it all right. She thought of all the women he'd been with. They'd have done *that* so many times before, they'd have known exactly what to do.

He leant in and suddenly, his mouth was on hers, in one of his swift, drugging kisses that could make a woman forget her own name.

'Stop overthinking it. It was good,' he said, a bewitching smile dancing at the edge of his lips. 'Perhaps I could return the favour?'

He scooped her up and carried her to one of the couches. He divested them both of the remainder of their clothes and lay her down, gazing at her body with absolute reverence.

'Do you have any idea how beautiful you are, *chérie*?' he said, placing his mouth just beneath her ear. Goose bumps flowered wherever his lips met her skin.

He trailed fingertips over her collarbone then lower, gliding between her breasts. He dipped his head, to kiss each nipple, then added the graze of teeth until both were puckered. He licked them then blew gently on the gleam of moisture. Agnesse moaned. He turned his mouth to her stomach, kissing it with reverence.

'Look away, precious blip,' he said to her still-flat belly. 'Your naughty papa is about to do some terribly wicked things to your beautiful mama.'

Agnesse squirmed with pleasure as he kissed all the way

down her abdomen until his mouth was there. And his tongue. Hot and unbelievably exciting. Stroking and licking and sucking until she was a writhing ball of need. One leg was draped over the low back of the sofa. She still wore her shoes. Impossibly slender six-inch heels in burgundy suede. It felt so wanton again.

'I still have my shoes on,' she said when he paused long enough for her to catch her breath, or rather, for him to lift her left leg and drape it over his shoulder, the better to get at her.

'I've had so many fantasies about doing this to you, with you wearing nothing but your heels.'

She didn't get a chance to make any kind of coherent answer to that. His mouth was on her again and all she could do was gasp and moan.

Then he rose up, gathered her close, and slid into her. She was slick, so primed he was seated to the hilt in one move.

'Agnesse,' he sighed as breathless and needy as she was. *'Chérie.'*

He was caught up in this. Even if it was just sex, it was still sex with her and she'd celebrate that a little.

He began to move. Slow, deep thrusts that came dangerously close to tipping her over the edge each time. But he played her body as he'd played her father's piano, with skill and gentle understanding, and coaxed such drawn-out delight from her that she trembled in his arms, and their shared bliss, when it came, was beyond anything she'd ever imagined.

Afterwards he seemed content to just hold her. Their limbs entwined, his fingers playing idly in her hair, her hand on his chest.

'I know you've felt neglected,' he said. 'But I was worried I might be too rough and hurt you or the baby.'

'You know our blip isn't even the size of a peanut yet. And pregnant women have sex all the time. Some of us actually *want* it all the time.'

She felt the rumble against her cheek as he chuckled. 'Then in the future I shall try to oblige, *ma chérie.*'

At last. She offered up a silent hallelujah to the universe. 'My hormones will thank you for it,' she said.

Eventually, they had to move. People would be wondering where they were. He helped her into her skirt and zipped it up. She found his shirt and buttoned him back into it, at least after peppering his broad chest with little kisses. He collected her jacket and bag in one hand and twined her fingers through his other.

'Right, *chérie,*' he said. 'It's time you were fed. Let's go freshen up, then and find you some dinner, shall we?'

Well loved, her hand safe in his, Agnesse could have almost believed she floated back to their rooms that evening.

On the terrace below their suite Agnesse saw Carl and her husband, deep in conversation. What about? she wondered.

They often talked this way now. Her brother she knew appreciated the presence of another male in the family. He missed their father and while no one could ever replace him, Seb was doing a sterling job of being a big brother.

As for Isobel, all the trouble she had once caused seemed long forgotten. Now her outrageous sister delighted in teasing and taunting the newest Toivonen family member. But he threw it all back in kind. It apparently pleased them both.

Even her mother, her disapproving, exacting mother, was mellowing, leaving some sheet music for him on the piano. When asked, she dismissed it as just an old piece she'd found lying around. But one morning Agnesse saw her standing outside the music room, the fingertips of one hand resting on the door, the other pressing a handkerchief to her mouth, as a piece her father used to play floated out from Seb's skillful fingers.

Agnesse quietly turned back the way she had come and left her mother with her memories. But she'd hugged that moment close. Her whole family had accepted him.

Then there was the sex; *oh, the sex*. It was everything she'd dreamed of, and more. Though he never said it, sometimes she even believed he was developing deeper feelings for her.

There'd been no more panic attacks. She was managing her workload, just. A second pair of hands—an official consort for example—would help enormously, but hey, a girl couldn't have everything.

Agnesse curled her hand over her abdomen. Even her little blip was behaving and her morning sickness was under control.

She had everything to look forward to. Life was good.

CHAPTER TWELVE

THE WOMAN WOULDN'T rest and it was driving him crazy.

She was trying to do too much. Her mother knew it, Keert knew it, the whole palace staff knew it, but his wife was refusing to see it.

He'd joined her in her study that morning so they could co-ordinate their diaries for the next month. He wasn't at her side for official duties. But social occasions were another matter and he often accompanied her on any charity visits. He enjoyed them. And people seemed to enjoy his presence. So far he was even getting favourable write-ups in the press. It was probably just the novelty of discovering that a playboy prince also had a caring heart.

The job was done and she'd closed the calendar on her screen and brought up her task list. Seb, standing at her shoulder as the list appeared, nearly ground his teeth at the sheer number of items on it.

No wonder she looked weary.

Although he knew in part he was responsible for that. She wasn't getting all the sleep she could. When they retired for the night, when she woke in his arms in the morning, they couldn't resist one another and the sex, quite frankly, was incredible.

Yes, he had made love to his wife—over and over—and the sky had not fallen.

The thought of it tightened his groin. He could banish the

staff and take her over this desk right now. But after, he knew she'd go straight back to work.

She was already making so few concessions to being pregnant. At least she was taking breakfast now and the nausea had lessened. A small win in many fights he felt he needed to have. Back in Grimentz intervening would have been less problematic. He'd have told Leo he was worn out and needed to take a break. Not to be such a martyr and to get some rest.

That approach wouldn't run here. She'd be more likely to dig in her heels and work even harder. If that was possible.

'Your view to the gardens is impressive,' he said casually.

Without shifting her gaze from her computer screen, she said, 'It's one of the reasons I chose this room for my study.'

Really? Did she even look at them? he wondered.

'And how often do you actually get out there?'

'Out there?' Now she looked at the view for about five seconds. Then her attention was back on the screen again. 'Recently, hardly ever.'

'Seems such a shame. The guidebook waxes lyrical about the carp pond.'

Her head swung towards him in surprise. 'You read the guidebook?'

'I was hoping to impress you with my knowledge when you take me on the tour.' He sent her the crooked smile that he knew she found irresistible.

Even though he heard the hitch in her breathing, on this occasion the woman stubbornly resisted. 'You've just seen my diary. I really don't have the time.'

He stretched out a hand, gathering one of hers from the keyboard. 'Let's be spontaneous. It'll be fun. Surely, you can spare me a little time to help me settle in.'

'You've already been here a month. Isn't that sufficient settling-in time?'

He made a face at her. 'And yet, I'm still to see the much-vaunted carp pond.'

'Did you actually just pout at me?' she said, laughing.

Yes, he had. He wasn't beneath using underhanded tactics. It was his job to look after her and that included getting her to take some time off. So he'd gifted her with his best sexy pout. It did the trick. She got to her feet. Ten minutes later they were seated on the raised slabs that ran around the edge of the pond.

She sighed prettily. The first unrestrained sigh of content-ment he'd heard from her outside the bedroom. 'I'd forgotten how lovely it is here,' she said.

His *lovely* wife was a vision in the sunshine. There were small changes to her body that he'd noticed. A fullness to her breasts, and they were more sensitive when he ministered to them at night. A slight thickening at her waist but no real baby bump yet. In just over a month, she'd have her first scan. He was a mix of excited and terrified. Would she be okay? Would their baby be okay?

She leant over to trail her fingers through the water. 'Would you like to hand-feed the fish?' she asked.

Seb was surprised. 'They'll let you do that?'

'My father trained them. Even though Papa is gone, his fa-vourite fish, Gunter, still leads the others to this part of the pond. We could try.'

She beckoned to one of the gardeners working nearby. Min-utes later there was a tub of fish food on the slabs between them and she was showing Seb what to do. Sure enough, with Gunter leading, the carp were soon swiping pellets from his fingers.

'Sometimes my father would bring me here. He'd talk about looking after the fish, but he was really talking about our country. I think he came out here to help him find different perspectives to a problem.'

'Or maybe,' Seb said, 'he just wanted to indulge in the plea-sure of feeding his fish?'

* * *

Agnesse closed her eyes and tipped her face to the sun. She'd forgotten how restful this part of the garden was. No wonder her father had loved to come out here. This stretch of the garden bordered the wildflower meadows, and everywhere was alive with bees, the buzzing a drowsy soundtrack to the beat of warm sunshine.

She exhaled with a long, slow breath of contentment. When she opened them again, she met Sebastien's warm, knowing gaze. Oh, the sneaky, *sneaky* man.

'I've just been managed, haven't I?'

The corner of his mouth curved up into that crooked smile she adored.

'I did really want to see this pond. And I really wanted to see it with you.' He took her chin in his hand and drew her closer for a kiss. 'Thank you,' he said.

The gentle kiss to each cheek was all the more entrancing for being so chaste. Her eyes fluttered closed and Agnesse sighed, feeling more tension drain away from her. A bird trilled in a nearby bush; a breeze stirred through the grasses edging the walkway. Lavender and rose and Sebastien's sandalwood mingled in the air. And then there was the soft touch of his fingers caressing her cheek. She wanted to freeze this moment in time. The calm, quiet morning. The feeling, for the moment at least, of having nothing to do. The warmth and touch of Seb's fingers. Like he cared. Like this thing between them was real. Queen and consort. Husband and wife. The image was so irresistible to her, she spoke without thinking.

'You know I'd have more time for these sort of moments if you accepted the position of consort. We could share the workload.'

His fingers were instantly gone, and without opening her eyes she sensed the anger in him.

'I told you before we married that I didn't want that life. I'm supporting you in any way I can, but it will always be behind the scenes. No titles, no official role.'

'You attend social events and charities with me. How is that different?'

'No weight of expectation to live with,' he said, looking more grim and closed off than she had ever seen him. 'No judgemental family criticising your every move.'

He meant the von Frohburgs. But her family wasn't doing that. They'd embraced him; even her mother had warmed to him.

'You have a new family now,' she said, softly, wanting him to see it. He had her, and their baby when it came. Their own fledgling family. She could have everything she'd dreamed of. If only she could make him want it, too.

If only he wanted her.

'I'm doing my duty, Agnesse. I always will. That will have to be enough for you.'

'So you're content to let me work my fingers to the bone while you do *what*?'

She knew she was being unfair, but he was sitting there so calmly while she was getting more and more angry; it made her want to shove him backwards into that blasted pond.

'I work. You know this. I'm hardly idle all day while you slave to keep me housed and fed.' A muscle ticked in his jaw. Finally, she might be shaking that impenetrable calm of his.

The crunch of gravel announced Keert's approach.

'Ma'am, sir. Forgive the intrusion but the prime minister is on the phone.'

'Tell him you'll call him back.' Seb's narrowed gaze challenged her to do just that. 'We are in the middle of something.'

'No, we're not.' Agnesse shot to her feet. 'We're on the edge of something we *could* be in the middle of. Together. But you don't want it. Or can't even see it. You'd rather hide behind all the terrible things your family made you believe.'

She saw it so clearly now. Despite his soft kisses and tender looks, despite all his care of her, it was just duty to him. The sex was getting better and better but the real intimacy she craved was eluding her. The only thing binding them together was their unborn baby. Seb couldn't love her and he'd never really stand beside her.

She placed her hand across her belly, splaying out her fingers protectively. *In that case, we'll just have to love each other won't we, little one?* she vowed silently.

Then sent her husband the parody of a smile.

'Thank you for a lovely few minutes. But you've done your duty. I'm rested now,' she said nastily and stalked away before Seb could stop her.

Fifteen minutes.

Twenty, at most.

That was how long he'd succeeded in getting her to rest.

And then they'd fought.

As Gunter bobbed hopefully behind him, Seb remained perched at the edge of the pond, watching his wife depart.

She was dressed in a blue silk blouse and ivory linen skirt. Neat and prim. Except, as ever, for the shoes. Today it was black stilettos.

Agnesse had a fondness for vertiginous heels; Seb had developed a fondness for watching her as she moved in them. With her quick, purposeful step, the resulting sway of her pert behind always drove him just a little crazy.

Now anger was driving her; the sway was even more pronounced. He was torn between dragging her back here to finish their argument or dragging her to bed and putting an end to it that way.

He knew what she wanted from him. The same as numerous lovers had over the years. An emotional commitment. But he was never going there. He always kept that piece of himself apart. Safe. It was buried so deep he wondered if his capacity to truly feel even existed anymore.

In the meantime, she could get as angry at him as she wanted. Because he'd made no false promises. He'd married her and given her the protection of a husband. He'd saved her and the Ellamaese royal family from scandal.

And despite her ridiculous accusation that he was doing nothing here, his workload was mounting, and he was navigating that as best he could. There was no precedent for his role here, no rule book they could give to the husband of the first ever queen regnant. Particularly one who hadn't adopted any official title or duties.

Despite that, he'd received various petitions; a few of those had come from charities. He was sifting through them, deciding which he'd like to support. Others, businesses or lobbyists mostly, just wanted a piece of him so they could gain access to his wife. Those he'd deal with to ensure he stood between her and yet more pressure.

For now his main priority was to support the queen—his wife.

Again, his insides warmed at the thought of her. He could barely get used to it. The leap of his pulse when she walked into a room; the pleasure he felt when she reached out to take his hand, or even just smiled for him.

That smile was the kicker. He tried to steel himself against the effects of it, the heady mix of lust and a strange longing. She used a version of it on her people, as he'd seen Violetta do. Using a smile to bring delight to a sea of upturned faces, or charm overwhelmed staff. But the effect his wife's had on him was different. Agnesse moved him in ways he couldn't quite define. He'd convinced himself it was lust. Just lust and sexual yearning.

Nothing more. There was certainly nothing emotional behind it. He wasn't the kind of man to be *emotional* about a woman. He desired his wife. That was all. He desired his wife and he wanted to keep her, and their unborn baby, safe.

And then, just before she disappeared from view, and as if in slow motion, Seb's entire world view was torn inside out.

Because with a bone-chilling cry and clutching desperately at her stomach, Agnesse had just sunk to the ground.

The cramping pain was so sudden and fierce she'd folded double with it. Then another wave, even more excruciating, took her legs from beneath her.

'Agnesse!' She heard Seb's panicked yell and the thundering of his feet as he sprinted towards her. She was on her hands and knees in the dirt, gasping to breathe through the agony when he reached her side.

The next hour was a horrible blur. Seb carried her inside. Yelling for doctors, for her mother. For a car. As one screeched to a halt in front of the palace entrance, he climbed in still clutching her tight to his chest. He held her, his cheek against her hair, telling her over and over it was going to be okay, all through the short drive to the private hospital on the outskirts of the city.

Where they took her away from him. When all she wanted was to cling to him and never let go. Because she knew what was happening. Everything was about to change.

She was losing their precious baby.

CHAPTER THIRTEEN

THEIR PRECIOUS LITTLE BLIP, that precious new life.

Their baby.

Gone.

Agnesse lay huddled on the bed, her faced turned away from them all as the doctors gave her the worst news.

They were so sorry, they said; there was nothing to be done. These things happened but there was no reason she and her husband couldn't have a healthy pregnancy in the future.

'See, darling,' said her mother tearfully, chaffing her hand. 'It's going to be fine.'

She ached for that tiny bundle of life that had been too fragile to survive. And she ached for the father of their little blip. The man who hid his true self behind a mask, who stood when she entered the room, and who watched her with haunted eyes. And only poured his heart into the music his mother had loved.

'No, Mama, it's not.'

She'd dared to believe she could have some part of a normal life. A man to love, a child, a family of her own. Now fate was punishing her in the cruellest of ways.

Because the loss of that precious little life had taken even more with it.

She wasn't good enough to be queen. She was barely coping with her workload. And she wasn't even good enough to keep their baby. How, then, could she hope to hold on to Seb when he didn't even want a royal life? He'd *never* wanted this. He'd only married her for their baby's sake.

Now there was no baby, why would he stay?

There was no point in protracting the agony when it was all futile anyway. Better to get it over with and push him away before he left of his own accord. She was the queen, after all. She could make that choice.

Feeling too numb even for tears, she sat up, pulled the bed covers neatly over her legs, and stiffened her spine.

'Mama, will you ask Seb to come in now please?'

They'd sent him away, out into the waiting room.

When she'd asked for her mother, not him, Seb had been too distraught to insist otherwise. Because he thought history was repeating itself, that he was losing Agnesse: like his father had lost Fabienne.

And then Mathilde had come for him and the expression on her face told him his worst fears had come true.

'Agnesse will be fine, but I'm so sorry, Sebastien, the baby is gone.'

He barely heard the rest, something about a perfectly healthy pregnancy next time. Next time? There was only one thought in his head now.

He'd failed.

His one task was to keep Agnesse and their baby safe and he'd failed. His child was lost.

'Seb?' Mathilde had to get his attention by tugging at his sleeve. 'I said she's asking for you. But be gentle and make allowances, won't you? She's not quite herself. It's been a terrible shock for her.' She placed a palm tenderly to his cheek. 'For you both.'

He nodded and set off for the room where they'd taken his wife. In the corridor the walls were lined with large framed photographs. Restful images of gardens and wildflower meadows, filled with cornflowers and daisies. Seb stared straight ahead.

Christina hovered outside Agnesse's door and closed it behind him once he had crossed the threshold, giving the queen and her husband privacy. Not, he soon discovered, that it was required. There were to be no tearful embraces, no mutual comfort for their grief at the loss of a baby.

Instead, Agnesse sat calm and still in the bed, leaning against several plumped cushions. Her expression was haughty and cool, like she was granting an audience to an unwelcome stranger. He took a bewildered step forward.

'No. Don't come closer.' She swept a crease from the counterpane. 'As you hadn't accepted the position of consort you had only one reason for being here. One purpose for being part of this family. To be the father of my child. That's done now so Ellamaa no longer has need of you.'

Be gentle, Mathilde had said. Agnesse certainly wasn't being. She landed blow after blow on him.

'But we're married,' he said. 'The loss of our child doesn't change that.'

A flicker of pain flashed through her blue eyes but was swiftly mastered. She lifted her chin and stared down her nose at him.

'It changes everything. With the baby gone what reason could there be for you to stay? From the start you've made it clear this isn't the life you ever wanted.'

He opened his mouth to answer but he couldn't summon the words to contradict her. Not when he'd confessed to precisely that only an hour or so ago.

She smiled at him, a cheerless, condescending lift of her lips. 'I'm setting you free, Sebastien.'

The use of his full name was a knife plunged into his chest. With her next remark she grabbed the hilt and twisted the blade so it slashed right through his heart.

'And I want a divorce,' she said.

He reeled. He should say something, *anything*, to fight for her, but the words wouldn't come. All he could hear was his father's taunt. *She's not for the likes of you, boy.*

'The coronation is a month away,' Agnesse said. 'I'd be grateful for your support on that day. The people deserve a celebration after a year of mourning. Once that's done you won't be needed here anymore.'

He could fall to his knees and beg her to forgive him, to reconsider, but why should she? What had he done to deserve her forgiveness?

'Very well,' he said in a flat, cold voice he barely recognised as his.

He saw her flinch, like he'd landed a wound of his own, but she quickly recovered.

'And now leave me, please.' She called for Christina and the door behind him was opened again. His audience was over.

Even in a crumpled hospital gown, her face as pale and wan as the bed sheets she sat upon, she was still more a queen than any woman he'd ever met. And he could never, ever be worthy of her.

He obeyed her without question and with a bow and a click of heels turned round and strode away.

CHAPTER FOURTEEN

HE LEFT ELLAMAA that evening. Slipping away with as little fanfare as when he and Agnesse had first arrived together. There were no pretty views to soften the pain of his departure, no graceful parkland or fairy palaces to marvel over.

No ravishing queen at his side.

He left from a deserted, private airfield in the dark of a rain-swept night and, as he had been most of his life—alone.

Leo had said there'd always be a place for him in Grimentz but Seb couldn't face the thought of being around a couple so obviously in love. So he'd spent the past month in France instead, at his father's old estate. The one the prince had purchased when he'd married Fabienne. Where Seb had been born and where his ill-fated mother was buried.

Max had inherited the bulk of their father's wealth and possessions, but along with a significant financial bequest, this Loire valley estate, with its elegant chateau and profitable vineyard, had been left to his younger brother. As if in death, Prince Georg had tried to atone for his parental failings in life.

Seb would have traded it all for a father who wanted him, but though he might never forgive him the rejection, he was at least beginning to understand his father's pain; the excruciating agony of losing the woman you loved...

Leaving Agnesse had been like tearing his still-beating heart from his own chest. Without her in it, his world was nothing.

Since he'd arrived, Seb had tried to work, but often his feet had carried him to the small cemetery in the grounds of the chateau, to where, shaded by a line of poplar trees, his mother slept, oblivious to the pain her only son was suffering. If he'd hoped to find comfort there, or answers to why fate had dealt him such blows, none was forthcoming. There was only a kinship of tragedy and heartbreak.

Leo's father had refused permission for Prince Georg's ashes to be brought here to lie with his second wife, insisting a von Frohburg should only be interred in the family crypt in Grimentz. Seb would ask Leo to reverse that decision so his parents could be reunited at last. Maybe they'd even find each other again beyond the grave.

He could grant them the happy ending their son was to be denied.

Because there was to be no such resolution for him. He would see Agnesse only one more time. He was returning to Ellamaa tomorrow to fulfil her request to support her during her coronation.

Then it would be done and he would move on. Perhaps he would come back here. This empty chateau could be put to many good uses. Whatever he did he knew he'd have to keep moving forward. If he stopped, even for a second, the grief would crush him.

He loved Agnesse but he'd failed to protect her. His father had been right all along. Seb wasn't good enough for her. He never had been.

Perhaps it would have been better if he'd never been born, as his father had believed. Fabienne would have survived and another man would have been there to keep Agnesse safe and spare her the anguish he saw in her eyes that last day in the hospital when she'd miscarried.

The torment of that lashed him to his bones. He'd failed her. And their baby.

Seb sent up a prayer to whatever gods may be listening that

his mother and father be granted peace and that his lost child, *their* grandchild, be gathered into their eternal embrace.

Then he turned away, hardened what was left of his heart, and set his course back to the realm of the living.

Seb was back.

For two final days in Ellamaa before he left for good.

He was using her father's old rooms that lay at the other end of this wing of the Winter Palace. The dowager queen had had them reopened especially for the prince, and the staff had worked tirelessly for two days solid to bring them to gleaming perfection. What a wonderful mark of respect for your husband, Dorel had gushed, as excited as all the staff seemed to be at his return.

Agnesse had offered no comment. She was merely grateful the separate stairwells meant they wouldn't accidentally meet one another in passing.

She didn't care about her mother's newfound affection for her soon to be *ex* son-in-law, or the buzz amongst the staff at the prince being back amongst them. In a matter of days divorce papers would be drawn up and this sham of a marriage would head for the courts and be brought to an end.

Before that could happen she had her coronation to get through and she'd asked Seb to be there for the sake of her people. They deserved a day of joy and happy memories. Not overshadowed by their impending divorce. Her PR team had explained away his month-long absence as matters elsewhere that had unfortunately required his personal attention.

Meanwhile, Agnesse had presented the perfect public face. She smiled serenely as she waved to the crowds, shook hands, accepted bouquets. And if she was asked where her husband was, she'd lean in and with a laugh, *Oh, you know men*, she'd say, *off saving the world or some such*. And her subjects would commiserate with her and offer their hopes for his swift return to her side.

She did what was expected and required of her, and disguised the truth of it: that it felt like pain and longing were leaking through her pores and threatening to drown her in the misery of it all.

The Winter Palace sat at the heart of the city a mile and a half from the cathedral where her coronation was to be held.

She wouldn't look at him as they attended the rehearsal walk-through together. He reached out a hand at the appropriate moments, which Agnesse never took. And which none of the clergy or staff around them had remarked on, though she saw their expressions. Compassion, sorrow, regret. Call it what you will, it made no difference. After her coronation tomorrow, Prince Sebastien von Frohburg would no longer be part of her life.

On the day, she in a gown of ivory silk, he in a uniform of a colonel of the Life Guards, she sat beside him as they'd travelled together in her carriage. Neither spoke; both kept their gazes on the crowds gathered on either side of the route. If she breathed deeper to savour sandalwood and Seb, well, she was only human. But she was required to place her hand over his as she stepped down from the carriage, and to keep it there as they processed through the cathedral, and his hand was warm and steady beneath hers at all the moments when she needed it to be.

She thought the hardest part of the day was being trapped in the carriage with him as they rode to and from the cathedral.

She'd been wrong; that moment had come later, at the coronation ball held in the glittering reception rooms of the Winter Palace. An event stuffed with the crowned heads of Europe and the great and good from around the world.

But in that sea of faces Agnesse could see only one: that of her husband's as he walked up to take her in his arms for the first dance.

The solemnity and longing in his eyes was nearly her undoing.

Agnesse sealed herself to it. She placed her hand in his. She felt need race along her spine as his other settled at her back. As supportive as ever. But she couldn't lean on him. He'd only married her because of their baby. That briefest of lives that had broken both their hearts. She couldn't doubt that. Not when she saw the sadness in his gaze. That was all for their lost child, surely.

The dance was over. He led her from the floor and towards her mother, who was deep in conversation with a dashing young man. The second son of one of Ellamaa's most high-ranking dukes.

Seb placed her hand on the young man's arm. 'I really shouldn't monopolise the queen all evening,' he said. And when he asked the queen to dance, Seb had made his farewells.

'Goodbye, Your Majesty.' He bent low over her hand, kissed her gloved fingers, and with that little heel click, was gone.

It was only after he'd gone that she realised he'd said good-bye and not good-night.

On the surface she remained as calm as ever. No one would ever know what that cost her as inside she crumbled and broke.

She made her own farewells soon after that. Dorel was there, helping her undress, removing the tiara, the beautiful gown, the perfect heels, when her mother walked in.

'So you are still determined to push Sebastien away. Are you going to tell me why?' she said.

'It didn't work out. We can't all be as lucky as you and Papa. It wasn't a love match. He doesn't love me. And there's an end to it. I'm sorry if I've disappointed you.'

'I'm not disappointed, Agnesse. I'm angry that a daughter of mine could be so blind.'

Agnesse swung towards her. 'Didn't you hear what I said? He doesn't love me.'

'He deserves an award, then, because he's been doing an excellent impression of a man who's very much in love with his wife. Look at the photos from today, Agnesse. Look at any of the photos of the two of you since the moment he proposed to you in London. And then tell me if you feel the same.'

'I know you're wrong, Mama.'

'Am I? Then who, may I ask, sent these?' her mother asked, plucking the unopened note from amongst the bouquet of daisies that had arrived earlier that evening. 'And you haven't even read what he's written to you?' The envelope remained firmly sealed. Her mother opened the card and scanned its message. Her hand fluttered up to her breast as she gave a soft sigh. 'Well, that's really rather lovely.'

'What if he changes his mind?' Agnesse asked.

'And what if he does not?'

'I'm not good enough for him, Mama,' Agnesse said in a small voice.

'Where did you get that half-baked idea? You're the Queen of Ellamaa. You're a match for any man.'

She stroked Agnesse's hair. 'I know what the problem really is. You're afraid. Everyone is when they fall in love. Because how do you bear it if things go wrong? But it's a terrible shame to let that fear prevent you from loving in the first place, darling.

'I lost your father and it crushes me every morning when I wake up and remember he is gone. But I wouldn't swap even a second of those years we had together to ease the grief I feel now. Love is precious, Agnesse. When you find it, you must grasp it with both hands.'

She kissed her cheek and placed the little handwritten card in her daughter's palm. 'And I think you should read this.'

After the door had closed behind her, Agnesse looked down, read what her husband had written to her, and felt the sting of tears forming.

Your father would have been so proud of you today.
As was I. You were magnificent.
S x

Was her mother right? Agnesse snatched up her tablet and scrolled through the photos of the day's events.

In every one, *every single one*, Seb's gaze was on her, standing at her right shoulder. When she'd paused in the portico of the cathedral, taking a moment to compose herself before she emerged into the light and her people saw their anointed queen for the first time, his hand had reached out towards her as if to steady her. It was such as small move that it would have passed unnoticed if she hadn't actually been searching the photos.

Then she searched for earlier pictures of them online. And there he was. Often a pace behind, but always with his gaze on her, fiercely protective.

Standing closer if she needed him. Giving her space if she did not.

Agnesse closed her eyes as the tears fell. All those moments, the panic attacks, the fight outside that bar, the expulsion of her mother, his endless concern and care for her? He'd been helping her, supporting her, *loving* her since that night in Vienna.

What had she done?

Agnesse dropped the tablet, abandoning the images of her loyal, steadfast husband always there, two paces behind her, and ran from her suite.

'I did not have you down as a quitter, Sebastien.'

The dowager queen had sailed into his suite without announcement while his valet was packing the last of the uniform and regalia Seb had used that day.

'Good evening, Your Majesty.' Despite her amicable tone Seb didn't, on this occasion, bother himself to bow.

'My daughter is as stubborn as they come. I thought you knew that. So why are you moping about here while she is breaking her heart over you on the other side of the palace?'

'Excuse me?'

It had taken every ounce of strength Seb had to leave Agnesse in the arms of another man. He'd wanted to drag her away, to keep her safe. She'd looked so defeated and alone and he could hardly bear it. But she'd barely spoken to him since he'd returned. It was abundantly clear how she felt about him. Yet still, the dowager queen expected *him* to go to *her*?

'It's her choice,' he said, handing the valet an item for stowing. 'She sent me away, remember?'

Mathilde waved a dismissive hand. 'She'd just miscarried. She was fighting with grief and a maelstrom of hormones. And you, Sebastien, are quite dazzling, you know. Her father was the same. I was so in awe of him it took months for me to believe he hadn't just proposed because of who my family was.'

Seb was stunned by that confession. Incredulous. There'd been a time when Mathilde was anything other than the formidable woman he knew.

She looked him up and down with a shake of her head.

'I wonder if there's ever been a female who truly thought she was good enough for you. Agnesse certainly doesn't. Once she lost the baby, she thought she had nothing else to offer you.' She made for the door again. 'Perhaps you might think about that before you leave tonight.'

And then she was gone almost as quickly as she'd arrived. Leaving Seb rooted to the spot and almost laughing at the incomprehensible suggestion that Agnesse was not good enough for him.

When the exact and polar opposite was true.

A message arrived that his car was ready. His valet was to finish what was left of his packing and follow on later. There was nothing more to keep Seb here…except his feet wouldn't move.

He had run out of reasons to see her. Tonight had been the last time he'd have her in his arms, and the realisation was a dead weight crushing his chest.

Mathilde was mistaken. His wife didn't want him. If she was breaking her heart it had nothing to do with him.

Did it?

It made no difference. He'd had his chance to protect her and he'd failed.

At last, his feet obeyed and carried him from the room.

Seb had deliberately left her in the arms of another man tonight. And he'd chosen carefully. The second son of a duke, handsome, connected, and gazing at Agnesse like she were Aphrodite herself. But would he have had any more success preventing the miscarriage once fate itself had decided that the tiny life was too fragile for this world?

Even the doctors couldn't prevent that. No one could have.

He reached the head of the staircase leading to the palace entrance. Seb grasped the banister, worn smooth by centuries of use. How many had leant on it for support, trusting implicitly in its strength as they went about their lives?

Who could do more than that? Offer their strength to another, day after day. But still, people must have fallen on these steps. One could take all the care in the world, but accidents happened.

Beyond the portico Seb could see his car. His driver and security team stood close by, waiting his arrival. They were the best at what they did and yet, that night in London he'd ended up battered and bruised. It was impossible to protect someone entirely from life. But it didn't mean you weren't good enough.

His father had loved his young wife. He couldn't have loved her more yet still, she'd died. Violetta had suffered two miscarriages before this latest pregnancy. Leo hadn't been able to prevent those, either. But he'd been there for her. Seb had seen for himself how she had leant on her husband and taken great comfort from him. Could he be there like that for Agnesse?

But would she let him?

The driver held the car door open and Seb slid into the backseat. His team took their places in the motorcade and the palace gates swung open.

No man could love her more and wasn't that what she

needed in the end? Someone to love her for who she was. Not the queen, but the woman.

The engine purred to life and began to pull away.

He could do that. Surely, he was more than up to that. Agnesse was still his wife. He loved her. His world was nothing without her in it.

Agnesse. *Agnesse...*

Seb yanked his seat belt loose, reared up in his seat, and slammed his fist hard against the roof of the limousine.

'Stop the car!'

As she burst through the door to her father's old room, Seb's valet was zipping up a garment carrier. She recognised the uniform that Seb had worn earlier today.

Near the door sat a collection of luggage. An attaché case on top of the pile. Somehow, that hurt more than anything. The evidence that he'd worked here. The efforts he'd made for her. For her family, for her people.

It broke her heart all over again. How had she mistaken what he'd been doing these past months? How had she got it so badly wrong?

That pile of luggage, so recently unpacked, was on the move again with its itinerant prince. And where would he go? Who would be there for him, comfort him, *love* him? She couldn't let any of that happen without trying to stop him.

'Where is my husband?' She didn't even try to keep the desperation from her voice.

'I'm sorry, ma'am. But Prince Sebastien has already gone.'

'Gone?' Was she already too late?

'He was heading for his car but he's only left a few moments ago. You might catch him if you hurry.'

The last of that was said into thin air. Agnesse had already spun on her heel and flown back out of the suite.

She tore along corridors and to the grand staircase leading to the exit they'd used earlier today. Framed by the looming darkness of the night sky, a black car glittered dully in the lights spilling from the portico. And it was pulling away.

Stricken, Agnesse cried out. 'Seb! No!'

Then miraculously, the car halted. She flew down the stairs, wild with relief as the back door opened and her husband climbed out.

'Seb!' She sobbed, running towards him.

The sight of the queen, arriving in a state of some agitation—actually sprinting full pelt towards them—and in an even more startling state of undress, her hair streaming loose behind her, her dressing gown flapping open to reveal bare thighs and sleep shorts, was the unequivocal cue for the servants and security team to look away. That, and the sudden and electrifying focus of the prince as she skidded to a halt before him. Though several sideways glances were aimed at the couple and at least one 'About time,' was muttered.

'Agnesse.'

He didn't bow or use her title and that gave her hope. That, and the fact his eyes were devouring her whole. In a dark suit and white dress shirt he was dressed almost as he was when he'd helped her through that panic attack. He'd been helping her pretty much ever since. How had she not seen it? How had she not understood and valued him for the extraordinary man he was?

'Don't go yet. I have things to say to you.' She gathered her courage. 'What if I asked you to stay?'

'It would depend on your conditions.' he said.

That you love me. But she couldn't ask for that. Not yet. He had to hear the words from her first. He had to know how precious he was to her.

'I have no conditions. Because it's quite simple. I know I can't do this without you.'

His warm gaze settled on her. 'Yes, you can. You have been doing it without me all along.'

Drat the man for choosing now to be picky about details.

'But I'll do it so much better with you by my side.' It was time for a grand gesture to prove her sincerity. She sank to her knees. Yes, both of them. This man deserved it.

'Marry me,' she said.

There was a murmur in the shadows around them, and from the corner of her eye she was quite certain she saw her butler punch the air.

'You do know it's just one knee for proposals?' her husband said.

She reached up to grasp his hands in hers. 'Take it as a measure of my devotion that I've used both.'

'And we're already married.'

She lifted his hands to her lips and with great solemnity pressed a kiss to both of them in turn. 'Yes, but that's just bodies and minds. I want your heart, too.' She took a deep breath. It was now or never. She had to declare herself. 'Because I love you.'

Now there was a chorus of 'ahs.' And coming from Seb's decidedly burly, and usually taciturn, security detail no less.

'Greedy girl,' he said, lifting her to her feet, gathering her in his arms and kissing her.

Yes, she was, and she was done with hiding it. 'When it comes to you I'm finding I can't get enough. I love you,' she said. 'This is me being spontaneous. Ripping up the rules and going after what I want. In this case, the man I love.' She gazed up at him. 'Very much.'

He buried his face in her hair. 'I'll confess I wasn't leaving. I was coming back. To persuade you to give us another chance. Because I know I can't live without you. I love you and I want it all. Everything I could possibly have with you. Any title you care to bestow. Any work you want to give me to take the pressure off you. Every night falling asleep with you and every morning waking up with you in my arms.'

'You'll be my consort?'

'God, yes,' he said, sealing that promise with a kiss.

'I don't have much else to offer.'

'Are you crazy? Getting the chance to grow old with you is gift enough, *chérie*, but you've also given me a family who seems to like me, and whom I can actually stand. Yes, even Isobel, though she'd try the patience of a saint. And somewhere to truly belong. That's not something I ever thought I'd have.'

She smiled up at him. Marvelling at the unmistakable joy in his green eyes. 'You love me, then.'

'Body, soul, mind. Heart. I'm all in, *chérie*.'

She chewed her lip and buried her face in his shirt front. 'Children?' she asked.

'Yes, that, too. A palace filled with them. As many as you want. I'll love every precious one of them. As I will their beautiful mama.'

'Well, then, that's a deal. Though maybe we could wait a year or so for babies. To have some time, just for us first. Although in the meantime...' She gazed up at him from under her lashes, slid her fingers through his and started for the stairs. 'There's nothing to say we can't have lots of *practice* at making babies.'

He sent her a positively filthy smile. 'My darling wife, I think you've just read my mind.'

EPILOGUE

AGNESSE'S SECOND ANNIVERSARY DAY parade was going perfectly. Ellamaa's flag flew from every vantage point, bunting festooned private homes and businesses alike, and crowds, ten deep, had cheered their queen's progress along the entire route from the cathedral, where a service of thanksgiving had been held, to the Winter Palace at the very heart of the capital. Even the weather was being kind; the sun shone from a clear, blue October sky, showing the city at its best.

Agnesse rode through the streets in a State Landau. Her mother by her side and Isobel opposite. In a guardsman's uniform, and part of her military escort, Carl was on horseback to her left. Other family members and dignitaries, including Leo and Violetta, followed in farther carriages.

With a jangle of harness and the clatter of hooves, the mounted cavalry at the head of the procession were already passing through the palace gates. The formal celebrations for the second anniversary of her coronation had nearly concluded. Only the balcony appearance awaited.

And Agnesse would be doing that alone.

Seb had told her last night that he wouldn't join her. For the second year in a row.

Despite her protestations he'd also refused to join her in the open carriage, but at least this year he'd agreed to ride alongside as part of her mounted honour guard.

As much as she'd have appreciated the comforting presence

of his solid bulk beside her, the spectacle of her prince consort, in full military regalia and astride a great black horse, was quite the compensation. The sun glinted off his gleaming gold breastplate; the horsetail plume of his spiked helmet fluttered in the breeze. Between doing her duty and waving to her subjects, Agnesse sneaked lustful glances at him again and again.

Along the route there were excited shouts for her and her family. Isobel beamed at the crowd, sending them cheery waves. Perhaps Carl sat taller in his saddle, but otherwise maintained his martial countenance. Then the spectators worked out the identity of the other rider flanking her carriage.

'Prince Sebastien!'

'We love you, Prince Sebastien.'

Agnesse shot her husband a swift look but his gaze remained fixed forward, and the only betrayal of any tension was his horse becoming restive. It pranced sideways for a few paces as if the gloved hand controlling the rein had tensed. But Seb was an experienced rider and his mount was swiftly back under control.

She wasn't surprised by the crowds adulation. Seb had won the admiration of many in the past twenty-four months. He wouldn't have it, of course. He believed he delivered nothing more than basic royal patronage and charitable support. What those organisations actually got was a tireless campaigner and a charismatic royal ambassador. He gave his heart to anything he took on and she couldn't have adored him more. Neither, it seemed, could her people.

The carriage arrived at the palace courtyard where Agnesse alighted. With her mother and sister she took the stairs that led to the upper floor. But as she ascended she felt the onset of a warning breathlessness. This hadn't happened in a while and when it had, Seb had been there to lean on. But he was still caught up in the dismount of the honour guard.

She tried to focus on her guests who'd also left their carriages and were joining her in the salon—and not its open

French windows and the grand balcony beyond. But Agnesse couldn't help it. She eyed it with growing disquiet. The numbers below were swelling as more and more of her subjects poured into the square before the Winter Palace.

Seb arrived. Minus his gold cuirass and helmet but looking no less magnificent in a scarlet tunic. She wanted to run at him and hide her face in his chest. A handful of times in the past two years when she'd nearly had an episode, he'd pulled her back from the brink. Usually just by talking. Once…well, she still blushed to think about how he'd achieved that.

Instead, she stood still and sent him a tight smile. He strolled towards her, greeting guests on the way, but she could see the concern in his cool green gaze.

He bent his head to kiss her cheek.

'Chérie,' he whispered. 'Do you need a moment?'

He understood her well enough by now. He saw the signs and always helped her deal with these now-rare moments of anxiety.

'Yes,' she breathed. Her heart was racing, her hands clammy. The day had gone well but that crowd outside was getting bigger by the minute. Perhaps it was the sheer numbers, because she was daunted by the weight of their expectations.

Seb quietly took charge. 'If you'll excuse us, the queen would like to freshen up before her appearance. You know how our ladies are,' he said pleasantly to their nearest guests, and placing a comforting hand in the small of her back, guided her towards a small retiring room that sat on one side of the salon. A place specifically designed for the monarchs to use before those iconic balcony moments. He ushered her in.

Agnesse paced nervously to the centre of the room. 'I'll be fine. I know I just need to breathe.'

'It's all right, *ma chérie,*' Seb said, coming closer. 'I know exactly what you need.'

From the look in his eye Agnesse saw instantly what he intended and backed away from her advancing husband.

'No, not that. Not here…surely.'

Her behind landed against something solid.

A previous monarch had installed a wooden vanity unit, with a porcelain sink painted with elaborate sprays of roses and trailing ivy.

Seb spared the frivolous decoration a passing glance. 'One of your forebears might have been fond of their fancy porcelains but I'm grateful. This, however—' he placed his hands on the table, trapping her between them '—is the perfect height.' With a nudge of his hips he pushed her back so she was trapped between him and its edge.

'I have the perfect way to make you relax,' he said with a wicked grin.

'We couldn't possibly. There really isn't time.' She was breathless for a whole different reason now.

His green eyes flashed.

'We both know I can make you come in three minutes flat. And nothing is guaranteed to relax you quicker,' he said, hitching up the long, full skirt of her dress with his fingers.

She placed a hand to his chest. Not to push him away, she was already beyond that, but for the pleasure of touching him.

The Royal Regiment of Horse Guards, who'd been without their Colonel-in-Chief since the death of her father, had recently asked if her husband might take on the role. She'd persuaded him to accept.

For many, *many* noble reasons.

But mostly she'd done it for the pleasure of seeing him decked out in his scarlet tunic, shiny black boots, and skin-tight riding breeches that showed off his taught backside and long, muscular legs to perfection.

She was a terrible woman, shallow and obsessed, and may the gods strike her down for using her power so frivolously, but Seb was hot, hot, *hot* in that uniform. As he sank to his knees before her she nearly climaxed there and then.

His hands slid beneath the hem of her dress and up her

thighs. Thumbs hooked in the sides of her panties and peeled them down to her ankles. He supported her as she stepped out of them. Then his head and shoulders disappeared beneath her dress. One of her feet lifted from the floor as he shifted her weight to part her thighs. And then his mouth was...*oh*.

Right there. Doing to her what only Seb could do.

Agnesse no longer cared about the size of the crowd gathering outside. Only that the lace curtains at the windows were obscuring the view in. Though what would anyone actually see? The queen, looking a little flushed, leaning against a vanity unit.

Two and half minutes later she stuffed a fist in her mouth and stifled her moans as best she could. Her family and guests were gathered just on the other side of a dividing wall.

Seb reemerged. Rose up before her and made use of that pretty little basin and its scented soap. He dampened a washcloth and collected a towel to bathe and pat her dry. When he was done she went to scoop up her panties but he got there first. But instead of handing them over to her, he stuffed them in the front of his tunic.

Her mouth fell open. 'You wouldn't dare.'

He chuckled. 'I think this will focus your mind on things other than the size of the crowd out there.' And before she could stop him he'd opened the door so they could rejoin their family and guests.

Just hidden from view of the crowds below, Seb tucked a stray lock behind the ear of his flushed and thoroughly beautiful wife.

'Right, you have your public to meet.'

'I presume you still won't join me.'

'Correct.'

Her delectable mouth formed into a frustrated pout. 'Why do I have to go out there and you get to stay in here?'

'Because they don't want me. They want you.'

'Are you sure about that? Because I heard several shouts for you on the way here.'

He'd heard them, too, but they meant nothing. A fan here or there did not mean acceptance by the wider public. He'd taken the title of Prince Consort to support his wife, not for his own aggrandisement. And he wasn't risking any balcony appearance. That was for his queen.

He swatted her on the backside. 'What are you waiting for? Get out there, woman.'

She shot him an affronted look but nevertheless smoothed her gown and, he'd swear, grew by about three inches before sailing through the doors to the roar of the crowd below.

There was a soft snuffle from behind him. He swivelled round to see Isobel approaching with a baby in her arms.

'Here's Papa's best girl,' he said, collecting the infant from her aunt's arms and settling her in his own. Green eyes, that he liked to believe were just like his, focused up on him.

Her Royal Highness, Crown Princess Fabienne-Mathilde, three-month-old future Queen of Ellamaa, gurgled and cooed and worked her tiny rosebud mouth into a smile. And stole her besotted papa's heart all over again.

Her godparents approached, Leo and Violetta, carrying their own twenty-two-month-old daughter.

Isobel smirked. 'What happens in about seventeen years and these two are grown up and the playboys of Europe come calling?'

'That's evil,' Violetta laughed. 'You're frightening their doting papas. I'm sure both our daughters will be very sensible and heed their fathers.'

'I'm sure they'll do nothing of the kind,' Isobel taunted. 'Look at who their mothers are.'

Leo and Seb exchanged panicked looks.

'That's it,' Leo said to his daughter. 'You're grounded until you are at least thirty.'

Seb gave his daughter a little sway.

'And there won't be any men allowed near you, will there?' he said to his enchanted baby in a singsong voice.

Isobel snorted. 'Yeah, right. Like you'll have any choice. Just you wait.'

It could wait because that was all a long way off. As were her royal duties.

For now she wouldn't be making any balcony appearances. That was a job for her mama and grandmama, her aunt and uncle. Today she belonged only to her parents, to her family, and their friends. A lifetime of service was yet to come. But when it did she'd have him beside her. Every step he'd be there. Till the end of his days.

As would her mother.

He watched from the shadows as Agnesse waved from the balcony. Ten minutes ago she'd practically been in bits. Now there she stood, smiling, calmly acknowledging the cheers of her people like the queen she was.

While wearing no underwear.

God, how he loved this mighty woman.

Outside, the cheering had formed into a chant. One he'd never heard before. One that caused his chest to tighten in alarm.

'We want Seb!'

'We want Seb!'

Mathilde came to his side and scooped her granddaughter into her arms.

'Your methods might sometimes be unconventional.' She frowned at his jacket where a speck of ivory lace peeked out. Seb quickly stuffed it out of sight.

'But you've been good for my daughter, and for Ellamaa.' She looked to where Agnesse stood alone on the balcony. 'And now the people want to acknowledge you for it. So it's time to get out there.'

The chant was getting louder.

'We want Seb! We want Seb!'

But Seb was frozen to the spot. They couldn't mean it. Surely?

Violetta smiled encouragingly and Leo slapped him on the back. 'Go on,' his cousin said, giving him a shove. 'Or by the sounds of it we'll have a revolution on our hands.'

On shaky legs, Seb reached the step that led from the shadowy protection of the salon to the world outside. As he emerged into the light, the chant became louder. He reached Agnesse's side and she took his hand and kissed it. When she raised it aloft, presenting him to the crowd, a great roar went up.

Seb stood there, like a rabbit in the headlights. Where were the boos, the looks of disapproval?

'We love you, Prince Sebastien,' came a shout from the front of the crowd.

'It's okay to wave, you know,' Agnesse said, laughing. 'In fact, it's actively encouraged.'

He shot a jerky hand upward, and another roar went up. He stared out at the swirling, excited crowd below, to thousands upon thousands chanting his name.

His name. The people were cheering for *him*.

Agnesse's smile was pure sunshine. 'Breathe, my darling,' she said.

And he did.

As the terrible, twisted belief that his father had instilled in him shattered like smashed glass, Seb's chest expanded. Like he was breathing in fully for the first time—just as a new cry went up. A demand from the people to their prince consort.

'Kiss her! Kiss her! Kiss her!'

He and Agnesse had deprived the public of a balcony kiss with their private wedding.

'To hell with it. If they want Seb, they'll get Seb.'

He slipped his arm about her waist and looked to the crowd expectantly, hamming it up.

They screamed in excitement.

He tugged her closer. Another look to the masses below.

'Kiss her,' came the cry.

'Okay, hold on to that sexy little hat, *chérie*, because I'm coming in.'

As he swept her backwards, Agnesse's hand flew up to steady her flower-bedecked fascinator. She narrowed her eyes. 'I can see I'm going to have to take you in hand later.'

'Oh, Your Majesty, such promises. I can hardly wait,' he breathed. Then, as he gazed into the eyes of the woman he adored, the balcony and the red carpet beneath his feet and the crowd beyond simply went away. It was just him and Agnesse.

'I love you,' he told her. 'My beloved queen, I'm yours to command forever.'

She reached up to hook her fingers in his tunic and tugged him closer. 'In that case, to stop that crowd growing ugly, will you please get on with kissing me?'

And with a grin, and to the roars of a crowd gone wild with delight, he bent his head and obliged her.

* * * * *

COMING SOON!

We really hope you enjoyed reading this
book. If you're looking for more romance
be sure to head to the shops when
new books are available on

Thursday 22nd
June

To see which titles are coming soon, please visit
millsandboon.co.uk/nextmonth

MILLS & BOON®

Coming next month

PENNILESS CINDERELLA FOR THE GREEK
Chantelle Shaw

'I had the impression on the beach a week ago that you want us to be work colleagues and nothing more.'

His dark blue eyes were unfathomable, but she noticed a nerve flicker in his cheek. He sipped his wine before he said softly, 'Is that what you want, Savannah?'

She was about to assure him that of course it was. Anything other than a strictly work based relationship with Dimitris would be dangerous. But she was transfixed by his masculine beauty, and when he smiled she felt more alive than she'd done in ten years. 'I don't know,' she admitted huskily.

The band had been playing smooth jazz tunes during dinner, but now the guests had finished eating and the tempo of the music increased as people stepped onto the dance floor.

Dimitris pushed back his chair and stood up. He offered his hand to Savannah. 'Would you like to dance?'

Continue reading
PENNILESS CINDERELLA FOR THE GREEK
Chantelle Shaw

Available next month
www.millsandboon.co.uk

LET'S TALK

Romance

For exclusive extracts, competitions
and special offers, find us online:

- MillsandBoon
- @MillsandBoon
- @MillsandBoonUK
- @MillsandBoonUK

Get in touch on 01413 063 232

MILLS & BOON

THE HEART OF ROMANCE

A ROMANCE FOR EVERY READER

MODERN

Prepare to be swept off your feet by sophisticated, sexy and seductive heroes, in some of the world's most glamourous and romantic locations, where power and passion collide.

HISTORICAL

Escape with historical heroes from time gone by. Whether your passion is for wicked Regency Rakes, muscled Vikings or rugged Highlanders, awaken the romance of the past.

MEDICAL

Set your pulse racing with dedicated, delectable doctors in the high-pressure world of medicine, where emotions run high and passion, comfort and love are the best medicine.

True Love

Celebrate true love with tender stories of heartfelt romance, from the rush of falling in love to the joy a new baby can bring, and a focus on the emotional heart of a relationship.

Desire

Indulge in secrets and scandal, intense drama and sizzling hot action with heroes who have it all: wealth, status, good looks…everything but the right woman.

HEROES

The excitement of a gripping thriller, with intense romance at its heart. Resourceful, true-to-life women and strong, fearless men face danger and desire - a killer combination!

To see which titles are coming soon, please visit

millsandboon.co.uk/nextmonth

MILLS & BOON
True Love
Romance from the Heart

Celebrate true love with tender stories of
heartfelt romance, from the rush of falling in love
to the joy a new baby can bring, and a focus on the
emotional heart of a relationship.

MILLS & BOON

Desire

Indulge in secrets and scandal, intense drama and plenty of sizzling hot action with powerful and passionate heroes who have it all: wealth, status, good looks…everything but the right woman.